Rachel's books

Novels

The Serial Dater — 31 dates in 31 days

The Serial Dieter — 31 dishes in 31 days

Oh, Henry — the first in the Henry Houdini series

Short Stories

Various Henry Houdini long short stories

The Serial Dater

The first in the 'Serial' series –

31 dates in 31 days

Rachel Cavanagh

This book is dedicated to my father, Don,

who I know would have been so proud.

Chapter One – Hunky Dunky at the Picturedrome

They say it takes less than ten seconds to make a first impression.

"How's it going, Izzy?"

I look up and there, looming, is William, my boss. My boss-for-not-very-much-longer-if-I-don't-get-this-article-right boss.

"Good, thanks," I reply. "Have it done in no time," I lie.

"Excellent. First copy on my desk by two, okay?"

Every time he says it, I think how much easier it would be to email it to him, or let him get it off the server, but he's a rather old-fashioned editor and to him, paper is king.

I nod. "Sure."

As he wanders back to his office, I spot my colleague and 'BFF' Donna looking at me. She mouths what I think is an 'Are you okay?' and I smile and blow her a kiss. She giggles which sets me off. She never fails to have that effect on me and, not for the first time, I wish I could bottle her effervescence.

My readers know me as Isobel MacFarlane, but I'm Izzy Mac to my friends. The only people to call me Isobel are my mother and my boss, especially when I was little and being naughty (to my mother, that is). My boss, William Stamp, calls me Izzy when he wants something, which is most of the time, but if things aren't going his way… you get the idea.

Being one of the few single girls in the office, and because I write a technology column, he's instructed me to set up a profile on NorthantsDating.co.uk. Disguised as 'tallgirlnn1' – because I'm five feet ten, female (last time I checked) and the paper's based in Northampton's town centre – I'm to line up a date a night for the next thirty-one days and write about it, because it's never been done at this paper before. I can see why.

I should count myself lucky; Donna's latest task on her 'Health & Beauty' section is yo-yo dieting. She has to find a new angle as it's been written about to death, but so has dating, I suppose.

With my profile containing the barest of (very) loosely based facts up and running, I already have one message from DBvet:

1

'Hi. I see you've just joined. Me too! I'm local but not sure what to write, so will let you check me out.' Short and sweet.

Clicking on the 'view my profile' button, I learn that Duncan is thirty-two with his own vet's practice. I assume he's six feet as his profile says five feet twelve, which makes me laugh. A good start.

There's no photo, but I can't complain because I haven't uploaded one either. I'd come to the conclusion that if this were truly going to be a blind-date project then seeing photos would rather defeat the object. I work for a local rag and although my smiling portrait appears above my column six days a week, it's old enough and black and white enough to look nothing like me, and I figure the town's big enough to get away with it. Besides, people are only ever interested in what the article says, not who writes it, aren't they? But even so, I decide to play safe. I'll see how it goes.

I send a rather forward 'you sound nice, let's meet' message, and then read on. Duncan's interests include 'animals' (no surprise there), 'reading' (I'm a big fan too), and 'cinema' (who doesn't?). There's no mention of the other cliché, 'eating out', but unless he's a couch potato, that's going to be a tick.

He replies suggesting the Picturedrome, which does lovely food, yep, no couch potato. We're just meeting for a drink or two… the paper's budget only stretches so far and with thirty-one dates on the menu, it may end up being a drink or one.

I reply to his message and hit the 'send' button.

I'm about to return to my article, or what there is of it, when I sense someone hovering next to me. I smile automatically and look up, expecting a six-foot-four William but it's a five-foot-two-and-a-half Donna. My smile widens.

"Cuppa?" she suggests, grinning.

"Definitely," I reply, curious to know why she's even more bouncy than normal. She's one of those naturally hyper people who doesn't need any more than life to get high.

We almost skip arm-in-arm to the kitchen where she offers to be 'mum' and make us both hot chocolates, our daily treats.

She's an expert at multi-tasking so launches into a conversation. "How's it going, Izzy?"

I laugh at her Williamism and she frowns. "The article or life?"

She pokes out the tip of her tongue and I giggle. I'm wondering how much I can charge for a 100ml bottle of Donnaesque when she says, "You know…"

I do. "Not so well. Bit of writer's block. Nothing that a Donna-made hot choc can't fix." I hold up the mug she's given me.

She blushes, takes a tentative sip of very hot hot chocolate, and looks down at her feet.

"Are you okay?" I ask, wanting to give her a hug but not risking either of us getting a scalding.

The beam is back, and I know she'd tell me if there were anything wrong – she can't keep any kind of secret – and I relax. If only the article were that easy to fix.

They say it takes less than ten seconds to make a first impression.

I had hoped reading it again would inspire me, but sadly it doesn't do the trick. I sit and stare at the screen. The cursor flashes encouragingly, but like the page before me, I'm pretty much blank.

I remember Sarah, a friend from years ago, and her list of things she 'didn't do'.

"Shopping list. I need a shopping list," I mutter, but sense someone hovering over my desk. Surprise, surprise, it's William.

"Aren't you a bit too busy to be thinking about food? That's Donna's department."

I smile and pretend to type. He's not usually fooled, but I grin as he walks back to his office with the cup of coffee he's just made himself. His PA, Janine, has called in sick, which has made him even more miserable than usual. Not that I blame her.

I open a Word document of notes I've ingeniously called 'Notes' (to go with '31 dates art. 0105' for the article itself).
Remembering what Sarah did and didn't 'do', I create a table

with such neatness that it could be classed as inane (I did say I'm a techie). A journalist or secretary would understand, and for the next thirty-one days, I'm both: journalist by day and 'secretary', when quizzed about my profile, by night.

I start typing the list, but soon run out of lines, so add a few… then a few more. Twenty-five lines later, I'm done. I stare at the screen. The Don't column dominates the Do, so I fill in the missing Dos.

Don't do (in no particular order)
- Trainers with smart suit
- Greasy hair/dirty fingernails
- Too young or too old
- Too short
- No arse (I smile)
- Boring conversation
- Couch potato
- Nauseatingly smooth
- Geek or trainspotter
- Old-fashioned (I'm too young for pipe and slippers)
- Addiction of any kind
- Wants kids
- Smoker
- Moustache or beard (although I do love a goatee)
- Too feminine
- No hard drugs
- Too ugly or self-indulgent pretty boys
- Orange suntans/leathery skin
- B.O.
- Never left Northampton
- Beer-bottle glasses
- Slurps his drink (the image of a cartoon slurper pops into my head)
- Sweats like a pig (I grimace and want to oink but resist – the office is too quiet)
- Ignorance
- Scrounger

Do (in a very particular order)
- Tall
- Funny/good conversation (binman)
- Tall
- Non-smoker
- Tall
- Intelligent
- Tall
- Smart appearance (clean hair etc.)
- Tall
- Some ambition (i.e. not a layabout)
- Tall
- Keeps up to date with current events
- Tall
- Passionate
- Tall
- Likes similar music/interests etc.
- Tall
- Well travelled/interesting
- Tall
- Likes animals
- Tall
- Rugby physique
- Tall
- Pays his way
- Oh, and did I say tall?

I look at the reference to the binman and laugh. It's reminded me of a conversation I'd once had with Sarah where she wanted someone with money and I'd said I'd rather date a humorous binman than a tedious accountant. Being an accounts assistant, I don't think she found that very funny, which went to prove my point.

With the list complete, I feel slightly inspired, so continue with my article.

And this girl has thirty-one impressions to make, all within the month of May. If you're a fan of 'Sex in the City' or 'Bridget Jones's Diary', then we have your very own local version. If you've ever considered internet dating this is the column for you.

Let me experience it on your behalf. Follow me as I meet hot and cold men on hot and cold nights, the roller coaster of emotions and, at the end of the month… who knows? Will I find the man of my dreams or will it be one big nightmare? I'll let you know.

I add a shorter-than-planned review of the new eCopter 3000, and then explain that my usual column will be back in June. After my thousand words are done, I edit, then re-edit.

With the piece printed and safely stowed in William's in tray, Duncan and I exchange a couple more messages and he's confirmed as tonight's guinea pig. One down, thirty to go. I look at the clock and it's just after four. I need to line up more dates for the rest of the week, so do a search for some other men.

Being five feet ten, I decide to select the '6ft+' box, but untick it as I remember that it's for work and not for myself. Besides, knowing the lack of talent in Northampton from weekend jaunts with fellow singleton Donna, and having read a statistic once that only four per cent of the UK male population is six feet and over, I'd end up seeing Duncan every day of the month, although I suspect this wouldn't be a bad thing.

Speak of the devil, fourth one down is DBvet. The first three sound as dull as lard, and with so many (around two hundred) to choose from I can be fussy. Scrolling through the first five pages, I refer to my shopping list and backtrack a little. I've ignored the ones with photos, which are surprisingly few, but after having studied the pictures in more detail, I'm not at all surprised. Very good-looking men invariably know they are and it's usually the cute rather than stunning ones that are worth following up on.

I shake my head as I think about how clinical all this is, but realise this is how a woman's mind works. Take my friend Sarah, and her shopping list as long as… well, a shopping list, and if a man didn't conform to it then he was toast. And who did she end up with? A guy who ticked all the boxes? Correct. Sebastian ticked all the Don't boxes. It goes to show that what you think you want and what you end up with are usually two different things. But I'm not really looking, am I?

After sending a few 'winks' and a couple of messages, I decide I'm done for the day, lock my computer screen, gather up my belongings and walk out to the car park. I smile at Mike the security guard who waves me through. It's something he does every day and I never know why.

Jason who does the early shifts is a different being. He can chat for England and I've lost count of the number of times I've been late for work because I can give as good as I get. More recently I've done it to annoy William, which probably hasn't helped my job situation, but there's more to life, as Jason tells me. He's counting down the days until he's finished his home-study law degree and he's off. Can't say I blame him.

The weekend daytime guy, Klaus, is German and, although he'd be too young, I'm convinced he's a former member of the Gestapo, but what do I know? I've only met him twice (I usually submit two articles on Fridays instead of working weekends and have never met Sidney the weekend nighter who makes up the quartet). William wants me to do Saturdays this month, a month with two bank holiday Mondays at that, so I've drawn the short straw. Maybe if Klaus gets to know me, he'll like me. I live in hope.

As I drive out of the underground car park, I wave and smile at the security camera. I imagine Mike grunting back as he eats his doughnut. He's always eating. Donna says it's to maintain his security guard physique. I think she has a soft spot for him. It takes all sorts.

Ten minutes later and I pull up outside my house. There's a piece of mail sticking out of the postbox and I growl. My postman's lovely, but he doesn't have a clue about security – I dare say Klaus could teach him a thing or two – and don't get me started on littered red elastic bands.

I let myself in, hook my bag over the bottom of the banisters, hang up my coat and make a couple of slices of beans on toast. There's some garlic bread in the fridge that could do with using up, but I can't imagine my dates liking second-hand garlic breath, so I stick it in the freezer, making a mental note to use it early next month.

After checking I have no landline messages, I go upstairs and jump in the shower. I had one before work, but my hair's gone flat from being buffeted around at lunchtime. I make another mental note to take sandwiches instead of having to go to Boots for their lunch snack mega-deals, which always means I eat and spend too much.

Showered and changed, I grab my bag and look around for my keys. I live less than a mile away from the venue, but have decided to drive. I figure it's a quick getaway if I need… well, a quick getaway. I dumped the keys somewhere when I came in, but the exact location escapes me. Then I remember the toast and there they are… the keys… by the kettle. I hadn't made a drink, but yet, there they are. I read once that the brain goes into reverse when you hit the big four-oh, which means I've still ten years to go, so dismiss it. When I realise the light shining down into the hall is the bathroom's, I guess my mental age might be closer to forty anyway.

I'm a bit early, so stop at the corner shop on the way. I'd forgotten to buy a national newspaper at lunchtime and figure it might come in handy if Duncan is late. We get free copies at work, but William always hogs them; research, he says – we figure they end up lining his birdcage. He lives for that creature.

I find a parking space round the corner from the bar, and as I walk in the early summer night's breeze, I take in my surroundings. The old Racecourse Pavilion, now Jade, an oriental restaurant, has half a dozen cars outside with another pulling up. From the obscured view I have of the park, it's teeming with dog walkers and teenagers still enjoying a bonus day off school or college. It's been a beautiful day and I'm a little envious of the families by the sea or pottering in the garden, while I was slaving away over a cold keyboard.

As I reach the Picturedrome's front door, there's no one waiting outside. My mobile says seven fifty-four, so I go in.

There's a chap standing by the bar and my heart leaps. He's at least six feet four, my ideal height for a man, and a Matthew

McConaughey lookalike. I can't believe my luck, but remind myself to be cool. I smile and he grins and waves. My smile gets bigger and I wave madly. I'm about to speak when I realise he's looking through me.

I turn round and am face to face with a Gisele Bünchen replica. When she passes me I want to walk in the direction I'm facing: towards the door. I turn back to the bar and fake a smile. As Matthew and Gisele disappear through the middle doors into the lower part of the building, I see a man sitting on one of the bar stools. He smiles.

On first impression he's to die for, more dark and brooding than Matthew, almost an Antonio Banderas. I get all excited, until he stands up. Six feet in platforms maybe. We'd be the same height if I was barefoot or wearing flatties, but I've got on my favourite kitten heels, so I'm a couple of inches taller. My disappointment must be obvious as his smile fades. I immediately beam and his twinkle reappears.

He's impeccably dressed: a smart pair of black jeans, charcoal polo shirt with white collar, and over the shirt he's wearing a black tailored jacket. It looks like a Boss, but I'm no expert, unlike my colleague Karen. The whole ensemble looks a world away from what I imagined of a veterinary surgeon and enhances his big puppy-dog brown eyes. I laugh at the irony then look down at his feet, imagining scruffy trainers breaking the look, but am greeted with black highly glossed dress shoes. I'm suddenly aware he's speaking to me.

He smiles and repeats, "Would you like a drink?'

I see he has a Coke, so I ask for the same.

With our drinks in his hands, he points to a quiet corner with his chin. "That table looks good."

We sit and, after a sip of Coke, he asks me, "What is it you do again?"

I know he'll have read my profile. "I'm a secretary for a training company."

"Is that interesting?"

"Yes, it can be. We get all sorts through the door. Our courses are for top-level executives, but some people…" I try to be diplomatic.

"Don't make any effort?"

I smile. "You'd be surprised, but you can never judge a book…"

"By its cover. Yes, I know. It's the same with my job. The smartest of people with the scruffiest of animals."

"Look at Richard Branson – classy shirts, but never a tie and always wears jeans. The expensive casual look."

"As long as they're loved."

"Sorry?"

"The animals," he explains. "People spend a fortune on their pets."

"Except me."

"You don't spend a fortune?'

I struggle to recall what I put about pets on my profile and nothing springs to mind, so I avoid specifics. "No animals. We had dogs when I was growing up, but I work full time, so it wouldn't be fair."

"Ah, this is where I'm lucky. I can take mine to work and am surrounded by more."

I smile as I imagine William being surrounded by them all. He's allergic to nearly everything, alive or otherwise: nuts, gluten, hair, and especially pollen. Except for the bird.

"Something funny?" he asks.

"Apart from a bird he says he has, my boss isn't what you would call an animal lover."

"But you are."

I nod and change the subject.

The conversation flows and an hour goes by before we even get on the topic of music, and that's only because Oasis's 'Wonderwall' comes on and we mime to it. Weather is never mentioned.

When I can drag myself away from Duncan's soulful eyes, I notice he occasionally pulls down his polo shirt. I look at his trousers, wondering whether he's trying to cover up a stain, and then I realise I've been staring at his crotch for far too long and my eyes spring back to meet his.

I feel like Helen Hunt to his Mel Gibson as I recall a similar scene from *What Women Want*. Duncan smiles and I blush like a schoolgirl caught kissing the football team captain behind the bike sheds.

Finally, I break the pause in conversation. "Can I ask you something?"

"Sure. Anything."

"I've noticed you tugging at the bottom of your top. Are you nervous?"

He laughs. "A little, but more self-conscious. Or at least I used to be."

"Why?"

He leans in to me and whispers, "I used to be a bit of a heifer."

"Really? You don't look..."

"It was a long process. Weight Watchers."

"My friend Donna would love you!" I blurt.

"Is she single?" I can tell he's teasing.

"She is. Do you want me to...?' I say, half joking.

He puts his hand up. 'Thanks, but..."

"Were you very big?"

"Yes, huge. I still have my forty-eight-waist trousers."

"Forty-eight... inches?" I feel as if I'm being particularly thick, but he seems not to notice.

"Yes. We'd probably both get in them." Now there's an offer.

We smile and I see our latest Cokes are almost untouched. We drink at the same time and the same speed and the noise of the bar around us appears to resume. I'd forgotten Mondays were film nights, so the large bottom end of the building is closed off and presumably quiet, whereas our end makes up for it. I don't think either of us had noticed it getting so busy and, as we drink, I realise that talking so much, and at a higher volume, has made my throat quite sore.

"What were we saying?" I have a brain like a colander.

"About my weight."

"I'm sorry. I didn't mean to be so personal."

"It's fine. I'm happy to talk about it. I'm still not used to being this size."

"Do you mind me asking how you got so...?"

"Large?" He smiles.

"I was trying to be diplomatic, but yes."

"An unhappy relationship."

"Married?"

'Thankfully, no, but we lived together."

"For a long time?"

"Too long. We worked together too, which made things a bit awkward."

"Ouch."

"Exactly."

"So it was comfort eating."

"Very much so." He pats his stomach. "People think only women do it, but we're just as likely, except we can get away with more."

"How do you mean?"

"Look around. How many men have a paunch?"

I look. "A few."

"And overweight women?"

I look again. "Not many."

"Exactly. It seems fashion magazines keep women slim, but men can do what they like."

"What about the likes of *GQ*, *Men's Health*, *Men's Fitness*, and…?"

"You know your men's magazines."

Oops. "A friend of mine reads them."

"A male friend, presumably."

"Err, yes. Friend, yes," I say, not sure why I feel the need to add the last bit. Above the waterline I struggle to stay sane, hoping he won't notice my metaphoric feet paddling away furiously underneath.

He yawns.

"Am I keeping you up?"

"Sorry. Had a callout last night. Well, this morning. One o'clock and the phone goes. Someone's cat's been shot."

"No!"

He nods. "Air rifle."

"At one in the morning?"

He nods again.

"Is it going to be all right?"

"Oh yes, patched him up a treat. He'll be catching mice again in no time."

I've never owned a cat. "Do they really do that?"

'Mice and other things. I used to have one, it brought a frog in once."

I winced. "Dead?"

"Oh no, very much alive. Hopping around the kitchen like a sucker toy on a spring."

"I used to have those."

"Weren't they fun? And Weebles."

"I'd hurt my fingernails trying to flick them over," I say, attempting to keep a straight face as Duncan sticks out his cheeks and elbows, and sways from side to side. I fail miserably.

He puts his arms back on the table and sighs. "Those were the days."

I nod, still smiling like Alice's Cheshire Cat.

Before we know it the barman comes over to collect our 'empty' glasses. We're knee deep in conversation and Duncan is the first to look up. He finishes his drink and hands over the glass. I look around the bar and realise we're the last two.

"I'm sorry, I have to… er," I splutter.

"That's okay. It's been a lovely evening. Thank you."

As we reach the front door, he steps back to let me out first, so I do a little 'thank you' curtsy. He laughs, and I melt.

We hover outside the bar as the door is locked behind us. The silence returns and we have the awkward 'do we shake hands or kiss' moment. We go for a peck on the cheek, his on mine, and I go to speak, but he beats me to it.

"Would you like me to walk you to your…?"

"I'm only round the corner, but thanks."

"Sure. Send me a message if you want to do this again."

I say a wimpy, "It's been fun," and my insides cringe. He smiles and goes towards the pedestrian crossing that connects the Picturedrome to the Racecourse's car park.

I watch him walk towards the pavilion and a dark-coloured Toyota RAV-4. As he unlocks the driver's door, he looks in my direction and smiles.

I lift a hand, then scuttle off to my awaiting Polo, feeling guilty that he might actually like me.

I'm the first to admit that I'm heightist, but remind myself this is only a work project and I won't be dating any of these guys properly, so it wouldn't matter if Duncan was four feet twelve and I'd get a chronic neck or backache looking down at him, because I'll never see him again.

"Onwards and upwards," I say, with the emphasis on 'up', as I zap the remote control and open my driver's door.

Chapter 2 – Tim the Weeble at the World's End

As I type the heading: *Miss Fussy meets Mr Short*, I feel rather guilty saying anything bad about Duncan, but remind myself it has to be an objective piece and starting the first article with pure praise isn't good journalism. I dismiss the 'had a good time' part of my brain and instead select the 'he was great, but…' part, and I'm now in mode.

William hovers over my desk holding a mug of something resembling coffee, or at least smells like it. He thumps it down on my 'Office Angels' temp company coaster. "Here, Janine's off again." I wonder what the two facts have to do with each other, but he continues. "I made this but didn't like it."

"Thanks." I smile weakly and debate whether I should tell him I don't drink coffee. Everyone knows that, including Janine, but it's the first time William's ever made me a drink… even though it wasn't.

"Liked your intro piece," he continues. "How did it go last night?"

"Good, thanks. Writing it up now."

William leans over and reads the nine words on the screen. "Looks like it. Ready by lunchtime then."

I sit there open mouthed, trying to work out why it's not the usual two p.m., when Donna bounces over. "Hiya!"

"Morning," I say, a tad subdued.

"Oh dear." Her face is covered in frown lines. "Didn't it go well with Hunky Dunky?"

"Who?"

"Hunky–"

"Dunky. I thought that's what you said. It went well, thanks." I couldn't help smiling.

"Ah ha!"

"No, not that good, Miss Smut. We went our separate ways." She fakes a Pierrot expression and I burst out laughing.

"So, you seeing him again?" She flutters her eyelids.

"No."

"Why not?"

"Because it's work. Research. A project. Not real."

"That doesn't matter."

15

"He's just–"

"What? Too ugly, too weird, too creepy?'

"Short."

"Oh? How short?"

"My height."

"Your height? Why that's huge."

'Thanks, Miss Five feet two."

"And a half. Don't forget the half. So, he's your height. Is that such a bad thing?"

"If I want to wear heels, yes."

"But you like him."

"Yes, but–"

"Ooh, sorry…' She points to William who's coming out of his office. "Fill me in later." She winks and heads for her desk.

I continue with the article as William walks past. He doesn't pay me or my computer screen any attention and goes back to the kitchen. Donna and I look at each other as a series of expletives follows a few seconds later.

How difficult is it to put an empty mug under a machine and press a button? This is William we're talking about though; he and technology don't exactly see eye to eye.

As he walks past my desk, the mug he's carrying drips onto the floor by my desk and I picture the poor cleaners cursing at… me. Thanks, William.

I eventually type again and out it comes.

Last night was date one of a series of daily dates for the entire month of May. Yes, that's right. If you missed yesterday's edition, my usual column of technology reviews and recommendations will be back on June second.

For this month, you can follow me as I swerve round the chicane of chivalry, sail down the slalom of speed dating (that was something I had never done, but thought it went well with 'slalom') *and…* I was running out of analogies… *and bait the barrage, no, barracuda of blind dates.* Or would oubliette of one-night stands be better? Oh yes, I've liked the word 'oubliette' since seeing the film *Labyrinth* with David Bowie in his tight leggings, so 'blind dates' has to go.

Last night I met a lovely man who I shall call D. We met at the Picturedrome on the Kettering Road, and the conversation was almost non-stop. Resorting to the weather proved unnecessary.

The bar staff were very pleasant and the surroundings immaculate as always. Although I didn't see anyone eating, the food is normally of a very high standard and all in all I would recommend this venue as a very convenient meeting place and a credit to the Richardson organisation.

I ramble a bit more about the place and avoid further commentary about Duncan and somehow manage to eke the piece to nine hundred and fifty words.

I dump it in William's in tray, pleased to be early, and go to the kitchen to make a cup of tea, the old-fashioned non-vending-machine way with a kettle and a teabag, discreetly pouring William's abandoned reject down the sink and placing his mug in the dishwasher.

I've just returned to my desk when William storms out of his office and drops my article on my desk. "What's this?"

"My article?" I offer.

"I know it's your article, but it's more like a restaurant review than a dating experience. The paper already has a food critic. Where's the juicy gossip I'm *paying* you for."

It's not difficult to understand why he emphasised the word *paying*. I should be grateful to have this job and I am; I love what I do, normally do, but equally I don't want to slate a man who was nothing but charming. William wants a mixed bag of good and juicy and I've just given him good. Okay, so it was Picturedrome-good rather than Duncan-good, but what does William expect? A line-by-line recount of our every word?

"It's not that I want every word that was said."

Boy, that was spooky.

"But I want more than this." He looks at the clock, which is heading towards one.

Just as well I brought in sandwiches today, I think, but just smile synthetically.

It's back to the drawing board, more or less. Losing any reference to the venue would lose eighty per cent of the words, so I'm reluctant to do that. An article of less than two hundred words isn't exactly what the readers, or William, expect, so I remember the shopping list and open up the Notes document for inspiration. I give it a quick read and return to the '31 dates art. 0205' file and scan the words.

Last night was date one of a series of daily dates…

I like everything until I waffle about the venue, so delete everything after *The bar staff…* and add *Earlier in the day I created a 'shopping list' of what I want, and what I don't look for, in a man. It may sound clinical, but as anyone having read John Gray's book will know, men and women really are from different planets.*

You can't tell me that other than looks (which we say we're not bothered about, but really are), we search for the same things in a prospective partner. Part of the conversation with D revolved around weight and, as he rightly pointed out, there is more pressure on the female species than the male. I did raise the subject of the 'new man' men's magazines, but, looking around the bar, I saw his point.

This article is about making a good first impression and the Picturedrome is the sort of place where you can get away with wearing almost anything. I had anticipated that D, working in animal services, would have worn casual smart, but he excelled himself with a very smart and co-ordinating dark James Bondesque ensemble, which suited his dark features perfectly.

I tweak one of the 'smart's and 'dark's then go on.

His manners were impeccable, naturally buying the first drink and offering the second, but I'm a 'pay my way' kind of girl (and on an, albeit small, allowance from the paper) and going Dutch seemed to please him. We talked too much to get to a third round.

We also touched on previous relationships, which is usually a no-no for a first (or even second) date, but the conversation with D was so natural that it fell into place with everything else. Before we knew it, the evening had come to an end. Again his chivalry kicked into place as he let me leave the bar first. He offered to walk me to my car and although it's a level of gallantry I could get used to, we went our separate ways.

What did I learn from last night? That there are still some nice guys out there, that the female population of Northamptonshire shouldn't write them, or themselves, off, and that, so far, internet dating is more than it's cracked up to be. Is D an exception to the rule? Maybe, time will tell, but with such an enjoyable date one, I can't wait for the other thirty.

So, I can tick the first two items on my 'dater's shopping list': Don't – too short (sorry D, we girls like to wear heels and still be able to look up to our man in an Officer and a Gentleman *kind of way) and Do – funny and great conversation. In fact he ticks a lot more Do boxes than that, but that would be greedy.*

I go to the Notes document and tick the 'funny/good conversation' Do box and 'too short' Don't box.

As this is the first article, I'm still not exactly sure what I should report on and leave out; it's a bit of a departure from testing mp3 speakers and digital radios. I guess the responses, if any, to my first article will lead me in the right direction… and of course William's editing.

With the article revised and left in William's tray (thankfully without him anywhere to be seen), I log on to my 'tallgirlnn1' profile and am stunned by: 'You have 22 new messages'. I click on the 'read messages' link and a gallery of photos appears. Reading and deleting the less than savoury ones, including five 'happily married' (not that happily if they're prepared to play away), I'm left with fourteen.

The first is from a chap called Tim who, at an astounding six feet seven, sounds like another nice guy. I send him a message and scroll down. I remind myself that while I need to meet a cross-section of the male population, I should be doing it from the point of view of a real dater, so include the men I'd normally dismiss. Besides, I have thirty more dates to find so, with just fourteen messages so far, I should be saying yes to them all.

I feel quite a thrill from the unfolding plan, although I doubt they're all going to be as easy to get on with as D. I then remember I'd planned to only date guys with no photos and if sticking to this rule I'd be left with eight, so decide to answer the non-photo non-weirdos for now and see if any more crawl out of the woodwork in the next few days, leaving the photo non-weirdos in reserve.

With messages sent, I press the F5 key to refresh the screen and already have a message from Timbo77. He apologises that he's busy at the moment (not too busy to be checking his messages), but is free tonight if that's not too soon (I'll let him off). I reply that I'm more than happy, and ask if he has anywhere in mind.

I scan his profile, which says he works 'in the meat industry'. Having visited an abattoir once for a previous job, I imagine living with someone who smells of dead animal twenty-four hours a day, although concede that a fishmonger would be ten times worse. I decide to add 'smell' to the shopping list, so Alt/Tab over to the Notes file and add 'and other smells' to the 'BO' line, then flick back to the internet.

I press F5 again and there is already a message from Tim. *Great!* it says. *How about the Picturedrome?*

What is it with that place?

I reply that it would normally be a great suggestion, but that I know someone who works there (well, I spoke to the barman for a few seconds last night). 'How about the World's End at Ecton?' In less than a minute, there's a reply. It turns out that TWE (as he calls it) is one of his locals, but he wouldn't mind if I didn't mind. We agree on seven o'clock as he has an early start tomorrow.

In the meantime, I've also received a message from a Lawrence (alias LorrieChi) asking if I'm free tonight. I've gone from Izzy No Mates to Miss Popular in a few mouse clicks. I send a message saying I'm sorry, but I have plans. How about tomorrow night and if so, does he have anywhere in mind? He then says Wednesday's fine and suggests the Bradlaugh pub.

I smile, thinking the Richardsons would be chuffed that I'm giving them more business, although I don't expect they'd plan to retire on a few Cokes and ice. I reply that it's fine and make a note of his details. I realise all this dating is going to get complicated, so make a diary in the Notes document, smiling again as the techno nerd side of me has its fix for the day.

I check my proper work emails – a mixture of review comments and supplier enquiries – until five o'clock and log off. It's been a good day and it isn't over yet. I'll be getting free drinks at a lovely eatery, part of a refurbished hotel, with hopefully a lovely man and all it would cost me is petrol, although I should speak to William about him paying mileage too. It is business after all.

Donna's engrossed on the phone, so I put a 'see ya' Post-it note in front of her (to which she smiles) then I do the usual waving at Mike (who nods like the Churchill Insurance dog) and go home.

I don't have time for, or need, another shower, so pull out a ready meal from the freezer; a low-fat beef hotpot, something else Duncan and I have in common. I eat my 'meal' (a word I use loosely as I'm still hungry afterwards, but put that partly down to an early lunch) while watching a rerun of *The Vicar of Dibley*. It's one of the last, a Christmas special I think, where she falls for the gorgeous actor who played Guy of Gisborne in *Robin Hood*. Richard something-or-other.

I realise I'm drooling when a blob of mince drops onto my right leg, just below my skirt line, and warms my skin a little too quickly. I swear, scoop it up and, carefully carrying the hotpot, go to the kitchen for a cloth.

It gets to the bit when she's tailing Richard and Keeley Hawes because Dawn thinks he's cheating on her, and she's about to disappear into the puddle, my favourite bit, when I look at the clock. It's six thirty. Swearing, I throw the hotpot tub in the kitchen bin and the dessertspoon into a mug on the draining board.

I glance up at the kitchen clock and I've lost another ten minutes. With a fifteen-minute journey ahead of me I grab my bag and car keys. Fortunately, I've left them on the ledge by the front door, so no repeat of the 'senior moment' of yesterday.

I run a couple of distinctly orange lights and arrive with seconds to spare. The World's End car park is pretty quiet and I spot a very cool-looking silver Porsche Boxster S convertible with a blue hood and keep everything crossed that it's Tim's. It would tick the aspirations Do box nicely.

I park my Polo next to the Porsche and casually walk past it, sniffing for several seconds. I'm not sure whether I seriously thought I'd smell dead cow, but I do get a whiff of leather, so I suppose I'm not far off.

As I walk up the stairs to the bar, Tim stands out a mile. That's because he's not only that tall, but he's nearly that wide. In fact he reminds me of a Weeble. I dismiss the Porsche theory and try to keep a straight face as I walk towards him, remembering Duncan's Weeble story of the night before.

Tim puts out his hand as I approach him and, after the Matthew/Gisele debacle, I turn behind me to check he means me. Behind me is clear air (all the clearer thanks to the smoking ban), so I feel safe to put my hand out. I feel like I'm greeting a politician although his smile appears more genuine.

"Hi, I'm Tim. I presume you're Izzy."

"I am. Hi."

He asks me what I'd like to drink and I request a pineapple juice and lemonade. It's the closest I get to Malibu and pineapple, and I need to keep a clear head to remember everything that takes place in the next couple of hours so I can report it the following day. I always keep a notepad and pens in my bag, but think it would be giving the game away if I dig them out now.

He orders a Staropramen beer (a new one on me) and we swap 'what do you do?' questions, with Tim explaining that he's a marketing manager for a dog food company. There's a theme running here and the inevitable pets question comes up.

It turns out he's got two cats, which surprises me considering his job, but he says he's not been there long. He says he used to work at a chocolate factory in Corby; I know the one he means, and I can imagine why he left. At least he won't be eating his way through the new company, but as the evening progresses I start to wonder.

I ask if there's an office dog and he says there are two and sometimes they fight like… well, dog and dog, but most of the time they're fine. "Chalk and cheese," I say, to list another cliché, and he nods. I later also wonder whether these are two menu items he'd not say 'no' to either.

We sit in a booth and I relax. It's all going swimmingly until he belches. I anticipate the customary apology, but it looks like I won't be holding my breath, which is a shame as I wished I had.

Next is the arrival of a huge 'share' mixed platter. Having placed the plate in the middle of the table, the waitress returns with two sets of cutlery and two serviettes, which she places on our left-hand sides.

I stare at the meal, then at Tim and say, "I didn't realise we were eating. I've already–"

"Oh, no," he interjects, "I ordered this before you arrived," which is fairly obvious.

"I've already eaten," I finish my previously planned statement.

"So have I," he says, "but my stomach rumbled while waiting for you, so I didn't think you'd mind."

I'm not sure how he would have heard, or felt, any rumbling. I feel mean and blush a little as I nod politely and he tucks into his 'snack'.

The whole experience is quite enlightening. Firstly, I've never seen anyone eat so quickly, maybe with the exception of Chinese people eating rice with chopsticks, but they're a hundred… no, a thousand times more elegant. Secondly, between bites, but not before masticating the chicken wings and mini sweetcorn cobs, he takes another extra-large (this man doesn't do anything in a smaller size) swig from his tankard (how old did he say he was?).

I look at his huge right arm lifting up the mini-keg and compare his bicep size with that of my right thigh, which is bigger than my left, having spent years doing step aerobics, right being my predominant foot.

I watch his arms compete with each other as they fight for access to his mouth and I look around the bar. No one appears to be watching other than me and for that I'm grateful, but I remember he's a regular and they've probably seen it a hundred times before.

With his mouth full of I sadly know exactly what, he says, "This seems rather unfair. Did you want some of this?" He points down at the plate; there isn't much 'this' to be had. The wings are bones and the dishevelled cobs devoid of corn. The stuffed mushrooms and onion rings were the first things to go and are remembered only by the presence of a few breadcrumbs. They would have been my first choices.

This may be one thing, perhaps the only thing, Tim and I have in common, other than we're both human, though at the moment I'm debating that too. There are a couple of potato skins, which I normally adore, but they look rather greasy. I'm pretty sure though that even a banoffee pie (my favourite food ever – something I would not only die for, but kill for) would be equally unappetising right now.

I shake my head, attempt a smile, and watch him clear the plate. Finally, he picks up the chicken bones and I expect him to eat them whole, but he licks them clean and drops them back on the plate. He issues another belch, this time apologising as he realises it was loud enough to draw attention to himself, as if the devouring of an African family's monthly intake wasn't bad enough.

Throughout the whole episode, there's not been a word of proper chat between us. He's been too busy eating and I've been concentrating on keeping my hotpot down.

As the last morsel of food disappears into the black hole, the waitress heads for our table, I assume to clear the platter away, but she's holding a plate above her left shoulder. I'm relieved it's not big enough to be another meal for two, although I wouldn't put it past him, but more like a standard-sized dinner plate. I will it to be nothing I would normally eat, but am sorely disappointed as laid before me is a double helping of, the waitress announces, "Home-made banoffee pie". I could cry.

I smile less than half-heartedly at the waitress who looks sympathetically at me before retreating to the kitchen, I assume to gossip about Table 14.

At the thought of the beautiful dessert being dismembered in a similar way to the platter, I look at Tim's eyebrows. I can't bear to look any further down as his nose is running and it's close to meeting the barbecue sauce on his upper lip. I've finally had enough and blurt out, "I'm sorry, but I've just remembered I've left my oven on." But I recall Duncan's battle to lose weight and feel guilty, until Tim's mouth gapes open revealing a mixture of toffee syrup and pastry, which threaten to spill over the edge like a coin cascade at a fair, and I can't bear to look anymore.

As I get up to leave, he splutters, "So, do you want to meet again?" I don't know what to say without hurting his feelings. I mumble a non-committal, "I'll message you," and almost do a Usain-Bolt sprint down the stairs.

As I walk to the car, I think of how proud William will be that I've not spent any of tonight's budget and equally proud I'll have such a wonderful story to recount. Again, I debate how much I should surrender to print, but for opposite reasons to the previous night.

As I start the engine, there's a tap at the driver's window. I look up and it's Tim. Tim with pie stains on his white Bolton Wanderers football shirt. I sigh at the waste.

I zip the window down and say a weak, "Hello."

He grins, thankfully with his teeth closed, although a strand of onion is trying to escape. "You don't talk much, do you?"

I don't know what to say, which is most unlike me. "Um," is all I can muster.

"I can talk for England," he says.

I'm so pleased he didn't and point to the restaurant, saying, "Have you done a runner?"

"Oh no. They know me. They know I'll be back."

"Ah." I wish he'd take the hint and return inside.

"Nice car," he says.

"Thanks. What do you drive?" I'm certain he won't say the Boxster, and he points to an equally sexy blue Mini Cooper S on the other side of the car park. It's exactly as I would have picked myself, and had done so a few months ago... well, to the point of going on the Mini website and 'spending' over twenty grand on a Mayfair model with the go-faster stripes and alloy wheels. I nearly cried when I had to close the screen without hitting the 'order' button.

I'm wondering how such a hulk of a man would fit inside the car, when he cheerfully repeats, "So, do you want to meet again?"

I realise I'm going to have to be a lot less subtle than 'I'll message you', so decide I'm going to have to hurt his feelings. I guess though, it wouldn't be the first time. "I'm sorry," I say. "You're a really nice guy..."

25

He looks crestfallen and I think maybe his skin's not that thick after all.

"I'm sorry," I repeat. "It's just that…"

"It's fine," he says. "I know how 'you're a nice guy' goes."

"I'm sorry." I can't help it.

"Okay," is all he says, and walks back towards the pub.

I feel like shouting after him that we could be friends, no hard feelings or another overused cliché, but I know the moment's passed. I try not to feel guilty because he probably would have been there having the meal anyway, but it's still a horrible feeling to turn someone down. I think I've been too hasty, but again remind myself it's for the paper and not to get personally involved.

I drive home in silence and the bleep of the car's remote, the flashing indicators and the squeaky gate are the only sounds to indicate I've arrived.

I need an animal to greet me as I open my front door to a cold hallway, and wonder whether Duncan would lend me one of his.

I swap my jacket for a jumper as I wait for the central heating to kick into life. Had I been away the anticipated two hours, plus travel time, I would have come back to a toasty house, but the kitchen clock tells me, as I fill the kettle, that it's been just over half that.

I take a cup of tea to bed and pick up Jack Myler's *Opaque*, a novel that's been patiently sitting by my digital clock radio for the last couple of months. Every time I read a bit more I keep thinking, *This is great, I should read this every night*, although parts of it scare me to death. I'm particularly looking forward to reading tonight as I've got to the end of a very long but enjoyable hundred-page chapter one, and can't wait to see what Elliot will do next. I'm hoping he will take my mind off Tim and his massacre of a lovely-looking banoffee pie. Something tells me I'll never again see it in quite the same light.

Chapter 3 – Lawrence at the Charles Bradlaugh

I've just unlocked my computer screen when William comes striding over to my desk. My face creases as I anticipate an ear bashing.

"Good work, my dear!" he gushes. "We've had floods of requests to meet this D."

"Really?" I'm quite astounded and, if honest, a little jealous. D was my find and I'm not sure I want to share him with my reading public, other than in print of course.

"Women love tall, dark and handsome."

"Oh, he wasn't very–'

"And they want to know what your shopping list consists of. And so do I. Two p.m."

I go to answer, but he turns and goes back to his office.

I look back at the screen and am logging on when I feel a presence hovering. I look up and it's William again. I'd love to know how he manages to appear as if by magic, like a scene from the 1970s cartoon *Mr Benn*.

"I forgot to say," he says, "we're renaming the column 'What did I learn from last night?'"

"Okay," I mumble, and he almost glides back to his office like the Martian Girl in *Mars Attacks*. I've never seen him like this and it's scary. He should have a chat with Klaus, that'll sort him out.

I first check my work emails and wade through the usual mix of round-robin crud which William would do his nut over if he was ever accidentally copied in on them. One is inane natter from Donna wanting to know all about D, although she only lives a few desks away from me, and we swap copious amounts of WhatsApp messages whenever we're not in ear or eyeshot of each other. Several emails are from companies requesting for me to review their latest gadgets, which is always lovely.

With those dealt with, I log onto NorthantsDating and guestimate my new messages to be around a dozen. I'm pleasantly surprised when it's twenty-three, although by the time I weed out today's weirdos, I'm left with an unlucky thirteen, so wasn't far out. I notice Tim's 'Timbo77' halfway down the list and click on that one first. I expect a barrage of abuse, but it's a gently worded few lines saying how lovely it was to meet me, sorry he wasn't what I was looking for, and wishing me all the best for the future.

I send a message back, thanking him for his understanding and saying I'm sorry too, making reference to the elusive 'spark', which I then delete. I wade through the others and one in particular leaps out at me. 'FelixP69'. I roll my eyes whenever I see the numbers six and nine together, but I note it's his year of birth, so let him off.

He sounds quite normal, so I send a message asking if he's free this week. I dismiss three others, giving them automated 'tallgirlnn1 has read your profile, but doesn't wish to proceed' replies, and move on to a guy who sent six messages, which is far too keen. Opening them up reveals photographs of various parts of his anatomy, far from photogenic, so I allocate them, and him, to the weirdos bin by clicking on 'block this user'.

This leaves four unread messages and I notice one is from Lawrence, alias 'LorrieChi', tonight's date. He's checking we're still on. I say I'm looking forward to it, which is less than honest after last night's experience, but hope my optimism shows in my typing. The other three include one guy I've already messaged but he says he's no longer available and should have pulled his advert weeks ago. "Why didn't you then?" I grumble at the screen.

The final two are from a Robert and a Nigel. I click on RobbieY69's first. Having given him the benefit of the doubt that he would have been born the same year as Felix, I'm proven wrong. Although his profile is littered with innuendos, there's something quite appealing about him, so I decide to send an innuendo-free reply.

'NigelEByGum' doesn't say very much… in fact just 'Hi. How are you?' so I make up for it by sending a rambling email back, referring to bits of his profile and asking if he's free this weekend.

With the online inbox cleared, I set about compiling today's piece. I remember what William said, and entitle it 'What did I learn from last night?'

I press the Enter key twice to leave a space and write the body of the article.

So, what did I learn? That you can't always judge a book by its cover (even if it's covered in banoffee pie); to either make it clear whether to eat beforehand or together; and to take something to read because your date is too busy eating to talk.

As I type, I regret not repeating Monday night's purchase of a newspaper, then at least I wouldn't have had to look at the car crash that was happening on the other side of the booth.

And what can I say about my date last night? Lots, but sadly little that my editor would allow to be printed. Let's just say T had a healthy appetite. We met at the World's End in Ecton, which, for those of you without good local knowledge, is near the area of town known as the Eastern district or the 'where you don't want to live' district.

The World's End bar, restaurant and hotel and Ecton itself are charming (if you ignore the smell from the local sewage plant – which is why no one ever drives along the A45 or A4500 with their windows open) and the venue did not let me down.

I delete the districts bit so not to offend locals, because the area's improved vastly over the years, but leave the sewage bit in because everyone knows it's true.

I understand from my editor that a few of you are interested in meeting D, mentioned in yesterday's article. Naturally, for reasons of national security… Data Protection Act 1998 (or is it 2003, I never remember) I can't give you D's details and because this article is ongoing I can't divulge to him that he was the first guinea pig in this experiment. I'm sure you understand.

We have also had some enquiries after the 'shopping list', so what I'm going to do is keep letting you know which ones each 'date' ticks in the Do or Don't do list and you can see whether it matches your list. What? You haven't made one? Maybe not on paper, but every one of us has, at some stage in our lives, made a mental note of what we seek from a potential partner.

Back to T and I at TWE.

T had the kind of figure where his stomach arrived before he did. It looked like he was either nine months pregnant or… but realise it's cruel, so I highlight it all with my mouse and press the 'delete' key.

T had a heart of gold. A heart that's made to work too hard. He'd ordered a mixed grill (I feel that's kinder than a 'platter for two to share') *before I arrived, so the first few minutes of our date held little conversation.* (True.) *It soon became clear* (because I said so) *that we weren't compatible and we went our separate ways.*

Scratching around for things to say about him other than appearance and pie-eating contests, I realise there isn't anything. What really happened is only known by Tim and I, and I debate making something up, but with so many dates to recount, I figure it's easier (and of course more ethical) to stick to the truth, so I return to the subject of the list and dating in general.

I realise when editing the first draft that it's very sparse, so click on Tim's 'Timbo77' profile for more inspiration about the man himself. A picture has appeared since my original look and it shows his sad eyes. It's obvious he's unhappy being the size he is, and I wonder why he doesn't do anything about it. I guess it's like being an alcoholic where the substance takes you over and you feel powerless to do anything about it. Duncan is living proof though, that it's possible to come out the other side. Maybe I could 'Ask Agnes' (aka Keith) about Tim and see what he, sorry she, thinks.

I realise I'm becoming too involved with these men. This is supposed to be fun, so I continue with the article, and add in some online dating tips.

When you're thinking about setting up a profile, do be honest, but don't give too much of yourself away. While you can hide behind a profile name, it's easier to use your real first name (surnames a definite no-no) on the dates themselves (especially if you're going to persevere after the first one). Any other slight inaccuracies you use have to be well remembered or they could come back to bite you on the bum.

Above all, don't take yourself, or other profiles, too seriously. There's a very helpful 'How to set up your profile' on the dating site I use (I'm unable to tell you which one for the duration of this project), but if you get stuck, the site usually has an FAQ section. Failing that, drop me a line via the email address at the bottom of this column.

Things to remember once your profile is set up and running: Men are more likely to lie about their age, height, (this is where I think of Duncan again and melt into a puddle of cornflakes – which reminds me, I should have put my sandwiches in the fridge as warm cheese is horrible) *income and marital status.*

While online dating has the advantage over face-to-face nightclub or pub dating of you being able to make a cup of tea and turn up the central heating, you often find photographs provided are either very old or of a handsome friend. It has been known for people, male and female, to scan in photos that come with picture frames or out of magazines, but they're only fooling themselves because you'll have to meet them eventually.

What they're relying on though, is that you'll have been so swayed by their charm that looks won't matter – and we all know that's bollocks. (I delete the last word and replace it with rubbish; bollocks would never get through the William sensor.)

While most dating sites will say you get far more responses if you include a photograph, you may get more honest messages if you don't. It's entirely up to you, but you also have to think about whether you want the world and his wife knowing you're looking for a partner.

Don't get me wrong, it's a great way of meeting people and there's little stigma attached to it these days, but some people have jobs where they need to be discreet (not something I'm known for).

If you create your profile and want to look for others before you get any messages, there are search boxes to fill in, but remember, the more specific you are, the fewer profiles you'll get to see. If you see a profile you like you can usually either 'wink' at it, which sends an automated she/he's interested in you, or you can compile a specific message. Depending on how interested you are or how recently they logged in (and therefore how interested they are in finding a mate), you can decide.

You can see from someone's profile whether they've logged on x days, x weeks or even x months ago. The chances are if they've not checked their messages for a month or more they've either found someone or lost interest, unless you're my boss, William, who has…

I hold the Ctrl key down and hit the backspace a few times deleting the last bit; it's never going to get past his desk, so I don't see the point in going any further. I replace it with… *unless he or she has been on an extended holiday or business trip. If that's the case then a 'wink' is the best course of action to avoid wasting your time or enthusiasm.*

Once the messages come in, you can swiftly weed through the weirdos – photos of any parts of their anatomies other than their faces usually give the game away – and see what you're left with. In my case today it was thirteen messages out of twenty-three, so if you work on a fifty-fifty ratio you're probably doing well.

Again you can decide on whether to have a quick chat or an involved 'deep and meaningful' exchange. If he's sent you 'Hi, how are you?' you don't want to reply with a long list of your aches and pains, or how your boss has been… (I backspace again, putting a full stop after pains) *Equally, if he's taken the time and effort to send you a lovely ramble about what he likes and dislikes and so on, you don't want to send a one-liner, unless you're really not interested. It's a good idea to have a few messages flying backwards and forwards before you agree to meet.* (Pot, kettle, black)

Meeting the opposite (or, of course, same) sex should be fun. Follow all the common-sense rules: meet in a public place and tell someone where you're going… yada yada yada.

That's me done for the day. Good luck with creating your profiles and if you're a bit further along in the process, good luck with your messages, or even further, good luck with your dates!

Oh yes, the shopping list. You want to know which boxes T ticks: Don't *– eat in front of your date who's already eaten, and* Do *– have a late-night (or midnight if the date goes well) snack in your fridge for when you get home. And spare your date's feelings – be very diplomatic, but honest when letting them* *down. They may have heard it before, but they'll want to know where they stand.*

I look at the clock and it's nearly two. I should have guessed from my stomach growling like a shredder. I take a quick scan of the piece, print it off and walk it over to William's office. He's on the phone with the door shut, but beckons me in. I put the article in his in tray and wait, but it's soon apparent he has no intention of finishing his call and I can tell by his expression it's not good news, so I make a run for it.

I go back to my desk and take the lukewarm cheese sandwiches out of my bag. They look as appetising as Tim's dribbled syrup and pastry, but I don't have time to go out, and the vending machine only has crisps and chocolate.

My sarnies taste like my old slippers (not that I've ever tried them of course), but I persevere. I still feel unfulfilled and am walking to the vending machine when Donna pounces.

"So," she pants, "how... how, did it go?" Her eyes are as wide as I've ever seen them. She reminds me of Tigger on something dubiously illegal and I can't help laughing.

She stares at me and it's obvious she's trying to work out whether last night's date was a success or failure.

"I've just submitted my column to William, you can read all about it tomorrow," which I know is untrue as there are so few lines about T.

"No! Don't do that to me. I want to know now! I want it from the horse's mouth."

"Have you had a lunch break?" I ask.

She shakes her head.

"Come on." I lead her to the kitchen and one of the sets of tables and chairs at the rear of the room. We sit with our backs to the wall so we can spot anyone, especially William, coming in, and Donna's already springing up and down like a child in a bouncer. I'm getting a headache.

I give in and she settles down. I relay almost blow by blow, and have her in stitches. By the end she needs tissues and is patting her eyes when William walks in. We can tell by his expression he thinks it's 'women's troubles' and he jabs at the button for coffee (Janine, it turns out, has the flu and is going to be off all week), grabs it as soon as it's done and shuffles out without a word.

When back at my desk, I check my messages again. There are equal numbers of work and pseudo-work emails: eight of each. I debate for a second which to answer first and decide that tallgirlnn1 is going to be more fun, so deal with the laborious Outlook inbox first.

There's one from Keith congratulating me on my first 'new' column and offering his 'Ask Agnes' services. I stand up and look at the right-hand corner of the office. Keith looks up and I wave. He smiles and looks down again. Despite his line of work, he's the shyest person I know, and I shake my head as I sit back down, wondering whether he ever takes any of his own advice.

There are two more messages from new suppliers and five from readers regarding the new column. I respond to the new suppliers thanking them for the offer of free items to evaluate, giving them the paper's postal address and the usual statement saying I can't guarantee to feature their items. I then click on the first of the readers' emails.

It's from a chap called Dudley. It gives me a scare for a second because I read it as 'Duncan' and think he's found out about me already, but as I read on I realise Dudley's just asking for advice about his unfaithful girlfriend. I reply, thanking him for his message, but saying it's not really my department and that I'll forward it to Aunt Agnes. I blind copy Keith in so he can deal with it without giving away his real identity to Dudley.

The next email is from Jenny who's just turned forty and hates it. All her friends are engaged or 'spliced' and she feels lonely. She says she's not sure whether to try internet dating, but all the conventional routes have been a nightmare. I realise my new column and Keith's are not that dissimilar.

I reply saying I understand how she feels (not completely untrue, albeit ten years younger), and that she's welcome to follow my column (I'm secretly not sure she should in case it ends in disaster) and/or I could pass her email on to Aunt Agnes who may be able to offer her advice in a more professional capacity. I get a swift reply thanking me, but saying she'll 'wait and see'. Oh, shit.

Reader email three is from sixteen-year-old Brad, which I suspect isn't his real name, who has tried gaynorthantsdating over the past six months and had a mixed response. Again, I mentally have Keith lined up as a fallback, but it's all good. Brad came out to his family and friends the year before, who have been incredibly supportive, and he's just wishing me luck.

I reply, applauding him, while trying desperately not to be condescending, for his maturity, and thanking him for being so open with me.

The last but one is from Ruby who says she's more than twice my age, is doing a course at her local library to use a computer and would like tips on setting up an online profile. I smile as she says she's there writing her email and has to ask the librarian how to send it, so she apologises if I have to wait a minute in case he's busy.

She goes on to say her husband of fifty-seven years died two years ago and she's just feeling 'ready to start again'. 'Terry wouldn't mind,' she adds.

I sit in a reflective mood as Donna bounces over. I swear she's on a spring. I've never known her to have a bad day and I'm jealous. I try to be a 'glass half full' person; sometimes it's difficult, but with Donna it seems so natural. Even when we go out, she's like a little bullet, a mini bottle of fizz. Our evenings are fun, and in a way I don't want her to be snapped up because it wouldn't be the same, and who goes out on the pull on their own? Someone braver than me.

"Hiya!"

"Hello," I say as cheerfully as I can.

"Has he contacted you yet?"

"Who?"

"Hunky Dunky."

I had thought for a second that she was going to say Tim, but my heart leaps when she mentions Duncan's name.

"No. Should he have?"

"I don't know. I thought you had a good time."

"We did. I certainly know I did, but he's not messaged me and I can't message him."

"Why not?"

"Because it's work."

Donna blows a loud raspberry, which makes our colleagues look up, even Keith way on the other side of the office.

I laugh. "Donna, you crack me up. Can I bottle you and sell you to my readers? They'd pay handsomely for liquid Donna, and I bet Keith would have a constant supply of customers."

She giggles as only Donna can and skips back to her desk. I should speak to Chloë in HR to check Donna's CV – I'm sure she's underage. I know for a fact that Donna's five months younger than me, which reminds me I shouldn't leave it too long to think about organising a party for her, but her brain age needs verifying.

I've always been a serious person and sometimes I wish I could relax. I can't pinpoint why I can't and think maybe I should make her a case study.

I look at the clock and it's half four. I double-click on the final reader email and it's from Penny. Her nine-year-old daughter has a computer in her room and Penny's sure she goes on the internet. She's worried about her daughter talking to paedophiles and would like some advice. I forward the email to Keith and ask him for his comments before I reply. It not only buys me time because I don't know what to say, but I'm itching to check my 'tallgirlnn1' messages before I leave.

I flick over to the internet. My session on NorthantsDating has timed out, so I log back in and am disappointed when there are no new messages. I had expected a couple. I click F5 to refresh the screen, but it's still zero. With half an hour to kill, I do more searching.

With only a date lined up for tonight, I'm panicking that this wonderful new column will end up being a total work of fiction, and while I've always had an idea for a novel rattling around in the space I call a brain, I've never put it down on paper, or in my case, onto the keyboard.

Before I leave the office, I have a quick final check of tallgirlnn1 and do a 'yay' when there's a message from Felix. He's free tomorrow night, Wednesday, if that's any good. I message back saying a cool 'Fine by me, where do you fancy going?'

I log off and go home, practising my nightly routine with Mike. However, Donna's already out there chatting to him, giggling like the proverbial schoolgirl, so I don't even get a half-hearted nod tonight. I think that if I even walked in with a camouflage rucksack on my back he wouldn't notice. He and Donna might actually be good for each other. He'd be a guinea pig for the 'Health' side of her column and she'd bring some sparkle to his seemingly flatline life.

Walking towards the car park, I think about how I got so cynical. Despite last night's 'blip' I have high hopes that the next twenty-nine days will prove me wrong. They have to, don't they?

Being a town centre pub, the Bradlaugh is heaving and I look around to see a guy on his own. I can't see anyone who fits the bill, so I wander. As I turn a corner, I see a tall thin guy standing in front of a pillar. He's so thin I can see it behind him. My clichéd heart sinks. He's tall, about six feet two, but must weigh less than me. I don't usually go for men who weigh less than me, something else to add to the Don't column.

He smiles, steps forward and I say, "Hello." He introduces himself as Lawrence and I do likewise (as Izzy, obviously). As he turns and walks towards the bar, I hesitate for a second, doing what all we girls do: check out the posterior. There isn't one. I should have guessed considering the lack of meat on him, but he's also wearing jeans that look a size too big (which begs the question as to whether they are the smallest size possible for someone as tall as him), so the denim wrinkles over what there is of his backside like the face of a Chinese Shar-Pei.

We go to the bar to order some drinks. I fancy a cup of tea, but have prepared the request of Coke with a dash of lime, when he says to the barman, "I'd like something hot. Do you do tea?" A man after my own heart, and I nod to order the same.

We aim for a table away from the speakers, and it's not long before the tea arrives.

I like my tea like gnat's… weak, so am delighted when there's a pot of water next to two unused teabags on a saucer. There are a couple of biscuits on a side plate, a small jug of milk and some sachets of white sugar and sweeteners. It all looks very civilised.

Like the gentleman he's been so far, Lawrence lets me be mum.

"I like my tea quite weak," I say.

"I have it however it comes," he replies.

I put one teabag in the pot, tip in some of the water, stir briefly and pour mine out. I then hold the other teabag over the pot and he nods. I let it fall and add the rest of the water.

While we sit waiting for his to brew, I drizzle a normal-sized portion of milk into my cup then help myself to a pink sachet of powdered sweetener, laying the empty sachet on the side plate as I watch him make his drink.

I will him to put in all six packets of sugar, but he also picks up a single pink sachet. I then stare at him as he empties the sweetener into his mug, almost counting the grains as they go in.

"They're calorie free, aren't they?" I ask, but I don't think he hears me.

I'm gripped as he trickles in a tiny amount of milk, as if he's counting the calories as each drop falls. It reminds me of an old advert for paint when, one by one, the millicalories of this white fluid hit the surface. I remember reading once that an average serving of milk is the same as an apple, about forty calories, so think he's had about a dozen.

Before Lawrence lifts the jug, I'm tempted to accidentally knock it with my elbow, but it's too far away. Besides, it might put him off having the drink altogether, so would be twelve calories that his body misses out on and I don't think it can spare them.

We drink and chat and, having forgotten to look at his profile again before I left the office, I bluff some questions to which I should have known the answers. Equally I have to recall what I've put in mine, but it all seems to fall into place.

The two biscuits are still waiting to be eaten, but he's not paying them any attention. I look at him then look at the plate, but it doesn't make any difference. Eventually I pick the plate up and offer them to him, but he shakes his head and pats his stomach.

As his hand disappears into the swathes of fleece, it hits home that not only does he weigh less than me, he also probably weighs less than the African child Tim's meal could have been intended for. I don't know what to say, but the silence is broken by Lawrence's stomach rumbling. It's so loud it drowns out the Stereophonics playing in the background and I say, "Are you sure you don't want the biscuits?"

I feel a bit like a mother who's convinced that their healthy child, who has just left home, isn't getting enough to eat, but I settle for asking him what he does for a living and he says he's a social worker. I wonder if any of his clients have reported him to the authorities for suspected malnutrition, but instead I say it must be a very rewarding job.

He puts down his cup, his face full of life for the first time. "It's all I've ever wanted to do. My mum was a nurse and father a doctor, so it was fairly inevitable I'd do something along the care line."

"And you obviously enjoy it," I say.

"Oh yes, can't see myself doing anything else."

"That must be lovely. So many people plod along in life and never have the guts to leave something they hate doing, taking even the smallest of risk for something they'd enjoy."

"I know what you mean. I see so many families trapped by their circumstances. Dead-end jobs on the minimum wage, but no get up and go to... well, get up and go."

A different barman to the one who originally served us comes over and puts our cups and plate on the tray. He looks at Lawrence and asks, "Can I get you anything to eat?"

I will him to say, "Yes, please I'd like a platter for two for one", but he just smiles and shakes his head. The barman then looks at me, and I do the same, so he takes the tray away. I then ask Lawrence if he'd like another drink and he asks for a Diet Coke. Trying not to be too obvious I say, "Ew, Diet Coke, don't you think it tastes tinny? I always go for fat Coke." I fail miserably.

"No, I find the proper stuff too sweet. I think you'll find the Coke is Pepsi here and they're supposed to ask you if that's okay, but no one ever does."

"Oh," is all I can muster and go to the bar.

As I'm waiting to be served, I look over at Lawrence who's looking more and more like a little lost boy. I want to fold him up like a piece of Origami, put him in my pocket and take him home. He reminds me of a tramp rifling through rubbish, and, working in the town centre, I've seen a few (and on more than one occasion have had to return to Boots after giving away my newly bought sandwich).

Having heard stories of people inviting strays home and then waking up the following morning with their valuables, and even their cars, gone, I always buy *The Big Issue* on a Monday lunchtime and love hitting the charity shops when I can.

When I get back to the table with the drinks, Lawrence asks to be excused to go to the men's room. I smile at his old-fashioned, but to be highly applauded in this day and age, politeness and watch the crumples of denim disappear into the corner of the bar. I'm not at all surprised that he has to go after only one drink as I can't imagine there's much food, if any, in his stomach to soak it up.

While I'm waiting, I sit and gaze at the other drinkers – a mixture of ages and sexes. I could people-watch for England and am still engrossed when Lawrence returns. He smiles and retakes his seat. We chat some more, taking it in turn to drink our Pepsis (his diet, mine fat). Our glasses are soon empty and, with a natural pause in the conversation, I ask him if he'd like another drink. Technically it's his turn, but I'm still one up from the previous night, so don't mind.

He pats his stomach. "I'd better not." I wonder whether it's a calorie factor (isn't there only one in a Diet Coke/Pepsi?) or that he'd have to go to the toilet again. I stay seated and he says, "Don't let me stop you having another."

I lift my right hand up to indicate that it's fine and he smiles. I decide it's not a bad thing as we seem to be running out of conversation and it must be close to chucking-out time. I'm thinking about what to say when the expected 'Do you want to meet again?' pause crops up.

Despite it failing miserably the night before, I decide on 'You're a nice guy', but he speaks first. "I've had a nice evening."

"Me too," I say, and wait.

"But I'm sorry, you're not really my type," he continues.

Because I have meat on my bones, I think, but say, "I quite understand. There needs to be a spark, doesn't there?"

He nods.

I now know for certain that I have to introduce him to Donna. She'd be fascinated.

Lawrence and I stand up, and he puts his left hand forward as if I am to leave first.

We do the usual pecks on the cheeks at the front door before going in opposite directions. I've parked my car at work, so don't have far to go, but it's raining – and not the odd drizzle, but a blanket. It's like God's done the washing-up and forgotten to turn off the tap. Somewhere more exotic, it would be like a tropical waterfall, except this is cold and damp rather than warm and inviting.

Apart from an easy conversation, nothing about this evening has been particularly warm and inviting. Watching Lawrence and his cup of tea, with his sucked-in cheeks as he drank, was like a scene from *Schindler's List*. Looking at him, I wanted to give him a hot meal. Tim could teach him a thing or two.

I wish Donna were here – it would give her column miles rather than inches. No doubt she'll 'Tigger D' over to my desk first thing tomorrow morning to get the latest rundown. She and I should have a little party and invite Keith, make it a mothers' meeting.

I arrive at the security barrier and wave at the screen. As far as I know, security changeover takes place at midnight so it'll still be Mike. I imagine him on his second packet of doughnuts (he rarely eats anything else, even at what would be his lunchtime) with jam or apple sauce running down his chin. I wonder again what Donna sees in him, but figure it might be motherlove and after Lawrence, I know only too well how that feels.

Driving home, I think about the article I'm going to construct tomorrow.

I arrive home at the same time as my next-door neighbour, Ursula. The rain's stopped, so we have a quick chat.

41

"Hi," she says getting out of her red Fiat Punto.

"Hello. You're late tonight. Just finished work?"

"Sort of. We had a callout. Family domestic."

"Oh dear. Nothing too serious I hope."

"Not really – a common occurrence with this particular family. I'm only there as a peacemaker."

"And I'm guessing they don't see you like that."

"No. It's difficult sometimes to get through to them, but when you do, it's worth it."

"I couldn't do it. I don't have the patience."

"Outside the job, I'm not as calm as some, but you have to be professional."

I debate whether to ask her if she has a colleague called Lawrence, but decide against it as I still have a cover to maintain. "I'd better go," I say.

"Yes, me too, I'm back on at six."

"Ouch, that's unfair. Can't you go in late because of your callout?"

"Sadly not. Such is the life I chose."

I smile and count myself lucky. An office job isn't for everyone, but you can't beat nine-to-five when it comes to a good night's sleep.

I'm pleased to see there's no post sticking out of the postbox, which either means there hasn't been any or my postman's finally got the message. I select the smallest key on my key ring and open the green metal door.

As I suspected, there's no post, but there is a pizza leaflet, which surprises me as they are normally particularly hopeless at pushing them all the way in (those who'll have gone past the sign on my gate displaying 'No leaflets or cold callers', which is usually most of them). Grrr.

It's rather late for another cup of tea, but I make one anyway. As I put the milk back in the fridge, I pull out the salad drawer and my right index finger hovers over the selection of fun-size chocolate bars. Most people keep salad in their salad drawers, and there is a little in there, but mine tends to keep house to far more interesting fodder.

I pick a mini Snickers, mini Bounty and the tea, and go upstairs. I like to read when I'm eating and/or drinking, so pick up where Elliot left off, and am soon quaking in my pyjamas. As I look under the duvet, I see my ample thighs quiver, and think of Lawrence and his skeletal bones.

I debate which is scarier out of seeing those naked or Elliot in the flesh, and conclude that Elliot would have to win every time. Lawrence could, I'm convinced, be mothered, whereas I don't think Elliot ever had one.

Chapter 4 – Felix at the Pavilion

I get to work and log on to my computer. I anticipate the Tigger D pounce, but there's no sign of her. By nine thirty I'm getting worried, so go out to reception. I expect to see Marion behind the desk, but early-shifter Jason's in her chair.

"Hi, Jason."

"Hello, Miss 'What did I learn from last night?' MacFarlane."

I blush and he laughs. "Only teasing. Can I help you with something? Were you after Marion?"

"No. Donna. Haven't seen her, have you?"

"Not seen, no. She rang in a few minutes ago. Running late. Hot date last night, I reckon."

"Really? The sly old fox. She didn't mention anything to me."

"Do you want me to grill her when she comes in? I do a mean frisk."

I laugh. "No, it's fine, although I'm sure she'd love that. I was just a little worried."

"Do you want me to buzz you when…"

"I'll come back later, but thanks."

We then have a chat about his course and plans thereafter, and I go back to my desk. There's no sign of William either, but I shake my head. She'd never go there.

It's ten by the time she comes in and she's very red-faced. I've checked and replied to my work emails and am about to log on to tallgirlnn1 when she rushes past me and goes to her desk, doing a quick recce of William's still-empty office en route. I stare in her direction until she's dumped her bag and taken off her coat.

She swings round as if she's suddenly remembered my existence. Waving at me like a mad woman, she's wearing the biggest grin I've seen, even for her. She mouths something like "I'll tell you all about it later" (I'm not the world's best lip reader) and slumps onto her chair.

I go back to the internet and type in my username and password. There are seven new messages and I'm keeping everything crossed that one of them will lead to a date for tomorrow night. I need to keep this train a-rollin'.

The first message is from Felix who I'm due to see tonight. I open it, dreading he can't make it, but he's suggested the Jade, which is great for me as it's opposite the Picturedrome. I reply with 'Yes, but can we just do drinks as I'm on a tight budget?' (I don't think William will be too happy stumping up for an oriental, although when I think about it, I've never been too sure about his taste in women.) I click on 'send' and move back to Robert, alias, RobbieY69.

Smooth as ever, he wants to know whether I'm free tonight. I send a reply apologising that I can't make it, but could he do tomorrow night? I take a sip of tea and before I've gone to the next message, there's already a reply from Robert. He usually takes his son to swimming lessons, but says he'll make other arrangements. I need him to say yes, but email back saying that he needn't do that on my account, especially if it means missing seeing his son swimming.

I take another swig of tea and he's replied again. This guy is slicker than John Travolta's Danny Zuko! Much to my colleagues' amusement, I punch the air when RobbieY69 comes up trumps by saying that it's not a problem as his ex-wife has been whingeing that she's not spending enough time with 'little Bobby', so she'll take him. I assume he has custody of the boy, which is a half Don't on the list. I like children, especially my niece, but even she can be a handful.

Robert suggests the Hilton at M1 junction 15. I say that's a good choice. Although I'm not a fan of corporate, I like clean, and it should be quiet, even on a Friday night. I imagine the wicked ex-wife, so add my sympathies.

I get a phone call from Marion to say I've got a parcel from Geek's Paradise and would I collect it 'at my leisure'? This equates to 'Now!', so I go ASAP. I arrive through the double doors and walk towards the reception desk, when I bump into, not quite literally but almost, Mike. For once he's not eating anything, but the colour of his face matches the jam filling that I often see adorning it and I put two and two together.

"Hello, Mike," I say, with a grin as big as Donna's. 'Did you two have a nice time last night?"

"She told you?" he splutters, and I'm grateful that he's in between meals.

"She hasn't, no."

"Shit!"

I smile, trying to look reassuring. "Why? Isn't a work fling allowed?"

"It's not a fling," he says rather too quickly.

I'm touched. I'm very protective of my Donna and realise that he does have layers, in more than one respect. I'm pleased he's human after all. "I wouldn't worry," I say, "I won't tell anyone."

"Thanks," he whispers, and then goes back downstairs towards the security office, I assume to relieve Jason, although he's rather early. It's not like him to be keen, but know his incentive to be on site.

I notice Marion behind her protective glass straining to hear what's going on, but she sits back in her chair as I approach. I collect my parcel, smile and leave.

As I approach my desk, I glance in Donna's direction. She's looking at William's office and I see there's still no sign of him. Rather than inflict another Marion session on myself, I ring her.

"Reception," she snaps, knowing it's me.

"Hi, Marion."

"Yes, Isobel." She's never called me Izzy.

"Any idea where our lord and master is?'

"Do you mean William?"

Yes, Marion, I mean William. "Yes, Marion."

"Vet."

"Nothing wrong, I hope."

She ignores my half question. "Anything else?"

"No, thanks, Marion."

And with that she cuts me off.

I sit and stare at my computer screen and occasionally look over at Donna. Finally we both look up at the same time and I mouth the word "Mike". She blushes then puts a finger up to her lips and I signal 'okay'. She should know I'm rubbish at keeping secrets.

I'm reading the next message when William comes stumbling by. I'm sure I hear sobbing, but he may only have a cold. He tunnel visions into his office, ignoring Keith who's walking two steps behind him with a piece of paper in his hand, trying to attract William's attention.

William slams his office door, nearly hitting Keith on the nose, and disappears out of view behind his desk. Keith peers through the glass, but there's a loud roar and he scuttles away. Good news it's clearly not.

There's still no sign of life when I've finished checking tallgirlnn1's emails. With Felix lined up for tonight, Robert tomorrow, and Nigel for Saturday night, I pray that my usual 'pulling' nights will be enjoyable or I'm going to have to think about having Sunday night off and making up half of Monday's column.

I'm giving myself the proverbial pat on the back when a message comes in from CXW69. What is it with that magic number? Are men's brains seriously only in one place? Figuring that two out of three men can't be that shallow, I click on his profile and find they are – he was born in 1975. He writes ever so eloquently though, so I have high hopes of an interesting date.

I'm writing a reply when Chloë from HR appears behind my right shoulder. "Shit, Chloë, you woke me up!"

"Sorry," she whispers.

"Why are you whispering?"

"Do you want some gossip?"

"Of course." I'm also whispering. "You should know me by now."

"It's about William."

"And you're telling me before Donna?'

"She's nearer his office, so I figure I can hide better here."

"Go on, dish the dirt."

"It's aspergillosis."

"William's got aspergillosis?" I ask a little too loudly.

"Shhh…. You know what it is?"

"Not a clue."

"Liver damage from eating fungally toxic peanuts."

"How do you know that?"

"My sister, Berni."

"She's a nurse?"

"Receptionist."

"So how does she know that William's got this asper…?"

"Aspergillosis. And no, William doesn't have it."

"But I thought you said…"

"No, Baby's got it."

"He's got children?"

"Baby, his African Grey. His parrot."

"Of course." It seems like a long time getting there, but I finally cotton on to where this conversation is going, and why I may or may not have heard sobbing. I knew he had a bird but it had almost become a bit of a myth because he's, normally, such a private person. I almost daren't ask the next question but I'm curious. "Is it fatal?"

"It can be, but it depends whether they treat it in time."

"Oh, God."

"In floods of tears apparently, when he left. He had his arms around the cage as if he'd lost her already."

"Her? Baby's a she?"

"She is, yes."

I feel sorry for him and can understand why he's so upset. I remember losing our dogs as I grew up and it was horrible. As far as we know, Baby's all he has and that must be twenty times worse. I dread to think what he'd be like if the bird did actually die.

Chloë walks back down the corridor to her office and I pluck up the courage to go to William's.

As I look through the clear top half of his door, I see that he's head-down on the desk. For all I know, he could have keeled over with a heart attack and he's getting rigor mortis, but as I open the door he looks up. His eyes are almost as red as Mike's doughnuts. He doesn't say a thing. I shut the door behind me and step forward.

"Would you like a cup of coffee?' I whisper. "I'll make it like Janine does."

He sniffs and nods, a vague smile looming.

I don't know whether I should say I know why he's so upset. I stay silent for now and leave, closing the door quietly, and go to the kitchen. I figure he'll tell me if he wants to, though I don't hold my breath.

I return a couple of minutes later and, as I pass her desk, Donna smiles at me, clearly oblivious to William's woe.

I tap lightly on William's door and he looks up again. I rest his mug on his desk and say, "My article's coming along nicely," hoping that the change of subject would take his mind off his troubles. He nods again and I leave the room. I don't suppose he'll drink any of it, but at least I've shown him that someone cares.

I've been back at my desk for less than five minutes when William comes over.

He puts his empty mug on my desk and says frighteningly cheerfully, "Thanks so much for the coffee, I'll tell Janine she's got a drink-making rival." That wasn't something I'd looked for to add to my CV, but I smile and he returns to his office.

I debate whether I'd put too much coffee in it considering the speed of his recovery and, as I look at his mug on my desk, I wonder whether its placement is a hint for a refill.

I check the clock and it's gone one. Looking over at Donna at her desk under the clock, I see her pointing to her mouth. Great minds think alike. I'm dying to get the gossip on Mike and swap it for aspergillosis, and can't wait a minute longer.

As I get up from my desk she does likewise, and we sprint for the kitchen like *Chariots of Fire* meets *Baywatch*. I'm ahead, so run past the kitchen, then swing round and our run becomes *Wuthering Heights*' Cathy and Heathcliff. Donna calls out a high-pitched "Heathcliff", and I do a low-pitch "Cathy", and we stumble through the kitchen in fits of laughter.

I grab my sandwich – home-made coronation chicken, which I adore – and have just sat down at our favourite corner table when I remember my article. Had William continued with his self-indulgent morose phase I might have got away with a later deadline, but if the last time I saw him is anything to go by, I don't stand a chance.

"I can't stay long," I say to Donna. "Not started my article yet."

49

"I'm a bit behind today too, after last night."

"Yes! Tell me, tell me. I want to know everything!' I then think for a second and say, "Not everything, just the censored version."

She tells me, in uncensored detail, everything that happened between her and the well-laden Mike. She's just getting to a particularly intimate moment when William walks in and sees her re-enacting the scene. He swiftly turns and walks back to his office. This obviously trumps 'women's troubles' as he doesn't even get as far as the machine.

I vow to make him a drink, but Donna's gossip is too juicy to miss, so I give her my undivided attention for the next six minutes and twelve seconds, which was, by the sound of it, not far off the entire timescale of their lovemaking.

I tell her what Chloë had told me about William's parrot, and Donna bursts into tears. I pass her a box of tissues and will William to return, but he doesn't.

Having finished my coronation chicken, I nip back to my desk and get William's mug. I make him a replica of my first effort, toning down the coffee a little, just in case.

I take it to his office and he's looking through his in tray.

"Mine's not quite there," I mumble as I place the mug on a coaster.

"You've got just under an hour."

"Can I…?"

"Close the door on the way out, will you?"

That's the William we know and, sort of, like.

I create a blank document and save it as '31 dates art. 0405', typing in 'What did I learn from last night?' Having given this some thought, I'm a bit more clued up than before, which, considering the time I have to do the word count, is just as well.

That men come in all shapes and sizes. While it's easy to judge a book by its cover and go with our first impressions, it's worth taking the time to dig a little deeper. There was an advert a few years ago for 'The Guardian' (thanks, YouTube!) called 'The Whole Picture' which sums up what I mean.

You first see a skinhead running towards you, but away from a car – you assume it's chasing him. The camera angle changes; you're following him as he approaches a suited gentleman (wearing a hat – those were the days) with a briefcase, so you assume that the 'thug' is going to rob him.

The final shot is an overview showing both men, but also a pallet of bricks outside a renovation project that's about to shed its load, and the skinhead pulls the gent back towards the building just in time to be saved from serious injury. The entire advert is less than thirty seconds but has such an impact.

While I couldn't remember what it was selling before checking YouTube (which would normally mean that it's not doing its job too well) – it has been over twenty years – I remembered how the clip played out. And this is why I mention it.

Whether a man is tall or short, fat or thin, he is likely to have a number of layers that are worth peeling back (metaphorically, on the first date, girls!) revealing the real him. Equally you might think about relaxing and letting small amounts of your true personality shine.

That may be easier said than done if you're nervous meeting for the first time, but I have found in the past that if I'd been unable to relax, I'd feel that he's not seen the real me when he's said 'Thanks, but no thanks'. As the dish of the day walks away, my insides are screaming, 'Wait, that wasn't me in there, I'm a lovely person really,' but the damage is already done.

Of course, attraction is a big part of finding a partner, because if you don't fancy them the first time in bed together, both shaved and smelling lovely, you're certainly not going to fancy them in x years' time when shaving was something that you watched on an Australian farming documentary, there are his and hers false teeth in tumblers on his and hers bedside tables, and you smell like… we won't go there.

You may like someone who's buff, tanned and gorgeous, but that won't last forever. If his exterior needs a bit of a repaint, that's just minor cosmetics, but if his interior needs a complete DIY home improvement then that's a whole Boots superstore. Me, I prefer a rugby player build to footballer. Peter Crouch is probably lovely, but ew, no. No meat.

I like a bit of meat, but given the choice of an intelligent, funny rake or thick-as-a-barge buff brickie, the rake would win *every time (although I'd still take the brickie's number for a few jobs I need doing round the house).*

So two more things to tick on my 'dater's shopping list': Do – take time to get to know the person beneath the skin (however saggy it may be!) and Don't – have sweetener in your tea when your body is crying out for full-fat hundred-calories-a-grain sugar.

I look at the clock and it's five to two. I have a quick skim read and print it off. Not knowing what mood William will be in when I get to his office, I prepare my battle armour (a fresh coffee), but he's not even there.

I put the coffee on his 'Newspaper Awards' coaster, and the paper in the tray, then turn to do a runner. Inches away from my face is William.

"Err…" I say.

"Hi, Izzy. Done?"

I nod.

"Thanks. I'll have a browse."

"Okay," I say, and walk back to my desk, making sure of course that I close the door on my way out.

I have a quick check of my tallgirlnn1 messages and there are a couple more. By the time I've read and replied to them, I have dates for Sunday (CXW69) and Monday (ReadyEddie) nights. Needless to say a lot of eye rolling was done when I clicked on ReadyEddie's profile expecting more of RobbieY69's smut, but he's a guy who hates to be late, so that can only be a good thing.

I have plenty of time to kill, so open the package from Geek's Paradise and play with a wind-up grasshopper. My colleagues are used to strange noises coming from my desk, but this one sounds like a vibrator and, given my current project, I quickly switch it off.

I look at the notes it comes with and type in the manufacturer's website link before watching a two-minute video of the thing in action. Pleased that I'd already muted my computer from my earlier internet trawling, I giggle away as the grasshopper walks its way along a long bench then stops as it gets to a purposely placed wall, flips over and walks its way back to the start.

I've had a few of Geek's Paradise freebies before, but none as fun as this, so play the video again before putting the grasshopper back in its package, with accompanying paperwork, and slipping it into my bag. I can't wait to get home and try it out for real.

After more admin, it's nearly time to go home when Donna comes bounding over, back to form.

"Who is it tonight?" she asks, her mouth almost drooling at the thought of me getting as much action as her.

"FelixP69."

She grins.

"He was born in 1969."

"Where are you going?"

"Jade Pavilion."

"Great, local."

"Indeed."

"To eat?"

"No. Just a couple of drinks."

"That's a shame. They do lovely food there."

"I know, but I'm on William's budget."

"You know the answer to that."

"What?"

"You get Felix to pay."

"You know I'm a Dutch girl."

With that, Donna flicks up the sides of her hair and teeters around my desk as if she's wearing clogs.

"Har, dcc, har. We'll see, but I highly doubt it."

"He'll be lovely: sleek and dark like Felix the cat."

"Or he'll bomb like the 1900 Alabama meteorite!"

"You've got such a brain in there, Izzy Mac. We should go to pub quizzes, you'd be great and we'd pick up some intelligent boys."

"You know how rare they are. Besides, aren't you spoken for?"

She laughs. "Tell me all about it in the morning."

"And you, missy."

Thinking of what Donna said, I have another low-fat meal, this time picking a non-garlicky chicken and lemon risotto, so I'm not too full in case Felix does insist on treating me.

After last night's rain, it's been a particularly hot day, so I have a shower while my 'dinner' is cooking (turning around on the glass microwave plate).

Showered, I slip on a dressing gown and go downstairs. My bag is hanging over the bottom of the banisters and I dig out the grasshopper. Collecting my dinner, which has cooled down nicely, I go into the lounge. Perched on the edge of my lilac sofa with dinner on a side table, I wind up the grasshopper and am in stitches when it bumps into the edges of the sofa, neighbouring chair and footstool.

As it's trying to tunnel its way through the corner of the room, I pick it up gently and place it in front of the radiator where it has a long run up to the dividing doors between the lounge and dining room. It goes full pelt before slamming into the woodwork, making a tiny dent in both the door and the toy's nose.

I pick it up and we stare face to face. I can't help smiling as it looks so cute, deformity and all. I could keep the items I test, but most end up at the local Red Cross shop or further afield. This one isn't going anywhere.

I lay it on the sofa next to me and put my hands out in front of me, Kung Fu-like, and say to my new housemate, in a distinctly average David Carradine impersonation, "You have failed no one, Grasshopper." My brother Mark is a film addict; I know the actual quote is 'You have not failed no one', but that's bad English and, like dropping litter, I can't bring myself to do it.

I look at the clock over the blocked-up fireplace and panic. I dash upstairs, throw open the wardrobe doors and pick something pretty (a long maxi dress – I rarely wear dresses), put on the war paint and tie my hair into a ponytail, but figure that to choose somewhere like Jade he'd be a long hair loose kind of guy, so I pull the band out and let it run free.

Felix is exactly as I'd imagined him. Like Tim, he's nearly as broad as he is tall, which in Felix's case is about an inch shorter than me, but unlike Tim there isn't an ounce of fat on him. I'd arrived just before him, so I'm standing at the bar when he walks in.

I try to keep a straight face as he comes towards me. It turns out he's a weightlifter and because his quadriceps ('thighs' to ordinary people like me) are so huge, he has to waddle one leg in front of the other, doing a good impression of the Michelin man.

I sit on a stool and his muscles bulge as he lifts his great weight on to his seat. He orders a Mai Tai for himself and I have a Virgin Colada. I spot him winking at the barmaid who I'm surprised has the job, as she's barely tall enough to see over the counter. I assume he's just being charming, but it soon transpires that he likes all the women here, bar one.

As we face each other and talk about the usual stuff that first daters do, it's quite obvious that he's a regular. Not only does the barmaid keep flirting with him, but so do all the waiting staff, female and male, when they walk past us to get to the kitchen.

A waitress, who seems capable of carrying only one item at a time because she goes past so often, is on first name terms with him and I get the feeling that there's some 'history' between them, and not too distant.

I distinctly feel like a spare part and wonder if he'd notice if I slid off the bar stool and slipped away. I say I'm going to the toilet to which I get a vague nod. I've been to Jade once before, so remember where I'm going, but he's not paying attention so it would be no use asking him anyway.

I finish my VC, discreetly (though there clearly was no need) grab my clutch purse and walk in the direction of the ladies toilet. Looking sideways so I still have him in my sights, I see he's chatting to Miss One-Item-at-a-Time Waitress and he hasn't a clue what I'm up to. I therefore leg it towards the entrance and out to my car.

Keeping in mind what happened at the World's End I wait, giving Felix a chance to redeem himself but, ten minutes later, there's still no sign of him so I drive home.

With the risotto long gone, I'm way past peckish. I want something more substantial than mini snack bars. After boiling the kettle for a cup of cherry and cinnamon tea, I make a couple of slices of toast which I smother with peanut butter and apricot jam, or jelly as the Yanks call it, and take everything upstairs.

I resume my liaison with Elliot, who doesn't get any less creepy, and heroine Natasha, and munch my way through the toast, which I wash down with lukewarm tea because I'm so engrossed in the book.

I end up falling asleep, waking up over an hour later with the book and remnants of toast scattered across the duvet. Fortunately, I'd already put the mug to one side, but omitted to take my glasses off which, I find out when I peer in the bathroom mirror to take my make-up off, have left an imprint in my right cheek, scar-like, something Elliot would be very proud of.

Once my teeth are squeaky clean, I yank the bathroom light-pull and go back to the bedroom. I swish the crumbs onto the floor, the hoovering's long overdue anyway, and put the book back next to the clock radio.

I apologise to Natasha that I have to leave her and Elliot alone again and switch off the light, muttering to myself that I must have a screw loose to be talking to an inanimate object, but if it's good enough for Prince Charles and his plants then it's good enough for me.

Chapter 5 – Robert at the Hilton

I wake up with a bit of a cold, so have another fruit tea and toast for breakfast. I eat, and then put my nose up to the mug, inhaling deeply. Misjudging the distance, tea shoots up both nostrils, which isn't pleasant, but clears the blockage nicely.

I stand in front of my mirrored wardrobes for what seems like forever, and peer over at the clock radio. Eight twenty. Better get a move on. I look at the black-and-red cover of *Opaque* and the figure behind the door. I've still not worked out whether the shadowy figure is Elliot or Natasha, but, even closed, the book gives me the creeps.

Wearing just my underwear, which would no doubt give Elliot a thrill, I walk over to the bedside chest of drawers and turn over the book. The back is a ghostly white with black-and-green writing, but still a distinctly more soothing option to the front.

The bookmark, on page one hundred and twenty-three (as far as I'd got before the crumbs-on-the-bed episode) peeks out of the top willing me to skip work and take it back to bed. I open the top drawer, put the book reverently, though firmly, next to a box of tissues and slam the drawer shut. Out of sight isn't totally out of mind; Elliot won't let me forget him completely.

I plump for a pair of grey trousers, sleeveless black shirt and red slim cotton scarf. It feels rather wintry for the beginning of May, but the weather still can't make its mind up. This is England after all.

Grabbing my red Kelly-type bag (I'm on a local rag's wages – everything I own is fake), I finish the tea, which is almost cold, and go out the front door.

Marion's prequel, Jason, opens his mouth to chat, but it's nearly nine, so I say I'm sorry and that I can't stop. Normally it wouldn't bother me, but I want to check on Donna, and for some reason I'm concerned about William's bird.

Donna's sitting in my chair and appears to be writing something. She looks up as I approach my desk, and puts down the mug, hers, she's just taken a swig from.

"Morning double-dee," I say. "How's things?"

This sends her into a fit of giggles, and the coffee she was drinking cascades from the sides of her mouth. I pull a stream of tissues from a box next to my monitor and offer them to her. I check the make of the box and wonder if I should buy some of their shares. Donna alone would keep me in the style to which I would love to become accustomed.

She moves to an empty desk next to mine while I log on to my computer. I make a cup of tea (Donna says her coffee's fine) while I'm waiting for the PC to open all the pre-selected software. I thank Bill Gates every morning for the time that 'Startup' saves me.

That reminds me to tell Donna a rude joke I know about 'Micro…soft', but I've forgotten by the time I get back to my desk. I have a dreadful memory and have a book at home somewhere about improving it, but can't remember where it is.

I continue the conversation. "So… did you see him last night?"

"Mike?"

I nod.

"Yes, we…" She's drooling again, so I move the box of tissues to her desk. "It was lovely. He…"

I put my hand up – I only want the barest of details – but she thinks I'm after the tissues, so gives back the box. I leave it on her side of my desk just in case.

"He was so gentle and caring. I never thought…"

I'm wondering whether I want to hear everything she's about to say when I realise that she's stopped talking and is looking behind me. I turn and William's standing there with a 'Do you two not have any work to do?' expression, but sees the stained tissues and scuttles off to his office without saying a word. I should buy those shares.

"So, Izzy Izzy, let's get busy… how did your night go last night?"

"Let's just say the Virgin Colada was the best thing about it. Two nights out of four I've not spent any of William's money."

"At least you didn't have very far to go. Was he not very nice, this Felix?"

"Oh no, he was lovely, that was the trouble. It was like bees round a honeypot, except king bee didn't notice queen bee

58

leaving and sitting in her car for ten minutes on the off chance that he'll have missed her… which he didn't."

"I didn't know bees had kings?"

Donna reminds me of the blonde from the Philadelphia adverts.

"You're not as dumb as you look, Donna."

"Thanks!" she says with her usual goofy grin.

"You're very welcome."

"So you won't be seeing him again then."

"No, I would imagine not. I'm about to log on and check my messages, but I don't expect to see one from him."

"Okay," she says, and goes back to her desk. I imagine that all the space there is in that little head of hers is currently taken up with Mike and I'm pleased for her.

He makes her even more inanely happy than she normally is, and while that could be sickly, I've seen her at some really low points, where the smile is close to disappearing. I sometimes wonder whether it's a defence mechanism, and I'm surprised Keith's not pounced on her before now as an agony aunt case study. That would be fun to watch.

I don't have any work emails, which is unusual, but leaves me more time to work through my tallgirlnn1. I log in but see 'You have 0 new messages'. The only thing left to do then is to start my article, a bit disappointed that I have to do some proper work. I Alt/Tab over to Word and save the blank 'Document 1' as '31 dates art. 0505', and type.

What did I learn from last night? That there are many different types of men in Northamptonshire, and many first impressions to be had. Take my date last night, for example. He was a very handsome guy, looked after himself, but had eye trouble.

I wear glasses (and suffered the 'boys never make passes at Izzy in glasses' taunt at school) and obviously sympathise with anyone with a disability, but the trouble with his eyes was that they wandered. Not in a Marty Feldman kind of way, but it turns out that I'm of the wrong nationality.

F had chosen the Jade restaurant for a reason, actually about a dozen reasons: all petite, all dark haired, and all letching after him. And of course he wasn't going to complain. If you read my article yesterday you'll recall my ramblings about physical attraction being a small part of a long-lasting relationship.

F obviously doesn't read my column. F is as shallow as the two-foot-six end of a swimming pool. I've sprained an ankle doing 'bubbles' (jumping in and pushing down both feet to make as much splash as you can) in the two-foot-six, and last night was even more unpleasant.

Can I ask that if you're a man reading this column and you're struggling to meet, or hold on to a woman, you ask yourself these three questions about the last woman you went on a date with:

1. What was the colour of her hair?

2. What was the colour of the top or dress she was wearing? (Okay, four questions: can you say what type of garment she was wearing?)

3. What colour were her eyes?

The chances are that if you can remember what colour car she was driving but nothing about her appearance, you're not going to score too highly. We like to be paid attention to. Not fawned over, but if you don't notice we've left the room, the chances are pretty high that there isn't going to be a second date. I wouldn't put it past F to still be waiting for me to return from the ladies toilets, assuming he's not been eaten by the Persian Piranhas.

I'm about to start a new paragraph when William walks over.

"How's it going, Izzy?"

"Good, thanks, William."

"And the money. You staying within budget?"

"Yes, surprisingly so. About petrol though…"

"Excellent. Usual deadline," he says, and walks off.

Sometimes I think I'm too honest. Bars and restaurants can give receipts for rounds of drinks, but, like the getting out of notepad and pens from my bag, asking for a receipt for a 'date' would arouse suspicion, so William's taking it on spec. I figure he's got other things on his mind, although he does look more cheerful; cheerful's pushing it, so I decide to leave the petrol issue for now, and see how things go.

If I have more dates like Tim and Felix, I'll be in pocket regardless of whether I claim for petrol or not. I would be if I filled in the expenses forms in my favour, but, as I said, I'm too honest... most of the time.

Now, where was I? Ah, yes, the Persian Piranhas.

The first thing to remember about a first date is not only to notice what she's wearing, but comment on it. And guys, please, positive. Even if you don't think she looks lovely, say she does, or say, 'I love the colour,' even if her pink hair clashes with her orange boob tube.

Unless you're embarrassed to be seen in the same room as her, getting out after one drink is fine if there's no chance of taking it any further. You can be a gentleman and say you don't think you're compatible. Unless you're the fiftieth guy she's been out with who's turned her down, she's unlikely to go nuts. It's a brave man who suggests dinner on a first date, but if you've had a drink or two and it's going well, you can play it by ear.

Remember that you always, always buy the first drink. Offer to buy the second, but if she's a modern woman, she'll insist on going Dutch. If she doesn't and also lets you buy the third without offering, you might like to question her motives. If you drip in gold, drive a flashy car, she may be interested in you for more than your looks.

If you drip in gold, drive a flashy car and look like the back end of a bus and she's still interested then this may tell you whether she's going to go Dutch on the haute cuisine and Bollinger you've just ordered. The words 'chance' and 'fat' spring to mind. Still, if she's hot it's still cheaper than a high-class escort...

I remember this is a family paper, so delete the final sentence.

If you're currently single all the relationships you've had to date are failures, aren't they? If you go on a date, you like the woman and think there's potential, it's worth the investment. If it doesn't work, you've only lost an evening of your life, a day's (a week's or month's) wages, but had a good time.

As the saying goes, you can't take it with you so you may as well spend it on someone with whom you had fun, and doesn't it warm your cockles to know that she'll be driving home with boosted confidence wearing a dress she wasn't sure about but someone who seemed like a nice guy said he liked?

If you're following this column and are building your dater's shopping list, the latest are: Do pay compliments and attention and Don't have wandering eyes.

If you're going on a date tonight, good luck and, you never know, it may just be with me!

I'm pretty happy with what I've written, so I give it a quick skim, make a couple of changes then print it off. William's at his desk when I drop it in. He leans forward, looks at my article, but doesn't say anything.

"How are things?" I ask.

"Good." He hesitates. "Things with you?"

"Good, thanks."

There's an unnatural pause for he continues. "Did you want something, Izzy?"

"How's your bird?"

He looks surprised. "Who told you about Baby?"

"I can't reveal my sources," I reply in a stupidly cloak and dagger fashion, trying to be funny and failing miserably. "Chloë's sister works at your vet." As I said, I'm hopeless at keeping secrets.

"Isn't there supposed to be client confidentiality?" He scowls.

"Sorry," I say, and go to leave his office.

"No, I'm sorry. You were asking about Baby."

"Is she going to be all right?"

"I don't know. It's fifty-fifty. She's on medication, so I hope so."

"How old is she?"

"She'll be forty in July."

"Wow."

"Did you have her as a…" I wrack my brains for Baby's baby version.

"Chick. No, my parents got her when she was six."

Doh. "When will you know whether it's worked?"

"I've got to go back in a couple of weeks."

"I'll keep everything crossed."

William just smiles and after a moment of silence, I turn to leave.

"Wait," he says.

I turn back and he's leaning forward. I wince as I think he's spotted something glaringly awful about my article, but he looks at me and mumbles, "Thanks, Izzy."

"No problem," I say, and leave, closing the door as softly as an Ikea glide drawer. I've got an Ikea kitchen and spent hours after it was installed playing with the drawers, all fourteen of them. I was like a child in a sweetshop, except with me it's gadgets. And sweets. Pick 'n' mix especially. Banoffee pie isn't the only thing I'd kill for.

Donna looks worried and mouths, "Okay?" I smile and walk back to my desk.

I look up at William's office and he's getting something from his filing cabinet. He sees me as he turns and smiles a brief but professional smile. He's all business, is our William.

I get back to the task at hand and refresh my internet screen. It turns out our server was playing hooky, and I have twelve messages. Seven are from idiots, so are deleted and blocked from ever contacting me again. This is great. It's like having your own judge to issue restraining orders. Have I said I love technology?

The other five include one from RobbieY69 saying that the old witch is having little Bobby and he can't wait to meet me tonight. I can see me being a rebound, but if it gives him something to look forward to, who am I to deny him that little piece of happiness?

NigelEByGum has suggested going to the cinema, which regular readers will know I love doing, so I answer him first. He likes arty films, and if that's all right with me will let me know what's on. I say I'll fit in with whatever he has planned. After all, I don't have a social life for the next twenty-six days, except I don't tell him that of course.

CXW69, alias Charles, alias Mr Sunday seventh May, is message number four. He's said although he thinks the lady should choose the venue so she'll feel comfortable, he adds that the Greyhound at Milton Malsor is nice. It's a favourite of mine, so I say yes, and that I would 'feel very comfortable there'. Although it's a chain, it's a lovely old pub oozing old charm, and it'll be nice to see it again. Tickety boo.

ReadyEddie cracks me up. He's so laid back he's horizontal. He's said he'll 'go with the flow' and is happy to do anything I suggest, unless it's jumping out of an aeroplane (on the rare occasions I'm in one, I strap myself to the seat when the seat belt sign illuminates, and it doesn't get undone until the light goes off, so why would I want to get off the plane until it's hooked up to the concertina tube that always reminds me of my dad's darkroom storage bottles), riding a camel (that I could do, providing I had even more padding on my backside than Mother Nature has already given me, and as long as I'm not at the front end when they spit, although it may be preferable to their back end), or going to the circus (I never understand why people are scared of clowns, but don't approve of the way some treat their animals).

Eddie, I think you're pretty safe on all three counts. Unless there's a multi-creatured festival in the grounds of Sywell Aerodrome, which reminds me that I've heard great things about the Aviator pub there, so I suggest that, promising myself we'll only be seeing the outside of planes.

NigelEByGum sends me a list of the films and times and the order in which he'd prefer to see them. He's spookily as geeky as me and, even better, he's suggested Cineworld (he lives in the modern complex at Upton, which I know well as there's a fairly regular Saturday morning car boot sale nearby).

I pick *After Jessica* because I've heard good things about it from a friend who's recently married a gorgeously funny Yank, lives in Washington, and, like all Americans, can see films way before they're shown here. They spend half their leisure time on the back row of a dark 'theatre'… I can't imagine why.

The fifth message is from an 'OMG69'. I roll my eyes. I immediately imagine that 'Oh My God 69' is going to be another Felix. I take a look at his profile and I'm not reassured. I like to think I'm fairly 'with it', but can't understand half of what he's saying. He loves Dizzy Rascal, or I assume he does as he calls him 'sick'.

He gets a tick in my (newly added) ethics box for 'dissing' (not approving of – I know that one already) 'disco biscuits' which londonslang.com tells me is ecstasy, a quote from the film *Snatch* apparently, which I would have known if I'd seen it for more than fifteen minutes (I do occasionally fall asleep at the movies – the last time was watching *Insomnia*, which I still find hilarious. Me falling asleep, not the film, which I've still not seen the end of).

Despite my better judgement and the prospect of needing a translator, I ask him if he's free next week. I make a note on my Office Angels (it's so cool having temps and getting free stuff) note block to add a 'Don't try this at home' bit in my next article – I'd have normally taken ages to get to know a guy before meeting them. In fact, the one and only time I had a profile on a popular international dating site, I spent the six months 'chatting' to half a dozen men and never met any of them, so that was a bit of a waste of sixty-five pounds, wasn't it?

I reply to RobbieY69 saying I'm also looking forward to going to the Hilton as it's been eighteen months since I'd been there last at a work's Christmas do (where Donna and I got off with two guys from another party, but that's another story), and I'd heard it had since had a facelift.

There's a message from Eddie, which has me rather speechless. He says he loves the Aviator, but is currently without a car. He can get a lift there, but could I take him home? He lives in Bellinge (the formerly dodgy Eastern district), so it's not that far, other than being the wrong direction for me, but I wouldn't know that because of course I've not told him where I live, although the NN1 would give him a clue.

It doesn't alter the fact that a complete stranger is asking to share my car, which, of course, is a big no-no. I could offer to pay his taxi home, which east-northamptonshire.gov.uk tells me would cost £1.35 a mile (I'm nothing if not methodical. Besides what's the point in having a technology column and all the software that goes with it, if I don't use it?), but I wonder why I should.

I stare at his message, but decide that as my budget's in credit and it should be a fun evening, especially as I can quiz him on Bellinge's improvements, I email him back with the taxi idea.

I'm reading Nigel's and Charles's confirmations when I notice my 'You have messages' number increase by one. It's Eddie also confirming, although he feels guilty that I should offer. I say it's not a problem and the deal is struck.

I sit back in my chair and smile. I have dates lined up to, and including, Monday night, so am well chuffed. I press F5 to refresh my messages back to zero, and it says there's another one. OMG69 suggests 'Groove' at the top of Gold Street, one of the town's shopping streets. I've only ever been in there when it was the Litten Tree, and it was okay.

I do a Google search and, in amongst results for barcode manufacturers, there's dontstayin.com, which I click on. Before me is a screen with wildly coloured side banners that wouldn't look out of place in a Black Eyed Peas video. As I love the band, I decide that OMG is the 'business' (the best euphemism my brain will find – I seriously need to do some homework before Tuesday). I reply that work's hectic (thirty-one men in thirty-one days isn't lying) and my only free night is Tuesday, would that be okay?

I go to my work emails and answer one from Donna asking me what I'm doing for lunch. I look up at the clock and it's just gone twelve forty. I reply 'Window shopping round the market?' and look over to see her grin, in her usual comic fashion.

I collect Donna and then my bag. I've brought sandwiches in for the fifth day in a row, and am well pleased with myself. I grab them as we walk past the kitchen. They're a bit too chilled to eat, so I stuff them in my bag and we walk towards reception.

Marion's at lunch, so Mike's covering. He cheers as we burst through the double doors. Not at me of course, just at the blonde on my arm. She lets go and runs over to him, kissing the glass that separates them.

Way to go, Donna. Play it cool, just like I taught you.

"I can go shopping on my own if you want to stay here," I say, not meaning it.

The normal Donna would have said, "It's only a man. I want to come with you", but this version says, "Do you mind?"

What can I say to that? 'Of course I mind. Donna, look at yourself. You're drooling. Just look at him. He's got stains down his shirt, his tie's half undone, he's a slob.' But I'm her friend, and she's happy. "Of course I don't mind. The shops will be there tomorrow." (Which of course they will, but so will Mike, so we'll no doubt be doing this all over again then). "I'll see you when I get back."

I think I lost her at 'don't mind' and she's already on the other side of the reception door sitting on his lap. If William ever went out for lunch, he'd be mortified. The reception area is one that has to 'maintain the business front at all times.

The leaflets must be stacked to perfection, the newspapers (ours) parallel to each other and in date order' (the latest on the top, as each issue is his baby and he gets prouder every day), and a five feet two (and a half) Health and Beauty columnist sitting on the lap of a twenty-something-stone security guard wouldn't be his idea of perfection. Or mine. Or anyone else's other than Donna's.

I go out to lunch and leave the lovebirds mouth-locked. I'm pleased for her, really I am, and a little jealous, if I'm honest, though not of Mike obviously. By the end of this month I shall have dated over thirty men, but life is about quality, not quantity, and I know which category Mike fits (or should I say squeezes) into.

I spend far too much money in town and come back with five bags of shopping. They call it therapy for a reason; I do feel much better.

There's no sign of the lovebirds when I walk back through reception. I hadn't thought to look in the security office beforehand, as I didn't think I'd been that long, but when I go past Frosty (Marion's real surname is Frist, but it doesn't suit her so well. I've never met her husband, but I imagine he has a constant backache from being under her thumb), she gives me an icy glare.

The clock above Donna's desk shows two thirty. Oops. William likes punctuality, but I figure I've skipped so many lunch breaks, and 'worked' so many evenings, that I've earned a particularly long one so don't feel guilty, especially as there's no sign of him in his office, but there's no sign of Donna either.

67

I've just sat down at my desk when Donna wafts past, adjusting her skirt. She winks at me as she heads for her desk. She throws her bag under it, wiggles her mouse to deactivate her screensaver, and then looks over in my direction, doing her Cheshire cat impression which doesn't match the rest of her.

Her normally neat bob is a mess, her blouse buttons mismatched, and I spotted a massive ladder in her tights as she walked by. She types something – I assume her password – into her computer then stands up and peers into William's office. There's still no sign of him, so she looks around the office before skipping in my direction.

"Tell you about it later," she whispers as she almost floats by.

I can't wait.

I lean forward and my gaze follows her bobbing figure along the corridor until she disappears into the loos. She comes out a few seconds later minus tights, winks at me again and bounces back to her desk.

My life would be so dull without Donna.

We spend the afternoon tied to our desks, tea-less, and I'm just finishing off the review on the grasshopper and am emailing the supplier promising that the article will appear early next month, when a curled fist appears on my desk and knocks furiously.

I look up and it's Tigger D.

"Can't wait any longer," she says. "I need tea. Coming?"

I look up at the clock. "But it's half four, we're going home soon."

"I'm bursting to tell you."

"About lunchtime?"

She grins.

"Give me two secs, just finishing an email. Put the kettle on and I'll see you in there." Needless to say, I can't wait to hear, blow-by-blow (pardon the pun), every sordid detail of what she got up to in the locked blind-down security office.

A blow-by-blow account is exactly what I get and just as she's getting to the juicy bit, William walks in. He stares at us, grabs a machine coffee and walks out shaking his head. At least there were no tissues involved this time.

I double-check my tallgirlnn1 emails just in case RobbieY69 has bailed, but there's nothing from him, or anyone else, so I log off, grab my bags and go home.

Marion's on the phone as I walk by. I smile at her but she pretends not to see me, or is too engrossed in the call. Going past the security office, I see the blind is up and that Mike's also chatting on the phone. He sees me, smiles like a five-year-old, waves like a two-year-old, and I smile back. I also lift my hand to wave, but do so like a thirty-year-old.

Sometimes I wish I could be as uninhibited as him and Donna, but comparing Mike's current behaviour to that of a couple of days ago, I think there's hope for me yet.

By the time I get home, I've got a few hours before I have to go out again. I skip the shower as I've sort of lost interest in Robert already. I'm not a fan of children, but preferring a blind date to seeing his son swimming, even if only a practice session, doesn't impress me much.

As I'm doing the washing-up, I dance around the kitchen using the scrubbing brush as a microphone singing Shania Twain's late-nineties hit 'That Don't Impress Me Much'. I remember the words until I get to the Brad Pitt bit, and hum the rest.

I 'cook' a full-fat lasagne and decide to put a movie on. I've got so many to choose from (working near a market has its uses), but plump for an old favourite: *Notting Hill*. Despite, or perhaps because of, my current project I feel like watching a love story and am, predictably, in tears by the end. I'm glad I'd forgotten to put any make-up on today, so go to the bathroom where I look up to the ceiling (I've heard it's a good way to stop tears quickly) and dab my face with cold water, after which I apply my warpaint.

The drive to junction 15 takes less than twenty minutes on the A45 ring road and I arrive at the hotel in plenty of time. I reverse into one of two spaces – I've always reversed since scraping a car a week after I passed my test by misjudging the angle – and debate whether to sit in my car or have a tour round the refurbished building, and I settle for the latter.

I've part-opened my door and am about to get out when a brand-new Ionian blue (I Google it later) Jaguar X-Type sweeps into the space next to me, forcing me to close it or lose it.

I growl at the driver through my now-closed door, but decide I don't want a confrontation to spoil my evening, so let him get out first. He's about late thirties with short dark hair swimming in hair gel, which reminds me of Tim's potato skins. This guy's also quite tall, around six feet I'd say, as his head and shoulders disappear above the top of my car, and of medium build. I can tell he's got money as it oozes through his perfectly tailored suit.

I'm walking towards the back of his car as he opens the boot and I spot a marine blue leather Louis Vuitton Keepall 45 overnight case in one corner of the vast expanse that is the boot. I sit next to the paper's fashion columnist, Karen, who's currently on holiday, hence the empty desk, so know it's the real thing.

Rather than pull out the whole bag, he removes a wallet from the top and zips the bag back up. Knowing it costs a couple of thousand pounds, I think I wouldn't leave it in the car, but I'd never be able to afford either. I'd rather have an XK anyway, or a Mercedes SLK and lots of change. Also on our side of the office is Gerry, our motors columnist, and I keep my ears open when it comes to cars. It's the techno geek in me. I can't help it. It's like Keith's gaydar.

The Jag driver's wallet would probably cost more than I earn in a week, but it's a hideous brown-and-black check design. I feel sorry for the cow that had to die for that monstrosity.

As I walk by, Mr Jag winks at me, and with his free hand sweeps back an imaginary stray hair from his potato-skin locks. I imagine a special effects star appearing by his teeth as he reveals a perfect set of pearly whites.

I hear the boot slam behind me, and footsteps, probably made by immaculate Louis Vuitton boots. I stride past reception and to an extension, which I don't remember being there during the Christmas party. I'm pleased when the footsteps divert into the hotel and I have a peek around the grounds.

It's about five to eight when I go into the hotel and veer off to the bar. Despite it being a Friday night, there are only a handful of people – five in fact, plus me. On the left is an elderly couple chatting away and looking at menus, which are inches away from their faces. On the right is what looks like a newly married couple as they are inches away from each other's faces. This leaves one person sitting by the bar: Mr Jag.

I pray (I'm only religious at moments like this) that he isn't Robert. I walk towards him and he winks. I sigh.

"Izzy?"

"That's me," I say, trying to contort my face into a convincing smile.

He offers his well-manicured right hand, and I shake it firmly. I've only just met him yet he already makes me want to stand my ground.

"What can I get you to drink?"

"I'm driving, so a soft drink please. Anything fruity."

That prompts another flash of his pearly whites and I immediately regret the unintended innuendo.

He orders an apple and mango J2O for me and a Bollinger for him. I assume he means a glass, but the barman brings over a bottle and two glasses. I'm about to say something, but the barman puts the bottle on the bar. "Thank you, Mr York, shall I charge it to your account?"

I look at the bottle, then at 'Mr York'.

"So," he says, "shall we have a drink here or shall we take it up to the room?"

"Sorry?"

"You said in your message you didn't want dinner?"

"I did, but…"

"I thought we might be more comfortable upstairs. I have an overnight bag in my car in case you want to make a night of it."

I can't think of anything worse. Even Tim with stains is appealing right now. "Err…"

"Don't worry, this one's for free."

Charming. I tap my right foot on the floor as I tell myself to stay cool. "I think you might have got the wrong impression…"

"Oh," he says, "but I thought that meant…"

I laugh. "So you think because your ex-wife has your son all night, that–"

"She's not my ex-wife."

71

"But you said…"

"Did I?"

"Err, yes."

"No, still married. We're sort of separated, but still share the same house. We stay together for the sake of little Bobby and we have to share a bed to keep up the façade, but nothing happens."

I put up my right hand, palm towards his face. "For one thing I don't believe you, and for another, what kind of man ditches his son for a blind date with someone he assumes is obviously a bimbo, who he thinks will roll over for him?"

"It…" he pauses and grins, "usually works."

"Nice," I say. "It'll be a double bed for one tonight then." And with that I ignore the J_2O, take the bottle of Bollinger, and walk out the door.

I see in the reflection of two huge mirrors on either side of the bar doors that he and the barman are speechless. I grin as I strut out past reception.

Chapter 6 – Nigel at Sixfields

My head hurts. Why did I drink it all?

I remember waking up on the sofa around two a.m. with the TV a black-and-white snowstorm (the Sky box switches itself off at one). I'd slobbered on the cushion, so was sleeping in a wet patch. It's been a while since I've done that. Happy days.

I'd put the empty bottle of Bolly in the sink, just in case it fell over (which, out of the two of us, it wouldn't be that), then stripped and got into bed.

Opening the curtains, I take a peek outside and squint as it looks like summer's starting. Knowing I'm still well over the limit, I decide to walk to work. It's just over a mile, so I might sober up by the time I get there.

Breakfast is less than appealing, so I pack a double bag of sandwiches, feeling decidedly iffy as I spread the crunchy peanut butter and jam on the bread (I've run out of cheese). I've swapped the Kelly bag for an over-the-shoulder blue and purple 'fit everything inside' hobo bag I bought from the market last year and adore.

As I walk down the Kettering Road and round the corner towards Abington Square, I get to the Jaguar garage. There in the front is an Ionian blue X-Type, registration plates out of view. I growl at it and immediately wish I hadn't as my brain growls back.

I give a subdued wave to Mike as I walk past the security office and he's still as cheerful as when I saw him last.

As I grab a machine hot chocolate (figuring the machine would be less noisy than the kettle and machine tea is foul), I slump at my desk and lower my head until it touches laminated wood, the movement not dissimilar to the aforementioned Ikea drawer. Even at a millimetre an hour, the impact is deafening. I decide not to do it again.

Then Tigger D descends.

As I metaphorically pick myself off the floor, she takes one look at me and yells, "My God, you look awful!"

"Please don't shout," I mumble.

"She's whispering," a voice to my right bellows.

I look up and it's Karen.

"I thought you were on holiday." The words reverberate around my brain.

"No, I'm back."

The penny drops. "But it's Saturday. I know Donna works some Saturdays, but you don't, do you?"

Karen looks up at Donna and I swing round, immediately wishing I hadn't.

"It's Monday, Izzy."

"What? I've lost two days? I've missed Nigel and–"

The girls burst out laughing, which doesn't help my mood.

"Sorry, we couldn't resist. Donna filled me in on your 'love life' and we knew you had plans."

I clamp my eyes shut as the room spins. I wish I'd stayed in bed. "You're horrible," I mutter.

Donna bends down and looks at me sympathetically. "Sorry, honey. I didn't realise it was that bad. I've only come in for an hour or two."

"And I was in town so I thought I'd see what I've got in store for Monday," Karen adds.

"You're too conscientious," I whisper and drink some of the hot chocolate. I shiver as I feel it descend through my insides. I'm not sure why as it's a warm drink on a warm day. Hey ho.

Donna gets me a glass of water and two paracetamol from the first-aid kit in the kitchen. I'm not sure how paracetamol ends up in a first-aid kit, but I'm guessing I'm not the first person in the office to feel like this.

She slowly places the glass down on my coaster and puts the tablets in my right-hand palm. I chuck them in my mouth and wash them down.

Donna, in her newly adopted mouse-like whisper, crouches between Karen and me. "Was it a good night then, last night?" Donna can't help smiling.

I nod slowly and croak, "It was great."

"Yes!" she claps delicately.

"Once I got home."

Karen grins like a naughty schoolgirl. "Oh yes?"

"Alone," I add.

"Oh," says Donna.

"Let's just say he was a bit too smooth."

"Eek," says Karen.

My head hurts, so I close my eyes until the imprints of their faces disappear into the darkness.

"I'm off." I recognise Karen's voice.

"Have a nice rest of the weekend," I say, eyes still closed. "See you Monday morning."

"And you. Don't do anything I wouldn't do." Karen's a married mother of three, so that doesn't leave much.

I open my eyes and squint as the fluorescence streams back into my eyes. "Okay, bye. Oh, and thanks for the mild heart attack."

"You're welcome. They say it does your heart good to have a scare once a day."

I sort of smile. I've always wanted to know who 'they' are so I can kick them in the shins!

I log on to the computer then go to the kitchen to get another hot chocolate. I put a mug under the nozzle and press the button, but a single puff of powder comes out. With the water dispensed, it looks like a muddy puddle, so I tip it down the sink and risk the kettle.

I set it going and go back to my desk to log on to my internet profile. There are a couple of messages and I open the first one, from a Metal Mickey. These guys, if nothing else, have good imaginations, although his profile looks pretty normal, which makes a change. He loves eighties music, keeps fit and is very unfussy when it comes to food.

The kettle boils and I'm grateful it's far enough away for the noise not to permeate too deeply. I make the tea, guide the mug onto the coaster, and lean over sniffing the warm steam. I now know the correct distance so my nostrils stay dry and I then turn my face so it warms my right cheek.

The next thing I know, William's standing by my desk.

"What, may I ask are you doing?"

"I've made a cup of tea."

"And what? It's talking to you?"

"No. Got a bit of a headache so it's warming me."

"You do realise it's nearly summer."

75

"I do, yes. Female logic, William."

He shrugs, clearly resigned to never understanding women, which I think is a very wise conclusion, as we gave up understanding men years ago.

The second message is from NigelEByGum saying he's off to town to do some shopping and will get the tickets on the way home. I send a message back saying if it's not too late he can hang fire as I have a season ticket and we could go early, collect the tickets and have a drink before the film starts.

I then reply to Metal Mickey's 'Hiya' message. A man of many words. I was an nineties teen but am nevertheless pleased we have something in common as I love eighties music. I reply with a bit of chat about 'me' and to drop me a line if he wants to know more.

Then a message from Charles comes in. We're on for seven as he has a business meeting in London at nine the next morning. I bet he's loving whoever set that up.

I'm about to start typing my article when Nigel replies saying he got held up by a phone call from his mother (please don't let him be a mummy's boy – at least they don't live together) and that he's happy to meet earlier. Say, six? I reply 'perfect' and that I'll see him later.

With my headache clearing and the office quiet (Donna crept out with a wave a little while ago), I get cracking on with '31 dates art. 0605'.

What did I learn from last night? That men never cease to surprise me. Never assume the communication lines are parallel when dealing with the opposite sex. And especially when it's the written word. It's like text messaging – the meaning can easily get lost along the way.

You're not there when the other person receives it to explain the emotion behind it. Many a friendship has been broken, patched up or lost in the short history of the text due to misunderstanding. And what happened last night was a miscommunication on a magnitudinous scale.

Who, in their right mind, would, before they've even exchanged a couple of 'get to know each other' remarks, ask the other whether they wish to 'have our drinks here or take them up to our room'? I suppose I should be flattered that he, R, would like me in that way, but with only our names exchanged, I felt it was a tad (like half a dozen dates) too quick.

*The fact he was also (supposedly) separated, having previously talked about his **ex**-wife, didn't help. She was painted as a nightmare he couldn't wake up from, but while he was attempting (and failing) to seduce me, his probably very lovely spouse was returning to an empty home with a note saying he had to go away on 'business'. Maybe she suspects, or maybe she knows, but however much money they have, and believe me he has plenty, I hope one day, soon, she asks herself whether he's worth it.*

Remember, I've been given the task of meeting an average (some more average than others) of one man a day/evening for a work project and I would urge ALL of you to take your time. Get to know someone before you meet and then get to know them in the flesh before actually seeing much more of that flesh!

I would imagine R is one of many many married men trawling the internet in search of 'bimbos', of which I'm not one. A man has to work hard for my affections. Friends call me fussy, and I am. I'm also heightist. At just under six feet, I, like most women I know, still like to look up to a man.

While partners of vastly different ages stand out a mile, so does a woman towering over her date. Sorry, guys, but unless you find a woman who's – like my friend D – a very special individual wrapped in a petite package, if you're less than five feet nine (five feet eight may be pushing it), you don't stand a chance. For all the personality in the world, if you're shorter than your date and she gets back or neck ache within the first twenty minutes, there's unlikely to be a second meeting.

That said, you can never have too many friends and we're not that shallow that we'd prefer a hunk over someone who makes us laugh, as a friend. So if you're a firecracker in a small gift box, there is hope. Anyone, tall or otherwise, who goes on a first date willing it to lead to romance and a permanent relationship is bound to be heading for a fall.

Leave home thinking you might have a bit of fun, good conversation or share a bottle of Bollinger RD (or in my case get the whole thing to myself in the comfort of my own home, thank you very much Mr 'this one's for free' Smoothie!), and you can only have a good time… with a bit of luck.

I wrap it up with a few more tips on the technology side of internet dating (the levels of membership and how to upload a photograph, should they be that brave), click 'save' then close the document.

With the article safely in William's tray ahead of the deadline (he's always in at the weekends – I think work is his first home rather than second), I decide to call it a day. He's disappeared, so I find a piece of scrap paper and pen from his desk and am writing a note to that effect when I notice a ring binder on a shelf with my name on it.

I do my meerkat impression – no one's looking in my direction and, better still, no William, so I pull out the file and open the front cover. It's everything I've ever done.

At the front is yesterday's computer-printed article with older ones behind it. I look at the shelf and then around the room, but there are no colleagues' equivalents in sight. I wonder whether he's got mine to hand for an appraisal, or something worse, and I feel sick.

I put the file back where I found it in, I hope, exactly the same position. I may whinge about my job and not be the most punctual of people, but from the feedback we get, my column's a popular one and I love what I do, so unless he's got someone else lined up, I should feel secure.

So why don't I?

I return to my desk to gather my things and am logging off when there's whistling from the corridor behind me. I turn round and it's William. He gives me a smile. As it's not something I see very often, I can't decide whether it's a 'her days are numbered' or 'I'm happy, yes it does happen sometimes' smile, so say something to help figure it, and him, out.

"You're looking pleased with yourself today, William."

"Baby's on the mend."

"That's great. I'm so relieved." And I'd never said a truer word. "I've left a note on your desk. The article's done and my work's pretty much up to date. Is it all right if I head off?" I figure this being a golden moment to ask such a question.

He looks around the desert of an office. "Have a good weekend. See you bright and early on Monday."

Not sure whether he means that literally, I smile and say, "And you, thanks."

After plodding home, I'm waiting for the kettle to boil when I remember my mobile sitting on my desk. I growl and flick the switch to off.

I grab my car keys and head back into town. After parking at work, I nip to Sainsbury's for the basics, or thereabouts – I always buy too much. I'm a nutty seedy bread fan and am gutted when my usual brand isn't there. In fact there's very little pre-packaged bread at all. I wonder if there's a world war looming that no one's told me about, and the population of Northampton have spent the morning stocking up and are building their shelters as I spend my less than twenty quid on a week's worth of shopping.

I decide that if the end is nigh, I may as well splurge the diet (not that I'm on one anyway) and get a 'tiger' French stick, three varieties of English cheeses and a four-pack of full-fat full-taste dips. I've got plenty of proper butter at home, so finally pick up a four-pack of Heinz Cream of Tomato Soup (only the best will do for my last days on earth).

If the world is going to end in the next few hours, I'm going to be sorely disappointed as it'll mean I'll be unlikely to meet OMG69, see the inside of 'Groove', or hold a conversation that would teach me a thing or three, if I understood a word of it.

Passing the drinks aisle, I stop and retrace my steps figuring that if I have a short time to live, I may as well be drunk.

Everything looks pretty much as I left it when I emerge from the centre and lug my emergency supplies back to my car. There was no sign of Klaus earlier, but he's now standing by the car park exit barrier.

"Good afternoon, Klaus," I say politely and go to push my pass into the slot.

"Guten tag," he replies. He speaks perfect English, but knows I have splatterings of his mother tongue.

"Und wie geht's heute?" I say.

"I'm good, thank you. How is your weekend going?"

79

He must have caught whatever happy bug William has, as this is the almost longest conversation we've ever had.

"It's going well, thank you. Just off home for a late lunch."

"Ah, good idea. I've just had mine."

"Anything nice?" I can't believe we're talking about food. Unlike Mike, I've never seen Klaus eat anything and he challenges Lawrence in physique terms, which is rather odd given his job. I can't see him chasing anyone round the block without breaking in two, but he is nearly seven feet tall with an imposing personality to match, so I suppose weight isn't everything.

"Wurst, cheese and crackers," he says patting his stomach. His uniform jacket disappears in a scene reminiscent of Lawrence's fleece. They are definite contenders for Donna's column. Anorexia may not be at the top of her list of topics to cover, but it seems to be a growing trend, especially with the menfolk of this town.

My mouth is watering as I realise Klaus is talking. I look up at him. "I'm sorry?"

"Oh, don't be," he replies in his strong Bavarian accent.

"No. I missed what you said."

"Just to have a good weekend."

"Thanks, Klaus, and you."

My car radio bursts into life as I leave the underground car park and I recognise Beethoven's Piano Sonata no. 14 in C sharp minor, Op.27-2... better known as the 'Moonlight Sonata'. I look in the mirror to see if Klaus has heard any of it, but he's disappeared back inside his office.

I'm pretty good at remembering modern song titles, but hopeless at classical. It's like having the words helps, which I suppose is pretty obvious. I only remember Ludwig's no. 14 as it's one I can play the first few notes of... that and 'Für Elise' (Bagatelle in A minor) as well as the intro to Deep Purple's 'Smoke on the Water' and, of course, 'Chopsticks'.

Despite buying a bottle of Disaronno liqueur (I'd seen the adverts and had tried it at Ursula and Max's housewarming/Easter holidays party), I have to stay sober and

take my luscious lunch into the lounge to set my *Jack & Sarah*
DVD going. It's one of my favourites – yes, I'm actually a slush-
bucket under this exterior – but I've not seen it for months and
can't wait to be reacquainted. If the world ended as the end
credits rolled, I'd be a happy woman.

With the aforementioned credits rolling, and Eileen Atkins firmly
planted in my memory (I think she's a great actress, but can
never remember her name), I look out of the window and, again,
everything looks as I left it, so I decide it's worth going upstairs
to get ready for Nigel. The Undertones song immediately pops
in my brain and I hum it (I only know the chorus) as I'm taking
my plates and mug into the kitchen.

I stand for ages in front of the wardrobe and nothing leaps
out at me. One day I wish it would, especially on a weekday
morning because when you work with a room full of colleagues
five, or currently six, days a week and sit next to the fashion
columnist, you want to make an effort. You can only team up so
many key pieces with other key pieces until your look gets a bit
tired. And so does your brain, having to remember what you
wore on each weekday for the past six months.

I finally plump for smart black jeans and a favourite
embroidered turquoise t-shirt. The latter wouldn't look out of
place on a Caribbean island beach and having had 'summer' for
two days in a row, I want to encourage the sun to stay out.

Nigel (or someone who I assume is, but desperately don't want
to be) is waiting for me outside.

It's Saturday night, the 'hottest' night of the week, the actual
hottest evening of the year so far, I'm surrounded by the hottest
people in Northampton, and on a date with Mr Nerd. The name
Nigel is often synonymous with trainspotters, but I have a friend
called Nigel who's lovely: tall, fair and handsome (and sadly, for
me, not interested in women), but this one is… a real picture.

His legs are whiter than mine, and that's saying something.
At the top of his anaemic legs are red, bright red, brighter than
a newly painted post box red, cycling shorts, tighter than an
Elizabethan corset and containing less than Eric Morecambe's
paper bags. At the other end of these hairy beanpoles are

81

yellow socks enveloped by brown open-toed sandals and cycling clips. His shoes don't look comfortable or practical enough to ride a bike in, but I guess he knows what he's doing.

Nerdy Nigel (mercifully no hint of a trainspotting jacket) is wearing a pink and orange Day-Glo cycling top. I had thought nothing could be worse than a Bolton Wanderers sports shirt, but I was wrong. If I didn't need sunglasses before, I do now.

I could, by rights, walk back to the car and leave – he's not spotted me yet – but I figure that after the drink (I'm hoping in a very dark bar, although no doubt his outfit is fluorescent), we'll be seeing the movie, so we won't have to talk much. Then it hits me. If the outfit is fluorescent in a dimly lit bar it's going to be positively radioactive in the cinema.

People are laughing at him as they walk into the foyer and I feel sorry for him, so I keep walking. He's oblivious to them, but spots me. I'm grateful he doesn't do any kind of wave (a Mexican wouldn't be a shock), but his eyes are concentrating on me and I feel distinctly overdressed.

As I make a beeline for him (and am surprised the real insects aren't congregating around him by now), he holds out his hand.

I shake it as he says, "Izzy, hi. I'm Nigel. I'm so pleased to meet you."

I muster a smile as bright as his outfit and say hello too.

"I must apologise for this…" He waves a hand at his attire. "My car broke down, so I had to go and get my bike. I hate being late or I would have walked here."

"I'm sorry to hear about your car and am grateful you went to so much trouble." I picture the sort of outfit I'd have been treated to if the car had behaved and think perhaps I prefer this one. If nothing else it's brightened my day (and the Sixfields complex) and will be something interesting for Tuesday's column.

We get the tickets and walk to Frankie & Benny's next door. Heads turn as we walk in. I'm getting a little peckish after my late lunch, and love F&Bs, but wouldn't want to do a Tim. We're shown a corner booth (no surprise) and given two menus.

"I know we said just a drink, but are you at all hungry?" Nigel asks.

"A little. You?"

"I wasn't, but having to push my car off the road, run home and get the bike has given me a bit of an appetite."

"I'm surprised you made it here before me."

"I'd left early to do some food shopping on the way here, but I guess it'll have to wait until the car's fixed."

"Oh dear." Part of me wants to say, "Throw your bike in the back of my car after the movie and I'll take you to Sainsbury's then home", but I resist. "Your profile name implies you're a Northerner? But you have a local accent."

"Ah, no. My surname's Edwards so Nigel E becomes…"

"Oh," is all I can manage. "So, do you have food in at home or…"

"No, but it's fine. I've got front and rear panniers."

Of course you do. "That's handy."

A waitress, who looks like she has constipation as she looks at Nigel's outfit, arrives and hovers to take our orders. Neither of us has even looked at the menu, so I ask for a couple of minutes. "Sure," she says before sniggering and going to a neighbouring table.

"Shall we just go for snacks then?" Nigel asks.

"Good idea." Needless to say the potato skins are not going to be my choice tonight and, despite Tim's assassination of them, I fancy onion rings and garlic bread, but neither are suitable for spending two hours in the dark with a complete stranger, although I can guarantee there won't be any kissing.

"Do you mind if I go for garlic bread and onion rings?" he says.

"Really?"

"It's fine. I quite understand… second-hand breath and all."

"No. That's exactly what I was going to pick."

"Great." He smiles a perfectly polished smile, then sticks up an orange-pink arm and the waitress comes scuttling over. There's one thing to be said about his attire, we won't have trouble catching anyone's attention.

He orders our food, a lemonade and lime for him, and lemonade and blackcurrant for me. We're deep in conversation when the waitress brings the food over. I scowl at her when it's apparent she still finds us hilarious and she looks down at the floor. If she was hoping for a tip, she can keep hoping.

We've finished the snacks when I look at my watch and realise we've got five minutes before the film starts. Again, finding the attention of a member of staff to pay isn't a problem. I assume it's his outfit as whenever I'm out on my own or with friends, I'm usually ignored or they look through me, which is odd because being five feet ten, I'm not exactly invisible.

We go Dutch, although Nigel offers to pay (which is very sweet), and we walk to the cinema. We get a small drink each, which Nigel does buy, and we take our seats, four rows from the back. He lets me sit on the outside, which is great because I love sticking out my legs, and we catch the last couple of adverts for forthcoming movies.

One is a gangster flick I'm not normally a fan of, but I loved *Lock, Stock and Two Smoking Barrels* and this one's done by the same people. The other is for a chick flick – they can be made by anyone and I'll still see it. That's the joy of the season ticket. Some people won't go anywhere on their own, but I don't mind. Pick a weekday daytime when people are at work and it's deadly. I love it. No one to shush at, no mobile phone screens illuminating the auditorium, and no kids asking 'why' every few seconds.

It's a 15-rated movie, so we get two out of three. Even in the dark I can tell Nigel's looking at me with 'should we do something about it or throw something at them' eyes, so I shake my head. "Better not," I whisper, "they might get funny", but wonder why we're all so scared of idiots who like to spoil it for everyone else, so add, "We'll see if they stop in a bit." Nigel nods, so we keep focused on the screen and try to blot out the numbskulls. Easier said than done. The numbskulls in question are a group of teenagers in the corner who are talking at normal volume about everything that's happening on the screen.

Nigel's right leg is bouncing, so I whisper, "Shall I go and tell someone?"

"Do you want me to?" he offers.

I'm grateful he's so chivalrous, but say I don't mind. I'm about to stand up, which is annoying because the film's started, when there's a loud "Shhh" from the middle of the seating and the teenagers stop. Nigel and I look at each other and I can tell we're both thinking, *That was easy*, when I see an empty cup being thrown from the aforementioned corner in the general direction of the 'shhh'. Big mistake.

A man, I presume the originator of the 'shhh', rises. And keeps on rising. He walks away from us, along to the end of his row, and then casually steps over the rows until he's reached the back and the group. He selects two of them, one in each hand, and marches them back to the beginning of their row, causing two couples to stand.

The whole audience is applauding and as he's 'escorting' them down the stairs, I hear snatches of what he's saying. I don't understand it all, but enough to realise that it's not English, enough to recognise the Bavarian accent. I turn to Nigel.

"I know him, the big guy. I'm going to see if I can help, do you mind?"

"Of course not. Do you want me to come with you?"

I think about it for a second, but that would mean both of us missing the film. Pointing at the screen I say, "Would you stay and tell me what happens?"

"Sure," he says a little too enthusiastically.

I'm about to step out into the aisle, but the rest of the teenagers have decided to make a run for it and come bolting down the stairs. I follow them, at a bit of a distance, and am rounding the right-hand corner into the tunnel, when Klaus appears. He realises it's me and we go outside.

"Hello, Isobel."

"Hi, Klaus. Good on you for doing that." It's only when I see him in civvies that I realise he's older than he looks at work. I'd not given it much thought before, and I'm even more impressed by his agility. "Are you here on your own?"

"No, with my wife. You?"

I'd never thought of a Mrs Klaus though I don't know why. I guess I see him so rarely that I don't picture him having a life outside of the paper. "Blind date. Project research for my column, but don't let on please, he doesn't know."

For some reason Klaus doesn't look surprised, but I get the impression little surprises him. It's like he has built-in armour and nothing, except for perhaps Mrs Klaus, gets away with it.

"We should go back. Heike'll be wondering where I am."

"So will Mr Project. Besides, I was enjoying the film… the little bit I saw." I look around the foyer. "What happened to the lads?"

"I frogmarched the first two to the manager's office. I think the others escaped."

He makes it sound like a scene from a war or prison film and I laugh. He frowns, so I apologise and open the door back into the movie. He bows, then pauses. "Please, after you."

I bow too, though there's no need, and say, "Thanks." It's all rather surreal. Before I go back in though, I have one more question for him. "How did you know where the manager's office was?"

"This happens very often. We're old friends by now."

I shake my head as I walk in front of him and wonder what the world's coming to.

After some very hushed filling in from Nigel, I really enjoy the film and when it's over make a mental note to look out for it when it comes out on DVD. I think about all these mental notes I keep giving my brain and wonder how many I would need to fill its filing cabinets.

They say you only use a tiny percentage of your brain in your lifetime, but there must be people, lawyers and the like, who use more than most. Something else I've heard is that your brain uses up more calories than any other organ in your body, something like a tenth of a calorie a minute, so if that's true I should be a waif, but I love my food, so it probably evens things out.

Nigel and I leave before Klaus and Heike, so we wait for them at the door. We do the introductions and Klaus winks at me before leading his wife towards the main exit. Heike is the opposite of him, diminutive in every way.

As Nigel and I walk out into the foyer and then to his bike, I'm working out what to say to let him down gently. I get as far as saying, "I'm sorry," when he sighs.

"I'm so glad, because I don't feel a spark either."

"Great," I say a little too cheerfully, then add more seriously, "Makes it easier, doesn't it?"

Nigel leans over, kisses me gently on the cheek, and walks to his locked green and yellow Day-Glo bike.

I walk to my car and take a quick look back at the bicycle racks. He's also looking in my direction, does a little Mexican wave, wraps the chain around the base of the seat, hops on the bike and races away.

With a smile and a little Latin undulation in my shoulders, I zap the car's remote and drive home.

Chapter 7 – Charles at the Greyhound

Having decided to stay up last night and watch another two movies (*Groundhog Day* and *Sliding Doors*), I have a ridiculously long lie-in. I don't think I've stayed in bed 'til midday since I was a teenager and it's fantastic. I wonder why I don't do it more often, but by the time I've set some washing going, made some lunch, had a shower, washed up, bought and read the paper (I use that term loosely as they only have the *Sunday Sport* left) it's gone four o'clock and there's little of the day left until I have to go and meet Charles, Mr CXW69.

I do some housework then, as we're meeting at seven thirty, I decide to get ready. It doesn't usually take long, but I've been struggling with outfits recently, so with warpaint, a sandwich and a twenty-minute drive, I don't want to leave it much longer. Besides, given the choice of looking at my colourful wardrobe or sorting more bank statements, which would win? Exactly.

I figure Charles for a skirt kind of chap, so pick a Long Tall Sally girlie floral number, a crisp white Gap shirt (one of my key pieces) and a lilac cotton jacket that matches one of the tones in the skirt. Again, I feel Karen's influence rubbing off on me. I add the warpaint, but subtle; I don't suppose Charles goes in for the full tribal effect.

With ten minutes to spare (twenty – I like to be ten minutes early), I grab my car keys and head out the door. Ursula's walking down her path as I walk down mine.

"Hello," she says. "You look pretty."

"Ah, thanks, Ursula. You look like you're going to work." I don't think that came out right. She's very attractive, but has casual clothes on – not jeans, but 'visiting a family' kind of clothes.

She laughs. "How did you guess? This is one of my 'trying to blend in' outfits."

"Oh dear."

"Just routine tonight. Regular visits, check-ups, that kind of thing."

"Good… well, enjoy."

"I'll try. You off anywhere nice?"

"Greyhound at Milton Malsor. Meeting a friend."

"Excellent. Lovely place."

"It is. Haven't been there for a while, so hoping it's still as nice." Lawrence pops into my head and again I omit saying anything. If they do work together I don't want him finding out he was a guinea pig, and even if she doesn't mention where I work, it would get too complicated. I realise I've been standing staring at her.

"Izzy?"

"Sorry. Miles away."

"Have to go. Duty calls."

"Me too. See you later."

Milton Malsor isn't far off M1 junction 15, so I growl at the Hilton as I drive towards it and take the turning for the village. Apart from the crematorium, the Greyhound pub seems to be the only memorable landmark. I think the post office is long gone, but remember signs for a school and think I've seen reports of football club matches (our sports guy, Andy, would know).

I'm driving into the pub car park when the clock on my dashboard flicks round to seven twenty-seven. Not bad.

Reversing into a space, I spot a Del Trotter lookalike to my right, repeatedly pointing a remote control at an old grubby grey Ford Mondeo without any success, so he eventually locks it manually. He's without the yellow Reliant Robin, but does do the 'sheepskin coat and bling' look. I'm warm in my cotton jacket, so he must be boiling, but I get the impression it's all for show.

As I get out of my Polo, I see he's hovering at the back of my car.

"Hello," I say.

"You must be the delightful Izzy."

"And you must be Charles."

"That's me." He grins a little too widely. "CXW69 at your service."

I grin too, the sentiment of mine probably not matching his.

"Shall we go in?" he asks, his arm round my waist, causing my body temperature to plummet. The entrance is narrow, so we enter single file.

I duck to avoid a beam as I walk to the bar and assume Charles isn't paying attention as there's a loud crack behind me. I swing round and he's rubbing his forehead. "Oh shit. Are you all right?"

"No," he moans, and I can tell it's not just his head that's taken a knock.

"Don't worry. I've done the same," I lie. When he removes his hand, there's a bright red stripe across his forehead and I have the prospect of talking to that all night. I surprise myself by keeping a straight face.

Because I reach the bar first, I ask Charles what he'd like to drink, and he orders a pint of Stella, probably the most expensive lager on the menu. William's paying, I remind myself, so hand over a crisp ten-pound note for the Stella and my J2O.

We find a cosy corner away from the main dining area. It's near the toilets and it isn't long before Charles is twitching.

"Anything wrong?" I ask.

"I don't like it here. I want to move."

He reminds me of Lola… my four-year-old niece.

"I don't like being on a flight path," he explains.

"Fine," is all I say.

We pick up our drinks, but can't see any free tables on this side of the pub, so walk to the dining area. All the tables are full. Sunday night appears to be family night and we do a whole circuit of the pub, but there isn't a space to be had, so we head back to our original table which is, of course, occupied. We therefore end up standing near the bar, but find that wherever we are, we're in the way, and have to keep apologising whenever someone wants to order a drink. I apologise; Charles just glares at them, like it's their fault the bar was placed where we decided to stand.

"Shall we go outside?" I ask, trying to be helpful.

"I'd rather not," he says.

"Oh." I wait for him to explain, but it's not forthcoming. The red stripe looks to be easing. "How's your head?"

"It hurts."

I give him the benefit of the doubt and assume that's why he appears to be in a bit of a mood, until someone accidentally bumps into him, making him spill his drink on his fake sheepskin jacket.

"Oy!" he shouts and spins round. The offender is nearly a foot taller than him, but that doesn't stop him standing on tiptoes (on his fake leather loafers), and demanding an apology, which he would have already heard, had he been paying attention. I feel I should butt in and say something, but the other chap apologises again and Charles spins back to me grunting, "I should think so too."

The couple behind him look at each other and the husband shakes his head, the woman saying something out of earshot. For the second time in twenty-four hours, I would love a cartoon Acme hole to appear in the ground, so I can jump in and disappear to a Toon Town somewhere, resurfacing as Jessica Rabbit's twin, so I can be 'bad because I'm drawn that way'.

Sadly, no hole appears and Charles is buying another round of drinks. This time he's ordered himself half a pint of local ale (the cheapest on the chalkboard) and he and the barman are looking at me, waiting for me to say what I want.

"Sorry. Just a Coke will be fine please. Is it Coke or Pepsi?" I say looking at the barman.

"Coke."

"Bottled or pump?"

Charles coughs, but I ignore him. I like my proper bottles of proper fat Coke, thanks very much.

"Pump, sorry."

"That's fine."

Charles is tapping his foot. Tonight is going to be remembered for all the wrong reasons and I can't wait to go home. I wonder how quickly I can down my drink and call it a night without being rude, even if Charles hasn't exactly been Mr Diplomacy.

I take a swig of tap Coke and some of it goes down the wrong way, so I splutter. More than a drop of Coke ends up on the front of Charles's coat and I needn't have worried about ending the date early as he takes one look at me. "That's it, I've had enough," and storms out the front door.

I'm left speechless until the barman says something. I turn round and he repeats what he said. "That'll be three eighty, please."

"Sorry?"

"Three eighty. One Coke, one Potbelly."

"Pot what?"

"Potbelly. The local ale that your… that the gentleman had."

Potbelly sums up CXW69 perfectly.

I hand over four pound coins and raise my hand to stop the barman when he attempts to give me the change. Seeing as my date has already left, I ask if I can have a receipt and the disgruntled barman presses a couple of buttons on the high-tech till (the only thing holding my interest) which prints one out. He hands it over with a glazed expression then moves to the next customer, smiling falsely.

I continue standing at the bar until I've finished my Coke and walk back to my car. The Mondeo's long gone; the only evidence of its existence is a trail of oil. A smile creeps over my face as I imagine hearing a distant bang as a certain Ford engine gives up the ghost.

I'd never noticed before how difficult it is to start a car with your fingers crossed.

Chapter 8 – Eddie at the Aviator

Didn't sleep very well last night. Thanks, Elliot.

I'd decided to reacquaint myself with him but woke up twice worrying about Natasha's baby. I'd assumed *Opaque*'s prologue was talking about her baby, but I've not got the explanation of that, so it's been at the back of my mind since the beginning of the story, which I guess is what prologues in this kind of book are good at.

I believe this is a first novel, so if I could write that well for my debut I'd be chuffed. I'm not a fan of children, but a missing baby – you'd have to be pretty hard not to be bothered by that, fictional or otherwise.

I drag myself out of bed and, remembering William's 'bright and early' comment on Saturday, fly around the house like a mad thing. It's already a quarter to eight, twenty minutes later than normal, and I'd like to be early today. Fat chance.

Showered, dressed and breakfasted, I only have to get lunch ready. I look at the clock and it's bang on half eight. Five minutes. I can do it.

Ursula's walking up her path as I'm sprinting down mine.

"Morning, Izzy."

"Morning. You've been working all time?"

She shakes her head. "A quick callout. I'm rostered on again at one, so going back to bed for a while."

"Can I join you?" I blurt out before realising what I've said. "I mean…"

She laughs. "I know what you mean. You had a nice time, at the Greyhound?"

I grimace. "Let's just say I got plenty of reading done when I got home. I should know better than to read a suspense novel after dark."

She laughs again and walks to her front door. "Have a good day."

"Thanks, have a good sleep."

I arrive with a couple of minutes to spare. There was no sign of Mike when I went past the security office, but Donna's already at her desk slaving away.

I look over at William's office and he's not there either, but Janine's back from sick leave, so I log on to my computer and wander over.

"Morning, Janine. Are you feeling better?"

"Much, thanks," the M distinctly like a B.

"Sounds like it. Are you sure you should be back already?"

"Oh yes, I'm fine. It sounds worse than it is. Besides, I've got so much work to do I'd never see my desk if I left it much longer."

I think of my fairly empty workload and empathise. On reflection I could have offered my assistance to William, in Janice's absence, and earned some brownie points, but too late now. "If there's anything I can do…"

"Thanks, but I came in early, so I've got a pretty clear idea of what needs to be done."

"Where's William?"

"He had to take Baby to the vet. Phoned me on his mobile while he was waiting to go in, which probably didn't go down well. Did you know Chloë's sister is the receptionist there?"

"Chloë did mention that, yes. I hope it's not bad news. He's so attached to her."

"I'm sure she's a great receptionist, but…"

"I didn't mean… ha."

"Baby is like a child to him."

I think of Natasha's fictional baby again and my heart goes out to them both. I offer to make Janine a drink and she nods furiously.

With two reports to write up today, I need to be more sparing with my prose and am looking forward to writing about Mr Nerd and Mr Synthetic.

I hang fire logging on to tallgirlnn1, although I'd love there to be a message from Charles. Armed with my gnat's pee tea, I get cracking on today's article. I want a lunch break because I need to buy some fruit from the market. I'm way behind on my five-a-day fruit and veg and feel the need for a big dose of vitamins. Besides, I like throwing grapes at Donna – we call it our 'feeding time at the zoo'. When William's out of course. So…

What did I learn from last night? That some people are too ready to take others at face value and usually think the worst.

I met N for a movie on Saturday evening and, as we were early, we had a drink and a snack first. As N had cycled to the cinema, he was wearing an outfit that I shall just say was rather 'loud'. It was a warm evening, so his attire was in keeping with the season, but perhaps not so with the occasion. He said his car had broken down (big brownie points for getting home, changing, and still getting there before me), so his clothes obviously needed to be comfortable, though I still don't know how he cycled in sandals.

As I walked towards him, I noticed everyone staring and laughing (he was blissfully oblivious). Most of us, myself included, worry what other people think of them, so it's so liberating and refreshing to spend time with someone who doesn't care about the 'little things'.

Every morning I stand in front of my wardrobe, then my mirror, wanting to look my best. Of course it makes me feel good, but I don't do it only for me. While I spend less time than most getting ready for work or an evening out, I want people – my colleagues, friends, complete strangers – to look at me and think that I didn't just roll out of bed.

We're all wearing masks to some extent. And there are the select few who don't feel, or are not aware, that they need one. And I say good on them. Let Sunday be no-make-up-slob-around-or-go-to-Sainsbury's-in-your-pyjamas day. Would the world be a happier place? Not necessarily, but if our little corner of it was, it'd make people like N examples to follow, not be laughed at.

Last night I met C. He proves my point to a tee. Mr Superficial was everything N wasn't. He cared about everything he did and wore. He was an offensive man whose surroundings had to be to his liking and we were the 'little people'.

Needless to say there'll be no second date. Our first encounter was cut short due to an unfortunate accident with a Coke-laden lung (mine) and a fake-laden jacket (C's). Mr Superficial as you can imagine was as impressed with that as with being unable to find a free table, apart from the one we had first sat at, which was en route to the toilets and therefore not suitable for a person such as himself.

So, following a rude encounter with a delightful couple who'd only decided to stand a little too close to him (not difficult in such a popular pub – we went to the Greyhound at Milton Malsor, by the way – if you've never been, you must. But watch out for anyone who wouldn't look out of place in an episode of 'Only Fools and Horses' and drives a tatty Mondeo – sorry, other Mondeo drivers), he declared he'd had enough and stormed out.

Having done so on the way in, I wondered if he would hit his head on a low beam on his exit, but he ducked before swinging the front door open and huffing out into the night. I expected a dramatic theatrical flick of the head before he left, but he failed his audience. A disappointing end to what could have been a disappointing evening, but I haven't laughed so much in ages. So, if you're reading this, C, thank you for being so entertaining.

I'm convinced that people who are rude and impatient are so because they don't get enough sleep. Tosh to anyone who says they don't need eight hours (I need nine). I reckon C probably stays up 'til the early hours staring at himself in the mirror, then gets up early (assuming he has a job to go to – we didn't get that far in the conversation, in fact we didn't get anywhere) to put on all his bling (which is probably as fake as his sheepskin, 'leather' shoes and whole personality) and prepare his act, before inflicting it on the world for another day.

So, today's two items ticked on my shopping list are Don't be afraid to be yourself and Do look in the mirror, and look deeper than your epidermis. We're all made up of layers, some of us deeper than others. You need to decide which you're going to wear on the outside, be proud of it, but subtle too.

I have a quick reread then print it off and put it on William's desk. There's still no sign of him and it's nearly eleven.

"Hi, Janine. Have you heard from William?"

"Not a peep. Doesn't look good, does it."

"Does Chloë know anything?"

"Haven't had a chance to speak to her yet."

"Do you want me to? I'm off to the kitchen for another drink anyway. Speaking of which, would you like a refill?"

"Thanks, Izzy. You're a star. The phone's been silly busy today, with William out, so I've not got very far."

"No problem. My article's done already, so I have a few emails to answer then I'm all yours. After lunch okay? Filing, photocopying, as menial as you like. I'm not proud."

Janine throws back her head laughing – the sort of hearty effort that I think I've only ever done half a dozen times in my entire life. I seriously think she, Donna and I should get together and they can share their secret. It seems to come naturally to them and I'm jealous. I'm sure men find me too... serious. That and my not being a size ten.

Men do prefer meat on a woman's bones (as do I on them – see earlier references to footballers v rugby players; why isn't rugbyers a word?). They say a man will love you for who you are, but that's generally tosh too. If we didn't care about a person's weight, I'd be on a second or third date with Tim by now, so I guess I'm as shallow as everyone else. After all, weight's just physical. Manners and personality are a lot harder to change and, to be fair, no one should have to change for anyone but themselves. I have a loft full of 'small me' clothes and if I'd seriously wanted to get back into them, I'd have done it before now. Wouldn't I?

I make another coffee for Janine, tea for me, and strong chocolate for Donna. It turns out Chloë's got the day off, so we're not enlightened on that score.

My emails take me nicely up until lunchtime. There's nothing from Charles; once again, he's a disappointment. OMG69 (who tells me he's called Ollie) confirms for nine tomorrow night. Nine? I'm sometimes asleep by nine, but who needs sleep anyway? With any luck I'll have a reasonably early night tonight, post-ReadyEddie, and save Elliot and Natasha for later in the week.

A fiver's worth of five-a-days (and twenty quid on half a dozen DVDs) later, I get a bowl from the kitchen and arrange half the fruit on the left-hand corner of my desk, the other half left in a recyclable bag destined for home.

Armed with a grape, I attract Donna's attention and hold the bowl up for her to pick at whenever she's passing. She smiles

97

and taps her watch. It's not like her to be too busy to chat; it must be serious – a Lawrence or Tim perhaps.

With all my emails checked and replied to, I spend the afternoon helping Janine play catch-up and am halfway through photocopying highly confidential board papers (which make very interesting reading) when Donna comes moping along.

"Hello. Sorry I haven't been over. I've got so much to do."

"What's wrong with you?"

"What do you mean?"

"Where's the Tigger bounce I know and love?"

"Oh, that."

"Well?"

"It's Mike."

"What's he done?"

"We had a fight."

"Oh no. What about?"

"Nothing really. I commented about how much he eats and he took it personally."

"I suppose he would. He does love his food."

"I know, but all that fat isn't good for his glycaemic index levels."

I've heard of GI from the labels on my Boots-bought sandwiches. "He does eat all the wrong things."

"That's what I told him."

"Maybe you could offer to make sandwiches for him?"

"I did, but he said I was trying to take over his life."

"What did you say?"

"That it's only because I care. And…"

I waited. "And?"

"And I said he was a heart attack waiting to happen."

"I'd agree. Is that what tipped him over the edge?"

"His father died of a heart attack."

"Not good."

"And now he's not speaking to me."

"I'm sorry. He'll come round. He must know you're just concerned."

"I'm hoping so. I didn't know."

"Of course you didn't. Do you want me to speak to him?"

She shakes her head and returns to her desk.

I check on Donna again before home time and she's not heard anything from 'him'. She still has work to do: a big review of hair colorants following a major hoo-ha in several leading nationals. I remember the pictures of a woman's frazzled scalp and am grateful for my natural highlights.

I've never been tempted to dye it (apart from an overdose of my mum's Sun-In in my teens, but that's another story), despite a friend, who's a different shade of red every time I see her, urging me to do so. I leave before Donna. William never made it in.

Mike's in reception, munching his way through a bag of Bombay mix. I'm not sure whether it's a step up or down from a doughnut.

I make myself a bowl of cereal and put on a DVD of another favourite: *27 Dresses*. As it ends, I glance at the clock. Oops. I'm meeting ReadyEddie in half an hour, so pull on my jeans, a deep purple close-fitting t-shirt and my white Gap shirt worn loosely over the top. I slip on a pair of black pumps and grab my keys.

The Aviator would usually be a fifteen-minute drive, but it's past a busy supermarket, so I'd rather be a few minutes early and sit in the car park than be in a queue, cursing that I hadn't left earlier (which I do on a regular basis and am kind of getting fed up with).

I arrive with ten minutes to spare and I'm getting out of the car when I see an old Volvo estate pull up outside the bar entrance. A man of about my age gets out then leans towards the driver, says something (presumably 'thanks') and slams the door. Although I have no plans to eat here tonight, I hope he's not the chef as he looks like he needs a good wash.

I zap my car's remote control and the indicators flash. I walk into the beautiful art deco building and am hit by the interior. I'm not sure what I expected, certainly not high-tech chrome, but this is delightfully charming. By the door there's a picture of before and after restoration works and an explanation that it was a clubhouse and Officers' Mess 'renovated to its former glory' where you can 'step back in time to a bygone age of aviation, style and fun'. It's a promise I hope will be fulfilled, but from the patronage this evening, I somehow find that hard to believe.

I walk up to the bar and wait for the barman to serve a smart businessman. I smile at the customer hoping it's ReadyEddie, and that his profile and messages were some kind of gold diggers' test, but he smiles weakly and returns to his table with two drinks, one for himself and one for his stunning blonde companion. Alanis Morissette's *Ironic* plays in my head.

The barman asks if I'd like a drink and I say I'm waiting for someone. Almost on cue, the scruffy chap I'd seen earlier comes out of the gents and walks towards me. I can smell him before he gets to me. I smile as he smiles, and hope I can hold my breath for the next hour or so. He puts out his hand, and given where he's just emerged from, I'm reluctant to shake it. I figure that as no food will be touching my currently clean hands, I'm fairly safe, even do so enthusiastically so he doesn't suspect.

As he's talking to me, I look at him in more detail. He has mousey brown hair that looks as if it's washed once in a millennium and cut with a pudding bowl… and badly. He resembles a mouse. Not a tame one, but one you see scurrying around hedges and rubbish tips on the TV. There's never an excuse for lack of hygiene and I feel compelled to say something, if only so no one else has to go through this, but despite my mean thoughts, I'm really not that cruel.

I buy us two Cokes and we move to a table in the middle of the room so we can 'find out about each other'.

One gem he parts with is that he doesn't 'currently have a car' because he's never had one. He's slightly older than me, doesn't drive, and has no intention or inclination to learn. Why would he when he can get lifts or taxis paid for him? He says he's too poor, but also doesn't have the intention or inclination to get a job, which is a real shame as he turns out to be a nice guy.

He's stuck in a rut and, like a mouse on a wheel, is going nowhere fast. He says he has a computer to keep him in touch with the real world as he doesn't have a TV in his 'bedroom', but also doesn't watch the news (even online) or read the newspaper (ditto). He says he should get glasses (I did wonder why he was squinting at me), but doesn't like the National Health ones and I can't say I blame him.

I remember owning two pairs when I was a child: blue plastic and pink plastic, and they were hideous. I dare say their freebies have come a long way since then, and it's his eyesight, but I think me saying anything would be a lost cause. He's like Lawrence: needs a good mother. This is when he confirms my suspicions that he still lives with his parents and it all slots into place.

I divulge everything there is to know about me (mostly the tallgirlnn1 version) and he seems impressed. He says he can't imagine how brave I must have been to not only leave home (I couldn't wait, and that was nearly ten years ago), but also move area (not a difficult choice given that Northamptonshire prices were a third of those down south).

He asks me what it's like to live alone and I want to say, 'You should get a job and try it', but I say it's great, that you can do whatever you like whenever you like, and hope he's inspired to do something with his life.

"I like the sound of that," he says as if the thought had never occurred to him before, then adds, "but don't you get scared?"

"Of what?"

"You know, at night."

"Err, no."

"I would be. Those noises. You can imagine all sorts."

I wonder at this juncture whether he's watched *Monsters Inc.* too often and see him as the child he so clearly is.

"Have you ever worked?" I ask, surprised at my lack of diplomacy.

"Oh, yes."

Great! I think, until he explains further.

"I was a paperboy when I was thirteen."

I muster some encouragement. "That was independence and fresh air."

"Gave it up after a couple of months. Too cold and had to get up early."

Okay. "Is there anything you'd like to do?"

He nods with a little enthusiasm. "I'd like to be a gamer."

"As in testing computer games?"

He nods again and I'm somewhat cheered.

"But I can't."

I despair. "Why's that?"

"I'm no good at it."

"But do you not practise?"

"All day every day, but I'm still rubbish."

Suddenly I feel really sorry for him. He spends longer at something he'd love to make a living out of than most people do at their careers, but has convinced himself he can't do it.

"Is there anything like it that you might be able to do?"

He shrugs and loses some of my sympathy. He feels like a lost cause.

I stare blankly out of the windows, wishing they were nearer so I could kill some time by drawing on them. I wonder if he'd mind if I got my pen and paper out of my bag.

I make a comment about the static planes on the runway, at which he looks out. Then, as my eyes refocus to my reflection, the windows stare blankly back at me.

"So," I say at last, "what time do you have the taxi booked for?"

"I didn't book one."

So it looks as if I'm taking him home.

"My dad's collecting me."

Yay! "Did you say a time or are you going to ring him?" I may be appearing a little too eager to get rid of him, but he doesn't seem to twig.

"Eleven."

We've been together about forty minutes. I think I'd commit hara-kiri (or seppuku to give it its proper Japanese title – I know this from a toy I tested) if I have to chivvy him, and the conversation, along for another three hours.

"I'm not sure I can stay that late."

"Oh… I can walk home."

Knowing how dodgy the roads are, I say, "It's rather a long way, especially when it gets dark."

"It's fine. I've done it loads of times before. Besides, I don't have to get up early. I'll probably stay. I like it here and my dad gave me a tenner so that'll last the evening."

However nice Eddie is, and he is, he needs more of a future than relying on pocket money. "How about working here, Eddie?"

His eyes light up.

"Have you never considered it?"

"I come here a lot, but I've never thought about there being any work here."

"I'm sure there are jobs everywhere at some stage. You just have to be in the right place at the right time. Why don't you come back tomorrow and have a chat with someone in the main office? You'd need a CV and to smarten yourself up."

He looks down at his worn jeans.

"Maybe your dad could lend you something?"

"I don't have a CV."

"Maybe I could help you. I have some paper and a pen in my bag."

He looks down at the bag and smiles.

With pen in hand, I start. "Now, I'll write 'personal details' at the top, so that's where you write who you are and where you live."

He nods.

"Then you'd normally put where you've worked with your current position and company details at the top and work backwards, but we may have to be a little diplomatic."

"What, lie?"

"No, you can't lie on a CV because they'll find you out, but you can elaborate on the things you enjoy doing."

I scribble down the things he's already told me, but soon run out of room.

"This is no good, the paper's too small."

He sticks up his hand like a student needing to be excused for the toilet, and disappears off to the bar.

Returning with a pad of A4 lined paper, he puts it in front of me and smiles again.

"Excellent." I smile. He has people skills. "Now, I'll lay this out exactly as you are to lay it out on your computer. Do you have word processing software?"

He nods.

"So you're okay with typing a letter?"

"Oh, yes. I do letters all the time for Mum and Dad, when they have to complain about something or we're sent Christmas presents through the post."

I smile again at his innocence, remembering when I was younger always having my 'thank you' letters out by New Year. "Great. So we've got your details at the top then the summary of what you're good at."

"Oh."

"No, be positive. You're resourceful and good at communication. You're eager. Putting 'eager to learn' is always good. CVs shouldn't be longer than a page or two anyway, so that will work in our favour."

He's looking at me like a child learning something new and in awe of his teacher.

"See, we've filled half a page already. So you come here a lot." That felt cheesy. "Do you know what the different planes are?"

"I do! There's the Tiger Moth, the Avro 504, the Hawker Hart, the Vickers–"

"Excellent. Then we put that you have extensive knowledge of the aircraft. And you don't mind hard work…" I punt.

"I don't."

I have no proof of that, but take his word for it. "Great, then we put that too. Put anything else you think they'd like to hear that's relevant to why you would want to work for them: you live locally, happy to do different shifts, that kind of thing."

He's bouncing up and down like Zebedee. Like Tigger. Like Donna.

"You'll also need a covering letter, again with your name and address, that says, "Please find attached my CV for your consideration…" and so on."

He looks blank, so I write it out for him. "Are you okay with all this?"

"Oh yes!" He claps his hands. In less than an hour he's gone from zero confidence to being on the verge of an interview. I'm thrilled with him, and myself.

Tearing off the top two pages, I pass the blank pad back to him to return to the bar. He stands up and lunges towards me. I pull back, but he throws his arms around me saying, "Thank you," repeatedly.

I have to look away as the smell of his musty t-shirt is overpowering. It reminds me of something I missed when I unloaded the washing machine and found a week or so later, by which time it, a particular favourite top, was past keeping.

He lets go, and I say he's welcome. He returns the pad to the bar, buys two Cokes and brings them back to the table.

"I don't wish to be rude," (there's no way around it) "but you'll have to have a shower before you hand in your CV tomorrow."

I feel guilty as he looks back down at his jeans.

"You'll need make the right impression." I try to sound encouraging.

"And I haven't done that with you, have I?"

"I'm sorry."

"No, it's fine. I'm grateful. I can't wait 'til tomorrow."

"Yes, good luck. I'm going to go now. Will you be all right?"

"Absolutely. Thanks again for everything."

"You're so welcome. Are you going to stay here for your dad, or do you want a lift home?" He seems charmingly harmless.

"Thanks, but I'll stay. I want to check the place out. Take a proper look round. Maybe find something else that I can say I'm interested in or good at."

"That's the spirit. I'm proud of you," I say, hoping I don't sound condescending.

He beams. "It's been a long time since anyone's said that to me."

"They should say it more often. Do something to make people proud and you'll feel fantastic." I think of how pleased my parents were when I got my job.

I stand and he goes to hug me again. I offer my right hand. "Pretend it's a job interview."

He shakes my hand with a firm grip. "Good morning, Miss Izzy. I'm so pleased to meet you. I wonder if it's at all possible to leave my Curriculum Vitae with you for your consideration."

I stand there agog. "My goodness. Do that tomorrow and you'll have no problem."

He blushes and mouths, "Thank you."

"Will you send me a message and let me know how you get on?"

He nods like a five-year-old.

The drive home is a delight.

I have a warm glow and one of my favourite songs, ELO's 'Ticket to the Moon', which I haven't heard on the radio for years, comes on.

Despite it being quite sad, and one of the songs I want played at my funeral (we all consider that, don't we?), I chirp along with it, thinking I might have changed someone's life.

Chapter 9 – Ollie at Groove

Tonight's venue is Groove the Retro Club & Bar with OMG69, so I don't envisage an early night unless we run out of understandable conversation, but I'm looking forward to going, and hope for the best.

I decide to try to get in the mood with one of the trendiest outfits my wardrobe can offer: a long bold red-and-black two-tone top over a pair of black leggings, and although Karen may say I'm 'so last season', I've been told red suits me.

I amaze myself by getting into work by eight thirty, despite having one too many Disaronno last night. I had something to celebrate, didn't I? I set the computer going and make a cup of tea.

The kettle's boiling when the kitchen door opens. It's William, and he looks awful. "William, you look awful."

"Thanks. You look great."

I feel my face matching the two-tone aspect of my top and say a feeble "Thanks", then see how pale he looks. "Has something happened?"

"Baby died."

"No! When?"

"Yesterday afternoon. I thought she was getting better over the weekend, but she was listless Sunday night, and even worse early yesterday, so I took her to the vet. They tried everything they could…"

I want to give him a hug, but don't think I should, until I see tears threatening. That makes the decision harder. Whenever I'm on the cusp like that, someone giving me a hug sets me off. I decide to risk it.

He backs away, so I stop, but he seems to realise my intention and moves. It's like a mini ritual dance. He steps forward and says, "Please," so gently I can't resist. It's the only time he's let me in and it's humbling.

We're still locked in a loose embrace when we hear the door from reception open, so quickly step away from each other.

William coughs. "And that's going well, then is it, Isobel?"

I say an instinctive, "It is, thank you. It's all coming together nicely."

We look round and it's Donna. She appears to be her old self.

"Morning! Don't mind me."

"There's nothing–" William starts to say, but Donna interrupts him.

"My goodness, William, you look awful."

Great minds think alike.

I fill her in. "Baby died."

"No!" Her face crumples. "Oh, William, poor you."

"Thanks." He looks so dejected and she puts her arms out to him, but he stands his ground and coughs again, saying, "Thank you, Donna, Isobel," before heading back to his office.

Donna and I are heading for our desks when I remember the kettle. "I'm making a drink," I say. "Would you like one?"

"I'd love a coffee. Thanks, Izzy."

"No problem. Coming right up."

My mind goes back to William and his bird. They say nothing compares to losing a child, but when someone, or in this instance something, has been a part of your life for so many years, it must be a terrible wrench. My heart goes out to him.

I put my tea on my coaster and take Donna's coffee over to her. She's on the phone, so we exchange glances. I look at William's office, but he too is on the phone. I go back to my desk.

Janine then walks down the corridor towards me as I go to sit down. I tell her about Baby and she bursts into tears. I offer her the tissues; she takes two.

"Can I make you a drink?" I can't believe how upset she is.

"It's fine." She snuffles. "I'll make it, and something for William. I think he'll need something strong. Besides, it'll give me time to get over the shock."

I suppose being a PA gives you a closeness, and then I think of all the times I've caught her looking into his office, and I imagine a cartoon light bulb pinging over my head.

Janine disappears into the kitchen, and I crack on with the day.

Remembering Mike's diet, I do some research on Google and find a hospital paper that lists a three-column chart on 'Not so good' food (they're being far too polite), 'Getting better', and 'Eating for your heart's sake'. I'm delighted to see the last column includes chapattis (I love Indian), porridge (my mum's a big fan, so I get that for breakfast whenever I visit), and even crumpets.

I think they mean the 'Let them go cold then put on the lowest-fat butter-tasting spread you can find on them' way rather than my 'Grab them both out of the toaster, spread as much of the real thing full-fat butter on them as you can, so it soaks right through and makes a not-so-little pool at the bottom of the plate, then threatens to drip all over you when you pick them up, burning your fingers' way, but which tastes nicer? I rest my case.

I come to the conclusion that because doughnuts and Bombay mix are in the same, let's be honest and call it 'As bad for you as eating ten McDonalds in a row' category, that they must be as bad as each other. I'm sure Mike will be as delighted as me that he can eat chapattis, crumpets and porridge as well as the other 'hearty' items such as nuts, which I knew were a good source of protein, but always thought they were fatty – I suppose it depends on whether you have unsalted naked nuts (boring) or honey-coated cashews (my fave). He can also eat fish (again I would say battered would be outlawed) and naked white meats… now that I can do, and a silly grin appears on my face.

I print off the page for Donna, and can't resist logging on to tallgirlnn1. There's one message.

Metal Mickey's got all chatty and sounds like fun. He's the eighties music lover, so I pause iTunes, type in 80 in the search bar and set a-ha's 'Take on me' going. I love the video, so go to the internet and find it on YouTube and am jigging away as the pencil drawings come to life.

Then there are half a dozen Outlook emails – one from Geek's Paradise asking how I got on with their grasshopper. I reply saying I wouldn't normally advise my findings in advance of a review, but in this instance I'd let slip that I thought it was awesome. If they wanted to send me other 'subjects' I'd be very happy to do some more trials, although I didn't say so exactly. As diplomacy isn't my forté, however, I might as well have done.

The others are feedback, thankfully all positive, on my '31 dates' column, and I'm done replying to the last one when Donna appears, minus spark.

"Hello, Donna. How are things with you and Mike?"

"He's forgiven me and we're speaking again."

"That's very gracious of him. Is that why you're a bit low?"

"Sort of, though I'm thinking about William's bird. Isn't it sad."

"It is. He's taken it hard. Actually, I need to run something by you."

"Oh?"

"Not here. Let's go into the kitchen and get another drink."

I tell her about my Janine suspicions.

"Ah, she has a crush. How sweet."

I look around the kitchen. "Donna! Don't you dare say a thing." But I know I'm speaking to the wrong person.

"Of course I won't. You know me."

"That's why I'm asking you not to. You're more hopeless at keeping secrets than I am."

"Isobel MacFarlane, I am not. I'm very good."

"What about the time when…"

"Point taken. Do you think there's anything going on then?"

"I don't know. I don't think so, but you're nearer them geographically. Have you noticed anything?"

"No."

I hadn't for a moment thought she had, because (a) she tells me everything that's going through her mind, especially when it comes to office gossip and (b) she wouldn't notice if Cupid himself landed on her desk and aimed his bow at her.

She makes the drinks (the only person I know who makes my tea exactly how I like it) and we go our separate ways. She has strict instructions to keep an eye out for any 'signals' and report back to me if she spots anything. I'm not holding my breath.

I open up Microsoft Word, save Document 1 as '31 dates art. 0905' and type.

What did I learn from last night? That you shouldn't give up on anyone or anything. You may know someone who you think is a waste of space, useless, or a lost cause. Give them the benefit of the doubt; they may surprise you.

Last night I met E. Although we didn't get off to a great start (he was dropped off at the venue by a parent he still lives with), the evening turned out to be an enlightening one.

Our conversation started the usual way with us getting to know each other – and then hit a rough patch: me, I'm ashamed to admit it, wondering how I could leave early. However, the next few minutes proved to change our lives – me in a small but distinctive way, and him, I'm hoping, drastically.

I'd initially written him off as having no future, and I'm sure I'm not the first person to have thought, or perhaps said, that about him. However, once we found the one thing that gave him passion in his life, he lit up.

In the years since I left home, I've changed enormously. Yes, I have the odd Bridget Jones-style weight fluctuation (who hasn't?), but my personality has been the one thing to have undergone the most dramatic transformation. I consider that I have grown as a person; I've become far more independent and confident, and feel capable of dealing with anything that life throws at me (mainly because I have no choice).

While I have been lucky to have very supportive parents, others have been less fortunate, and I believe E is one of those people. His parents may provide for him, but they don't appear to have pushed him to be independent. Perhaps they're not ready to let him go.

They say nothing compares to losing a child, and when someone has been a part of your life for thirty years it must be incredibly difficult to let them go out on their own. E's parents have to remember they will see him again, and the more freedom they give him, the more he'll appreciate it and the happier they'll all be.

So today's two items ticked on my dater's shopping list: Don't assume that lack of money means lack of potential, and Do give someone time to surprise you. They could well be worth a second chance.

I reread, tweak, then print off the article and head for William's office. He's on the phone again (I assume not the same call), but beckons me in when he sees me standing the other side of his door. I open it quietly then close it behind me.

"Yes, sir. I think that's a great idea. Of course. No, it's never been done before, but it could work. Sure, I'll get my best reporter on it. Thank you. I'm happy with the way it's all going too. Yes, sir. Goodbye."

I'm itching to know what that was all about, but wait for him to say something. He obliges.

"That was the chairman, Sir Edward."

I smile at the irony of his Edward being the chairman of a multi-paper chain and my ReadyEddie potentially being on the bottom rung of the aviation corporate ladder.

"Oh?" I say, hoping William will dish the dirt.

"Some hare-brained scheme. He comes up with them all the time. Ways to increase circulation, but he doesn't have a clue. He'll have forgotten all about it by the time he goes off to play golf."

I've always admired a man who doesn't get caught up in red tape.

"Anyway, Izzy."

"Yes, William." He's got my full attention again.

"About this morning."

"Yes?"

"I wanted to say sorry for blubbing all over you like a child."

"It's fine. I understand."

"Would you keep it to yourself?"

"Of course." And I'm certain I will.

"And Donna?"

"Won't breathe a word." Oops.

I walk back to my desk and refresh the tallgirlnn1 page. It takes a while for the internet to kick in. I look up at the clock. Twelve thirty. Might have guessed. Everyone's on their lunch break and they're checking their social networking sites, the ones that are allowed anyway. We can go on anything; research is a wonderful excuse, especially when writing a technology column.

When my profile finally appears, I'm astounded that there are thirty messages. The last one to come in is from ReadyEddie, so I eagerly open it first. He's typed up his CV and covering letter and wants to thank me for my help and encouragement last night. He's about to drop off the paperwork and has even rung them to get the name of the contact in HR and has addressed it directly to her. I'm so impressed. He adds that he can't believe he didn't see what was right under his nose.

I reply, wishing him well. I try to be a glass-half-full person, but add that if they don't have any vacancies, or they feel he doesn't have enough experience, he should not be disheartened. While he's got to learn what life is going to throw at him I don't want to put him off completely, and when I press 'send' I wonder whether I've done the right thing.

Of the others, I recognise OMG69 and Metal Mickey. Ollie's confirming nine tonight, and I think it's pointless to pretend to be the slightest bit cool, so reply saying, 'That's fine.' Mickey, or Mike as he signs his message, is up for meeting me, and suggests Chicago's. I haven't been there for over a week and am getting withdrawal symptoms, so say that's a perfect choice. I suggest eight o'clock, to give us time to chat before it gets busy, not that it gets particularly busy on Wednesdays.

I work my way through the other twenty-seven messages and delete twenty of them. The others are two from the same guy, DR1NK, saying the same thing, but one is addressed to me and the other to a girl called Sindy. Although it's clearly his standard pattern, his messages are quite funny, so I delete Sindy's and answer mine.

I then reply to BlackJack, HarryRoberts, SingleDad5811, AdamKzz and AlexC17. My head hurts and I'm wondering whether I've taken on too much when my Outlook email pings.

I Alt/Tab over and see it's from William. The only time I get emails from him is when it's a round robin, talking about ways to increase circulation figures (presumably post-Sir Edward phone calls) or announcing a departmental meeting to talk about ways to increase circulation figures.

I double-click to open it and read. It's short and sweet.

Dear Isobel,

Thank you for your article. It was very well written, as usual, and I know that the last-but-one paragraph was about Baby, and I'm touched.

113

Thanks again.
W

I stare at the screen, concentrating on the 'W'. William rarely abbreviates anything, especially his own name. I look over at his office, but he's on the phone, looking down at his desk. I think like many people he's misunderstood, although he doesn't help himself, but there's some of that in all of us.

Donna and I go into town and do some girlie shopping, which is lovely. We chat about Mike then William and Janine, and we're no further forwards on any of them. Mike, I reckon, is hard work, but Donna seems smitten again, so I suggest she treads carefully, and if it doesn't seem worth the hassle, it probably isn't. I can be like a dog with a bone, but if I'm in a relationship that isn't working then I've learned the hard way to cut my losses and pull the cord.

When we get back, I tuck my bag under my desk and wiggle the mouse to disable the screensaver. I type in the password and it comes up with my tallgirlnn1 account. There's a message in from ReadyEddie. I'm hoping it's good news, but can't look, so go and make a drink. I gesture to Donna to ask if she'd like one and she nods. I guess, as it's a warm day, that she doesn't need hot chocolate, so make her a refreshing fruit tea. She's easily pleased.

Having put off the inevitable, I double-click the message link.

I punch the air, as not only has Eddie gone for a chat, they've offered him a position. It's just as an odd-job man – sweeping the yard, taking deliveries, that kind of thing – but he's over the moon. He adds that his parents are thrilled, which makes me see them in a new light.

There are also a couple of messages back from the new guys, BlackJack and SingleDad5811, so I read and reply to those.

BlackJack asks if I like going to the dogs, and I assume he means the hairy variety not 'letting myself go'. I email back and say I've only been once, but had a great time… and even came out with more money than I went in with.

I'm just replying to SingleDad5811 when I see BlackJack's replied already, so I flick to that. He says the nearest to

Northampton (it's obvious from my NN1 on the end of tallgirl that it's where I live, so he's on the ball) is Coventry, but he prefers Peterborough. Plus he lives in Rushden, so it's his regular venue.

He goes on to say that Friday is the biggest night and he wants me to see it at his best, especially if I'm going to be a 'lucky charm'. I remind him that I've only been to the Peterborough track once (and on another occasion, driven through Coventry, which I understand is the best thing to do), so can't guarantee a repeat performance, but, under his tutelage, will do my best.

I still have Thursday to fill before slotting in guys for the weekend, and am going back to my message to SingleDad5811 when a promo pop-up appears on the screen. NorthantsDating has a speed-dating service and there's an event next Monday. 'Click here for more details' it says, and I'm usually a good girl, so do as I'm told.

I always thought that speed-dating events were held towards the end of the week, the norm for meeting the opposite sex, but their events are dedicated to the beginning of the week and, according to their website, sell out quickly.

I fill in an online form then I receive an email ten minutes later to say that I'm booked and to ask for Rosie at The Cock Hotel, Kingsthorpe, seven fifteen latest for a seven thirty start. It's not far from my house and a lovely old building, so a great choice. I just hope the men will be as inviting.

I shake my head as I remind myself that the Cock's not been a hotel for years, probably decades if not centuries. *The Cock, the Cock*, I think and smile.

I finish the message to SingleDad5811 asking if he's free Thursday night. Although being rather forward, it's the only night I have this week as 'work is so hectic', which is sort of true.

I flick over to my normal emails until curiosity gets the better of me, so I go back to tallgirlnn1. SingleDad5811 has replied already. He's sorry, but his oldest has drama class and it's the dress rehearsal. How can I compete with a dress rehearsal? I say it's no problem. I'm about to resume proper work when he's replied already.

Apparently his sister is visiting for the weekend, so he might be able to pop out for an hour or so on Sunday – how does that sound? It sounds great. We agree five p.m. at the Cock (a coincidence, but I don't mind going there two nights in a row), as he lives in Kingsthorpe Village. It's a little earlier than I would have normally plumped for, but it'll give me an evening in, so I jump at the chance.

I only have Thursday and Saturday left to fill, and DR1NK, alias Keith Adnams (I had a boyfriend who loved Adnams beer, so understand his profile name now) and HarryRoberts do the honours.

Keith suggests Thursday at The Moon on the Square in the town centre (again giving me the dilemma of 'do I go home first or, heaven forbid, work late').

Harry, on the other hand, has gone for Saturday at the Britannia on the Bedford Road which is the same chain as the Greyhound, but still also full of character. "Good choice, guys," I say a little too loudly.

It's not 'til then that I realise Karen has been looking over my shoulder for a while.

"Having fun, Izzy?' she whispers.

"A roller coaster, while you've been sunning yourself."

She can tell she needs to take my comment with a whole heap of salt, so changes the subject, still whispering. "Did I miss any other gossip?"

I think of the William/Janine 'are they aren't they' scenario, Mike and Donna's on-off-on again romance and Baby's demise, but shake my head. "No, it's been a pretty uneventful week."

"And these men. Are you really seeing one a night?"

I look at the kitchen and say, "Tea, ten minutes, I'll fill you in."

She winks and we get back to our respective computers. I reply to tallgirlnn1's Keith A and Harry, before going to put the kettle on.

We're at Mr Nerd when Donna comes in.

"I thought there was something up. Are you telling her about Baby?"

"Donna! He doesn't want the world to know."

"I thought everyone knew."

Karen looks at me. "He who? Baby who?"

"I promised William that I wouldn't say anything to anyone, so you mustn't pass this on."

"Cross my heart." And she does the action just to convince me.

"William's had an African Grey parrot all his life, but it died yesterday."

Karen gasps. "It must have been really old!"

"It was, Karen," I say, "about ten years older than us."

That shuts her up, for a moment anyway. "What did it die from?"

"Err..." My super-unreliable memory fails me.

"Aspergillosis," Donna chirps.

We both look at her, astounded.

"Aspergillosis," she continues, "is the name given to a wide variety of diseases caused by fungi of the genus aspergillus. The most common forms are allergic bronchopulmonary aspergillosis, pulmonary aspergilloma and invasive aspergillosis. Most humans inhale aspergillus spores every day, which is a leading cause of death in acute leukaemia and haematopoietic stem cell transplantation."

If it were possible to be any more gobsmacked than a moment ago, we are now.

"Where did you get all that from?"

"Wikipedia," she announces proudly. "When you mentioned it before, I remembered that I'd heard of it. My uncle's ducks had it."

"I didn't know your uncle had ducks."

"He did. A pair – Mr and Mrs Duck – but they died."

"Of asper–?" I start.

"Oh no, a fox... or old age, I can't remember."

"Ahhh," I say looking at Donna's sad face. And as if by magic, she returns to her childlike innocence. She's full of surprises and, as I've said before, too good for Mike the all-you-can-eat security guard.

We return to our desks as it's gone four, but I can't concentrate. Having done my meerkat impression so no one who matters (William) is looking, I nip over to Donna's desk.

"Donna?"

"Yes, Izzy." She looks at me as if she can't cope with any more responsibility, but bends down a little and whispers, "What's so secret?"

"Are you doing anything on Monday night?"

"Why?" She's still whispering. "You want me to do one of your dates for you?"

"Kind of."

She sits up straight, claps and squeals. She's never been one for subtlety. "Can I? Can I really?"

I still feel the urge to whisper, despite everyone in the office knowing what I'm working on. "I'm going speed dating at Kingsthorpe. If there's still a space, do you want to come with me?"

She claps again. "Yes please." But her smile disappears. "What about Mike?"

"Mike's an idiot, Donna."

"No, he's lovely."

"Think about it. If he was so lovely your first instinct wouldn't have been to get so excited, would it?"

"Err, no, I guess not."

"Then that's settled. I'll let you know if they say it's okay."

They did.

Donna and I leave at the same time and walk through reception arm in arm like we're about to walk up the yellow brick road. Marion stares at us as we sail past her, smiling like synchronised swimmers.

Through gritted teeth I say to Donna to keep that pose as we walk to the security office and she does me proud. Mike stares at us with a bead of jam dropping out of the doughnut in his left hand and onto his blue uniform jacket.

Donna giggles as we walk to the car park. She lives round the corner from the office, but I offer her a lift home so we can talk about my forthcoming dates.

Wearing another trendy outfit (same leggings, but a silver version of the red top), I feel like a fish out of water as I walk into Groove. Firstly, I'm a bit older than most of the occupants, not old enough to be their mother but not twenty either, and I am somewhat underdressed. Or rather overdressed in respect of having too many clothes on (I wonder what their mothers really think), but it's too late to do anything about it now.

There doesn't appear to be anyone on their own, so I wait at the bar with a clear view of the front door. No one else has leggings on and certainly not a top like mine. I thought it was trendy – I've seen Fergie from the Black Eyed Peas wearing the same thing (though no doubt twenty times the price) – but I guess by the stares I'm getting that my nine-month-old top is out of fashion again.

I'm not sure how much slower I can drink my Coke. I guess I'll have to try.

There's nothing for it. I'll have to get another one. I need the toilet, but I'll lose my seat if I go and he'll probably come in and think I've gone home already and leave again. I can hang on.

I really need to go and am wiggling in time to the music.

It's no good. I've got to…

"Sorry, dude," Ollie says as he sways up to me. Last time I checked I wasn't a 'dude', but smile anyway.

No problem, bro, I want to say, but drop the 'bro'.

He's everything I imagined him to be. He looks like a backing dancer in an Eminem video: the epitome of hip-hop with baggy trousers and CXW69 Charles fake bling, although at least Ollie's looks more realistic.

"It's a banging tune, innit," he says, and I nod enthusiastically. In fact my whole body is enthusiastic, except he's not to know it's not about him.

"I'm sorry. I'm going to have to go to the…" I rack my brains for a cool word for the ladies and fail miserably, my task to learn an entire slang dictionary forgotten. "Loo."

"Sure, cool. Wan me to gitcha somat?"

"Sure." I hesitate. "Cool. I'll 'ava Coke. Fanks." I sound more cockney that 'hip and happening', but he dips his head in true gangsta style, although to me it looks a bit more Kevin and Perry, and tries to attract the attention of the bar staff. I can't take my eyes off him, sadly for all the wrong reasons. No one is paying him any attention and, for once, I'm glad I'm wearing what I am, because at least people notice I exist. And, for once, I wish Nigel and his Day-Glo clothes were here.

I just make it to the toilet and thank every god under the sun that there's no queue.

When I get back out, there's no sign of Ollie. I assume he's taken one look at me and decided I'm not 'dude' enough, but I spot him sitting on a sofa in a left-hand corner, talking to some of his mates. He's surrounded by at least half a dozen people who look exactly the same as him: baseball cap (worn backwards of course), baggy trousers... sorry, 'bagging pants' – that's one I remember from the little research I did – and black chunky sneakers (trainers), but more alarming is that they're all around the same age as him, some ten years younger than me.

None of them have noticed my return, but they're likely to if I make a run for it. I'm debating what to do when one of the bar's bouncers, a guy who would make Tim look tiny, heads for the door, so I walk on his right and am completely shadowed. I make some inane comment to Mr Massive as I get the feeling he's sussing me out, then hang a sharp right and walk up College Street, past one of the greatest fish and chip shops in town.

I'm not at all hungry, but the adrenalin currently pumping through my brain and the smell wafting out of the door are irresistible, so I end up a breaded haddock and chips richer, but six pounds poorer. I walk back towards the office and my car, and as I take the first bite it's like sinking into an edible cloud. I've never eaten cooked cloud, but if I could, I guess it would taste something like this. Simply heaven.

Chapter 10 – Mike at Chicago's

What did I learn from last night? To double-check a guy's age before entering into serious 'conversations' (i.e. swapping messages) with him. The guy I met last night, 'O' (I say 'met' in the loosest terms – we exchanged thirty-three words with each other. Literally. I wrote them down later), looked ten years younger, if not more. So no, I won't be going there again. The Litten Tree, as I knew it when I went last (so long ago that it had become Bar Code in between), attracted a mix of ages, tastes and music, but 'Groove' was outside my comfort zone.

I can only assume that O (because I didn't stay long enough to ask him. Sorry, O, if you're reading this) 'digs' older women, but I 'dig' older men. Not much older, you understand, anyone beginning with a four is pushing it, and more than five I'd probably have to push him in years from now, but even the thought of 'pashing' (that's kissing to us non-streetwise dudes) a boy doesn't do anything for me.

Having checked O's profile on my return to work, I see that he's given his age as ninety-nine. I suspect that's a default for anyone who doesn't want to specify, but if that's his real age, then O, please contact me again – I'd like to buy some of your face cream.

It's amazing how generations vary. O's slang is an entirely different language to mine. I'm sure we both spoke English, but one is so far removed from the other that I feel we'd have needed a translator as a chaperone... or we would have done if we'd spoken more than the thirty-three words.

So, girls, as much as I would urge anyone to beware of men pretending to be boys, because there are undoubtedly plenty of them, double-check that your date isn't still wearing nappies or, as in my case, 'bagging pants'.

There's such a thing as 'young at heart', but when the heart that's beating in a potential date's body is at least ten years younger, or double the age of your own, you might like to think twice.

Therefore today's two items to be ticked on my dater's shopping list: Don't date anyone young enough to be legal offspring (I know I'm exaggerating), and Do have breaded haddock and chips from the College Street chippie more often.

I'm rather pleased with today's article although the word count goes far short of filling the space I'm usually allocated. I therefore add some more techie internet dating stuff, because that's what my readers, and William, expect.

After, I check emails until I'm interrupted by Marion phoning for me to collect another parcel from Geek's Heaven (did I say I love my job?), so I end up playing with the almost-silent 'camera disguised as a cigarette lighter'.

There's no sign of Donna yet and no one knows where she is, so I go to reception to face Battleaxe Frist.

"Hi, Marion."

"Yes, Isobel."

"Do you have any idea where Donna is?"

Silence. Marion's waiting for something. What have I forgotten?

The penny drops. "Please, Marion?" How old am I? Five?

"She went to see Mike then came back up here in tears."

"And you didn't ring me?"

"It's not my job to be nursemaid."

No, Marion, it's your job to be rude. I say nothing, and go to the only other place that Donna can be: the ladies.

As I swing open the door, it hits the wall and I hear a squeak.

"Donna?"

"Izzy? Is that you?"

"Yes."

She whimpers.

"What's he done now?"

"We…" She's still crying. "We had another fight."

The door to the middle cubicle is shut, so I go in the one past hers, lock the door, and lift the toilet lid before sitting down. I never trust the plastic to hold my weight, although it's probably designed for larger bottoms than mine.

"What about this time?"

"His eating."

"Oh, Donna. You know that's a no-no."

"But why does he keep doing it?"

"He's like a smoker, or an alcoholic. They have to keep their mouths busy."

"I like keeping his mouth busy." And with that she giggles.

That's better. Too much information, but better. "How did you leave things? Obviously not well."

"I went downstairs to tell him I'd like to cook him a healthy dinner and I caught him eating his way through a whole plastic tub of brownies."

"That makes a change from doughnuts," I say rather unhelpfully.

"But they're not healthy are they?"

"Oh, they're… no, they're not, Donna. Not good at all."

After some persuasion, I finally get her to come out. Her face looks as if two spiders have crawled down a rainy window, so I clean her up and place her, face first, beneath the electric hand dryer.

"We'd better go back before William sends out a search party."

"Uh huh."

We get halfway down the corridor and I stop outside the kitchen.

"You go ahead. I'll make you a nice cup of hot choc."

"Thanks," she says, trying to smile.

"Mike's an idiot. He'll realise it when it's too late and you'll have moved on to Mr Six Pack and be deliriously happy with eight children in tow."

She giggles and walks to her desk. Knowing her, she'll already be thinking up names for them all.

I'm staring at my wardrobe for the umpteenth time. I never have this problem with Chicago's normally, but tonight I'm stuck. I want to go for something retro, to fit in with Metal Mickey's favourite era, but think it would be too clichéd.

I could do something with my hair (loose or ponytailed are usually as daring as I get), but don't think the permed frizzy look is really me. Nor are puffballs; I'm so glad I was too young the first time and too sensible the second… and shoulder pads – mine are broad enough without them, thanks very much. I go for safe leggings and a glitzy top, teamed up with my kitten heels, and I'm away.

He says he's going to wait for me outside, but when I get there, there are about fifty people in the queue. All nightclubs and trendy bars do it, keep everyone waiting because they're so popular and it's the old 'one out, one in' rule, except you never see anyone coming out and when they do finally allow you in, the place is half empty.

I see a group of girls wearing leggings, so I'm pleased I'm not an outcast two nights in a row, until I notice that one has exactly the same top as me under her denim jacket and I wish I'm wearing a jacket too. Not denim, of course.

Then I see him: the eighties throwback. If I hadn't known he was into that era already, I'd have thought it was a themed evening, but he looks so serious, like a sixth member of Spandau Ballet. His lower half is aerobics shell suit with the trousers tucked into a pair of the loudest sneakers I have ever seen. I think they're Converse and remember Will Smith wearing a pair in *I Am Legend*, except Will wouldn't be seen dead in these.

Nigel, on the other hand, would be proud, or jealous, I can't think which as my brain is too frazzled by Mike's top half. It's straight out of a *Jackie* speech bubble comic strip: an orange shoulder-padded nylon zip-up jacket with... no, it can't be. It is. A 'Frankie says relax' t-shirt underneath it. Is this guy for real?

It turns out that he is. And he's actually very nice, but I can't take him seriously and neither can the others at Chicago's. If the rest of the month carries on like this, I think I'll need to be carted off to a mental institution, and it wasn't long ago that Northampton had as many of those as shoe factories. Nowadays they've been converted into apartments, or are derelict with a 'Sold' sign, waiting to be turned into a 'des res'.

As I put my key into my front door lock, I can't help smiling. I've had such a wonderful night. I never thought I would have, having looked at the queue and spotted the odd one out, but we had a ball. He can't dance for toffee, but nor can I, and we became so engrossed in having a good time that I forgot why I was there.

There were moments when I wished Donna had gone with me. I was tempted to ask for Mike's number or give him mine, but he explained that he was not long out of a serious relationship, and was sorry if he'd given the wrong impression, but he's only looking to get out of himself. I wonder whether he's currently 'in', but reckon it doesn't matter, as he was clearly having a great time being single and who am I to interrupt him?

So we went our separate ways, but agreed to look out for each other whenever we're there again, and I definitely want Donna to meet him. Mike vs er, Mike. No comparison.

Chapter 11 – Keith at the Moon on the Square

What did I learn from last night? That if something was bad in a certain era, it's bound to still be bad over twenty years on. However, what maketh the clothes, doesn't necessarily maketh the man. And M was the man. Smart (though not exactly in attire), funny, and with no inhibitions (I'm so jealous), he was entertaining and enlightening… in fact a sharp breath of fresh air. Sadly, there was no spark on either side, as is often the way, but we parted as friends.

As the month progresses, I am seeing a different side to the men of Northamptonshire, and a different side of me. I, like many people, can be judgemental, but once people let their guard down (although I don't think M has one), we're all alike, and yet so different.

People are complex on one side of the coin, but on the other, we all want the same things – to share and be shared and, if we're truly honest, to grow old disgracefully, but not alone. Anyone who knows me can tell you that I'm fussy when it comes to men, perhaps because of the independence I've had in recent months, but I can't see myself going grey, as Eric Carmen sang, all by myself.

Meeting these guys is an experience I have my boss to thank for. It's given me a perspective on the human genus that at first glance I would have bypassed, but given the opportunity… no, privilege, to meet these characters (and boy, are some of them characters), I see who they really are (as much as I can in an hour or two) and would urge anyone to go beyond the Lycra or nylon to the person beneath the skin and the heart that beats within.

Today's two items are Don't worry what people think about your dancing, and Do allow yourself to have fun every now and then. It doesn't hurt.

Both email systems have gone nuts, and I end up with no lunch break and am even pushing it to leave by five. I check tallgirlnn1 before I switch off and there's a message from Keith. It's strangely familiar, overly so, and I wonder for a second whether it's 'Aunt Agnes' Keith, but the profile description is nothing like him. As I type a reply I stand up and look over at AA's desk. It's empty. I stay standing until I get a reply and his desk is still a void. I notice that he's in William's office getting a dressing down, so that confirms they're two different people. I feel sorry for our Keith for whatever bawling he's getting.

It's another evening in town and normally I'd not bother going home, but I overslept and didn't have a shower (thankfully the weather's cooled down), so need to get my skates on if I'm going to meet DR1NK at seven. I thought that was early, but he says he goes there after work, so I assume he must be a workaholic (which is still an 'olic', but deemed better for your health), and he only goes to the pub to be sociable. One shouldn't make assumptions. But I do.

I first see this Keith sitting on a bar stool in a corner of the main lobby of The Moon on the Square. The red carnation in his lapel gives him away – a corny but attractive flower, which sadly matches his not-so-attractive nose.

He looks a little glazed and rather unsteady on the stool when I walk over to him, but when he stands up he nearly collapses in my arms which, had he been in the slightest bit appealing to me, I would have welcomed with… well, open arms, but he's not, so I don't, and I help him to a table.

I leave him there and go to buy a couple of drinks. Needless to say, both are non-alcoholic.

Drinks in hand, I walk back to the table and to Keith who's wearing the goofiest of grins.

Here goes nothing.

We struggle our way through a mostly one-sided (me) conversation. There is something strangely familiar about him. I don't recognise his face, but something about him, and the little he's saying, gives me the creeps, like an eye through a bathroom spyhole.

I've just been punched in the stomach. Not physically, but it feels the same. I realise where I know him from. A couple of times at the swimming pool, he'd been 'passing by' as I'd come out of the building, saying something about purple being nice. I have a purple costume.

"Keith?"

"Yes, Izzy." I'm rather surprised, given his current state of inebriation, that he remembers my name and wonder if he knows more about me than I realise.

"Keith," I say more firmly.

"Huh?"

"Say the word purple."

"A game? I like games. Purple!" he shouts out loud, like a bingo player with a winning line. Needless to say, nearly everyone in the bar looks round.

It's him; the swimming pool stalker.

"Do you remember me, Keith?"

"Sure."

"From where?"

"From our messages."

"Nowhere else?"

"No… have we met before? Like, in a previous life? Are you into all that mumbo-jumbo reincarnation stuff?" He's acting his shoe size again.

"No. More recently."

"Errr…" His eyes are having trouble focusing and his face is a few inches from mine. He backs away and hiccups. Lovely. "No, my belle. Enlighten me."

"The swimming pool?"

His glazed look is replaced by a blank one. "I can't swim."

"But you've been there."

"Have I?"

"Outside."

"Maybe. I live in the town centre."

"You don't remember?"

Another blank look. No doubt in the morning he won't remember anything about tonight either, and I feel sorry for the guy. He isn't a stalker; a bit creepy maybe, but I don't think that he means me, or probably anyone else, any harm. He's his own worst enemy, another perfect candidate for Aunt Agnes, except I'm guessing that Keith Mk 2 doesn't admit to having a problem of any kind. He strikes me as a guy who has issues, but drinks until he's numb enough to forget them and everything else.

The glazed look is back and I watch him as he wavers. It isn't long before he gives up the fight to stay awake and his head falls down onto the table, producing an almighty crash which wakes everyone else up… if they'd been asleep, which of course they weren't, but it's another reason for them to look in our direction.

If they hadn't seen me earlier, I could have done the 'he's nothing to do with me' act. I wish for the first time in my life that I smoked so I could go outside and light up. Within seconds, they're all back to their own conversations and I can't see anyone looking at me. I do the next best thing to a ciggie and dig out my mobile phone. I pretend to tap some numbers and am soon having a 'conversation' of my own (with myself), which of course I 'can't hear' and have to go outside.

Sorry, Keith, but I'm sure someone will wake you up when it's time to go home.

Chapter 12 – Gary at Peterborough Greyhound Stadium

What did I learn from last night? That any addiction, whether drinking, gambling or worse, is only solvable from within. Own up to having a problem, and you're more than halfway there. Admission gives you the willpower to do something about it. However numb your 'tonic' makes you, it's only temporary. You still have to wake up in the morning, face whatever crisis that's driving you to your solace and not bury your head in the sand.

K strikes me as a man who drinks until he can't feel anymore. We all have 'off' days and resort to some kind of crutch, but usually it's a quick fix like a portion of banoffee pie or half an hour down the gym (guess which one I go for).

It's not a good look to share your rock bottom with a complete stranger, and especially not if it's supposed to be a date – unless you want her to feel sorry for you. And that's not a good look either.

I left K fast asleep in The Moon on the Square. There are a few bars to choose from around the market, but I would guess not many containing a thirty-something business-suited guy with a sore head – in more ways than one.

So if you're feeling down, think about the things you enjoy. If you honestly feel better after you turn to your 'friend indeed', and you won't regret it later, then do what makes you happy. Life is too short to take everything seriously and, while we have the necessities such as work and bills, everything else should be enjoyable. You shouldn't need a bolster to prop up whatever's wrong in your life – go out there and make it right.

Today's two items: Don't do negative addictions and Do make sure that if there's anything troubling you, take a good look at your life and see what you can do about it before inflicting it on anyone else.

With the article added to and safely installed in William's tray (no sign of him, nothing unusual there), I'll get to go on a non-rushed lunch with Donna. It feels like it's been ages since our last proper chat, albeit that being through a toilet wall, but she seems happier today, so I'm not too worried.

At one p.m. precisely she's standing by my desk, tapping her right foot impatiently. I look up and she's wearing sunglasses.

"Is it summer already?"

"Can we just go?"

We walk the corridor in silence, and past Marion in silence (who duly says nothing in return). We get near the security office and I can't keep it in any longer. "What's with the sunnies and silent treatment?"

"Shh." She even puts her finger to her mouth.

I stop walking. "What's going on?"

Donna, a couple of paces ahead, stops and turns to face me. She lifts her sunglasses and I expect to see a black eye or at the very least runny make-up, but she's her usual annoyingly flawless-skinned self.

"So?" I say.

"I don't want him to see me."

"Who?"

"Mike, of course."

"Why not?"

"Because I lied to him."

I resist a laugh. "What about?"

"I can't tell you here, he might come out at any second."

"Do you seriously think that sunglasses are going to hide your entire being? You're the only five-foot-two blonde working here. He may not be the smartest cookie in the jar, but even he wouldn't mistake you for anyone else."

"Don't forget the half."

Talking of smart cookies, I've decided that Donna's aspergillosis narration was the real Donna kept hidden, but behind a desk and cupboard full of make-up, weaves and wigs (for an earlier issue on alopecia), I find the sunglasses very… well, Donnaesque.

As soon as we're outside, I can't wait to grill her. "Stop, Donna, stop walking."

She looks nervously back towards the security office, which I know can't be seen from where we are.

"He can't see you. Tell me."

"Let's just go into town."

"Donna!"

"It's stupid really, but Mike wanted us to go out Monday night and I told him I couldn't."

"And?"

"He got a bit…" She looks down at the floor.

"Donna. Is he giving you grief again?"

"No."

I'm not convinced, and it must show in my face as she looks up.

"No, he isn't. It's just that he wanted to know what I was doing."

"And what did you say?"

"Nothing. I couldn't tell him that I was going speed dating with you, could I?"

"Well…"

"We're still going, aren't we?"

"Oh, yes. Looking forward to it."

"Phew."

"So what will you tell him?"

"Don't know. I'm too angry at the moment. He can stew. Let him think I'm out with someone else."

"Which you will be."

"Yes, but he doesn't need to know that."

"Obviously."

We start at Boots then the market, and hardly say a word the entire hour. We're back at our building when out come the sunglasses again in readiness for 'is he or isn't he there' Mike.

"This is ridiculous," I say, as she puts them on.

"I'm not being bossed around by him."

"But you are. You're hiding from him. Just tell him you're going out with me, and he can like it or lump it."

"Yes, boss."

That's me.

I leave work early to get to the Peterborough stadium for six. Donna and Mike have patched things up and she seems happier. I'm not holding my breath for them to still be a couple by the time I see her next, but I did tell him what I'd do to him if he didn't look after her, so that might have helped. Not that I'm a patch on Mike's build but, like a puppy, I have big eyes and know how to use them.

I've forgotten to bring any CDs and the car radio's been playing up for ages. It keeps losing reception and I forget how to take it off AF (auto find – you'd think I would, seeing as I run a technology column, but I only ever remember when it's dark and I'm driving) and I'm growling at it by the time I've hit the A45, ten minutes from home, so imagine what I'm like when I get to Peterborough, some forty-odd miles away. Not a happy bunny.

I think the problem is that the radio's got one of these removable fronts and I'd only had the thing a couple of days when a spring came off (which probably got vacuumed up on the rare occasion that it sees a clean, usually the day before I go to my mum's – she spots everything) so now the front doesn't connect with the rest of it properly, and it tries to retune every few hundred yards. There's little point in having the radio on, but I like company and intermittent AF company is better than nothing. I may need reminding I said that.

I get there in plenty of time, thanks to my lovely lady satnav, and am sitting in the car park. It's already very busy and I'm surprised by how many families there are. I see a couple walking in with a papoose and a little Chinese baby. I'm not known for my sentimentality when it comes to children, but he, or she, is very, very cute. I assume he/she is adopted because the parents are what is politically correctly called White Caucasians.

I glance at the clock on the dashboard and it's five fifty – about right – and I wander in. I can't see anyone waiting outside, so walk through the turnstiles. Now, I like my food and am a typical yo-yo dieter and sometimes, in my bigger phases, I bump into things. I don't know why my body doesn't realise how big it is and accommodate.

I'm not too big for the turnstile, although I see a chap along the row struggling and he's not particularly huge, so maybe the stadium should rethink their equipment, but I'm hitting the sides like a pinball machine and am so glad when no one seems to be paying attention.

Inside, there are so many guys on their own that it's impossible to work out which is Gary, but as there aren't many solo women, he spots me and comes running over.

"Izzy?"

I nod.

"Hi. You made it. Quick!" he continues before I have a chance to respond. "They're going to start in a few minutes. We need to work out a plan for the evening. You're my lucky charm tonight, remember." He grins like a man possessed, not in an 'evil clown' sort of way, but in an excited 'child at a birthday party who actually likes clowns' sort of way.

He grabs my arm, which surprises but doesn't unnerve me given his enthusiasm, and pulls me towards a table which already has a part-pint and full Coke sitting on it. Good guess, although I don't know anyone of my generation who doesn't like Coke, so perhaps we're predictable.

"I've covered the first race. Blind Bessie. Fifty each way."

"Fifty what? Pounds?" My limit on any kind of bet is usually two or three.

He nods.

"Great! Let the games begin," I say enthusiastically, but he just stares at me. I can tell this is going to be another fun evening. A Mr 'No Sense of Humour' and two addicts in a row. I know how to pick them.

The evening, as it turns out, was great. I arrived with £32.50, or thereabouts, and left with £92.03 exactly. G, on the other hand, lost about five grand.

We didn't share a kiss goodnight, him being in a strop. I don't recall him even saying 'Goodnight', but did that spoil things for me? Not in the least.

He opened my eyes to his personality, not from losing the money, but from how tightly wound up he was throughout the evening. Apart from shouting in my ear every inch that the dogs were running, he slammed his beer glass, his fifth, down on the table (losing some of the contents) and got very depressed when his dog lost (which all bar one of them did).

I was very proud of myself when my dogs won; I didn't rub it in, but did a much quieter 'yay' whenever they romped home, versus his roar when his one and only crossed the line. The highlight of his grumpiness was when the delightful couple with the Chinese baby, who'd been on the table next to us (we'd chatted when Gary had gone to place the bets), had been unable to placate their crying child and Gary had seriously lost his rag.

It's good to be home. The heating went off hours ago, and the house is chilly, so I put on some fingerless gloves, which I keep in the hall meter cupboard. It's been months since I've had a kebab (Mike would be jealous, and Donna tutting right now) and it's made me thirsty. I decide to dilute the calories, should have something healthy, so go to the kitchen and lean forward to the gap between the washing machine and sink, pulling up a blue-topped litre bottle of orange-flavoured water.

Deciding that a full-length movie would be beyond even me, I scan the selection of TV DVDs. I fancy something girlie and am nearly halfway through when I spot *Love Soup* (yes, they're A-Z), which I've only ever seen on TV. I remember Alice's love life being quite disastrous and that appeals. What I had forgotten was that the episodes are an hour rather than half an hour, so I'm struggling to stay awake by the time the first episode ends. I zap the remote and the whole thing shuts down.

I take a swig of the water. Anyone looking at me would think I'm mad, and I feel like a Dickensian character but, unlike them, I have money in my pocket won legitimately. Gary will have arrived home and is probably drowning his sorrows, but presumably on something more heavy duty than mine.

So I go to bed. Too late for an interlude with Elliot, but tomorrow night is Harry Roberts at the Britannia, so even if we get on brilliantly, I should be home by eleven-ish and as it's not a 'school' night, I can share my bed with Elliot, Natasha and Mr Häagen Dazs's Banoffee ice cream. A foursome – I like it.

Chapter 13 – Harry at the Britannia

What did I learn from last night? That there are different levels of gambling, but when it goes from being a bit of fun to a way of life, you may need to ask yourself whether you have a problem. Of course, some people do make a very successful living out of it, but they tend to be the racetracks, betting shops and, more recently, online gaming websites.

I met G last night and, while I saw it as an evening's entertainment, for him it was serious business; quite scary to watch. He did what a lot of punters do; he followed the form, weighed up the odds and then went for the 'sure' bet. I, on the other hand, did the girlie thing – going for names I liked or the colour of the greyhounds' coats… jackets? There's probably a proper name for them. I didn't like to ask.

He'd invited me there as his lucky charm and, while it turned out I was lucky, that luck didn't rub off on him.

During the course of the evening, I watched him change from a mild-mannered individual to a Hyde-like character, overreacting because of his losses and taking it out on the family sitting near us. Given the choice of who I'd have liked to spend the evening with, there would have been no contest.

I would like to think that G learned from last night but I suspect he didn't, and that others like him won't. It taught me that taking anything that seriously, especially when money changes hands, is a dangerous game, and one I'd rather play with matchsticks… dead ones of course.

If you've been following my column since the start of the month (I can't believe we're nearly halfway) you'll have been living the ups and downs (mostly the latter) of my 'dates'. What do you look for in a man? Have you found 'the one' online? I'd like to hear your experiences in the world of online profiles and virtual relationships, so drop me an email at the address above and I may include some of your tales, anonymously obviously, for the world (or at least the county) to share.

Unlike the office, my email system is a hive of activity. With Harry tonight, SingleDad5811 tomorrow, then the speed-dating thing on Monday, I've yet to line up more guys for the rest of the week and thereafter. Messages from AdamKzz and AlexC17 suggest Tuesday and Wednesday respectively, so I'm chuffed.

I need to add more to my column, but William's not in today (maybe he does have a life after all), so I guess there's no hurry unless, in the absence of an official deputy, he's left Janine in charge, but we're New Best Friends, so there's nothing to worry about on that score.

Speaking of whom... "Hi, Janine."

"Hey, Izzy. How's it going?"

"Good. You?"

"Uh huh, good. So it's going well?"

I nod.

"Excellent, on my desk by lunchtime then please."

I watch her as she returns to said desk. This power thing's changed her walk and it's scary. So much for NBF. I'm learning a lot about people this month, maybe I should write a column.

My date with Harry is another early one. Apparently he's flying to Germany on business ridiculously early in the morning (who works on a Sunday?) and is staying at one of Heathrow's hotels. So he's driving, which means sober, and that's fine with me. His profile says he's a sales director for a printing company and he's obviously not bothered that people know he's on there.

A lot of people, especially senior management, remain decidedly vague, and certainly no picture, as it's 'not professional', but presumably Harry has nothing to hide. In fact every box on his profile is completed. Again people tend to leave the options as 'not selected'. I can't talk as there's very little on dating sites that's complete, or true.

Anyway, I've cracked on with the article and it hits Janine's tray with a few minutes to spare. Of course lunchtime can mean anywhere between twelve and two, but I play it safe and get it there by twelve thirty. That means after replying to AdamKzz and AlexC17, I'm pretty much done.

Donna's not said a word since yesterday lunchtime, which is not like her. Like me, she's not normally in on a Saturday, so I go over to her desk to try to drag her out. She says she's got too much to do and I assume it's because she doesn't want to do the sunglasses routine again (although I spot a bright red wig on her desk which is likely to be just as obvious), but I won't take *no* for an answer.

After a hurried exit (Donna looks like she's running for a bus) past the security office, thankfully without the sunglasses (or wig), we escape the building and walk to the café in the Grosvenor Centre, two minutes from the office.

It turns out Mike's been off sick the last couple of days, but given everything that passes through his system, I can't say I'm surprised.

We nab a corner table, and I go to buy the drinks.

"We've split up," Donna blurts out when I'm about to sit back down, tray in hand.

"Oh." I don't know what else to say. Great! About time. He's no good for you anyway, but she looks upset. "Is that a good thing?"

She nods, but looks like a wounded dog.

"Who did the…?"

"Me."

"Wow. That must have been hard."

She nods then shakes her head. I see that getting much more out of her today is going to be a tall order.

"Shall I buy some cake?" I've always seen food as a real tonic – Mike should be a walking medicine cabinet.

The nod is back. "Anything special?"

Head-shaking takes over.

"I'll surprise you." I smile.

She sighs.

When I get back, she seems a little more cheerful. The slice of Death by Chocolate (the biggest piece on offer) and Key Lime Pie may have something to do with that.

I've never been a big chocolate fan, and am willing Donna to go for the 'death' option. As I put the tray in between us and our hot chocolates, her eyes light up at the slab of cake, so I put it in front of her, take the pie, and put the tray on an empty chair beside me.

The café is filling up, so it's a little difficult to hear, but our Mike conversation is far from over. I gently dig for more information.

"I'd just had enough," she says.

"I can understand that, honey. No man is worth crying over and it doesn't sound as if he's going to change."

"You're right, but I still love him."

My heart goes out to her. "This is probably a stupid question but how did he take it?"

"Okay, I suppose. We'd not been together long anyway."

"So you can go speed dating with me on Monday with a clear conscience."

"I guess so."

I try cheerful. "You might meet the man of your dreams."

"Maybe."

I need another approach. "Or just have a fun evening."

"That'll be nice."

We smile and tuck into our desserts.

She eats like she hasn't seen food for weeks.

"Nice?" I ask.

She closes her eyes and 'mmm's in schoolgirl-like delight then, with mouth part-full, says, "Just what the doctor ordered."

Touché, Donna Clarke.

We walk back to the office, chatting about anything other than Mike, then hug as we reach the building. I walk to my car and she heads to her desk, no doubt doing a Speedy Gonzales past the security office.

After a relaxing afternoon and a microwaved portion of pasta in chicken and mushroom sauce with two lightly toasted granary slices, I arrive at the Britannia just before six. Harry is waiting outside the pub and is drop-dead gorgeous. I've made an effort, but wish I'd made more.

As I walk over smiling, he looks disappointed. With nothing to lose, I put out my hand. "Hi, I'm Izzy. You must be Harry."

"Hi," is all he says, ignoring my proffered hand. He turns towards the pub's front door and walks in first. Fine.

I follow him and he goes straight to the bar.

"What do you want?"

I was always told off as a child for asking 'Do you want' instead of the much more polite 'Would you like', but he's clearly in a strop, so I resist correcting him and am extra polite. "Can I have a pineapple juice and lemonade please?"

"Sure." This is going to be a barrel of laughs.

He pays for the drinks and we aim for a free table in a quiet corner. It's by an old fire, but being quite a warm evening, it's unlit. It's a very romantic setting, but I get the impression there's going to be none of that tonight.

We sit and wait for one of us to start the conversation. The first thing that springs to mind is the weather, but I'm not quite that desperate. Yet. "So, you're off to Germany tomorrow."

"Yes."

Great. A yes man. "Have you been there before?"

"Yes."

The words 'teeth' and 'pulling' spring to mind. "I have friends in Germany, near the Black Forest."

"Nice."

I'm going to call him 'One-Word H' in my column on Monday. "Do you speak German?"

He nods.

Make that 'Half-a-Word-on-Average H'. "I speak enough to hold a decent conversation."

Nothing. The word count average is decreasing by the second. I'm surprised because most salesmen I've met, and in my job that's been a few, can't stop talking.

Figuring he must travel a lot, I ask, "Do you speak any other languages?"

"Japanese, Spanish, Danish and Russian."

Of course you do, I think, but just say, "Wow."

Silence ensues and I still resist weather. "Have you ever seen *A Fish Called Wanda*?"

He shakes his head.

"Jamie Lee Curtis is turned on by Kevin Kline speaking Italian and then John Cleese speaking Russian."

"Yes, I know the film."

But not seen it. How picky can you get? I take a large mouthful of my drink and will him to do the same, so I can get another one and keep plying him until he goes to the toilet and I can escape. Dirty trick, I know, but I've had my fill of sneaking out with the guy still in sight.

I've nearly finished my drink and he's not started his. This isn't fair. I'm going to have to go to the ladies if I have another one.

He finally decides to speak, tells me he doesn't normally 'do' women over a size ten, but thought he'd make an exception in my case because my profile sounded interesting and that he'd have bought me a gym membership if I looked like a good bet. I can tell by his reaction so far that I don't. He's not wrong.

As a barmaid walks round clearing the empty plates (they do lovely food here) and glasses (not ours – I'm still eking mine out and Harry's had about a millimetre of his), she approaches our table and picks up speed as she sees Harry. She smiles broadly, but reduces pace and enthusiasm when she sees his thunderous look. She veers away from our table and walks back to the bar.

When she's not quite out of earshot, he says loudly that she looked like a fat (presumably a size twelve plus) girl running for a piece of cake. If Donna had been here to hear him comparing himself to Death by Chocolate she probably would have belted him, and I'm tempted to, but just glare.

I needn't have bothered as he's too busy looking around the bar, perhaps to check that no one he knows can see him, or maybe there's a supermodel he might be able to escape me for.

I'm tempted to do him a favour and leave, but I persevere. Why should I put him out of his misery? I'm so glad I don't as I'd have missed the best bit.

I'm taking my last dribble of drink when a family of four sit down at the table nearest to us, on the other side of the fire.

Harry glares at them. He seems to have a limited range of facial expressions, and could learn a thing or two from Donna.

"Do you have children?" I ask. I remember he's divorced.

"God, no."

That explains the glaring.

With the exception of our strained conversation, everything's fine until the boy, aged about six or seven, plays up.

The expression on Harry's face gets even gloomier.

Then their pink-enveloped baby starts crying. That, it would appear, is the final straw.

Rather than lean or walk over to the parents and have a quiet word, he lunges at the children and shouts at them to behave and shut up. This actually works as he stuns them into silence. For about ten seconds.

The baby then bawls at the top of her voice, and the boy screams as if his favourite toy has just been crushed by a bulldozer. Although knowing most boys (Karen's got three and another of my neighbours has four), he'd probably love to see a bulldozer up close.

The parents are glaring back at us and I'm trying a 'he's nothing to do with me' expression, but seeing as I'm sitting opposite him, it doesn't hold much weight.

The family then gather up their things and with still-screaming children in tow, move to another table at the opposite side of the pub.

"Good," Harry grumbles. "Let them go and annoy someone else."

I'm tempted to say something like 'this is a family pub', but see it's futile. Instead I push my empty glass towards him and say, "Thanks for the drink, but I've just remembered I'm supposed to be babysitting my sister's eight children."

I don't have a sister; and just the one niece, Lola, but he's not to know that.

I do love it when I can shut my front door and have an evening to do with as I wish.

Harry will be on his way to the hotel and is probably grumbling about the waste of time. I thought it was hilarious to see a man who loves himself so much behaving like that. Younger than the boy with the proverbial crushed toy, younger than Moon on the Square Keith's shoes, and I think even the Chinese and pink-wrapped babies had more maturity.

I, on the other hand, have my second date of the night, with the sofa, a bottle of Asti and a good book. Elliot, get ready to rock 'n' roll.

Chapter 14 – Rick at the Cock

I love Sundays. There's a car boot sale at a local pub car park and the weather's good, so I decide to walk.

I arrive just before nine and it's already a hive of activity. I pass a couple walking back to their car carrying an old exercise bike. I can guarantee it'll get used twice then end up in the shed. I sold mine years ago, but still have a fold-up cross trainer in the dining room and trampoline (with its six feet in a plastic bag) in the shed 'just in case'. And, of course, they're used all the time.

I'm only after books, DVDs and a particular type of Bedford-made porcelain pottery that I like. I soon find a couple of anthologies (I rarely read novels, but the cover of *Opaque* did it for me) and half a dozen chick flicks. I can't believe my luck – they're all from the same stall and I get the lot for a fiver. The next few stalls are mainly tat or children's toys, although I do spot a great mini theatre I think Lola would adore. She's always telling me stories when I visit. The thing's still in its box and even comes with five puppets.

The stallholder says her children have grown out of it and would five pounds be okay? I usually haggle if I think something's a bit too expensive, but I know this is a bargain, so calmly say (in a Babe-like 'that'll do, pig' voice), 'That sounds fine, thanks very much,' then plod back home with my loot. I should have brought my car.

As there are still more stalls I've not seen, I return – still walking, it's too nice a day not to – and do another circuit and find, in a box of oddments, a small piece of the pottery I collect. I turn it over and on the bottom is the GP mark, although I know from the colouring grooves round the inside that it's a piece of Bedford-made POG. I pay the extortionate 20p, find nothing else, so return home again.

Once back, I dump my goodies in the lounge and head over to the shops on the Kingsley Park Parade, specifically to go to the Co-op to buy some fruit bread.

Still in bargain mode, I pop into the British Red Cross shop, en route to the Co-op, and am glad I brought a bag for life as I pile up stacks of six-for-a-pound paperbacks on the shop's counter.

As I pay for those and a taupe-coloured glass dish – destined to hold sweets on my lounge's coffee table, I chat with the manager, Christine, who I think is mad for opening on a Sunday, especially when she says she doesn't have to. Being bibliophiles, we discuss books and, before I know it, I've volunteered to help with theirs. I fill in a couple of forms and say I'll pop in early next month.

I'm not a fan of the classics but John Steinbeck's *Of Mice and Men* is a thin read (just over 120 pages – I check) so that comes out when I take a window seat at Heather's, a charming independent café nestled between a florist's and dry cleaner's, and below a photocopying shop (yes, we have everything we need here... and could probably even buy a kitchen sink from the DIY shop further along the parade).

Having ordered a hot chocolate, I tuck the bag of books and bread under the table and am a couple of pages in when my drink arrives. I thank the lady, who I assume to be Heather, and make a mental note to call in again, perhaps often, as I don't have somewhere that knows me by what I drink. I've always envied the characters of *Cheers* where they are not only known by name, but their favourite tipple – mostly lager, from memory – is waiting for them. I'm not sure I'd want to be that predictable but somewhere in between would be nice.

I finish my so-delicious-it-must-be-a-thousand-calories hot chocolate, thank Heather, and take my books and bread home, humming a mixture of Adele, Coldplay and Pink Floyd.

Having made myself some lunch, I put on a DVD and spend a while playing with my car boot 'toys' (including the theatre). *The Accidental Husband* is just finishing when I notice it's gone four. I'm supposed to be meeting SingleDad5811 in less than an hour, so quickly do the washing-up and go upstairs to decide what to wear.

The Cock is another family pub, so I know I don't need to do glam. I'm also figuring that a single father won't be ultra chic, so go for black jeans, a shades-of-beige top, and brown flat leather shoes.

I'm looking forward to tonight because anyone with children will have lots to talk about. Donna reckons I'll end up with someone with children because I don't want my own, but I can't see it myself. I wouldn't mind as long as they're old enough to leave home by the time we've had our third date... that's me and their father obviously.

I'm five minutes late as I burst through the pub door. Everyone stares at me. I hate being late, even by five minutes. I can't see anyone who I think SingleDad5811 might look like, so walk towards the bar. The barman raises his eyebrows at me as if to ask me what I want to drink, but I say I'm waiting for someone. With my back to the bar, I look around. No one's stepped forward, so I assume I've beaten him to it.

After ten minutes of feeling like a lemon, I decide to get a drink. I go for the predicable Coke and am sipping it when SingleDad arrives. I can tell it's him by his worn-out expression, an expression that changes to 'sorry' when he sees me. That and the presence of a little boy clutching his left hand.

"Hello. So sorry. Babysitting glitch. My sister changed her plans at the last moment, so I called the usual babysitter and she was late. Then my oldest couldn't find her iPod, the middle one couldn't find her Pony World DS game and then Zak here said he wanted to come with me. I hope you don't mind. He wouldn't have settled if I'd said no."

"No problem," I say hesitantly. "How many children do you have?"

"Just the three, but they're five, eight and eleven, so a bit of a handful."

Zak is wiping his nose with his left sleeve and my expression must be one of revulsion as SingleDad looks down at his son. "Zak! How many times do I have to tell you?"

"Sorry, Rick."

I look gobsmacked at Rick. "He calls you Rick?"

"Yes."

"I thought you were his father."

"I am."

"You don't mind him calling you by your first name?"

"No, they all do. We're a very liberated household."

I can tell, although liberated isn't the word I would have chosen.

"Anyway, I see you have a drink already. Can I get you another or…"

"Thanks, but it's okay. I'll wait until the next round."

Rick drags his son to the bar and orders a pint of lager and half of lemonade. He carries the lager and his son, and I take the lemonade and what's left of my Coke to a table by a fruit machine.

"So, Rick, are you a full-time dad?"

"Yes," he says proudly. "I only rely on outside help at times like this. I have to have a life, don't I?"

"It sounds like it's a very hectic one."

"Oh yes, but I wouldn't change it for the world."

"That's nice. So many fathers shirk their responsibility."

"Don't they," he says, shaking his head vigorously. "I've been there since the minute they were born."

"And your wife?" This, I see, is a conversation killer. In the seconds that remain unspoken, I notice there's what looks like breakfast splattered down Zac's t-shirt.

"Zak, you go and play on the fruit machine." Rick hands him a few coins and the boy wanders off.

"I'm sorry. It's none of my business," I say when Zak's out of earshot.

"No, it's okay. If we're going to be dating, it's only fair you know."

News to me… that we're dating. Technically this is a first date, but he's being somewhat presumptuous. Maybe he's recently single, so I wait to be told.

"I've told everyone she died."

"I'm so sorry." But it hits me what he actually said. He's *told* everyone.

"Oh no, she didn't die. She left me for… for someone else."

I can only say, "Oh," and wait for him to continue, but he doesn't. "Won't they find out it's not true? What about her funeral?"

"There wasn't one."

"I guess not, but they'd have expected one, surely."

"I said she was working overseas and was eaten by a big animal on safari."

"And they believed you?"

"So far."

I'm not sure what to say next, so go with, "When did she leave?"

"Last week."

"Last week? And you're dating again?"

"I need to find a new mother, don't I?"

Not here, you won't. "And there's no chance of her coming back?"

"Absolutely not. Doesn't want anything to do with us."

"But what if her new man feels guilty, realises his mistake or kicks her out."

"There's no chance of that. She's not a he."

Now I'm confused. "Your wife."

"No, the new 'man'."

"Oh… your wife has left you for another woman." I say it a little too loudly and realise that young ears are listening.

Zak stops hitting the buttons and picking his nose and comes running back to his father. He starts bawling and I catch, "What was the bad lady saying? Where's Mummy?"

Rick grabs him by his hand, gets up from the table and glares at me.

I try to look sorry, but it's not washing with either of them.

"See what you've done!" he hisses, and storms out of the pub.

Oops.

Chapter 15 – Speed Dating at the Cock

Mike's back from sick leave, although he doesn't look very sick to me especially given the food he's still stuffing down his throat.

Donna's back to her chirpy self. I'm at my desk but haven't yet taken off my jacket when she comes over. "Hello! Can't wait 'til tonight."

"Oh good."

"You don't seem too excited."

"It's work and, to be honest, it's getting to be hard work."

"But think of all those lovely men."

I am, comparing them to the fourteen I've met already and it's too depressing, but I put on a smile just for her and she skips back to her desk.

What did I learn from last night? That children provoke many different reactions. Saturday evening was spent in the company of H. We met early as he had to fly to an overseas meeting the following morning (only serious businessmen work on a Sunday – and boy, was he serious).

We were in a delightful pub (the Britannia on the Bedford Road), but I got the distinct impression from the off that I wasn't his cup of tea. Conversation was hard going, thanks to his one-word answers. He was, however, far more vocal on the subject of children – or rather at two excitable children who were with their parents at the next table. His behaviour made them leave and I wasn't far behind them.

Mr Sunday Afternoon, however, was the complete opposite. I so wish I could get these two together. No need to buy any fireworks. R2 brought his youngest offspring, who was suffering from a bit of a cold. While I admire single parents, I felt less empathy for R2, who wasn't exactly being truthful about the 'loss' of the children's mother.

Still, that's something he's going to have to deal with at some stage. She may have cut them out of her life for now, but it's very early days, and she is likely to change her mind. Besides, the children will ask questions and will want to go to visit their mother's grave. When they find out there isn't one, he may wish he'd been a little more honest.

Finding new ways of being diplomatic is proving difficult. Fortunately tonight's event is speed dating, so I shouldn't have problems with word count. Donna's picking me up en route and has promised not to be late. She's late for everything. Except work, strangely.

Where is she? It's just gone seven and she's not here yet. She's been here loads of times, so she can't be lost. I decide to wait outside. It's not the warmest night of the year, but it's dry.

Ten past.

Donna, where are you?

"Hi, Ursula. You look nice."

"Thanks. And you. Going anywhere special?"

"Not really, just out with a work colleague. You?"

"Same, kind of. Meeting some friends," she says.

"Have a great time."

"Thanks. And you."

At last. Donna and her trusted steed (a Ford Focus).

"Sorry. Sorry. I know we're cutting it fine."

"We are. Never mind. I don't suppose we'll be last."

Rosie lives up to her name: a wide red-lipped smile and badge on her lapel giving her name with 'ND Speed Dating' above it and 'Soul-Mating' underneath.

She ticks off our names and slaps a pink number seven on my chest and eight on Donna's, before handing us a form and pen each. Rosie then smiles plastically and points us in the direction of the bar to get a drink before we begin, while looking at the clock as if to make a point.

The place is busy for a Monday and after we order our drinks, Donna whispers, "Have you done this before?"

"No. You?" I whisper back.

"Why are you two whispering?" a voice behind me says.

I turn round and there's Ursula.

"Hello, neighbour," I say, then look at her chest. "I didn't know you were coming here, number four."

"Me, neither, number… seven. How funny, if we'd known we could have shared a car."

149

"We could."

"And this is your work colleague… friend?"

"Hi, I'm Donna." Donna thrusts out her hand, and Ursula shakes it firmly.

"This is Ursula, my next-door neighbour. I thought you and Max…"

"We split up a little while ago. He didn't like my irregular work patterns, so I thought I'd come here and see what happens. Bit of fun."

"Me too, but Donna here is more hopeful."

"That's not fair. You wouldn't mind…"

"But more realistic," I chip in.

Rosie appears and chivvies us into a back room and towards two rows of eight tables, with thirty-two chairs, in pairs, face to face. It looks like an informal Spanish inquisition, but I suppose that's exactly what it's going to be. She beckons a few more people over until we're all gathered around her like a coach group and their tour guide.

"Good evening, ladies and gentlemen." She pauses.

We twig and say, out of unison, "Good evening."

"Welcome to the Cock."

Donna bursts out laughing and I nudge her with my left hip, which shuts her up.

Rosie coughs and starts again. "Welcome to the Cock Hotel and to ND's Speed-Dating Soul-Mating event. We are just waiting for one more who I'm assured is on his way. When he arrives we shall have one more gentleman this evening than lady, but our blue numbers eleven and twelve have very kindly offered to rotate as a pair and, for that very reason, we will have three and a half minutes per pairing instead of three minutes.

"When the bell goes, you will have a few seconds to write down any comments you wish to make, but you will need to be quick, please, then move on to the next table. The ladies will stay seated and the men move.

"You can ask the other person, or persons, any question you like and if you wish to exchange contact details simply write that person's number on the form and hand it into me at the end of the evening. That way, there will be no embarrassment – I shall contact you by email with the numbers of the gentleman or gentlemen who have requested your details. Only those who both wish to exchange details will be able to do so."

I'm following this, but Donna is frowning, so I translate. "If you think he's hot, tick his number on the card. If he thinks you're hot, he'll do the same and then Rosie will send you his details and him yours."

"You *have* done this before."

"No, a lucky guess." Though why you can't just have a chat afterwards and swap then is beyond me, but Rosie's the expert.

I look at the group of men we're going to be meeting and it's not looking good. According to the website the age range is thirty to forty, but I would say it's more like twenty to fifty. And twenty might be pushing it. Karen's eleven-year-old son, Simon, looks older than number thirteen.

We take our seats and are about to start when the missing man bursts in and I laugh. Donna, who's a table ahead of me, turns. "What's so funny?"

"It's Hunky."

"Yes, isn't he?"

"No. It's Duncan."

Donna looks none the wiser.

"The vet?"

Her eyes light up. "Ah, Hunky Dunky!"

He's looking in her direction then spots me. "Hi, Izzy. How are things?"

"Hi, Duncan. Good, thanks, and you?"

"Oh, you know. Busy. Only just finished work. Had to change at the surgery. Couldn't come here in my scrubs, could I?"

I've lost Donna.

He looks back at her. "Hello. Are you okay?"

Him speaking seems to snap her out of her trance and she sighs. "Hello."

"Donna, Duncan. Duncan, Donna."

"Hello," she says again, giggling, and holds out her hand to him.

He shakes it warmly. "Hello, Donna."

I almost see a flash in Donna's eyes and it's clear Mike's forgotten, albeit for an evening. She winks at me then mouths something, and, for the first time, I know exactly what she's said. *He's a keeper.*

I feel someone standing over my right shoulder and turn round. It's Rosie.

"Duncan, I presume," she says, slapping a blue number sixteen on his Hugo Boss shirt.

"Yes, sorry I'm late. Duty called."

"We're about to start." She looks at numbers eleven and twelve, twins in jeans and pastel-coloured polo shirts and they take a seat together a few tables down from me. She then points to the empty chair in front of me and Duncan takes his seat.

Donna smiles at him then turns to the fifty-something man sitting opposite her. A serious look takes over her face and, pen in hand, she's already asking him questions when the 'begin' bell goes.

"So Isobel. What would you like to know?"

"I don't know, Duncan. What is there about you I don't know already?"

'Did I tell you I've been on *The Weakest Link*?'

I lean forward. "Really?"

"Yes."

"Did you win?"

"Sadly, no. I was in the last three though – two women and me, so they voted me off."

"That's not fair."

"It was actually because I just got one question right in that round and I forgot to bank twice, so I only got them twenty pounds."

"Oops, but you got that far."

"I did."

We then chat about work (his real and my fake) and I'm about to change the subject when the bell goes. "God, that was quick."

"Good we've already met then." Duncan smiles.

"Indeed. Have a fun evening."

"Am already. See you later."

152

Next up is fifteen, the fifty-something. I look at Donna who's studying her form intently. I then look at the geek sitting in front of her and feel sorry for her until I realise I'm getting him next. Great.

I sit mesmerised by Baxter 'OCD' Ingells as he rolls his hand like he has a ball or sweet wrapper in it, but there's nothing there, unless it's an imaginary friend. He turns his upside-down beer mat (with a very cute picture of a dog on it) round the right way and then every few seconds lines up his pens so they are central to his marking card.

Everything about him is coordinated, probably even down to matching underwear. We've not started talking yet, but I'm willing the 'move on' bell to go. It doesn't get any better.

Sport fanatic Phil is number fourteen. He's a professional golfer (yes, I imagine him dolled up in his plus fours pushing his trolley and it isn't a pretty sight, especially from the neck upwards), but his big passion is football. He's 'tried out' for a couple of major clubs (he won't tell me which ones as he's signed confidentiality agreements… do I look interested?) and has played for numerous amateur clubs (again, so not interested).

He keeps looking down at his crotch.

"Something wrong?"

"No." He looks up. "Sorry."

I then see a flash of light that can only be a mobile.

"Are we keeping you?"

"The Everton Chelsea friendly starts in twenty minutes. Think I might skip the last few women, they don't look like they're worth it." Knowing that will include Ursula, he plummets even further in my estimation.

"If you want to move on now, don't let me stop you."

"All right, darling, keep your frillies on."

I'm no women's libber, but I'm certainly not his darling and I don't wear frillies. "Looking at all the women here," I say, "you'd probably be doing them a favour."

Number thirteen, unluckily for me, is Rebel Hell. Yorath is very forthcoming with information. He left home at sixteen (which, judging by his acned complexion, was about six months ago), lives with a mate (Ollie by any chance?) in a flat in the

153

town centre, works as a nightshift shelf stacker at Sainsbury's and has just had a tattoo done on his arm – of an eagle.

He proudly shows me, but all I can see is a very red-and-black blur underneath some very unattractive looking cling film. I quite fancy having a small pawprint or barcode on my wrist, so that conversation takes the remaining two minutes, at the end of which I make a note not to go to the same tattooist as him.

Next up are twelve and eleven, the twins Xabiere and Xantes Xardel, the definitive mother's boys. They're thirty-five and still live at home, talk about 'mummy' and won't have a bad word said about all mothers. They go everywhere together, so are presumably grateful that we're a woman short, and *I'm* grateful that I get them over and done with in three and a half minutes instead of seven.

Rosie, in the meantime, is walking around the room scribbling away on her clipboard. I can't think what she's writing about, but she looks like she has a headache, though it may just be concentration. She's the only person I've ever seen who can frown and smile at the same time. Still, an almost full house at twenty-five pounds a pop would make anyone happy.

The next contestant is number ten – Waffler (Zeek Townsend). We're a match made in heaven. I can talk for England.

"Hi, I'm Izzy."

"Hey, Izzy. I'm Zeek, Zeek Townsend. Bet you're wondering how I got the name? It originates back to…"

I look at the clock: one minute and counting.

"…and a funny thing happened today at work. Did I tell you I'm a glazier?"

He did.

"I went to fit some new windows for an old dear and…"

I look past him to see how Donna's getting on, tilting my head while pretending to be listening, and she's deep in conversation. A two-way conversation.

"I'm sorry. I should let you say something. Which reminds me…"

It would appear everything reminds him of something else. He'd make a good comedian. They never seem to pause for breath, with endless ammunition ready to fire out at their audience – bam, bam, bam…

There's a pause and I go to speak, but the bell goes.

Quiet Mr Nine, Nick, works in a library, so I'd expect him to be quite sociable. Wrong. He's like Harry from Saturday night's Britannia; I string along a perfectly good question, which deserves a perfectly good answer, and what do I get? Yes's and no's.

"So you work in a library?"

"Yes."

"Do you enjoy it?"

"Yes."

"Have you been there long?"

"No."

"You must read a lot of books."

"Yes."

"Have you been to one of these before?"

"Yes. You?"

I'm trying to think of another question when it dawns on me that he's asked me something.

"No. This is the first one."

He doesn't say anything to that. I look at his hands and they're beautifully polished. I don't know what that has to do with the price of fish. I should google it to see where that expression comes from. Probably nothing to do with fish.

"Do you work?" he finally asks. He's coming out of his shell.

I nod. "I'm a… a secretary for a training company." Oops, nearly slipped up there.

He nods, going back into his shell. Damn it.

I'm saved by the bell. Literally. Our 'conversation' has been so drawn out that the three and a half minutes has flown by. Ish.

I can smell number eight before he leaves the neighbouring table. Sidney, the smoker, appears to be a pack of nerves. He sits down and before long his right leg is shaking so much that it keeps hitting the table. I wonder whether it's me or the whole experience making him anxious.

"Are you all right?" I ask. It's not going to be a fun three and a half minutes if the table, and therefore my Coke, is going to get pummelled.

He nods, but looks at the door.

"Are you waiting for someone?"

He shakes his head. Great, this is going to be more painful than number nine. "Do you need a fag?"

He nods.

"I guess there'll be a break at some stage – we'll need to get a drink, won't we?"

He shrugs.

"You've not done this before?"

He shakes his head again. It's obvious he speaks English as he's nodding and shaking in all the right places, assuming they are the right places, but something's obviously got his tongue.

"Have you met anyone nice so far?" It's a bit of a shame that in such a short time the conversation has already moved on to someone else.

"A couple."

He does speak.

"There was a girl a couple of people back who was quite funny. She's a horse-riding instructress. I don't know anything about horses though…"

I let him waffle on and it's not long before the bell goes.

"Thanks for that, Sidney."

He smiles, stands up and walks past me to the next table. Ho hum.

I'm seriously beginning to lose the will to live, until the bell rings twice and Rosie steps forward.

"Ladies and gentlemen. We shall have a ten-minute recess and you can talk to one another, but remember you have another seven partners to meet, so reserve judgement until the very end of the evening please." She makes it sound like a courtroom; we're the jury that she's trying to plead her case to.

We return to the main room and Donna sprints towards me, waving her card furiously. "Isn't this fun?"

"Uh huh."

She then rushes over to number seven, who I'm due to meet next, and chats to him. I can't say I blame her as, apart from Duncan, who she'll meet last, none of the ones I've met so far merit a second conversation. I shake my head as I listen to myself. I've become so cynical in the past two weeks and have another two to go.

"Are you all right?"

"Hi, Duncan. Yes, I'm fine, thanks. Are you having a good time?"

"It's something different to do, isn't it? Beats the telly night after night."

That sounds so appealing right now, but he's right. It's good to get out and meet people. I'm taking it far too seriously, but that's me.

"Would you like a drink, Izzy?"

"Thanks. Just a Coke please. No… as I'm not driving, do you mind a Southern Comfort in it? Medicinal, of course."

He smiles and puts his hand up to attract the attention of the barman, which he succeeds in doing almost immediately. I'm so glad he's here.

Donna's back and even more excited than ever. "You'll like number seven. He's lovely."

"I'll take your word for it."

"Hey, Donna," Duncan says. "I'm getting Izzy and me a drink, would you like something?"

"Hi, Duncan," she drools. "Can I have a lemonade and lime please?"

"Sure. No problem." He orders the drinks and we move away from the bar to let in others. "So you're having fun then, Donna?"

"Oh, yes. It's wonderful. Taking my mind off… things."

"Oh dear."

I butt in. "She's been seeing an idiot who doesn't appreciate how truly wonderful she is."

"A one-woman Donna fan club," Duncan says, and Donna giggles. Duncan smiles at me and I want to kick myself for letting him go the first time we met.

Rosie appears like a Border Collie, rounding everyone up to go back into our pen.

We three are the last to go in and Donna makes an excuse for Duncan to go in front, saying she wants a quick word with me. We walk behind him and watch his Levi 501s sashay towards the back room.

"He's gorgeous," Donna whispers.

I nod.

"And he really likes you."

"Really?" I take a swig of my drink. "Do you think?"

"Oh, yes, I saw the way he smiled at you back there."

We follow him and his little red Levi label, and resume our seats.

Blue number seven, it turns out, is Walter the anti-smoker. Not just casually, as most of us non-smokers are, but he's strident in his beliefs. He can't take his eyes off blue number eight and isn't concentrating on our conversation, which is fine by me because nor am I.

We get as far as swapping professions. He tells me he's a biological researcher and I stick with the secretary role, hoping Donna doesn't forget, especially blabbing to Duncan when they come to meet properly. Not that they'd talk about me, of course, but I can live in hope.

Walter is a little man, about my age, but gives off an aura of maturity. That's me being polite. He's as dull as watching *Big Brother* at four a.m. What Donna sees in him I'll never know, but there's no accounting for taste, although she does find Duncan gorgeous.

Number six, John, spends the whole three and a half minutes trying to drum up business for his struggling electrical company. 'I've set fire to a couple of houses, but the police never pressed charges' doesn't exactly fill me with confidence, so I make up a handyman neighbour and John soon loses interest.

He looks like a labourer. His hands are rough and he's 'weathered'. I feel sorry for him until the bell goes and he tries his patter on the girl behind me. She's laughing, so sounds like an easier target.

It soon becomes apparent that number five is not only unemployed, but unemployable. Frankie has never had a job and doesn't want one. He's made little effort and it looks like he had the same breakfast as Zak. For a second, he reminds me of Aviator's Eddie, but there's no hint of a spark in Frankie's eyes.

I assume he's after a woman to 'keep him' and it appears he can read minds when he says, "You may wonder why I'm looking for a woman if I've got nothing to offer her."

"Well…"

"Oh, but I have."

You could have fooled me.

"I'm quite wealthy."

Which is why you've been wearing the same t-shirt all week and your jeans have non-intended holes in them.

"I inherited some money."

"Oh." Is all I can muster.

"Yes, from a rich aunt."

That old chestnut.

"She was a writer."

Now that does sound interesting. "Oh, who's that?"

"She… err… erm… Have you ever heard of Margaret Allingham?"

"Do you mean Margery Allingham? Author of *Campion*."

"Err, yes… we weren't close."

Clearly. "Margery who died in the 1960s." I like my crime writing.

"There was a trust."

"And you're part-Canadian?"

This time he's saved by the bell. Hadn't banked on someone who actually reads, had he?

Bottle collector Paul is number four. My mum has a few old bottles and especially the 'cod' variety with the marbles, so it's something we can talk about, although I make the mistake of saying, "That sounds like an interesting hobby."

"No, you misunderstand. It's my career." Not a job, but a career. "Oh, yes," he continues, "I sell on eBay, but travel all over the country to buy them. Car boot sales, jumble sales, charity shops, you name it."

159

"Antique fairs?" I offer. He did ask.

"No. They're always too expensive. That would be like *Bargain Hunt*."

I look at him blankly.

"You know, that programme where they buy from antique dealers and sell at auction, and wonder why they never make any money. They don't because that's where dealers buy the stuff in the first place."

I just think he's getting more like a cartoon character when he says, "Doh!" and then spends the next minute or so that's left telling me all about the different types of glass and stoneware bottles, which are the most valuable (I assume the oldest ones, but I'm soon put right), then, as he's telling me all about his membership with the Antique Bottle and Pot Lid Collectors Web Ring, the bell goes. I've never been so pleased.

Thirteen down, three to go.

Number three is Mr Chilled, alias Quent, short for Quentin. I'd never have guessed. He's a surfer dude out of place, given that we're probably at one of the most inland points in the UK. He's named after his granddad and very proud of it.

He's not making any notes and has no numbers ticked, and answers the questions with "yeah, you can do" or "I suppose so". I can picture his bedroom (or flat, house, cardboard box – we didn't get that far) being a shambles. He seems very 'earthy', so I imagine the place being full of plants, except they all died months ago and he's not noticed. I feel rather wilted myself.

Last but one is Maurice, a not-so-happy-snapper photographer. I have an uncomfortable feeling about him. My dad's a retired photographer, so I usually like them, but can't bond with this one. He's a candidate for the most overdressed – not in your dinner jacket or tuxedo way, but too many layers of clothing.

It's a mild evening and I can count at least four. There's a t-shirt under his shirt, which is a very nice blue check, then a not-so-nice patterned jumper, and an olive-green trainspotter type jacket. He's also wearing nerdy glasses with detachable shades (which he's wearing up, of course, because we're inside, but they're called detachable for a reason). Has no one told him it's summer?

"Aren't you warm in all that clothing?"

"A little, but you never know what the weather's going to be like in May, do you?"

Checking the weather forecast or looking out the window might give you a clue. "No, I suppose you don't. It is England after all."

The conversation runs out of steam, just like me. I look at Rosie who's nowhere near the bell and is looking at a couple at the far end of the room who seem to be getting on well.

I'm desperate. "So, have you photographed anything nice lately?" Nice is such an insipid word but, as I said, I'm desperate. I feel like adding 'underage children or trains' but resist the urge.

"Oh, yes." At last, some passion. "I took a lovely picture of a door the other day."

"A door."

"Yes. It was lovely."

There are lots of things in this world I would call 'lovely', but a door isn't one that springs to mind. "And where was this door? Somewhere nice?"

"My goodness, yes." He's beside himself and I'm wishing I wasn't. "On the top of a skip."

It just gets better. Maybe it was a skip on a beautiful tropical island. I dread asking. "And the skip was…"

"At the tip."

"Oh."

"I know what you're thinking."

I bet you do.

"Not the most romantic of places."

"That thought had crossed my mind."

"But you can take some wonderful pictures of rubbish." He's nearly orgasmic now.

Right.

"One person's trash and all that..."

Is it still trash if it's in a skip and not being saved?

This is the longest three and a half minutes of my life.

161

I look at Rosie again and she's walking back towards the bell. She stops. No! I will her to step forward. "Just a few more paces."

"Sorry?"

"Err… there must be a few more places you've found to take wonderful pictures." I'm talking to him, but my eyes are fixed firmly on Rosie. She finally glances at her watch and looks horrified. She sprints to the bell and rings it as if her life depends upon it. "Yes!" I say a little too loudly and Maurice grunts before getting up and moving to his final table. Poor Miss Number Six.

Last but not least is number one, a teacher. He hasn't told me he's a teacher, but he can't be anything else. Who else wears tweed? He sits down opposite me and stretches out a long scrawny arm. I shake his hand and tell him my name.

"Hello, Izzy. I'm Quigley, Victor Quigley. I teach 7VQ… Year 7 physics."

I was rubbish at physics. At my first parents' evening, my physics teacher told my mum and dad I should give it up. I was only too glad to do so.

I glance behind Victor and see Donna and Duncan getting on very well. Duncan then spots me spying and smiles. I can't really see what Donna's doing, but it looks like she's writing furiously on her card. She's got her other elbow on the edge of the table and is looking dreamily at him. I love her to bits, but I'm willing her elbow to slip in a classic *Only Fools and Horses* moment.

"And what do you do? Hello?"

"Sorry. My friend's sitting behind you. She's a bit nervous," I lie.

Victor turns and Duncan smiles at him. This makes Donna turn round and say, "Hiya."

Rosie comes over. "Victor, please turn round."

"Sorry." The teacher blushes like a naughty schoolboy as she walks away.

"What did you ask me, Victor?"

"What you did for a living."

"Sorry, yes. Secretary for a training company." I've said it nearly thirty times and am beginning to feel that's what I do.

"So we have a lot in common then."

He waits for me to agree, which I don't because I don't have a clue what he's talking about.

"We help people learn. Take an empty shell and fill it with enlightening information."

"Yes, I suppose we do," I concede.

Victor's telling me all about their latest experiment when the bell goes. I think I remained conscious throughout, but either can't remember or understand a word of it, and say, "That sounds interesting. I'm sure my friend Donna, the one sitting behind you, would love to hear all about it. Nice to meet you."

"Oh, yes, I had her first. She was lovely," he says then gets up and heads for Rosie, marking his card as he walks. I look down at mine and the empty boxes. Just to have something to hand in, I tick box number sixteen (Duncan).

As Duncan also walks towards Rosie, Donna turns to me and claps. "Wasn't that great?"

"Yes, delightful."

"Come on. It was fun."

"I suppose. Definitely different. Lots of fodder for tomorrow's article."

With that, she slaps her hand over her mouth.

"What have you done?"

"I might have said something to someone."

"Who?" Please don't say Duncan.

"Number…" She looks at her card.

"Yes…?" I'm slightly relieved, it can't be Duncan because she would have said his name not his number.

"Well…"

"Donna."

"I think it was either number three or number ten."

Looking at my card with the notes I'd written in the margin that signified 'Chilled' and 'Waffler', I think I'm pretty safe. I don't figure Chilled for someone who'd put two and two together, and Waffler, if Donna had managed to get a word in, wouldn't have been paying attention because he'd be too busy concentrating on what to say next.

"Don't worry, I'm sure they won't say anything."

163

"Oh, and number one... Victor. He was really interesting, telling me about a new microscopy technique that's allowed researchers in the US to make the first measurements of the earliest stages of crystallisation. He said the technique could help scientists gain a more complete understanding of how materials crystallise – which might eventually lead to high-speed computer memories based on crystallisation."

She, and her auditory memory, never cease to amaze me. "Only Victor and Duncan know we're friends and unless the two of them are... no!"

Donna swings round in the direction I'm looking. Victor and Duncan are heading for Rosie at the same time and they're chatting like best friends. I feel sick. I can't imagine Duncan making a big deal of it, but Victor might. 'Take an empty shell and fill it with wondering information.' I know it still applies to what I really do, but most teachers abhor lying and I've told a few whoppers here tonight.

Cards delivered, they're pointing in our direction. Uh oh, they're walking over.

Victor puts out his hand in Donna's direction and she shakes it warmly. "It was so lovely talking to you." He then does the same with me before whispering, "I've put both your numbers down. You were delightful, truly lovely."

I don't know what to say other than a feeble, "Thanks." He pauses as if waiting for me to say that I've also put his number down, but he's got a long wait. "Nice to meet you too," I continue. "Have a safe journey home." He takes that as his cue and walks to the bar.

"That was mean." Donna sees the best in everyone.

"Not intentionally, but I couldn't tell him I wasn't interested."

"Have you put my number down?" Duncan asks.

I slap the card to my chest, blank side out, and smile. "Now, that would be telling."

"I have!" Donna bounces enthusiastically.

"Thank you, Donna. I've done likewise. In fact..." He leans in closer between Donna and I. "You're the only two numbers I've put on my card."

We're both speechless.

"Well, ladies, I'd better go. Donna, a pleasure. Isobel, a re-pleasure."

Donna sighs again as we watch the little red label walk out the door, then she slaps me with her card. "Why didn't you ask him out?"

"We've already been out."

"I know, but you like him."

"So do you."

"You got there first."

I wonder whether I only have feelings for him because I had to share him with fourteen other women including my best friend. I'm not into mumbo jumbo, as Keith Mk 2 put it, but decide to let fate take its course. Rosie will send our details and if it feels right, then I will.

I look around the room for Ursula, but she's chatting away to Nick the librarian and I'm surprised when I see he's giving as good as he gets. She's found a topic that gets more than the monosyllable, so we leave her to it.

Donna can't stop talking on the way back to my house. She relives the last couple of hours in her mind, except it's spilling out through her mouth. I find it hilarious though as her take on the evening is so different to mine, but to me it's still work and to her it's excitement, Donna style.

Chapter 16 – Adam at the Red Lion

I can't wait to log on to my emails to get my matches from Rosie.

One name, and it's not Duncan's. Seeing as I'd only requested him, I email Rosie saying I think she's made a mistake. She has.

Sorry. Thought you'd requested Victor too. That means that there were no matches for you both ways. Sorry again.

I can't believe Duncan said what he did and then didn't request me, so I send him an email via tallgirlnn1. A nice one of course. I figure he'll be at work, so don't expect a reply today.

With so much to type up from last night, I make a large mug of tea and get cracking. I'm nearly done when William comes over.

"Hi, Izzy."

No Isobel? "Hello, William. How are things?"

"Good, thanks. Can I see you in my office for a minute?"

Uh oh. I smile and say, "Sure."

I follow him to his office and he steps back, letting me go first. I say, "Thanks," and he follows me, closing the door behind him. I stay standing, but he goes behind his desk, sits, then indicates that I should do the same.

I sit, but say nothing, letting him go first.

"Now, Izzy."

Here we go.

"I've been reading through your articles this month…"

Yes, and they're a load of rubbish. You're fired, clear your desk, and to add insult to injury, I'm going to get Mike to walk you out of the building.

"…and they're great."

Oh. Great.

"There's just one thing."

Here we go. A compliment first, dull the pain, then wham!

"Rita's given me your expenses to sign off."

You did give me the okay beforehand, and I've not…

"You're not spending very much money." I can't decide from his expression whether he's complaining or congratulating me. "Is everything all right?"

"How do you mean?"

"From the articles it looks like you should be spending more than you are. You're not using any of your own money, are you?"

I suppress a laugh. Me, spend money on work? Not happened so far. "No. It's worked out on some occasions that the guy buys the first drink and then we don't get to a second."

"Oh."

"Is that bad?"

"No, not at all. You're producing great work – quality, quantity. No complaints from me."

"Great."

I'm debating whether the conversation's over and that was my cue to leave, when he asks, "How did it go last night?"

"Good, thanks. Writing it up now."

"Speed dating, wasn't it?"

"Err… how…?"

"Receipt for the reservations."

Then it hits me. I'd also booked Donna's place with the company credit card. "I'd meant to pay for Donna's…"

"No, Izzy, it's fine. She's a colleague. It was a work event, sort of. It's fine. I've signed it off."

"Thanks. It was going to be my treat to her though, honestly."

"It's fine. All gone through. Besides, you're ahead by more than that in the first two weeks of this project."

That was true, and it did make me feel better.

"And you're still okay about the whole thing? Not getting too much?"

"Not at all. Having a blast." That was a bit of an overstatement, but it was fine. Makes a change from testing boys' toys (the best aspect of my job) and I get to go to places I've either not been for ages or have always wanted to visit. Other than thirty-one dates in thirty-one days, when would I get the opportunity to do that again? Actually, forty-five in thirty-one days, but who's counting? Yes, I am.

Donna looks worried as I leave William's office, so I give her the thumbs up and she smiles.

I make a fresh cuppa to help me finish the article (I'm on Mr Unemployable and boy, is he fun to write about) and have just sat down when Tigger D comes bouncing over. If history didn't have to follow chronologically, I'd swear AA Milne's character was based on her.

"What did William want? What did he want?"

"To fire me."

"No!"

"No."

"Oh."

"Don't seem disappointed."

"Of course I'm not. No, really, what did he want?"

"He likes my articles."

She claps her hands (they must be so sore because she does that at least twice a day, and that's only the times I see her do it). "I think he likes you."

"Donna, don't be so ridiculous."

"No, I think he does."

"You think everybody likes me, and me them. Besides, I still think it's someone a little closer to home he's got his eye on."

"What, you know his neighbours?"

"Donna, for someone with a photographic memory, you can be so blonde sometimes."

"Eh?"

"By someone closer, I mean geographically."

"Like a neighbour."

"No. Someone geographical at work."

"Me?" She looks horrified.

William's not that bad. "Donna!"

"You mean Janine?"

"It wouldn't be Keith, would it?"

"I don't know."

"Yes, Donna, it's Janine."

"You did mention something the other day. Do you really think…?"

"Yes, Donna."

So, the theme of today's article is 'quality not quantity'. *And the two ticked boxes? Don't write someone off on a first date if you*

168

have a good time and could, at the very least, be friends (however clichéd that sounds) and *Do go out there, have fun and circulate.*

You're never going to meet anyone staying at home (although I'm looking forward to a night off… in fourteen nights' time. That sounds ridiculous. Two weeks. Get a grip. Lots of people work night shifts fourteen days in a row and spend their whole day sleeping, so this is no different is it? No, Isobel, it's much better).

Three boxes… and do *try speed dating. While you run the risk of meeting a dozen or so oddities* (I scrub out '*oddities*' and replace it with *'men you have nothing in common with'*), *the chances are that there will be one or two people you do get on with and even if you don't want to swap details, you can have a fun evening.*

I'm looking forward to tonight. I've not been to the Red Lion for ages and it's quite posh, so he… (I look at my notes to remind me of his name), Adam, must be 'of good standing' as my dad would say. That reminds me, I'm due a visit to the olds on Sunday so ring to confirm. Plus I have to pack the theatre away (fortunately all the bits are there – I had to take it out of the box to check, didn't I?) and take it for Lola. L O L A Lola.

I can rarely resist singing the Kinks song whenever I say her name (although Ellen, my sister-in-law, says she was named after Ludwig the First of Bavaria's mistress Lola Montez because she studied her in Bavarian history, but I know my brother is a Kinks fan).

Yes, the Red Lion. The last time I went there was for a hike (leisurely walk in my case) then lunch (a former boyfriend was a fitness fanatic; needless to say we didn't last long) and it was delicious, but I've never been there in the evening, so this should be a new experience.

I'm not wrong. Adam, it turns out, suffers from narcolepsy. Everything starts well; he's charming, with old-fashioned values (pulls out my chair for me), but we're halfway through a conversation when he falls asleep. I've seen a programme recently where someone did this, so I guess what's happened.

What I can't remember though, is what to do about it. Should I wake him up? Leave him be until he wakes of his own accord? What if that's hours? It's like Keith Mk 2 all over again.

I needn't have worried.

"Sorry. Did I fall asleep?"

"You did."

"I'm so sorry. I get no warning when it happens. I had an early night last night, but it often doesn't make any difference."

"It must be very difficult to live with."

"I've had it for years, so I'm quite used to it, but…"

There he goes again. This time it's a bit longer, about quarter of an hour, so I'm glad I've brought my iPhone with me so I can play some games. I get bored with Sudoku, move on to FreeCell and have just cracked level ninety-five with my personal best score when Adam wakes up.

He's drooled on his top, so I offer him a tissue.

"God, I'm so sorry. It's not been this bad for a while."

"Are you nervous?"

"A little. I wasn't, but I suppose I am now."

"Don't be. I don't mind." And I don't. "You can't help it, after all."

"Not really, no. I've used a CPAP then BiPAP machines, and acetazolamide helps."

"Wow. It is serious."

"But I don't snore."

"You don't? Are they related?"

"Usually, but I sleep alone. I don't wake myself up snoring though, so I assume I don't."

I don't know what to say, but I'm quite impressed that we're getting a decent, and interesting, conversation. I'm about to ask if anything can be done surgically – I remember a little boy who went to the States for treatment – when I realise I'm talking to myself.

We'd not got around to getting a drink; I'm not sure why. He was sitting at the table when I got there, so I leave him where he is and go to the bar. I order a couple of Cokes (I'm going to have to think of something more original as I'm getting sick of them) and have just put them down when he wakes up with a jolt, catching his right hand on the table and spilling some of his drink.

"Man. I'm so sorry. You must think I'm a complete idiot."

"No, it's fine. This is going to sound heartless, but if it wasn't so sad, it would be funny."

"I used to get laughed at when I was at school."

"That's terrible. It's been going on that long?"

"Over twenty-five years." He's older than me, must be almost forty.

"What caused it, do they know?"

"I'd always been quite a big child…"

He looks all right to me.

"…and it kind of crept up on me. I put the tiredness down to studying hard, but it's never really gone away."

"And you've learned to live with it."

"Had to. I have an incredibly understanding boss."

"What do you do?"

"I work for a chocolate company, on the factory line."

I only know of one chocolate company in the area and my thoughts go back to Tim. Like Duncan, Adam's battled with weight and won. "Do you do shift work?"

"I do. Nights mainly."

"Which doesn't help."

"No, but it pays better."

"Money isn't everything. I'm sorry, that sounded…"

"It's okay. I rather overstretched myself on a house with my ex and had to buy her out."

"But it's affecting your life." Again my size eight feet engage mouth full force.

"Yes, but I'm doing something about it."

"Really?"

"I've told my bosses and they've been great. The company doctor's recommending me for surgery."

"Must be a good company to have their own doctor."

"He works in a local practice, but we're on a health scheme which he supports."

"Does it affect your driving?"

"That's the downside. I have a licence, but can only drive short distances and when I'm not feeling tired. I usually like to

171

have someone with me, but it's not always possible. If it gets bad, like it is at the moment, I get someone else to drive. My brother drove…"

He's nodded off again. Poor thing. This time it lasts a few seconds and he wakes up talking as if he was mid-flow. "Oh yes, I'm very hopeful."

"That's great." I don't know what else to say. My heart goes out to him. "I saw a programme a while back on it and it was fascinating."

"My family and I had never heard of it until I was diagnosed and obviously research has gone a long way since then."

Having exhausted, pardon the pun, the conversation, I'm glad of an opportunity to divert it. "And I love the way technology's gone in the last few years. It's all amazing and you wonder where it's going next."

"A girl after my own heart."

Now we're talking. "I was playing with a wind-up grasshopper the other day and it was simple, but such fun."

"Oh?"

I couldn't have expected him to say anything else, could I?

"I can't get over how you cope with…" I realise I'm sounding like a broken record and would send anyone to sleep, which I duly do. As I sit and wait for him to wake up again, I wonder how he gets any work done at all if he falls asleep so often. I couldn't see William lasting long with me if I had it. I dig out my iPhone again and restart FreeCell.

I get through level ninety-six and pause, hoping Adam will wake, but smash level ninety-seven and he's still asleep. He looks pretty comfortable and, despite what he said earlier, he does snore… in fact quite loudly. People are looking at us and I have a distinct case of déjà vu.

Half an hour and a cup of tea later (it makes a change from another Coke) he's still asleep. I decide to wait another ten minutes and see what happens.

Fifteen go by and he's still snoring, so I pull my notepad and pen out of my bag and write a note. He can't be too surprised that I wouldn't hang around forever and I make it as polite as possible: that I had a lovely evening, but I had to go, and for him to take care.

I feel rather guilty as I leave the note tucked under his glass, but assume he's arranged a time with his brother, so he'll no doubt wake him up.

Driving home, I think about how easy I have it. I may whinge about not having a spare evening for a couple of weeks, but can pretty much do what I like, whenever I like. As the saying goes, I got it good.

Chapter 17 – Alex at the Red Hot

I come into work to an email from Duncan.

Hi, Izzy. Sorry about that. I said it really for Donna's benefit. I thought she'd be upset if I said I'd requested her and not you, but you have my details already, so we didn't need to request each other, did we?

He has a point, but I'd still requested him. And he'd requested Donna. I shouldn't have been surprised.

My date tonight, with AlexC17, is set for the Red Hot World Buffet on Sixfields. It's not 'til eight, so I reckon I can squeeze in a movie beforehand, making the most of my season ticket. If I can get something for around six that should slot in nicely.

I go on the Cineworld website and plump for *Hitman Sam*, a comedy about a trainee hitman. It starts at six, so with the usual twenty minutes of adverts, timing should be perfect.

In the meantime I have to crack on with the article and have loads of emails from people reacting (mostly positively) to this month's column. William's in and looks a bit stressed, so I opt for the article first.

What did I learn from last night? To have a good night's sleep.

I met A last night and it was a lovely, if rather frustrating, evening. Frustrating for both of us because A suffers from narcolepsy. In a good way, I'm hoping that last night was an unusually bad night for him as he fell asleep four or five times on me (not literally 'on' me, but you know what I mean)…

I delete everything from 'on me' onwards and continue.

… five times. I knew a little about the condition, but seeing it for myself made me realise how difficult it must be to live with. I'm a very independent person and can't imagine having to rely on others for the most basic of day-to-day care. While a lot of sufferers live perfectly self-sufficient lives, others with more severe forms of illness…

I'm struggling to make this not sound condescending or preachy, so I Shift/F7 to bring up the thesaurus and change illness to ailment, then to complaint and back to illness. I'm still not happy with it, but hope that inspiration will strike during the editing process.

... must have to rely on family and friends to live as normal a life as possible. A child growing up with narcolepsy will know no different, but what happens when the child grows into a teenager and wants their independence? Given that nearly eight per cent of the population (in the US anyway) have it, you'd think we'd see more people falling asleep around us. There is medication and a variety of techniques to sleep better and therefore lessen the chances of falling asleep during waking hours, but as yet there is no cure.

So if you're feeling tired and whinge that you didn't sleep very well last night, spare a thought for those who struggle, day in, day out, to stay awake.

I save the draft and Alt/Tab over to tallgirlnn1. It's suddenly dawned on me that after AlexC17 tonight, my well of dates is dry. I shouldn't panic as I've set up late-notice dates before, but with nothing on the horizon, I get worried.

I'm pleased to see there are seven messages from guys I've not corresponded with yet and fire off replies.

DodgeNitroSXT (which I Google and find is a cool-looking gas guzzler) sounds like fun. He's 'up for anything' and is 'not afraid of a challenge'.

SoftieBear on the other hand sounds like... well, a softie. There's a picture of his dog, a puppy, which is really cute. Apparently she's a red merle Australian Shepherd, which I've never heard of, but has the weirdest blue eyes and huge black irises. A non-animal lover would think she's creepy, but to me she's a bundle of fluff and I want to meet her as much, if not more so, as her owner. I think about contacting Duncan to borrow one of his dogs, but I can't tell him what I really do until the month is over. I could, I suppose, but keeping shtum would make life easier.

QuincyJ's profile doesn't say much, which is fine. A lot of them don't. At this point, I can't be too fussy.

CloudSpirit seems a little away with the fairies, although I'd rather have a deep and meaningful experience than a struggle for conversation with a brain-numb bumpkin.

Another guy with a horizontal attitude is JakeT. Like Dodge, he's happy to do anything a partner suggests, but does sound as if he can't make a decision. Just a feeling I have.

Then there's another Eddie: EddieG. If it wasn't for the name I'd have thought I was visiting a woman's profile. There's no picture (I've so far still managed to pick guys who don't have one of themselves and it's proven fun to have no idea what they look like, so it's more of a true blind date), but it's a very pink and fluffy profile. Nice, I guess, for a man to show his feminine side for a change.

The one I'm keen to meet is TechnoGeek. Just the name is Izzy territory and his profile lists gadgets he's bought recently and thinks are 'cool'. I recognise all but one and have tested most of them. I wouldn't have bought a couple of the computer games that he did, but he's a bloke and I'm not into gaming. I listen to technology podcasts, but glaze over when it comes to that kind of stuff.

It takes quite a while to go to each profile then reply, and by the time I've done EddieG's and finalised my article, it's one thirty. I'm surprised Donna's not come over before now to drag me out to lunch, but see she's not at her desk. I do my meerkat impression and she's in William's office. The door is shut, so it must be serious.

I stay standing for a minute or two before dropping back down to my seat when William threatens to look in my direction. I rise slowly, peering round my blue cloth-covered partition and watch Donna nodding and leaving his office, closing the door again behind her.

She skips back to her desk. I'm relieved it's good news and am sorely tempted to go rushing over to her desk. I sink slowly back onto my chair, but keep looking in her direction.

"What are you doing?" Karen whispers.

Without turning, I reply. "Donna's just come out of William's office with a huge grin. Something's happened."

"And you want to know what."

"Of course. Wouldn't you?"

She nods. "Go over and speak to her then."

I don't need telling twice.

"I saw you in William's office. What did he want?"

"I can't tell you."

"Donna Clarke, don't give me that."

She clenches both fists, screws her face up and wiggles on her chair. "All right, but not here. And you've got to swear not to tell anyone."

"Of course. You know me. I'm great at keeping secrets." Next to her, I'm the world's worst, but she'll go blabbing it around the office anyway, so I won't need to.

She grabs her bag and we walk to my desk. I half whisper, half mouth, "I'll tell you later," to Karen and she nods.

I'd forgotten to print off my article, do so now and nip it into William's office, but he's on the phone, so we exchange smiles and I rejoin Donna.

We go to the Fishmarket Café for lunch (I got up too late to make a sandwich, which would have been difficult anyway as I hadn't got any bread) and by the time we've got our fruit teas (we both plump for blackcurrant), order our food and sit at a corner table, she's fit to burst.

"William wants me to do an exposé on the cost of glasses – why it's so much more expensive in shops than getting them off the internet… which reminds me, I've got two dates. It's going to be all about customer service versus quality and do you get what you pay for because you can't try on what you're buying online."

I'm not sure which she wants me to comment on first, especially as I can't see how the exposé is top secret, so I go for the juiciest. "With whom?"

"Boots, SpecSavers, Vision Express–"

"No, the dates. Who are the dates with?"

"Walter the anti-smoker, Nick the librarian, and…" She pauses.

"Three? Who's the third?"

"Duncan."

"Of course."

"I won't if you don't want me too," she blurts. "It's just that we both requested each other, and… he emailed me."

"No… I mean yes, it's fine." I'm not sure whether it's fine or not, but she seems so happy and he isn't mine to say 'yes' or 'no' on, so I change the subject. "The exposé sounds interesting. If you want any help with the internet research, let me know."

"Ah, thanks. I didn't like to ask, I know you've got your hands full."

I know who I'd like to have my hands full of, but say nothing and smile at the waitress as she brings our chicken and ham salads. "Thank you."

I open my sachet of salad cream and squeeze the end like a toothpaste tube, spluttering it across the plate.

Donna puts her sachet on a side plate and smiles. "So, Izzy Belle, who are you meeting tonight?"

I tell her all about AlexC17 and the week's worth of men I'm hoping to line up, and she eats while watching me with rabbit-in-headlights eyes.

"Wow! I wish I had your job."

"You're not doing so badly yourself. At least you know what you're letting yourself in for. Although I can't see what you see in Walter, Nick was nice. A little quiet for you perhaps, but genuine."

"Walter was funny."

"Really? He didn't make me laugh." It takes a lot to make me laugh, unless you're called Donna.

"And he's so clever. Nick was nice. I don't know."

"What don't you know?"

"Which one I prefer."

"Does it matter? Besides, there's Duncan to think about too." As if I'm not.

"Yes, but…"

"Don't not see him just because of me. I had my chance. Besides, if he was 'the one' I'd have felt it, wouldn't I?"

"I suppose, but…"

"No buts. You have a good time."

"I'll try." And, knowing Donna, she'll do exactly that.

By the time we finish our salads, share a jam doughnut and get back to the office, there are five tallgirlnn1 messages.

DodgeNitroSXT is set for The Romany pub (my nearest – perfect) tomorrow night. SoftieBear suggests we meet at

178

Abington Park Saturday afternoon while CloudSpirit (Callum) opts for a Sunday mid-morning walk at Delapre Park, and JakeT says there's a pub quiz at The Four Pears at Little Houghton on Tuesday (a change from their usual Sunday, apparently). EddieG is flamboyant to say the least. He, Edgar, says he would be delighted to meet with me and that I'm his first message, so he can't wait.

That just leaves QuincyJ and TechnoGeek, and I will TechnoGeek to reply. He's not logged on for 'over a week', so I'm not hopeful, but QuincyJ checked his messages in the last twenty-four hours, so perhaps he'll come back with something. From his profile name, it's a toss-up between him being my favourite 1970s pathologist or the Motown guru, but of course I know he's neither.

It's nearly five when I've finished replying to the work emails. My head is swelling from all the lovely comments I've had from readers about my dating experiences, although I'm brought down to earth again by two saying I'm not being fair to the guys I've met and that I'm too glass half empty. I make a note to weave a line into the next article to remind my readers that, while I try to be fair to my 'subjects', the column can only show my version of events and is not to be taken too seriously.

I check tallgirlnn1 again before I shut down and there are two messages, the first from QuincyJ who's free on Monday and suggests the White Elephant. He explains he lives in Derbyshire, but works in Northampton's town centre in the week, lodging round the corner from the White Elephant, so it's the only pub he knows. It sounds fine to me and, in fact, is likely to be the easiest of all the guys as he's just 'passing through' (and the pub's another of my locals). I confirm for eight p.m. and move on to the next message.

AlbertE1879 says he thinks I'm gorgeous (which is hilarious as there's no picture of me) and would like to get to know me better. I look at his profile, which is even barer than QuincyJ's, and am about to reply, against my better judgement, but I've got no one lined up for Friday night, when I notice his location is Africa.

I don't think, even being in credit, that William's budget will stretch that far. I'm amused by the profile name as I assume the

179

E to stand for Einstein and am suitably impressed when Wikipedia tells me that Mr Einstein was in fact born in 1879. Instead of a proper message, I click on the 'You're very kind, but no thanks' automated reply and log off the computer. I'm rather disappointed that TechnoGeek hasn't replied but, as the saying goes, tomorrow is another day.

Nipping to Morrison's to fill up the car with petrol, and me with food, means that by the time I get home, I have to get changed and go straight out again.

Hitman Sam is hilarious and another film that I'm going to get when it comes out on DVD. Because I've picked up so many cheap DVDs, the cupboard underneath my TV in the lounge is packed, so sorting out a few to sell at a boot sale would be a good plan for the weekend. I can't this Sunday morning as I've got Callum's walk, but providing the weather holds out, could be something for the following weekend, especially as it's another bank holiday.

It's ten to eight by the time I leave the cinema, but have about a hundred yards to walk, so take my time.

The car park is packed, so I'm glad I parked near the restaurant before the movie. I spot a man who looks very similar to Zeek the Waffler (average height, average build and, in my fussy opinion, average looks) although when I get closer, I see he has the most brilliant green eyes. And I can't tear myself away.

He steps forward, putting out his left hand. "Hi. I'm Alex."

"Hello. I'm Izzy."

"Izzy, yes, right. That's it, Izzy."

He opens the door for me and I walk through first, with him repeating my name under his breath. Another fun evening ahead then.

We wait our turn and, when we get to the maître d's rostrum, I turn to Alex expecting him to say something, but he stays silent.

"What name is it please?" the maître d' asks.

Of course I don't have a clue what his surname is. "Alex?"

"Oh." He looks at me blankly.

"Did you book our table?" I have visions of going to McDonalds next door instead.

"I think so."

"The name please?" the maître d' repeats and he looks over my shoulder. I turn round and there's a queue forming.

"Alex?"

"The name please!" The maître d's face is getting redder.

"Connor!" Alex blurts back.

We're shown to a tiny table for two by an emergency exit (I suspect probably not the one we'd originally been intended for) and we sit. We're about to get up again to help ourselves to food when a waiter comes shuffling over to take our drinks order.

Alex orders a bottle of Peroni Nastro Azzurro beer and I go for a white wine lemonade spritzer. I don't usually have any alcohol when I'm driving, but knowing how much food I'm about to eat, I figure I'm safe.

We each pick up an empty plate and go in different directions. Alex starts with the salad bar, progressing to the Italian mains, whereas I go straight for the curries, sweet and sours, and rice.

I walk back to the table, but Alex is looking a little lost. I wave at him and point to the table. He still appears vague, but comes over and sits down.

"Hi, I'm Alex."

Déjà vu. "Hi, Alex. We did meet outside."

"Ah, yes. Sorry."

"No problem. So, Alex, what is it that you do?"

"I'm a doctor."

"Wow. GP?"

"Yes, partner in a local…" He trails off as he stares at a woman sitting at a table on the other side of the room.

"Alex?"

'Sorry. I know her."

"Really? Friend, or someone famous?" We never see anyone famous in Northampton. We have a couple of local celebs on the paper – a historian called Tony Hind who does our 'On this day' and 'In Hindsight' columns (and was a consultant for Channel 4's *Time Team*) and Percy Thrower's former PA, Nettie Phillips, who does our weekend gardening pull-out, but apart from panto stars at the Derngate and Royal theatres and visitors to the office for promotional events, I don't think I've ever seen, or at least recognised, anyone famous in the town… with the exception of Alan Moore, who is so normal looking that he doesn't feel like a celebrity. I've always had the impression he's uncomfortable with his fame.

"Friend. Yes, pretty sure she's a friend."

I seriously wonder whether Alex is suffering from Alzheimer's, when the 'friend' who we've been staring at stands up and walks in our direction.

"Hello," she says cheerily.

"Hello," I say, then look at Alex.

"Hi, Alex," she says.

He looks at me then back at her. "Hello." I can almost see his brain whirring.

"You must be Izzy," she says to me, so I turn back to her and shake the hand that's offered. "I am. I'm sorry I don't quite…"

"I'm Oma. A friend of Alex's here."

"Oma?" Alex says, clearly still trying to work things out. She nods.

"Are you German?" I ask her.

"No, Irish."

"Oh. I thought because Oma means grandmother in German." It's probably a European thing but…

"My grandmother's name was Olive and mine means the colour of olive," she explains.

"That's nice. Mine's religious, Isobel, which didn't please my mum too much when she found out, because she's not."

"But it's a nice name."

"Thanks." It's an odd conversation to be having on a first date, especially not with my actual *date*, but I'm getting much more out of her than Alex. "You're welcome to join us if they'll let us have a bigger table," I offer, willing her to say yes.

"Thanks, but I'd better not."

"Alex, do you mind?" I ask, and he shakes his head slowly, as if unsure what the correct answer is.

"I'm on a table for four – come and join me."

"That would be great, thanks." I go to stand up.

Alex, meanwhile, is watching the play unfold and trying to take it in.

Oma attracts the attention of the waiter and tells him what's going on, while Alex and I move to her table, taking our part-eaten dinners and drinks with us. Her plate is nearly empty, but she has an untouched glass of wine.

Once we're seated, Oma turns to Alex. "Alex, I'm Oma, your sister-in-law. I'm married to Barry, your brother."

It takes a second for the penny to drop. "Ah, Oma. I went to the wedding."

"You did."

I must be looking as puzzled as I feel because Oma then looks at me. "I'm sorry, Izzy. Someone should have explained in the messages to you. Alex suffers from antegrade amnesia."

I know amnesia, obviously, but the antegrade loses me and I'm curious to know who the 'someone' would be.

"He was in a car crash just before Christmas three years ago," Oma continues, "and hit his head on the dashboard. He can remember pretty much everything up to then, although he's not good with faces, but his short-term memory only lasts a few minutes."

"How awful."

"He remembers where he lives, so he can get home, but I offered to come with him to explain the situation to you in case things got…"

"Tricky."

"Yes."

"Thanks, Oma," Alex says, clearly caught up. "Izzy."

"Yes, Alex?"

"Sorry."

"For what?"

"For confusing everything."

"It's fine, but it must feel very strange."

He nods.

"Alex," Oma chips in. "Your dinner's cold, why don't you go and get a new one." She pulls his plate towards her, puts the contents of hers on top of his, and slides the empty plate under the full one. Considering that most of his was salad, I think it's an odd thing to say, but soon realise why once he's out of earshot. "His brother died in the accident…"

"Oh, no!"

"Please don't say anything. He doesn't remember."

"Of course. What happened?"

"He and Barry were business partners and had been to a work's function. While Alex stuck to orange juice, Barry was knocking back Buck's Fizz, which obviously looks the same, so Alex didn't notice. Barry insisted on driving home and…"

"How awful."

"Apart from the bump to his head, Alex walked away without a scratch. And we've been trying to lead as normal a life for him as possible ever since."

The conversation ends as Alex returns with a fresh plate of food.

"I'm so hungry. Oh, hello, Oma, who's your friend?"

"Alex, this is Isobel."

"Hi, Isobel." He looks at my plate. "That looks nice. I think I'll have that next time."

I look at his plate which is more or less a replica of his previous one, and smile.

After that we chat, eat and have another round of drinks each. With the exception of a couple of re-introductions, you'd never know there was anything untoward. We split the bill when it comes and chat briefly in the car park.

"It was lovely to meet you, Izzy," Oma says, while Alex catches us up from a visit to the gents. "And I'm sorry about… you know."

"God, no, don't apologise. It's been enlightening."

"Hi!" Alex thrusts out his left hand, and I shake it warmly.

"Hello, you must be Alex."

"I am." He looks questioningly at Oma.

"Alex, this is a good friend, Isobel."

"Hello, Isobel. Oma, you kept her quiet."

Oma and I smile at each other, before she leads him to the driver's door. "I'll tell you all about her on the way home. Thanks, Izzy, for everything. You could have left when you had the chance."

"I wouldn't have missed it. He's so lucky to have you. I'm not sure I would have the patience."

"He's Barry's brother, his twin. He reminds me of my husband every day, the good side, and some wives don't get that. I'm the lucky one."

Driving home I think about what's happened. The whole scenario reminds me of the theme of the film *50 First Dates* and I can appreciate how difficult it must be for Alex's family to break the news to him every time the subject of his brother is mentioned.

Again, I'm reminded how wonderfully uncomplicated my life is, and for the umpteenth time, I'm looking forward to writing my next article and telling Donna, and my readers, in differing proportions, of a charming man and his devoted sister-in-law.

Chapter 18 – Dodge at the Romany

What did I learn from last night? That dedication comes in all shapes and sizes. Last night I met a couple living their day-to-day lives, but in very extraordinary circumstances. An accident had changed their existence beyond all recognition. They'd lost a loved one and were living with the consequences. The man I met last night suffered from antegrade amnesia, giving him short-term memory loss. He remembers everything up to the accident and fragments thereafter, but building new memories proves impossible, with anything learned soon forgotten: people, places and so on. If you've seen the film '50 First Dates' you'll know what I mean.

The gentleman and I met at one of my favourite restaurants. I'm a big fan of buffets, and, after a complex start, we were joined by his sister-in-law who explained the situation. They were both charming, upbeat, and inspirational, and I will cherish meeting them.

I have been reminded by a couple of readers that I should perhaps be more objective about the men I meet. Like any review, I don't reveal who I am and why I'm meeting them and while that may seem rather unfair, I don't ask or agree to see them again. I'm sure there won't be any hearts on Northamptonshire floors just because I didn't want to, or couldn't, get to know them better.

So, this article has been designed as a warts-and-all guide to online dating; to show you the Dos and Don'ts, and for me to be like a big sister who chaperones you before leaving you to your own devices.

I'm in serious need of a cup of tea. I've come into the office early, which is not like me, and people are filtering in.

Jason had handed me a couple of parcels when I arrived and, as a grateful distraction from all things dating, I unwrap them. I sigh – one is a bundle of PlayStation 3 games and with only one that appeals, I put the rest aside to offer to Karen.

Her boys always jump at the chance of testing them and are undoubtedly better reviewers of car chases and platform games than I am. Plus they love getting their names in the paper. I've always been more of a fan of brain training and simple 2D games like Space Invaders, Jetpac, and more recently FreeCell and Sudoku.

The other parcel contains a 'Storm of London Circuit' watch, which resembles the front grill of Knight Rider's car, and all it seems to do is tell the time (in, admittedly, very futuristic vertical red LED lights), but to be able to give my professional opinion, I need to test it fully.

"Ah, Trevor. Just the person." Although I'm not sure whether watches come under the 'Homes' attribute of his 'Homes and Gardens' job description.

"Yes, my dear."

"What do you think of this watch?"

"It's a watch?"

"Thanks, Trevor, that's all I need to know."

No, seriously, I'll look at it later.

Donna walks past without saying hello, so I walk after her.

"Hello? Earth calling Donna?"

She spins round. "Hello. Sorry."

"So, spill."

"I met up with Nick the librarian."

"And it went well?'

"It did." Her smile two-folds.

"Very well?"

"Oh yes."

"Donna Clarke!"

"No, not that well!"

"So you won't be seeing Walter or Duncan?"

"I will. Nick and I are just going to be friends. I'd better get to my desk. I've got a lot to plan with this new project that William's given me."

"Sure. Have fun."

"Always." She almost dances back to her desk.

I think about properly testing the watch, but before that, I've got a shed-load of work to get through. There have been so many emails about my speed-dating article that it takes forever. With the exception of a quick break for lunch and chat with Donna, it's not quite forever, but 'til half four. I check tallgirlnn1 messages and there's one. And it's definitely quality not quantity: TechnoGeek.

He's sorry it's short notice, but he's going on a two-week holiday (boo) at the weekend, but he's happy to meet up tomorrow lunchtime if that's okay (yay). He says he's dropping off some gadgets in the town centre and he'll be parked in the Grosvenor Centre car park, so if it's not too corny, we could meet in the café at the top of the stairs by BHS upper floor.

With no other 'date' for Friday and happy to talk shop with a fellow techie, I book him in.

I've got ten minutes before I have to go home and prepare for my date at the Romany, so take a peek at one of my favourite websites: gizmodo.com. It's a (very) honest look at gadgets on the market (mostly in the US) and I'm hooked on their 'All Barcodes Should Be This Creative' section. They're hilarious.

They're barcode designs as you'd never normally see them. Instead of the bog-standard vertical stripes in a conformed rectangle, there's a sumo wrestler, clapperboard and waterfall. I think the sleeping man is my favourite. I look at the bottom of the boxes I've received. One is bog-standard, whereas the other is of a curvy bench with a character reading a book under a tree. How cool is that?

I'm ready for the off. I shut down the PC and gather my things (including the watch in case tonight's date is a short one). Donna's slaving away, so I walk to her desk for a quick goodbye. It's covered in paperwork and magazine cut-outs.

"Hey, Donna."

"Hi."

"You look rather overwhelmed." I'm good at stating the obvious.

"A bit."

"Anything I can help you with?"

"Thanks, but it's okay. Tying up some loose ends before I get on with the..." She lowers her voice. "The new thing, you know." She even winks at me.

I lower my torso and voice and say, "I do. I can come in early tomorrow if that'll help."

"Thanks, but another half hour and I should be done."

"See you."

Having decided on wearing blue Levi jeans, a simple black top and black loafers, I toast the crust and first slice of last night's bought seeded batch, while a tin of Heinz tomato soup is rotating in the microwave.

It's a bit of a fiddle as I set it going for a minute, stir it, then set it for another thirty seconds, but it's done to perfection, and with the butter still melting on the toast and offcuts/oddments of vintage cheese sinking into the dark orange liquid, I put it on a tray and take it through to the lounge. I don't have time for a DVD, so watch the national then local news.

I walk down the path and notice I'm in tandem with Ursula, who's tapping into her mobile. "Hi."

"Hi, Izzy."

"Work or speed dating?"

She laughs. "Neither. Visiting a friend in hospital."

"Oh dear."

"Nothing major. She'll be fine, but I think she's bored."

"I meant to ask you when the thing finished on Monday, how did you get on?"

"All right. How about you?"

"Just the one guy."

"Number sixteen?"

I laugh. "How did you guess?"

"No contest really, was there?"

"No."

"I had a couple of matches. Sadly neither was him."

"Oh?"

"Nick the librarian and a guy who talked a lot…"

"Zeek?" I ask.

"That was it. I'm somewhere in the middle, so not holding out much hope, but it's a bit of fun, isn't it?' Wiggling her mobile, Ursula says, "I'd better go. Sorry."

"Me too. Have a good evening."

"Thanks, and you. You know, we should go out. I hadn't realised until you said you were single, I thought…"

"It's a recent thing, but a long time coming. We thought a change of scene would do, but…"

"I know how that goes. Anyway, I should be…"

"Indeed. See ya."

Ursula drives off and I make my way to the Romany. I'm going to be a minute or two late, but I'm sure he won't mind.

As I walk through the car park, I notice a group of rough-looking guys standing outside puffing away. It looks so unattractive that I'm glad I started and stopped smoking in the same week.

I'm approaching the steps into the lounge when one of the guys steps forward.

"Hello," he says.

I smile politely and say, "Hello," back, but keep on walking.

"Are you Izzy?"

Oh no. I should say yes, but I'd much rather say no and keep going, but I'm a good girl, so I nod and besides, what have I been saying all along about not judging a book by its cover?

This particular book is a hardback, rock hard, with solid 'GOUDY STOUT' lettering. The jacket's rather tatty and the pages look well thumbed. Judging by the people he's with, he's clearly part of a serial, but I can't decide whether a sequel or prequel.

He sniffs loudly and throws his cigarette on the floor. Behind him is a stub container, but I resist saying anything as he looks the sort to throw me on the floor and stub me out. Again, I remind myself about the 'judging book by cover' bit and smile.

He walks up the steps first, I assume to open the door for me, and he does, but not for me. He marches through and lets go so it nearly hits me, and I hear a cackle from his cronies behind me. *It's only a job*, I tell myself as I grab the door and march into the bar after him.

He slightly redeems his lack of brownie points by asking me what I'd like to drink, but loses them again when he obviously doesn't approve of my costly request for a Southern Comfort and lemonade. I don't usually go for a short when a man is paying, but I'm walking and everything about him so far is far from gentlemanly, so I may as well make the most of the situation.

He reluctantly hands over the four eighty-five for our two drinks. His pint of Great Oakley Gobble, I see from the ales board, is fifteen pence more than my drink, so he can't complain, although he looks like he wants to.

"Pool?" he says.

"Sure." I used to play a mean game of pool, but I'm so out of practice that if it's anything like my darts and bowling, it'll go one of two ways: rubbish to start then warm up until it's mediocre, or great then go rapidly downhill. I figure it's probably best to let him win anyway – he looks anything but a good loser.

We take our drinks and walk through into the public bar, where there's football playing on the TV in the corner. I'm delighted as he's wearing a dark blue Scotland football shirt (I only know that from the badge), and it may put him off his game.

He digs around in his jeans for a coin and holds it in his hand waiting for me to call.

"Heads," I say, and he throws it into the air then slams it on one side of the pool table. It's tails.

"Yes!" he shouts, fists flung in the air. I can't imagine him coming second at anything.

As I wait my turn for the table, I think about how to describe him to Donna, which I'll no doubt have to do when I see her next.

He's bald, and has piercing blue eyes. I'll then explain the hardback's dust jacket and she'll think I'm exaggerating. When he grins, which he does whenever he pots a ball (we've had three smiles already), he has surprisingly good teeth, other than the ones that are gold or ruby encrusted. I've never seen the sense in that.

He's also got tattoos everywhere, including D O D G E over the knuckles of his left hand, and I expect to see M S on his right to spell out my favourite fairground attraction, or even H A T E (L O V E would be beyond him), but they're bare and I'm rather disappointed.

As he pots his fifth red, I suspect he only invited me to play pool to show off, but he misses the next one, and I step forward, holding my rather tatty and chalkless cue. I pick up the cube of blue chalk from the corner of the table and wiggle it

191

against the cue's end. I hear foot tapping and am not surprised when it's Dodge.

I take aim at one of the many yellows and misjudge the angle (him hovering at the end of my line of sight didn't help) and, while I graze the yellow, it goes nowhere near a pocket. I console myself that at least it didn't approach the black, but realise I spoke too soon when my second shot (after two more reds go down) sends the black ball heading in the direction of a corner pocket. Dodge lets out a shriek of laughter, and I can't help glaring at him.

His gaze is fixed on the white ball, so he doesn't see my face crease as the shot looks a dead cert, but I smile (he growls) when I realise it doesn't have enough power.

I've finished my drink, so ask him if he wants another. Fortunately, he's been too busy to drink much of his, so I don't give him the chance to say yes, which I feel he's going to do anyway.

I buy a replacement SoCo (I've always thought it a daft name) and lemonade and return to my 'date'. I go to put the drink on the edge of the pool table, but he barks at me.

"Don't you dare!" He lunges towards me and I recoil as he puts both arms forward to grab me.

"Sorry, love," he says. "Instant reaction. They're very protective about the felt and if anyone knocks your drink over…"

"No, you're right."

"Guess I shouldn't have been so reactionary."

I agree, but the damage is done. "Is it my go?" I say coolly and he nods. I play my shot and we take turns until he wins with four of my yellow balls left on the table. Again clenched fists (his) are thrust in the air. He took longer getting the last few balls in, perhaps to let me catch up, but it was inevitable I'd lose.

By that time though, I couldn't care less.

Chapter 19 – Louis at the Grosvenor Shopping Centre

I'm really tired by the time I get to work, partly thanks to Elliot and his latest literary antics, but also through sheer lack of enthusiasm for my current project.

Donna, on the other hand, has enough for both of us and nearly crashes into me as I get to my desk.

"So, so, so… how did it go?"

"You're a poet and you didn't even know it."

"Eh?"

"Never mind. I presume you're talking about last night."

"Of course."

"Waste of time."

"That's not good."

"It wasn't great. He was not what you would call charming or debonair."

"Unlike the lovely Duncan."

"Poles apart." I can tell by her expression she's brought up his name for a reason. "Go on, tell me."

"What?" She does her 'Miss Innocent' routine.

"You've got a date with Duncan, haven't you?"

"Yes, Sunday."

"That's great." I try my hardest to be sincere, but can't help wallowing in self-pity. I should be happy for her. I am, really I am. I sound as earnest as Judy Dench in *Jack & Sarah*, but wear my biggest smile. "Are you going somewhere nice?" I half expect her to say the Picturedrome, but they're meeting at its older, more mature sister bar, Auntie Ruth's, and I'm so jealous. It's for members only and I'm not (an ex-boyfriend was).

Donna can see my mind's elsewhere.

"I'm a bit concerned."

"What about?"

"My cover being blown."

"Oh, yes. I'd forgotten about that."

"You haven't said anything, have you?"

"No, but…"

"But?"

"I would have done if you'd not reminded me. You're going to have to fill me in on what we do before Sunday. Cuppa?"

"Cuppa."

And we got to the kitchen.

William walks in as we've just sat down and looks at us with a 'you two are always here' expression.

"Just helping Donna get her head around the online aspect of buying glasses."

"Sorry?"

"I'm just helping Donna with…"

"Great. Erm…"

I obviously needn't have pre-empted him as he's clearly on another planet. We watch in silence as he fumbles for a mug then drops it on the floor where it disintegrates, and he stands staring at it as if nothing like that has ever happened to him and he needs to be told what to do.

We rush over, Donna to him, and me to underneath the sink to get a dustpan and brush. Donna ushers him back to his office with a promise that we'll make a drink for him (we assume there's no Janine yet) as I sweep up the bits. I shovel them in the bin as Donna returns.

"He's got it bad," she says.

"Sorry?"

"He's got a serious crush."

"On…?'

"You."

"Don't be silly."

"Has so. You didn't see him looking at you before he dropped the mug."

I've never noticed him looking at me. In fact, he usually avoids eye contact. No. It couldn't be true. "Maybe he was looking in my direction, but was thinking about work and the mug slipped."

"You mark my words. He's got a C.R.U.S.H."

"Yes, mother, whatever you say. You've promised him a drink, so you'd better deliver."

"I've got a better idea. I'll make it, but you deliver."

"Nice try, but I've got work to do." I pick up my tea and walk back to my desk.

"Chicken!" she shouts after me.

"That's me," I reply, and squawk, much to Karen's amusement.

"Hey, my boys have tested your games."

"Already? What did they think?"

"Simon loved the car one, but thought the egg hunt one was boring."

"He's your oldest, right?"

"He is, but Thomas loved the egg hunt and got to…" she digs a piece of paper out of her bag "… level nine."

"Wow." I don't know if that's good, but it's higher than I'd got on any of my iPod games and he's her youngest. "And Ivan?" I impress myself this time by remembering her middle son.

"He kept crashing into Thomas's car, which is probably why Thomas lost interest. He thought the egg game was stupid, but he thinks everything's stupid at the moment, so I didn't persevere."

It's at times like this I'm glad I don't have children. I'm sure they bring sheer joy on the odd occasions, but the thought of managing a household of four 'children' (I've met her husband) doesn't fill me with any particular desire to add to the human race, although I admire Karen hugely for her having done so, and still clearly enjoying the whole experience.

She hands me the piece of paper from her bag and, as I'm deciphering the children's writing, it soon becomes clear I have competition for my job. "This is great."

"Really?"

"Yes. Who did this, Simon?"

"He and Ivan, I think."

"Wow." I'm back on my broken record mode again, but it's all I can think of to say, so I say it again. "Wow." I look at her bemused face.

"I'll tell them you're pleased. They'll be chuffed, especially Ivan. He reads your column every day without fail. He hates Sundays."

"Really?"

"No, not really, because he doesn't have school on Sundays."

"Thank you for boosting my ego, and thank you so much for these."

195

"Given the choice of doing their homework or playing games and writing about it, there's no contest."

"I suppose not, but I wouldn't want to…"

"They do their homework first, but miraculously it takes a fraction of the time it normally would, so you're doing me a favour, plus it keeps them out of my hair. Anyway, better get on. Fashion waits for no one."

"As does technology… or doesn't." I'm confused.

I set about writing the article on Dodge and am struggling to say anything positive about the whole experience. Even the 'judging the book' scenario fails to amuse me. I've got quite a lot to do today and I need a favour.

"William?"

He looks up from his desk and blushes. Maybe Donna's got a point. "Yes, Isobel." (Ah, we're back to 'Isobel'.) Maybe not.

"Can I be a bit late with my article today? It's just I have a lunch date…"

"Oh?"

"Techno Geek, Grosvenor Centre, twelve thirty."

"Ah."

"I'm a bit behind writing up last night and want to see if I can do Techno Geek after lunch instead of coming in tomorrow."

William looks nonplussed.

"If that's okay."

No reply.

"Not coming in tomorrow?"

"Sure. It's your day off, it's only fair."

"Thanks. What time do you want the piece in by?"

"Can you get the first one done by three and then the other by close of play?"

"I'll do my best."

"I'm sure you will, Isobel."

"Thanks, William," I say hesitantly, and leave the office. Something's troubling him and, contrary to Donna's earlier comment, I don't think it's me he's got on his mind.

I'm particularly excited by TechnoGeek; I think out of everyone so far, he's going to be the one I'll have most in common with.

I get the majority of Dodge done by quarter past twelve and rush to get to the Grosvenor in time.

I'm racing along the outside walkway when I see the upper mall is shut.

'Shit!' I don't know what to do as I don't have TG's mobile number.

I race back towards the down ramp and burst through the double doors by Beattie's. The lower floor is packed with people and as I reach the 'up' escalator, I see it's cordoned off. There's a centre security guard in front of me, so I tap him on the shoulder and he spins round.

"What's going on?" I ask.

"A flood."

"Eh?"

"The toilets at the top of the stairs flooded and made the whole floor dangerous. Got as far as the café. Not a pretty sight."

"I'm supposed to be meeting–"

"Doesn't matter, love. You can't go up there."

"But I don't–"

"If you want to wait an hour or two it should be re-opened once they clear up the mess."

"I can't, I'm on my lunch break. Besides, I don't think he'll wait that long."

"Impatient type, is he?"

"No, it's a bit more complicated than that."

"Oh?"

I don't normally confide in complete strangers, but he's the only one who's talking to me, and he works in the centre, so I cling on to the hope he might be able to do something.

"Ah." He twigs. "Blind date, is it?"

"Err…"

"Sweet."

I'm about to tell him he's wrong, and save face, when I feel tapping on my shoulder. I turn round and look up.

"Hi, did I hear right?"

I'm lost for words as I look at the most gorgeous black man I've ever seen.

"Are you on a blind date?"

"Err…" Donna would be proud of the way I'm keeping it all together.

"Then you're Izzy?"

I've died and gone to heaven. "Techno Geek?" I whimper, then rub the corners of my mouth as I'm convinced I must be drooling.

He smiles and my legs almost wobble. You see guys on TV with brilliant teeth and a comic flash as the person smiles, but this is literally blinding. He'd easily give Simon Cowell a run for his money.

"What have I missed?" he asks.

"A flood."

"Really? How biblical."

I laugh, a Dawn French *Vicar of Dibley* kind of exaggerated laugh, and if I had a pair of legs that worked properly, I'd use them to kick myself.

It's obvious to anyone that he's not going to get another word out of me, so it's up to him to speak. "So if we can't go upstairs, is there anywhere else?"

"McDonalds?"

"That'll do."

"Oh."

"Oh?"

"It's upstairs, although there's a lift."

"Never mind. Anywhere else?"

"There's a cookie place or a smoothie bar."

"Not very healthy."

Yes, Donna would approve. "There's a nice place along Fish Street."

"That settles it."

As we walk side by side towards the nearest exit, I feel like telling the whole world 'he's mine' at the top of my voice.

We talk as we walk and he, 'Louie', apologises for being late as his satnav sent him the wrong way and then he got stuck on the outer ring road.

I stopped paying attention after his name. "Were you named Louie after the song?"

"Song?"

"'Louie, Louie' by Iggy…"

"Richard Berry and The Pharaohs, but no, Louis Armstrong."

So Louie is a Louis Louie. "Ah, right. Yes, I love his 'Wonderful World'… reminds me of *Good Morning Vietnam* whenever I hear it, and 'All The Time In The World' gets me going every time."

"Really?"

"I've got them both on a list to play at my funeral."

"That's a bit morbid."

"It is, isn't it, but I'm a practical sort of person."

"I'm sure Louis would be chuffed."

"Do you reckon? I think if I wrote songs I'd rather have them played at weddings."

"So what is it that you do?"

"Secretary for a training company."

"Do you enjoy it?"

"Most of the time, yes. Where do you work?" I'm willing him to say Gizmodo, but I know they're an American company.

"Gadget Shack in Leicester. Been there since fourteen, no, fifteen years, and my house is packed with toys."

Again, out comes the Dibley laugh. Shoot me now.

I'm dying to talk toys, but he speaks first. "So, which is your favourite?"

"Probably something simple like a wind-up grasshopper."

"No!" He looks at me as if I've just told him off. "I've got one of those."

"You have? Really?"

I grin like a badly drawn Cheshire cat and am feeling like Alice, the Vicar's dopey sidekick.

As we arrive at the café we're next in line to order, so I can only hope he's forgotten how inane I'm being, and we can start from scratch when we get seated. This proves difficult on both counts as the pavement seating area outside is packed and we fare no better when we return inside.

We've both gone for a sandwich and juice, so at least it's easy to eat standing, although the café itself is sardined like a tube train and I'm seriously regretting wearing a white Gap shirt and ordering a bright orange, distinctly packed with colourings, orange juice.

I picture a scene from *Notting Hill* where I'm Julia Roberts and Louis is Hugh Grant and we bump into each other, so I have to go back to his gadget-crammed house to get changed. Knowing my luck, he'd have a lodger like Spike with a hideous t-shirt I'd have to wear.

Louis, however, is the sort of person who looks über cool in everything he wears or does and I'm getting a case of serious stalker yearning. He's been nothing but charming. He bought my shirt-threatening juice, my chicken coronation on granary (which is another no-no for anything white) and lets me ramble without looking bored. He's tall (six feet six – I asked), dark and handsome: a typical Mills & Boon hero.

As we talk techie, he's like a walking gadget dictionary – a gadgetionary. I thought he'd be worth giving up a lunch break for, but never imagined the internet would house someone like him.

I'm thinking things couldn't get any better, when in walks Miss Blonde Supermodel from ReadyEddie's Aviator. I know I have nothing to worry about because she's already spoken for, but Louis' eyes almost pop out. It would be funny if not so depressing. She smiles at him provocatively and it's as if I don't exist.

I don't know whether to say anything. I feel I should because it's our date, not hers, but I've never been any good as a jealous bunny-boiler, so I continue where we left off. "A friend of mine gave me the grasshopper as a present." I don't see the harm in more lies at this stage as he's not paying any attention to me, but I have to say something. And something I know he'd be interested in.

"Yes?" he says, but still isn't looking in my direction.

I should be pleased because at least he's listening. "Yes, it was hilarious. Don't you think?"

"Uh huh."

I need to up the ante. Supermodels are famous for being nice but dim. Surely Louis is above all that 'looks' stuff, but I see his expression intensify and realise he's not.

And he can't have missed the rings on her left hand. The engagement ring's stone is bigger than the rock of Gibraltar, but it doesn't seem to be stopping her either.

I can't watch. It's like a scene in a movie when two star-crossed lovers meet for the first time and you know they are destined to be with each other.

It's Mr Supermodel I feel sorry for. And, if I'm honest, myself. I've only known Louis a matter of minutes, but I like him. Really like.

Feeling like a right lemon, I quickly finish my lunch while they're still staring at each other. Although I know I'm talking to a brick wall, I try nonetheless.

"I'd better return to work."

"Huh?" He's still facing her, with his back to me.

"Work. I have to go."

He reluctantly turns round, leaving Miss BS to order her lunch. His is still untouched. Anticipating an 'I'm sorry, I'm being so rude', and quietly hoping for an added, 'She's just eye candy. You have depth. It's you I'd rather be with', I know I'm going to be disappointed.

"Sure," is all I get, and he turns away from me.

If I had any drink left, I'd be sorely tempted to pour it over his head, but I'm not that much of a drama queen, even for someone as hot as him.

Needless to say, I can see there's no point in me staying any longer, so I leg it. One good thing to come out of it is that he bought me lunch, and I've got an article that's going to be a bit of fun. Plus if I get it done I won't have to work for a third Saturday in a row.

What did I learn from this lunchtime? Yes, that's right. Today was a lunch date. L2 is a stunner. Sadly just from the neck upwards. And what was above the neck was easily turned. So she was drop dead, but she's also married, and that didn't stop either of them. If we single girls are having trouble finding a single guy we like and who likes us, then double that if they're quite happy to date women who are already taken.

And what's to say L2 isn't married himself? Why is it that ninety-nine-point-nine per cent of married women wear a ring (or in this instance, two – the engagement ring probably worth the same as my house) and yet it's perfectly fine for men to not wear a ring? Isn't it a little sexist in these days of equality? What does it say about a woman who insists her new husband wear one? That said, statistics of married women having affairs are startling, and why do we think it's worse for the wife to be the guilty party? If a man has lots of women in tow, he's a stud, whereas we all know what is thought of the woman if she has more than one man.

So, today's episode proves that attraction doesn't stop just because you're wearing a token of your partner's affection. Who's to know that their affection isn't being sought elsewhere?

Apart from the free lunch (who said that it doesn't exist?), we did have a fun conversation about technology and have a wind-up grasshopper in common (review to follow next month when normality – not necessarily sanity – resumes) and he was a funny guy. It's just a shame I became invisible once Mrs Supermodel appeared on the scene.

Other than being superficial, L2 is a real catch (typical tall, dark and handsome) and if he is single then he'd make someone a great husband – but don't expect him to wear your ring, or if he does, to still be wearing it when another Mrs S catches his eye.

Thank you for your feedback on this column. While it was an unexpected project, it has been an enlightening experience and one that appears to strike a chord with you. There are tales of woe, and others of triumph, but the ones in between provide hope that there are many normal men out there for us (dare I say 'normal'?) girls in here.

So, today's two items ticked on my 'dater's shopping list': Don't – let your head rule your heart and Do – watch out for a suntan circle on his left hand. I remember that from an old episode of Home & Away; *Donald Fisher's daughter Bobby, and I visualise their conversation – I have a better memory than I thought... for the important things, clearly.*

With fresh cup of tea in hand, a little disappointment in my heart and article safely in William's tray (he didn't look up – just said a quiet "thanks"), I crack on with answering tallgirlnn1 messages. I'm surprised to see one from Louis. I read it and burst out laughing.

Where did you disappear to? I thought we were getting on well. Is he serious? I run it all through my head again. Could they have known each other already and were just friends? Nah. That was lust, pure and simple.

I press the black 'X', which deletes the message and the next one pops open. It's from SoftieBear checking we're still on for three p.m. tomorrow. I reply that I am.

QuincyJ says he may have to postpone as he may have to stay in Derbyshire and travel down on Tuesday, but he'll let me know. I'm keeping everything crossed.

There are three left and they're all new. Yay. The first is KromerG (Garth). He's a chatty little soul and his profile looks like he could be fun, but I know from recent experience that looks can be deceptive. Still, I like to be optimistic and reply equally heartily.

Next up is ScotInNorthants. Innes lists the Shipman's Public Inn on the Drapery as his 'second home'. I Google it and see it's one of the few Scottish pubs in the town. It's also reported to be haunted, which will at least make for an interesting conversation.

I reply and suggest it as a meeting place. Apart from The Moon on the Square and Chicago's, I've never been in any of the pubs around the Drapery/Market Square and this one sounds like fun.

Last but not least is VABellinge. I assume his initials are V and A and he lives in Bellinge, and I'm right. Vance says it's a great place to live and I'm delighted. Despite living in the town for a number of years, I've never really been there and it's so easy to be swayed by the media (although I should know better).

By the time I'm ready to leave the office, KromerG and Innes have replied. Dates are therefore set for Thursday and Friday respectively. I'm hoping to slot Vance in for Saturday, so email him again saying it's the only evening I have free (which is true). It's a bit forward (and emailing twice borders on stalkerish), but it's a popular night and I have to see someone, and what would be better than to see Bellinge on a busy night. Now, where did I put my body armour?

Donna's so engrossed in her new project that she's forgotten all about my lunch date, so I pop over to see her.

"Are you having fun?"

"Oh, yes," she gushes, "it's amazing the differences in price. I'm so glad William gave me this task."

"And me mine, kind of."

"Ah yes, Lunch Boy. How did it go?"

"You're busy, so how about you go on to the network and read my article if you want a break. I've put a hard copy in William's tray as usual."

"I've always thought that's funny."

"What?"

"That you're the only one he asks for the hard copy of."

"What?" I say, recalling my solitary file.

Donna nods.

"Are you sure?"

She nods again. "Do you see anyone else trailing into his office, paperwork in hand, early afternoon day in day out?"

"Now you come to mention it… Maybe he finds more mistakes with mine?"

"Do the published versions look very different?"

"No, not usually."

"Well then."

"But there must be some explanation."

"Of course there is."

"What?"

"Doh."

"What do you mean, 'Doh'?"

"Remember the mug incident this morning?"

"Yes…"

"Izzy. Sometimes you can be so thick." Pot, kettle, black. "He's got the hots for you."

"You keep saying that, but it's ridiculous."

"Why else would he do what he does?"

"He doesn't trust me."

"Think about it. William's got a crush all right, but it's not on Janine."

I shake my head, but it does make sense. I've never thought of him in that way, but he has shown a more vulnerable side to himself lately and I must admit, it's kind of sweet.

"No, Donna, can't go there. He's the boss. And he's… he's William. No, definitely not."

"Methinks the lady doth."

"I'm going now. Get ready for the next date."

"Which is…" She looks at the clock. "In about twenty hours' time."

I don't have an answer, or another excuse. "See you Monday."

She looks suddenly miserable.

"What?"

"Am I not seeing you over the weekend?"

"I thought you were busy with your speed-dating guys?"

"Not really. Saw Walter last night…"

"Did you? You didn't say. How did it go?"

A shake of her head says it all.

"And of course there's still Duncan. He'll be a breath of fresh air compared with Mike the Slob."

"He's not that bad."

"Donna!"

"But his heart's in the right place."

"And it's covered in lard."

That sets her giggling and it's lovely to see her happy again. If she and Duncan are meant to be then I will truly be happy for them both. I'll keep telling myself that.

Chapter 20 – Bear at Abington Park

I'm pretty pleased with myself when I wake up. Last night I watched two DVDs back to back and only munched my way through a small bag of popcorn. I was also in bed by ten and that's pretty good for me.

I set a load of washing going, do the washing-up, and have a shower. I pay homage to my combi-boiler on a daily basis as it pumps out ready-to-roll piping hot water (eventually) whenever I want it.

Wrapped in a cosy dressing gown, purple of course, I'm about to make a cup of tea when I realise the milk's past its due date. I open the top, sniff and recoil. I lift the washing-up bowl (there's nothing worse that its underside smelling) and tip the milk down the sink. I use the word 'tip' loosely. I swill the remnants away, wash out the empty plastic bottle and leave it to drain.

Fortunately my local store is a three-minute walk away (roughly, I'm not sad enough to time it), so I get dressed and take enough cash to buy some milk, bread and a paper. I never get why the weekend papers are so much more expensive than the daily ones – the tabloids usually look the same.

Today there's a free DVD of *No One Knows* with the *Guardian*, which I'm tempted to get despite already having the film on my shelves. I buy it with the excuse of being interested in the Arts Review (which I am, I've still not forgotten that I'd like to write a book someday) and decide to send the DVD to a friend in Germany.

I'm just walking out of the shop when I see Ursula locking her car on the opposite side of the road.

"Morning."

"Hi, Izzy."

She looks knackered. "You look well, Ursula."

"Thanks. Bit tired."

"Late night?"

"You could say that."

I can tell by her smile there's gossip to be had.

"Yes?"

"Saw Nick."

Her smirk says everything. I don't need to ask, but I can't resist. "And it went well."

"Kind of… on my way back from his house."

"Good girl. So Zeek's out of the picture then."

"Seeing him tomorrow night."

"Ursula!"

"I know, but I'm waning. I really like Nick. He's not as quiet as he seems." The smirk returns.

"Too much information."

"Zeek was cute, but…"

"He's no Nick."

"Indeed. And you?"

"Ticking over. I'm meeting a friend shortly, so I'd better go."

"Have a nice time. I'll no doubt see you soon."

I'm glad I don't have to explain (lie). June and normality, here I come.

The first thing that gets me about SoftieBear is that he's tiny. He can't be more than five feet and his dog is up to his hips. She is gorgeous. I love dogs anyway and she's the one I'd want to put in my bag and take home. She's obviously too big, but I'd still try.

Abington Park's usually full of squirrels, so I can imagine SoftieBear being pulled over if his dog decided to chase one. For someone so short, he's pretty skinny. Nowhere near Lawrence proportions, but too thin for my liking.

Another thing that strikes me is his lack of confidence. A lot of small men I've met have been larger than life to make up for it. Softie has bright ginger hair with equally loud eyebrows that meet in the middle, and nearly as much hair as his dog.

As they walk towards me I stifle a laugh as they both have bow legs. They make a fine pair, like a Queen Anne table. From the way he's talking to his dog, he's an animal lover, so that's mega brownie points.

He introduces himself as Bear Patrick, so I call him Patrick, assuming he'd done the Bond, James thing, but he says, "No, my first name's Bear." I wonder what kind of parents called their son Bear, but remember there's a TV presenter called Bear. At least this Bear's surname isn't Paddington or Rupert – now that would be funny.

"Is it really your name?" I ask stupidly.

He rolls his eyes, pauses, then bursts out laughing, so I relax.

"Sorry, I get asked so often. No, it's not. I'm Edward, but I've been called Bear since I was a baby. I only use Edward at work, for new clients, and so on."

"Oh…" is all I can think of saying, but I'm relieved he's got a sense of humour. This is the third Ed I'll have met by the end of the month. He's nothing like ReadyEddie and, I suspect, worlds away from EddieG.

The fine spell we've been having appears to be at an end as dark clouds loom overhead.

"Sod's law, isn't it?" I say, as I look skywards.

"It's just water."

Another brownie point: he's glass half full.

"Doesn't your dog mind?"

"Sheba? No, she's not bothered. Good as gold."

When she hears her name, she nudges his hand with her nose and I melt. If Duncan and she were paired, I'd have trouble concentrating, but I have to admit Edward does nothing for me. If someone could bottle chemistry they'd make a fortune. Despite the obvious shortcomings (pardon the pun), there's no spark.

"Hello?"

"Sorry, miles away. She is lovely, isn't she?"

"I've not had her long, but we've bonded so well."

"I can tell. What's she like when you wash her?"

"Again, she loves it. We went to Hunstanton the other day and she was in and out of the water."

"You're lucky. We had dogs when I was growing up and they'd refuse to go out when it was raining, tolerated the bath, and preferred the sand and other dogs to the water." I then spot there's no sign of a lead. "And she doesn't run away?"

"No. I obviously put her on a lead…" he pats his jacket's left pocket, "when we're in the street, but she never goes far."

We walk round the top half of the park, which is packed, mainly with other dog walkers.

And we have a wonderful time. He's easy to talk to and so funny. As we make a fuss over other dogs, we're oblivious to what's about to happen.

It starts to bucket and we run towards the bandstand for shelter. It's soon crammed. A teenage couple stands right next to us, and we can't help staring as they lock lips. The rain's continuous and so is the kiss. I look at my mobile's clock.

"Do you have to go?" Edward asks, and I'm tempted to say no, but can't see any point in going round the park again, especially not in this weather.

"Sorry, but I ought to."

"Oh, sure." He looks rather dejected and I look down at Sheba who's wearing a similar expression. They're so suited it's scary, and I wonder whether he needs another female in his life when this one loves him so much already.

Being surrounded by people, neither of us makes any reference to being on a date, but just say we'll see each other soon, and then I make a dash for the car. I was going to walk, but by the time I'd left the shop after seeing Ursula and put away the dishes I didn't have time, and I'm glad for that now. Like Edward, I think 'it's only water', but when you're soaked through and it takes forever against a radiator to get warm, it's not much fun.

I drip on the upholstery as I get in the car and whack the heating up to full blast. An old parking ticket flies off the dashboard and flutters to the floor.

I'm about to start the engine when there's a knock on the window. I half expect it to be Edward, but it's a woman of about seventy. I zip down the window. "Hello?"

"Hello, dear."

I wait for her to say something else, but she seems somewhat lost. The rain's eased off. It's still spitting, but it doesn't seem to bother her.

"Can I help you?"

"Are you that girl from the paper?"

"Possibly."

209

"The one who's going on all those rendezvous?"

I whisper, "I am."

"I saw you in the park with a man, was he one of them?"

"I can't say."

"I bet he was."

"I'm not at liberty…" I crack like crazy paving. "Please don't say anything to him. It's supposed to be secret."

Her eyes widen excitedly. "Like an undercover operation?"

"Sort of."

"I think you're very brave."

"Really?"

"Oh yes, dear."

"Thank you. And thank you for reading my column."

"I've only been reading them since you've been doing these ones. It's much more interesting than all that high-tech gismo mumbo jumbo."

"Thank you." I think.

"My grandson's got one of those little computer things… a top something…"

"Laptop?"

"Yes, a laptop. And he said he's going to set up a page for me with my details on it, so I can do what you're doing."

"A dating profile?"

"Yes."

"Wow."

"I've been on my own, you see, for a little while and he thinks I'm lonely and sometimes I am. I have my garden, the bridge club, the salsa lessons, swimming…"

"My goodness. Do you not meet men when you're out doing all this?"

"Yes, dear, but they're so old. I don't want someone my age. Oh no, they're too fuddy duddy."

"Will you let me know how you get on?"

"Really? You want to know?"

"Please. I don't think I'll stop writing about online dating just because I've done the month. Not for a while anyway. I've had so much feedback that it's obviously something people are interested in. And I'd especially love to know how the… er, different age groups get on."

"The old and wrinklies."

"I wouldn't put it like that. Besides, you certainly sound far more active than even people my age."

"I have to stay active. Can't sit and rot, can I?"

"It doesn't sound like you have time to sit, and good on you. I only hope I'm as sprightly."

"Keeps the brain going too. Better get on. My daughter-in-law and grandson have gone on with Bertie, that's their dog, but I had to stop and say something."

"I'm very flattered you did."

"My pleasure. It's not every day I see someone famous."

"But I'm not…"

She looks towards the bottom section of the park and waves. "Coming!" she yells then turns back to me. "Better go. Got some catching up to do. Bye, dear."

"Bye and thank…" but she's gone, striding down the path like she's on a mission. Just watching her makes me tired.

Even though I could murder an early night, Donna and I have arranged to meet at Chicago's at nine, so I've got a few hours to kill. I start the car and wonder what I'm going to do. I've not read the paper yet, so that sounds great, alongside a bath and… no ice cream. A quick stop to Morrison's is called for.

As I head in that direction, I think of what Mrs Setting Up a Profile to Find a Toy Boy said. Me, famous? I burst out laughing, much to the curiosity of the driver who's pulled up next to me at the lights.

211

Chapter 21 – Callum at Delapré Park

After a fantastic night out with Donna, leading to a three a.m. turn-in, I'm up at nine and am knackered. I'm supposed to be meeting Callum at eleven, so don't have much time to get ready.

We've not said anything about lunch, although I'm not hungry having had the ice cream for lunch yesterday and a kebab midnight snack with a burger buster meal in between. Donna, you'd think, would be mortified, but she matched me mouthful for mouthful for the last two and won hands down. I'm such a lightweight.

I decide on a couple of slices of toast to keep me going. Delapré Park isn't huge, but if we get on well and do two laps, the sound of my rumbling stomach probably wouldn't win him over.

Callum's standing by his vehicle when I pull into the car park, and he's exactly how I imagine a cloud spirit to look. He has pre-*About a Boy* Hugh Grant floppy hair and brown corduroys, brown loafers and a teacher-style jacket. The vehicle is something else I've always fancied getting: a pale blue VW camper. It's the Scooby Doo model and so cute.

He grins and shows smoker's teeth. I then notice the fag in his hand and am glad we're outdoors. I dated a smoker in my early twenties and it was, as they say, like kissing an ashtray – I don't want to go through that again.

I'm still feeling jaded from last night and know I'm not going to be my usually chatty self, but manage to utter an enthusiastic, "Hi."

"Are you fit?"

I feel far from it, but say, "I am," and we walk towards the park.

"Do you want to go clockwise or anticlockwise?"

Does it matter? "I don't mind. Surprise me."

"Okay," he says cheerfully, and it's clear he's chosen anticlockwise as we head for the right-hand bottom corner.

We haven't got very far when he stops. "Bugger."

"Forgotten something?"

"Yes, in the car."

"Shall I wait here?"

"May as well. Won't be a second."

I watch him return to the camper and open the boot. He pulls out what looks like a suitcase and blanket, then slams the boot shut before walking back towards me. As he gets closer I see the suitcase is a picnic basket, and I'm glad I only had toast for breakfast.

"That looks nice."

"A few things I threw together."

"Isn't it a bit early for lunch?"

"Brunch?"

"Sounds good to me." Despite my initial reservations, I'm warming to the guy.

We get to the top and he stops again, turns and looks at the bottom of the hill and Delapre Abbey. "This is the spot, perfect." He lays the blanket on the ground, putting the basket in the middle, and we sit on either side.

Before he opens the basket, he lies flat on his back and looks up at the sky. He's silent for a minute then says, "Wow!"

"Wow?" I say.

"Look at the sky and tell me what you see."

I played this game when I was five and feel a bit old for it now, but do it to please him, although I stay seated and look up.

"I see two lines, like a vapour trail."

"Yes, but what do you see?"

"A race track? Vertebrae? Heart monitor?"

"Oh, no, it's far more exciting than that. It signifies parallel worlds."

"Sorry?"

"Oh yes." He's getting quite excited. "One line signifies everything that's wrong with the world and the other, everything that's right."

I can't see it myself, but give him an agreeable murmur and nod.

"You see where they run in sync? That's the times when there's no hardship, no wars, but the lines soon wobble or veer apart and that's when there's…"

"Hardship and war."

He claps his hands. "You get it."

I don't at all, but give him another nod. In fact I can't ever remember a time when the world was as he describes. Right from Adam and Eve there's been conflict and hardship and if there's any world that's trouble-free, then Callum's certainly living in it. I watch him as he unpacks the crockery. The food looks amazing.

"It must be very frustrating then for you to watch all the bad news on TV."

"I don't own a TV."

"Online then?"

"Don't have a computer either."

"Then how did you contact me?"

"My kid brother. He thought it was a good idea." Which implies he doesn't, but I don't say as much. "I don't have a mobile either. They fry your brain, you know." I think his brain wouldn't stand a chance, mobile or no mobile. "Why would you want any form of man-made technology when you can get every fulfilment from nature?"

"Nature is amazing," I concede.

"Oh yes, you see…" He loses me after that although I do pick up "…the main issues associated with meeting the challenges of international development, in the context of changing global, political and economic circumstances."

When he's finished, I'm still none the wiser, but say, "Wow," again, which pleases him. "Where did you learn all that?"

"BA / BSc (Hons) Environmental Studies. University of Hertfordshire. Got a First."

"Gosh," I reply lamely. I don't know what to say after that, so pretend to cloud watch, *um*ing and *ah*ing as they drift by. I rack my brains for something else and reckon he must at least read newspapers, so I ask him who he thinks will win the next election.

"I don't know. I don't follow politics."

"But doesn't a change in government affect environmental issues?"

"Probably, but they're as bad as each other." He pauses. "What?"

"Sorry. I find it amazing that you can spout so much, and yet you don't keep up with the everyday."

"Spout?"

"I'm sorry. I didn't mean…"

He bolts upright. "Spout!" I watch him as he packs up the basket, closes it and grabs the handle. He stands up and stomps back down the hill. I pull up the blanket and fold it as I follow him, at the same speed, but purposely keeping a few feet behind.

"Sorry!" I shout after him.

His pace increases; he quickly reaches the camper and unlocks the boot. I catch up with him and silently hand him the blanket.

"Thank you," he says quietly.

"I am sorry."

"I have to go."

"Okay." And there's nothing more to say.

I watch him drive away and wonder how long he'll feel sorry for himself. He'll probably tell his brother to remove his profile unless his in-touch-with-reality sibling persuades him that the right woman is out there for him. She probably is, but she won't be online to see his profile because she'll be too busy lying on her back at the top of a hill somewhere. Those were the days.

At least having a short date gives me time at home before driving to my parents.

I don't have to be in Olney 'til four, so have three and a half hours. The sensible thing to do would be to catch up on my sleep, but I'm not sensible. Instead I curl up on the sofa under a throw and veg out on soup, more toast and two films.

There's ringing in my ears.

When I come to, I realise it's the phone. I go to grab the cordless handset and notice the clock on it says five ten. Urgh. I press the green 'accept' button.

"Hello?"

"Isobel?"

Who else would it be? "Yes, Mum."

"Are you coming over today?"

"I am, but I fell asleep on the sofa."

"Don't be long." And she hangs up.

That's my mum, short (well, five feet six) and sweet (most of the time).

I arrive at their house just before six and Lola runs out to meet me. "Aunt Izzy! Auntie Izzy!"

"Hey, pumpkin."

"I've got a new horse!"

"Really?' When I walk into the house, I expect to see a stuffed animal, Barbie variety or rocking horse, but there's no sign of anything. "Where is it, Lola?'

"Where's what?"

"The horse."

"In the field, of course."

"You've got a *real* horse?"

She nods vehemently.

This makes the theatre seem very tame and I hesitate retrieving it from the boot, but there's no sign of any toys in the spotless lounge, so figure it would be nice for her to have something to play with. I hear voices from the kitchen, so go through, leaving Lola to stare out through the patio doors.

"Ah, there she is."

"Hello, Dad." We hug, then I turn to the others.

Mum's cooking the evening meal while Mark and Ellen lean against the work surface near the dining room.

"Hello, everyone."

They say hello but stay put, engrossed in something.

"Sorry, have I interrupted?"

"No, it's fine," Mark says, before turning to his wife.

"I heard about the horse," I say and add before I can help it, "It's very extravagant."

"Yes, it is." Mark's glaring at Ellen.

"She wanted one," Ellen says.

"But it's far too big for her."

"She'll grow into it."

"In a few years. By then she'll have got bored with it."

"It's an investment."

"A liability."

216

"We've been over this a hundred times."

I feel like I've transmuted into the middle of a war zone, with my parents as onlookers.

"Can you ride, Ellen?" my dad asks.

"Oh, yes. I already have a horse at the stables."

"Two horses?" my mum pipes in.

"Yes," Mark growls.

Dad looks at me and changes the subject. "How's work, Izzy?"

"Good, thanks. The column's going well."

"Mark's been offered a promotion," Ellen butts in.

"That's great," I say, but Mark seems less than chuffed.

"Thanks. Means more travelling."

"Is that bad?" I ask.

"No," Ellen blurts, "we get to go with him on the long hauls."

"That's good," I say sincerely.

"Mmm," Mark says, unconvinced. "So they won't be around to ride the horses."

Ellen's face flushes. "Are we going back to that?"

Mum taps a wooden spoon on the edge of a dish, which successfully kills the conversation.

"I've got something in the car for Lola. Shall I get it?" I offer.

"That sounds lovely, dear," Dad says as he follows me out of the kitchen.

"Mark seems a bit stressed," I say, standing by my car.

"I think they've got money worries."

"So they go and buy a horse?"

"I don't think he's letting on to Ellen."

"But she'll find out, won't she?"

"I gather this promotion will sort it."

"So he works himself to death while she gallivants around the countryside on her thoroughbred."

"I don't think it's a thoroughbred."

"Knowing her..."

"She means well. Anyway, what's this present for little Lola?"

"Oh, yes. I got it from a boot sale last Sunday." I zap the remote and lift the boot.

"Look at that. She'll love it."

"I hope so."

"Shall I?"

"Sure."

Lola's eyes light up as her grandfather brings the box into the lounge. "Wow! Is that for me?"

"It's from your Auntie Isobel."

She looks at me and grins a 'Donna' smile, then rushes over and throws her arms round me. "I love it! I love it!"

Her parents appear from the kitchen. Mark walks over to Lola, kneels beside her and helps her remove the contents.

Ellen, however, stays in the doorway and seems less impressed. "That looks expensive, Isobel."

"Don't worry," I say, "it was from a car boot sale. They're great when you're a bit strapped for cash."

Mark looks at Dad, who shrugs, then at me. I nod and his gaze returns to the theatre.

It's set up in no time and father and daughter are left to do a 'dress rehearsal', so we return to the kitchen, which is full of delicious smells.

"Dinner won't be long," Mum announces.

"Isobel's bought Lola a theatre," Ellen tells her.

"A lovely one," Dad adds.

"A lucky car boot find," I say. "Do we have time to watch their play before dinner?"

"They've got one prepared already?" Mum asks.

"Oh yes, Lola is quite the storyteller," Ellen gushes.

"Of course. Let me turn this down."

There's a 'Ready' from the other room and we wander through.

We're treated to a mini version of Snow White and the Seven Dwarfs, except in this adaptation there are only four dwarfs and they're not particularly small.

A deservedly rapturous round of applause is given when the curtain closes and Lola curtsies while Mark bows.

"I'll dish up," Mum says, and Ellen and I follow her into the kitchen to help, leaving the men to congratulate Lola.

As I take the cutlery and glasses through on a tray to the dining room, the men are discussing finances.

"Dad, I wish you hadn't said anything to Izzy."

"She suspected. It was obvious there was a problem from the way you two were talking."

"I'm going to sort it out."

"Your mother and I can lend you some–"

"No thanks," he says too swiftly. "Sorry, Dad, but it's fine, really. We should never have bought the second H O R S E."

I poke my head round the door and see Lola with a glove puppet on each hand; St George is arguing with the Prince about how best to slay the dragon, which is hiding between two cushions propped up at forty-five degree angles, making a tent-like cave. The pink Princess is lying abandoned by the box. I suspect, like her, the horse is going to be a white elephant.

I return to the kitchen as Ellen and Mum bring through serving dishes.

"Can I help?" I ask.

"Do you want to get the plates?" Ellen suggests.

"Sure," I say, and she smiles.

I fetch six warm dinner plates and serving spoons, by which time the men have joined the others. There's no sign of Lola.

"Where is she?" Ellen asks.

"Still playing dungeons and dragons," Mark replies.

"Shall I get her?" I offer.

"Yes, pl–" Mark starts to say, but Ellen cuts him off.

"Can you leave her for a minute. I've got some news."

All eyes turn to her. I keep my fingers crossed that it's good.

"Lola turns five in August, so I thought that when she goes to school in September, I'd go back to work."

Mark looks as stunned as the rest of us. "Really?"

"Yes. I'll have more time on my hands and…" She looks round the table. Mum and Mark look clueless, but Dad and I guess what she's going to say. "We need the money."

"You know?" Mark asks.

"I guessed by your reaction to Lola's horse and the prospect of your new position."

Mark's about to speak, but she continues. "And we can sell the horse, or both of them. I don't care about them. We're not happy and we should be. I want to do something before it goes too far. You're right. She's not interested in the horse. I bought it so we'd have something to do together, but she's happier playing dress-up and theatre…" She turns to face me. "Thanks, Izzy, by the way, for that. It's lovely."

And I think she means it.

"Is there anything I can do?" I ask. "I don't have much money, but…"

"Thanks, sis, but we'll be fine," Mark says.

"Yes, thanks, Izzy," Ellen adds. "That's settled then. You turn down the promotion, we sell the horses and I go back to work."

Mark goes to speak, but Ellen puts her palm up. "I want to see more of you, not less, and travelling with you would be too disruptive for Lola as she's starting a new school. I could get a secretary job nearby or even at the school. If I'm honest, even being at home while Lola's at nursery is driving me nuts. There are only so many times you can clean the house."

I'm surprised. We all are. Their house is always spotless, but I don't think we'd realised why.

"Okay…" Mark hesitates.

Lola charges in with the pink Princess on her right hand, and runs up to her mother.

"You're going to have to take her off, poppet."

Lola shakes her head.

"But how are you going to eat dinner with Princess on your eating hand?"

"Easy. I'll eat with the other hand."

"Can you do that?"

"Yes, Mummy."

Ellen looks quizzically at me. I shrug, but smile at how I was wrong regarding the Princess, and we all watch Lola sit on her chair and tuck into her child-size chicken roast dinner with an expert left hand. Princess Annabel, as Lola introduces her, oversees the whole operation and is suitably impressed.

After dinner, we're treated to another show. This time it's a mixture of the *Shrek* films, where St George is Shrek (which makes sense as he was after the dragon in the first film), Snow White is the Queen, the Prince is the King, and the Princess and Dragon played themselves (except I think Lola's dragon is male, but I don't suppose he minds).

Again, Lola is magnificent, but it's Mark who surprises me, and I think Ellen's seeing him in a new light.

After much deserved applause, the theatre set is packed away. While Mark heads to the car with their belongings, Ellen fetches Lola's coat then returns to the dining room.

"Time to go home, missy."

"Please, can we staaaaay."

"Sorry, but Daddy has work tomorrow and he's got a big meeting with Uncle Roger, so he has to get lots of sleep."

I've met Mark's boss, and turning down the promotion isn't going to be taken well, but I can see why he wants to. Who wouldn't want to spend more time with a woman like Ellen and a daughter who's going to be a worldwide superstar before she reaches double figures?

"Go kiss Grandma, Grandpa and Auntie Izzy goodnight."

Lola, this time wearing St George on her left hand, walks round the table kissing everyone. As she reaches me, she yawns and sets me off.

"Bed too for Auntie Izzy then," Ellen says.

I nod. "Bit of a late night last night."

"Work or pleasure?" Ellen smiles.

"Definitely pleasure."

"Nothing to do with the article then?"

"No…" I say, hesitantly.

Mark walks into the dining room. "We're set. Ready, munchkin?"

Lola nods a sleepy head as does St George, so Mark picks her up and walks out into the hall, closely followed by Mum and Dad.

I'm about to stand when Ellen says, "I love your new column."

"Thank you." I'm building up quite a fan club. "So you've caught it?"

"We get the paper delivered especially and keep every column."

"Really?"

"Got files of them."

"Wow."

Ellen stands up. "I'd better catch up with the others."

"Ellen."

"Yes?"

"Thanks. For everything. Mark's lucky."

"I'm the lucky one."

We walk out to the hallway where the others are saying their goodbyes. Lola is talking sleepily to St George who's moving slightly, so presumably talking sleepily back to her. It's at times like this that I wonder whether I should have children, but think, nah. I'd have Lola any time, but I'm sure even with someone as cute as her, I'd be happy to give her back eventually. They're only in Bedford; I should see them more often… maybe via the pottery.

"We should see them more often," Dad says as they drive off.

"Great minds think alike," I say.

"They're only in Bedford, after all."

"They have their own lives to lead, Don," Mum says.

"I know, Jane, but I think they struggle sometimes."

"You heard Ellen, she's bored."

"But you also heard her say she wants to spend more time with him."

I go into the lounge to get my bag, say goodbye, and leave them to it.

The drive home is uneventful and as soon as I get in, I make a cup of tea. It's still early, so I sit up in bed, propped by four pillows, and pick up where Elliot and Natasha left off. I get a few pages read before my eyelids droop, so put the bookmark back in, finish my tea and go through to the bathroom.

I see an old woman staring back at me. I used to be quite proud of my wrinkle-free skin, but I spot minor crow's feet around my eyes and a distinct hint of dark circles. Next will be bags and I'm not letting that happen. Even if my life depends upon it.

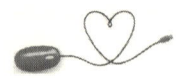

Chapter 22 – Jamie at the White Elephant

What did I learn from the weekend? That sometimes you can judge a book from the cover. E2 was the shortest man I've dated so far and was utterly charming. His dog was beautiful and so devoted.

We had a lovely walk around Abington Park until the heavens opened and we took shelter in the bandstand. Our 'date' was therefore brief, but I would recommend him to any of you petite single girls who would like someone thoughtful, polite, who is a major animal lover.

I also learned that age really is only a number. I met a lovely retired lady who, despite being of some years (I daren't guess as to how many as she reads this column), had far more energy than me.

So that was Saturday. Sunday was a different kettle of fish.

The saying goes that 'simple things please simple minds', but C was not simplistic. He was far too complicated for me – another man living in his own cocoon. He doesn't have a clue what's going on in the world around him, and yet his surroundings are all he seems bothered about.

That said, he was a very generous man. He'd brought a picnic and a blanket, and we walked to a romantic spot at the top of Delapré Park… or it would have been romantic if I hadn't opened my big mouth and put my size eights in it – and off stomped C with uneaten picnic.

Electrical items that many of us take for granted are not owned by C. He has no television, no computer (we have his brother to thank for setting us up) and no mobile phone. C seems like a very intelligent guy, and if you live on Planet C and want to talk about nothing but his cocoon, then he's the man for you.

So, the latest two items ticked on my 'dater's shopping list': Don't speak your mind if it's likely to hurt someone's feelings, even if it's well intended, and Do get to know someone before making your decision.

I'm about to type the nerdy bit of the article when Donna creeps up behind me.

"Morning."

"Ouch."

"Oh dear. Did someone get out of the wrong side of the bed, or the wrong bed?" She laughs.

I turn round.

"Oh dear," she repeats. "I shouldn't probably say this, but you do look awful."

"Thanks, friend."

"I've probably got a serum for your dark circles…"

"And an early night, Doctor Clarke?"

"They have nothing to do with sleep."

"Really?"

"Oh yes. It's all to do with blood capillaries."

"Oh."

"It's caused by a complex interaction between your body and a chemical reaction similar to that which produces bruises."

"Donna Clarke, you never cease to amaze me."

The cheesy grin returns. She peers at the screen, so I turn back to face it. "You're hard at work already," she says.

"I've got a lot to do, so I thought I'd come in early."

"How very conscientious of you. Not trying to score any brownie points?" She looks over in the direction of William's office, which is empty.

"No. I'm not. Lots to do."

"If you say so."

"I do, stirrer. He'll go nuts if he hears you talking about him like that."

"Who?" a voice asks behind me.

I spin round in my chair, nearly hitting William's ankles with my feet. "Oops."

"Morning, ladies. Are we well?"

"Yes, thank you, William," I say.

"Oh yes." Donna beams back. Which reminds me, she went out with Duncan last night and I'm dying to know how it went. I did text her before going to sleep, but had no reply.

William walks to his office, trendy black leather briefcase in hand, and we watch him go before resuming our conversation.

"So, serum?" Donna asks.

"Why not. First though, the goss. Did you get my text last night?"

"Ah, yes. Sorry, I did mean to reply except–"

"You were busy."

She blushes. "Er, yes."

"And how was Auntie Ruth's?"

"Surprisingly busy for a Sunday night. Not as busy as a Friday or Saturday, I would imagine, but…"

"Details, Donna. Give me the juice."

"He collected me…"

"Good."

"I know. He's a real gentleman."

"Does his car smell of animals?"

"No. I was surprised. You'd think, wouldn't you? Seeing as what he does…"

"Donna."

"So anyway, he collects me in his new car…"

I envisage his RAV-4 then twig she said 'new' and is waiting for me to react, which I do, overdramatically. "A new car?"

"Blue BMW Roadster," she replies, emphasising each word.

"Ooooh!"

"I know. He said he wanted something more fun."

"I'm so jealous."

"I'm sorry."

"No, I mean of the car."

"Oh, okay."

"I've seen or heard about my three favourite cars this week and I don't own any of them."

"You will if you become Mrs Stamp."

"Donna! You still on that one?" Mrs Stamp. Sounds like a children's cartoon character.

"Sorry. I'll drop it."

"Thank you."

"But you would look cute…"

I glare.

"I'll shut up now."

"Back to dishing the dirt on date with Duncan please."

She laughs. "So we go to Auntie Ruth's and he's got a space reserved for him. Don't tell me how…"

"Maybe he knows the Richardsons."

"Yes, maybe. So anyway, we park up and there's a queue outside, on a Sunday, but we walk straight in like we're royalty. The bouncer even calls him Duncan. It was so cool. Everyone looking at us."

"I bet. And…"

"He buys me a drink, and we spy a couple who have finished theirs, so nab the seats as soon as they get up. After they've got up obviously, otherwise we'd be sitting on their laps…" She doesn't pause for breath. "And we chat about the speed dating and then about work, and…"

"Hold on. What did you say about work?"

"What I do."

"Shit."

"What?"

"So he also knows what I do?"

"Erm…"

"Donna. I begged you not to say anything."

"He already knew."

"He did? How?"

"From when William took his bird to the vet. The cage had our newspaper at the bottom and he said he saw your face. Quite funny really. Your face all covered in…"

"I get the picture." It had never occurred to me that William's vet could have been Duncan. They live on different sides of town, although William did move house a few months ago when he and his then wife separated. "So Duncan's known for a while."

"A couple of weeks or so."

"Before the speed dating?"

"I suppose so."

"Sneaky devil."

"Why?"

"Because he didn't say anything, did he? He let me waffle on about being a secretary when all along he knew all about the column. Why didn't he say anything?"

"I don't know. Do you think that's why he didn't request you?"

"I don't think so. Besides, he's got the hots for you."

She looks down at her feet and moves her right foot from side to side before patting the carpet, as if stamping out an imaginary cigarette.

"Donna. Next?"

"Let's just say the hours flew and… I don't think I should tell you any more."

"You can't stop now."

"On the way home, he drove past Abington Park. The moon was shining on the water, it was very romantic."

"Sounds idyllic."

"It was lovely. So quiet, especially when he turned the engine off."

"Go on."

"He asked me if I'd mind if he kissed me."

"And you said…"

"Yes please, that would be lovely."

"How sweet."

"Isn't it? He's so lovely. Then we went back to my house and…"

By her grin, I can guess the rest and she changes the subject. "I'd better get to my desk. William will be on the prowl soon. He's not come out for coffee yet or sent Janine over."

"I'm glad you had a good time."

"Really?"

"Of course. I'm happy if you're happy."

"I am."

"And how did you leave things?"

"After breakfast." She giggles.

"No, I mean, you're seeing him again."

"Yes, tonight."

"Oooh. Serious."

"He's got a busy week, so…"

"Look out, Janine's coming."

Donna scuttles back to her desk and Janine walks past with a smile in my direction.

"Morning, Izzy."

"Morning, Janine."

She keeps walking and disappears into the kitchen.

With Donna safely installed at her desk and Janine heading back to her domain with a coffee in each hand, I fetch a drink for Donna and me, and leave hers on her desk. She's on the phone, so just smiles and nods. It sounds like she's progressing well with the glasses project.

I log into the tallgirlnn1 account and am surprised there are only three messages. Having been offline for the weekend, I had hoped for more, but at least they're useful ones.

Much to my relief, QuincyJ has emailed to say the Derbyshire drama has been averted (something very dull, he says) and he'll be there 'by hook or by crook'. I love these old English sayings. I reply that I'm pleased and look forward to seeing him. In fact I'm more than pleased as it would have left me one man short and I would have had to either make up someone or do a general column about 'my experiences so far' and meet two another day.

Vance's message is just to say he's fine for Saturday. He was supposed to be going away, but he's rather skint, so I'm a good excuse to stay. I'm glad I have my uses.

The other is from a guy called UlverTheIrish. It's a quick intro email, as if he's checking I'm still available. Assuming he's Irish, I do a Google search on Irish pubs in Northampton. We agree on Sunday and the Swan and Helmet on Clare Street 'as I've never been' (which is true).

With that done, I'm back to the nerdy bit of the article. I'm finding it more difficult to think of original things today, but reader feedback is coming in thick and fast, so kills a chunk of the morning. I therefore decide to take a different tack and comment on some of them. It's rapidly turning into an agony column, so I email Keith to warn him, but promise to end each piece with a reference to him being the best place to go for real advice and he's pleased.

It's lunchtime before I know it and Donna announces she needs to hit the town and do some research. She has twenty-twenty vision, so I'm the perfect candidate. My glasses are only a few weeks old (bought as a 'treat'), but they're not to know that, are they (she says)?

"Are you just doing glasses or are you covering contact lenses too?"

"Izzy, that's a brilliant idea! It'll be an extra gold star from William. He likes initiative."

That's very true. Anything above and beyond the call of duty is back-patting as far as he's concerned. And after this month, I'll have earned some of that.

She's done a yell.com search and there are over twenty opticians in Northampton. Fortunately only eight are in the town centre, but that's still too many to do in a lunch break, so we agree on two a day with Friday off.

"There's a cross-section of national chains and independents," she says. "I'll be doing the same sort of number online, so that's bound to be plenty. The article's only going to run for a week or so. Are you sure you don't mind coming with me and using up your lunch breaks?"

"Of course not. It'll be fun putting them through their paces."

"Oh yes," she says, rubbing her hands. I can see that, like me with my project, this isn't work to her, but something to get her teeth into.

We start with the nearest two, a national (Vision Express for contact lenses only – me being a glasses customer there) and an independent (for both) in the Grosvenor Centre and they're pretty much the same. The service is good in both, although the independent does feel less clinical, but you can't beat hygiene.

The prices are what you'd expect – I'm as blind as a mole without my glasses and don't go for the Mr Magoo look, so get a quote for ultra-thin. There's a maze of free this and half-price that, and neither of the shops has a price list as such (I suppose because their offers change so often), so we have to memorise the options then plonk on a bench on one of the centre's walkways to jot them down.

When we're done, we pop to a juice bar where Donna orders a mixed veg smoothie (which has never appealed to me, but she assures me is delicious) and I go for a mixed fruit, which looks and tastes gorgeous.

Drinking as we walk, we head back to the office and Donna's looking at the notes.

"I can't believe they're so expensive," she says.

"I have got a ridiculously high prescription."

229

"Yes, I know, but over three hundred pounds and that's including free second frames."

"Which is why they have to last a couple of years or so."

"Two years? That's a hundred and fifty a year."

"I know. A cheapie gym membership."

"Jeez."

She does make me laugh. "But they're essential," I continue. "You've got to look after your eyes."

"I know, but they must play on that, even to some extent."

"The equipment and set-up must cost a bomb."

"Which is why online is so much cheaper."

"Exactly. Lower overheads."

"But probably poorer quality."

"That, Detective Clarke, is what you're going to find out."

"I'm not sure how – I'm not planning on ordering any."

"William must expect you to spend something. Can you get freebies somehow, like I do with my gadgets?"

"I suppose so, however, it wouldn't be an exposé, would it."

"I guess. I don't always give good reviews. Just as well you're not doing the world of laser surgery."

Her eyes widen.

"You'd not thought of that?"

"Ooh, no. It's got to be covered, hasn't it?"

"It *is* very popular."

"So why spend three hundred pounds on glasses when you could get your eyes lasered and it's sorted for the rest of your life?"

"Is it, though?"

"What?"

"Forever."

"I don't know. There's more to this than meets the…"

"Ha, ha. Also…"

"There's more?"

"How do you know by going to the cheapest place for the lasering, like the adverts on TV, that you're going to get trouble-free vision? Surely it's better to go somewhere private. I used to work with someone who got it done on the cheap and had real trouble."

Donna screws up her face. "Really?"

"Yes. It wasn't pleasant."

"Ew."

"Exactly. So it pays to not mess with your eyes. I'd have it done if it was a hundred per cent, but no procedure is that safe."

"Mmm." I can almost hear her cogs whirring.

We arrive back at work and Mike's on duty. Donna walks slightly ahead of me and I catch a half smile as she turns towards him. I give her a gentle shove and she looks forward.

As we walk up the stairs to the main reception, I say, "You're not over him, are you?"

"I am."

"Then what was all that about?"

"Just being friendly."

That's her trouble, she can't be anything but. And it's why everyone's mad about her.

Marion's on the phone. She's moaning about something or someone, so we're grateful to escape it coming in our direction.

We've not been back at our desks long when Donna springs over, waving a piece of paper in her hand. "Look at this!"

"What?"

She plonks it on my desk and I see it's a printout from the Three Shires and she continues talking. "It says 'Excimer laser surgery (photo refractive keratectomy or PRK) involves using a laser, which is computer-controlled to reshape the cornea… The surgery is carried out by a consultant ophthalmologist and is designed to treat imperfect vision.'"

As she speaks, I'm reading the article and she's relaying it word for word, with the exception of 'the clear surface of the eye in front of the pupil' as she knows that I know what a cornea is, and 'refractive errors' because 'imperfect vision' speaks for itself.

"Donna?"

"Yes, Izzy."

"Has anyone ever told you that you have photographic memory?"

"Huh?"

"You've just repeated this word for word without looking at the text."

"It's a skill I have," she says proudly.

"But you could do so much with it."

"I suppose so."

"Donna, you could do anything you wanted to. You could be an actress…"

"I'm doing what I want to do."

"Really?"

"I love my job. Can't imagine doing anything else." And she can't lie.

I hand her back the piece of paper and she scuttles off to her desk. I spend the afternoon replying to reader emails, including two from irate men who think they've met me, which I assure them I haven't (if I had, they'd have emailed tallgirlnn1, wouldn't they?).

A skim of tallgirlnn1 reveals two messages: one from UlverTheIrish saying Sunday is fine. He may be late as he's away for the weekend, but he'll be there for eight thirty. I'm quite pleased as it'll mean a quick escape if things don't go well. I've learned over the past three weeks (has it been that long already?) that early dates aren't wise if I need an 'I have work tomorrow' excuse, so eight thirty's great and I reply accordingly.

The other is from a weirdo called WellHung69. I know what's coming (pardon the pun) as soon as I see his profile name and, sure enough, he lists everything he'd like to do to me. I make a mental note for future reference elsewhere, but use the familiar block option and don't even bother with an automated 'Thanks, but no thanks'.

I've just pressed the block button when my Outlook email pings and I switch over to see a message from William. I expect it to be another round robin, but it's addressed solely to me, and it's headed 'tallgirlnn1 project'. I anticipate a Marion-style ear bashing, but I'm pleasantly surprised to see a one-liner, *Thanks for today's piece. How's it all going?* I think he'd be able to tell from my articles, but it's nice that he's taken an interest, so I draft a slightly longer reply.

Hi, William. Thanks for your email. I think it's going well, thank you. I've received mostly positive reader feedback and it's been a very interesting project. Thank you for the opportunity. Perhaps we could have a discussion at month-end and see where, if anywhere, it should be taken from there.

I delete the gushy 'Thank you for the opportunity' and click on 'send'. I gaze into his office, but he's on the phone. I keep watching for a few seconds and see him look at his screen; he then glances over at me and smiles. I immediately look down at my keyboard with what I hope is an engrossed expression, but I know he saw me, and I feel myself blushing. It's something I can't help doing, and it happens rarely, but when I do, I know I go bright red.

There's one solution: kitchen – cup of tea.

As I flick on the kettle, Donna comes rushing in. "I've got an appointment with Three Shires!"

"To have a chat about laser surgery?"

She nods.

"And they don't mind?"

"They won't, no."

"That's good."

"They won't because you'll be coming with me."

"Oh?"

"As a potential patient."

"Erm…"

"William said it's okay. Sorry, I was too excited."

"No, it's fine. When's it set for?"

"Ten tomorrow morning."

"Wow, that's quick."

"I said we wanted the best."

"I would."

"Great, thanks. Can't stop." And with that, she disappears back to her desk.

I make her a coffee and drop it off. She's on the phone again talking lotions and potions, so I don't stop.

By the time I've replied to more reader emails, it's nearly time to go home. Donna's on the phone again and it looks like it's going to be a long one, that's why I send her an email saying I'll see her in the morning and hope she enjoys date two with Hunky Dunky.

The White Elephant's in between casual and smart so I opt for blue Levi 501s and a plain black top. A pair of black slip-on shoes get their first airing for a while and I pull my black Levi jacket off one of the hooks in the hall on the way out.

We've arranged to meet outside. When I get there just before eight, QuincyJ's already there. Although wearing quite casual clothes, he looks ultra-smart and I can tell he has money.

We exchange greetings and he opens the door for me and, unlike Dodge, waits until I've gone through. I thank him and walk towards the bar.

"Call me Jamie, by the way. What would you like to drink, Izzy?"

I must look puzzled trying to connect QuincyJ to Jamie because he explains. "I'm a Quincy Jones fan and the J is for Jamie too."

"Nice. I'd love a Southern Comfort and lemonade with a little ice, if I may."

"Of course you may." A great start.

A barman's waiting so Jamie requests mine, adding a pint of Guinness for himself. When the drinks are ready, he pays with a crisp twenty-pound note and slides the change into his, I would guess, designer jeans pocket. At this stage, I can't look at the label on his backside without being obvious. Something to look forward to.

I pick a discreet corner table away from the speakers and other clientele. So I can people watch, I sit facing the bar and he sits to my left so he doesn't have to watch people surfacing from the toilets, a wise move.

I start the conversation. "So how long have you worked down here?"

"A couple of months."

"And you work in the town centre?"

"I do. For a small practice law firm, but it's very up and coming. They headhunted me and it's working out well so far." For anyone else I'd have said he was bragging, but I get the impression he's not like that.

"That's great. It's so important to have a job you like."

"And what do you do?"

"I'm a secretary for a training company."

"Really? What sort of training?"

"Business management, that kind of thing."

"Great. We're looking for training courses for our executives. What's your work number?"

I tell him and he taps it into his BlackBerry. I will him not to try it as I've given him our old fax number at the paper. Thankfully, he puts his device back in his pocket and takes a sip of his drink. He's got a bit of froth on his upper lip, so I point it out to him, not anticipating what would happen next.

"You women are all alike! Point out our failings whenever you can."

I say, "Hold on a second," but he storms off to the gents.

By rights, I should leave, but he's back before I've decided.

"I'm so sorry. I shouldn't have said that. I had a ridiculously late night last night after a horrendous journey down the M1."

"Okay." I'm glad this is work, as I don't do short-tempered.

He flicks back a stray lock of dark mousey hair and plays with the collar on his blue Ralph Lauren polo shirt. He smiles, but I can tell this isn't over.

He insists on buying the second round too, which I accept to keep the peace, and he goes to the bar to place the order, returning a few seconds later. "They're bringing them over, letting the Guinness settle."

We make polite, but strained, conversation.

A young barmaid brings the drinks over, putting mine in front of me first, then with a quivering hand putting his down. I get the impression she recognises him.

"What do you call that?" he barks.

"You ordered a pint of Guinness?" she squeaks.

"It looks like foam to me, get me a fresh one."

I'm astounded but watch her pick up the glass and return to the bar. We've not spoken a word by the time she returns.

The original looked pretty good to me, but if I had to say there was a difference, the replacement appears to have a few millimetres less white on it.

"That's better," he mumbles.

"Thank you," I say in a normal tone to the barmaid, who smiles weakly at me before returning to the bar.

He reminds me of Dodge though without the wolf's clothing.

I can't help speaking. "Do you always get personal service?"

"I like to get my way."

I'm tempted to say something sarcastic, but remember Delapré Park and resist. "So, the emergency's averted."

"Oh, that. Yes. My wife started a new job today."

"Your… wife?"

"She wanted me to be around. What's the big deal?"

He's a walking cliché: under the thumb at home, so has to be in charge elsewhere. "Oh, nothing," I say. "I'm relieved it wasn't a real emergency."

He grunts and takes a very ungentlemanly swig of his Guinness, but I swiftly find out there's very little about him that is gentlemanly.

Another silence is followed by another swig, so I drink mine quickly, though more ladylike. We're both nearly finished when he announces another trip to the gents and I see this as my cue to do a runner.

"Okay," I say, smile sweetly and watch him walk away, no Levi tag on this one. Delving around in my bag, I fish out my trusty pen and paper and write out a note.

Had to go. I've left my husband in charge of our sixteen offspring.

That should do the trick.

236

Chapter 23 – Jake at the Four Pears

What did I learn from last night? That a wolf can appear in sheep's or wolf's clothing. The jacket on this particular book was probably designer-made, but the inside pages were substandard and I would vote to reject the whole thing and return it to the publisher for pulping. After all, he thinks he's God's gift, so why not make him one?

Q (sadly nowhere near the gentleman of the Bond movies) is a tall man with a very short temper. I get the impression he's under the thumb at home (I didn't know he was married when we booked the 'date') as he treats other women appallingly.

First impressions were impeccable – door opening, drink buying, great manners – but as soon as something didn't go his way, he bellowed his objections about all things female to me and a poor barmaid. Needless to say, I scarpered at the first opportunity. Two free drinks and an early night. Thank you very much, Q.

I've received some more feedback (thank you everyone) on this column and wanted to share…

I get thus far and remember the appointment at the Three Shires. It's twenty-five to now. Donna's on the phone, so I sidle up to her desk and wait until she's finished.

"So, are you ready for our ten o'clock?"

"Sorry, Izzy, I meant to tell you. There's no need."

"Oh?"

"I've cancelled – Duncan had it done there."

"Okay. No… problem."

Since my last chat with Donna, I'd been giving her and Duncan a lot of thought, and come to the conclusion it's her being with someone that I'm jealous of, not who she's seeing. He isn't the one for me and I'm clearly not the person for him so, as QuincyJ put it, what's the big deal?

"I had an interesting chat with Ursula last night," I say, pointing towards the kitchen.

Donna nods and we walk. "Ursula?"

"My next-door neighbour. She was on the speed dating…"

"Oh, yes."

"She said her father used to tell her off for putting herself down – for telling your brain a negative thought so you believe it."

"Yes! Self-belief begins with self-worth. It's a well-known mental health mantra."

Donna, I realise, has so many layers that she'd win a vegetable competition hands down. Pity the men before Duncan hadn't realised what a gem they'd had. I smile at the unintended lettuce pun.

"So tell me more about Duncan's eyes." Before she has a chance to open her mouth, I add, "The surgery. I know they're brown."

"Couldn't you just… his surgery, yes."

I make the drinks and, as she watches me, she tells me everything he told her about the process in eye-popping gory detail. This is one occasion where I curse her photographic memory. I stare into her mug of Nescafé granules and sugar and imagine an eye staring back at me. It screams for help as I pour on the water, and is no more as I whisk the spoon.

We talk as we walk back to our desks, hovering by mine as she describes the removal of the bandages. I don't remember there being any bandages when I've learned about such procedures on the TV or radio, so expect some Clarke artistic licence is at play of Elephant Man proportions.

I crack on with the article and finish it with…

Today's two ticks on the 'shopping list': Don't – be swayed by charm and money and Do – stand up for yourself. If your date treats you anything less than as an equal, you have every right to stand up to him (her). If he's (she's) not worthy of you then feel free to walk.

I'm feeling more and more like Aunt Izzy every article. Watch out, Keith… no, it's fine. Your job is safe. I'm sticking to my gadgets. They can't talk back. Or if they do, they have an 'off' button.

There are no messages on NorthantsDating, so I blitz my Outlook emails. I like to keep my inbox clear, so I know I've dealt with everything that's come in. I create a new folder for 'tallgirlnn1' in Archive and drag all the relevant emails in there.

This'll keep our IT department happy – they keep reminding us to declutter the server. And if IT is happy, William's happy.

I double-check the article and print it off. I wonder why I bother, given his 'clear desk' and 'paperless office' mantra, which is hilarious considering what we do.

With papers in hand, I walk to William's office. Janine's in there with him, so I wait outside, but he beckons me. I nod and go in, holding up the article to show him what's about to go in the tray.

They stop talking as I lay the sheets on top of some very colourful bar charts.

"Thanks, Isobel."

Before I can answer, I yawn like a lion and clamp my hand to my mouth in a vain attempt to stop. Janine smiles sympathetically.

"Late night, Isobel?" William asks.

"A few, yes."

"Is it getting too much for you?"

"It's fine. Besides, I'm on the home straight."

"Let me know."

"Thanks, but no need."

"Well…"

"Yes. Thanks. Bye, Janine." She winks at me and I make a rapid exit, closing the door behind me.

I look at the clock and it's just gone one, so I hover around Donna's desk until she comes off the phone. "Next two opticians?"

"That would be great. Are you sure you don't mind?"

"Of course not. This open-plan spying is fun."

"It's helping me no end. I'm a bit stuck on the online stuff. I've found a fair amount, but I'm sure you being the technology expert…"

"No problem. Leave it with me. I'll have a look when we get back."

We plan to hit the pedestrian area, Abington Street, again aiming for a national optician and an independent. As we walk down Lower Mounts, I look at Donna's list. "How come some are ophthalmic, others are dispensing, but some are both? Do you know?"

Knowing Donna as I do, it's a foolish question.

"That stumped me too, so I looked it up. Ophthalmologists undergo twelve years of undergraduate and medical or osteopathic education and residency. It prepares them to understand the relationship between your eyes and the rest of your body, how certain conditions, such as diabetes, can affect your eyes. That's the American version anyway."

"And the English version?" As she draws breath, I raise my hand. "It's fine."

"It's pretty much the same."

"Donna, you are so wasted… okay, I won't say it again."

"Do you think I don't enjoy my job because you don't enjoy yours?"

"Eh?"

"You don't enjoy your job."

Do I not enjoy my job? There are aspects that I love – testing the gadgets, and I'm loving the reader feedback… not the dates so much, but that's temporary and tiring – but has she picked up on something else?

"Izzy?"

"Yes?"

"Can we grab a sandwich on the way back? I didn't bring anything in and I'm starving."

"Sure."

We stop off at a bakery and she gets a pasta salad.

"I thought you were going to get a sandwich."

"This is much healthier."

I could never do her column. Apart from the odd night-out binge, she's always being good and never leaves the house without a hint of make-up, which is probably why she's so delighted when the free samples come in.

Whizzing past Marion again (we're getting good at this), I duck into the kitchen and grab our corner table while Donna fetches her notes on the online opticians. We spread them out across the table and are engrossed when William walks in.

"Hello, ladies."

Donna looks up first. "Hi, William. We're going through all the online stuff, it's very interesting."

"Excellent. I look forward to reading your first piece. I'm aiming for Monday – is that okay with you?" He manages to put the mug under the machine without any damage this time. My effect must be wearing off, especially as he's not yet looked in my direction.

"No problem. We're doing the last shops on Thursday so plenty of time."

"Great. Hello, Isobel."

"Hello, William," I say to his back as he walks off.

Donna looks disappointed.

I pre-empt her by saying, "You should be thinking of your love life, not mine."

With that, a huge smile radiates from her face and we resume the paperwork.

By the time my computer archiving's done, another workday is over. Donna's already typing up her first article and all I get from her is a wave as I walk out the door.

I'm standing in front of my mirror wearing the old faithful 501s, a green top and thin black leather jacket. The black slip-ons get another airing and I'm ready to go.

Counting on more traffic than there was, I arrive at The Four Pears with twenty-five minutes to spare before the quiz starts. Better early than late for the 'collect paper, pen, pay your pound and meet your blind date' routine. Should be fun.

I get the last space in the tiny car park next to another purple Polo, except this one has three doors instead of five.

As I get out of my car, so does the owner of the twin – a thirty-something with a faded denim jacket and a tour t-shirt.

I zap the remote and walk slowly towards the front of the car. He does likewise.

"Nice car," I say.

"Thanks, yours too."

I smile. "Jake?"

"The very same. You must be Izzy then."

"Hi."

"Have you brought your brain with you?"

"I hope so. Are you any good at these?"

"Not bad," he says.

That turns out to be the understatement of the year. I hadn't realised it was a music quiz and he answers everything post 1960s. I get a few, but he's already written them down. The only rounds we struggle with are the fifties and sixties, but I know some from what my parents used to play when I was growing up. In the end, we come second to a team of seven who could easily take on the Eggheads.

We win twelve pounds, which Jake and I split, although I insist on only taking a fiver as he answered more questions and had paid the pound each to enter.

As the quiz finishes just after nine, we stay and chat. It's the first opportunity we get because we've been so engrossed in listening to the questions and remembering the tunes of the ones we're struggling with when the quizmaster speeds on to the next question.

We start with the usual, "What do you do?" He works in a pet store and I tell him what I 'do', then say, "I couldn't do what you do."

"Work with animals?"

"No. I'd want to take them all home."

"So, you're an animal lover."

"I am, but don't have any pets 'cause I work full time. It's a shame because I grew up with dogs."

We skip the redundant 'What sort of music do you like' question and move on to hobbies.

"I love reading," Jake says.

"Me too. I'm about halfway through a crime story at the moment."

"Which one?"

"Jack Myler's *Opaque*, do you know it?"

"Sorry, no."

"It's a real page-turner."

"Okay."

"What do you read?"

"Romance usually."

"Really?" I know men do read romance, but he doesn't look the type. Something to do with his Rolling Stones t-shirt.

"I used to read horror, but I found it too…"

"Horrible?"

"Exactly. My mum got me into romance. She reads a Mills & Boon a day."

"They are very popular."

"I find the romantic ones the hardest to read."

"Because they're too slushy?"

"Absolutely, I burst into tears."

How I keep a straight face then, I don't know, so I change the subject. "How about films?"

"Love them. Grittier the better. You?"

Great, he's redeemed himself. "I like pretty much everything, although comedy and chick flicks are my favourites."

"Can't watch chick flicks."

"Are they not like romance books?"

"Yes, that's the trouble. I can't stop crying at them."

What can I say to that? "They can be very realistic. I'm a bit of a slush bucket."

"I know when it all started."

"Oh?" All we need now is a black leather couch and I can ask him how it makes him feel.

"When my dog died."

"Sorry…"

"We'd had her since before I was born."

My maths is pretty good, so I'm fairly sure of the next answer. "And how old were you…"

"Ten."

I was a couple of years out. "Oh, bless." I can see tears welling up in his eyes again. "Do you want to go?"

Unable to answer, he nods, grabs his jacket, mouths "Thank you" and leaves.

I smile at the bemused quizmaster and go home.

Chapter 24 – Edgar at the Boston

There are still no messages for tallgirlnn1 and I'm panicking. Not seriously, because I'm 'dated' 'til Monday, but I don't want to leave it much longer to set up the last few before getting my life back. I like the thought of that.

What did I learn from last night? That even hard toffees can have soft centres. I met J last night for a pub quiz (we came second, thanks mostly to J) and then stayed on to have a chat. The rock group t-shirt he was wearing gave me no indication as to what lay beneath.

J's a lovely guy, but can't handle serious conversation about delicate subjects. While being soft-natured like C, his emotions are far rawer. We touched on the subject of animals – he works with them – and when dogs were mentioned, he went into a mini meltdown. It transpires he lost a family pet when he was ten and has never fully recovered. I only hope none of the animals he works with dies.

That said, I'm all in favour of men showing their feelings. There's a wonderful advert with a man sobbing while watching a soppy movie (which I admittedly do), but I'm sure even he doesn't still get teary when talking about it decades afterwards. There needs to be a happy medium. Happy mediums make happy relationships.

Today's two items ticked on my 'dater's shopping list': Don't assume a hard exterior equates to a hard centre; they may be the favourites in a box of chocolates, but the soft ones are worth it too, and Do wear your psychiatry hat when dealing with anyone who has any emotional baggage (which, if we're honest, is all of us).

I turn in the article, with added techie bits, and Donna and I do the other two Abington Street opticians. They're all pretty much the same and, in a way, it amazes me that so many keep going. Are there that many people in Northampton wearing glasses? Maybe they make their money on contact lenses and we'd just never know. No doubt Donna will enlighten us.

I plough through my work and it's five before I know it. I have a quick check of tallgirlnn1 before I leave and there are still no messages. I'm going to have to do something if there's no joy tomorrow, but tonight I shall concentrate on having fun.

Dressed in a suitably glitzy outfit (silver shimmery top and black satin jeans – it sounds horrible on anyone other than a skinny rake, but I'm surprisingly pleased with the combo), I decide to take a taxi into town so I can let my hair down.

As taxi drivers always do, he doesn't stop talking and I've not said a word until we approach the town centre and he asks me where I want dropping off. Because of the one-way system, I say anywhere near the bus station, so he asks me if I'm going somewhere nice. Before I can stop myself I say, The Boston, and the rest of the journey is spent in silence.

He's not overly impressed either when the fare comes to two pounds sixty and I give him three pounds and tell him to keep the change, but knowing exactly where the pub is, he's dropped me the wrong side of the bus station, so I think he's done well. I've now got to walk on a pavement-less, dual lane, one-way road through a major set of traffic lights. Thanks, mate.

Edgar's waiting outside. I think it must be him, as I mistake him for a very ugly woman. He's wearing a pink puffball skirt, orange skin-tight Lycra top and has dyed pillar-box red hair, which matches his bright red lipstick. He looks like a colour-blind traffic light and I struggle to keep a straight (pardon the pun) face.

"Edgar?"

"Yes?"

"I'm Izzy."

"Are you?"

"Yes. We've arranged to meet?"

"I don't think so."

"Your profile name is EddieG?"

He nods, but still looks confused.

"You sent me some messages on NorthantsDating."

He looks mortified. "But you're a woman!"

"Last time I checked." I laugh, but his expression hasn't changed.

245

"You're not supposed to be a woman."

"I think I am. You could ask my parents, but…"

"No! I messaged a man."

I don't know how from 'tallgirlnn1' he thought I was a man. "No, sorry, I'm very much a girl."

"Oh."

"I'm happy to still go in if you like."

"I suppose."

Needless to say, I'm heartened by his enthusiasm.

So we walk into the Boston and it's everything I'd imagined it to be. It's packed with same sex couples and a variety of groups. The music is lively and loud, but goes with the atmosphere and I'm astounded it's only a Wednesday night.

It occurs to me that people might think we're a couple, despite being of opposite sexes, but it's very much 'everything goes' and that's what I love about the place.

I look around and EddieG's disappeared. We didn't even get to a first drink or talk about the weather. Under normal circumstances I'd be annoyed, but the next thing I know, I'm overshadowed by a six-foot-four hunk who looks like he could be the seventh member of the Village People.

His non-green Incredible Hulk hands grab mine and whisk me onto the dance floor, which is packed with gyrating bodies. I don't recognise the song, but I love the beat and become part of the rhythm, especially when Goldfrapp comes on to a wall of cheers. Again, it's not a song I can name, but I have it on my iPod, so sing along to it, as does nearly everyone else.

I spot Edgar in a corner chatting to someone equally brightly dressed (head to toe in turquoise) and I see a match made in heaven. He clearly didn't need NorthantsDating, but I'm so glad he tried it or I wouldn't be having such a wonderful time.

"I'm going to get a drink!" I shout to Village People number seven who nods and turns to his neighbour who resembles a very short Cher. Again, I'm proud of myself for not crumpling into hysterics.

I order my usual Southern Comfort and lemonade and see a list of cocktails behind the bar. Not having to drive opens up a whole new world and I'm a little overwhelmed by it all. I down my drink in two massive gulps and slam the empty glass down on the bar like I've seen in movie drinking competitions. I'm on a roll.

"Same again?" a voice behind me asks. It's Cher Mk 2. Knowing there's no possibility of him hitting on me, I nod, mouth still full of gulp. I swallow the drink and hold my hand up. "Can I try one of these cocktails?"

"Sure, love," he says in a very broad Scottish accent.

I look at the list and don't know where to start.

"The Spanish Screw is very nice. Very mellow, slips down your throat a treat." And he winks.

"What's it got in it?" I ask, although at this point as long as it's alcohol, it'll do.

"Sangria and Anis del Mono, mainly."

"I know Sangria, what's the other one?"

"It literally means 'the monkey's Anisette'."

"I'm not sure if I'd like anything that comes from a monkey." He laughs. "It's aniseed."

Sangria and aniseed isn't a combo I'd put together, but if the Chinese can make sweet and sour tasty, why not try this? "Why not!" I shout in his left ear.

He turns to the barman, who's as tall as VP7, and leans over the bar to take his order.

"Two Spanish Screws please."

The barman winks and wiggles to the cocktail shaker. It looks far too staged to be real and I'm pretty sure he's straight, but Aunt Agnes could tell me. The customers clearly love the barman and I'm having the time of my life.

We all watch as he replicates a one-man version of the Tom Cruise and Bryan Brown iconic *Cocktail* scene and everyone's clapping and whooping. The guy (I think he's male although I can't be sure) Edgar was talking to jumps on the bar and gyrates in time with the music, which is 'I believe' by Cher, so her 'twin' next to me is euphoric.

I thank Cher Mk 2 for the drink, but he's engrossed in conversation with VP7. Edgar, in the meantime, is on the dance floor with his new companion. They're entwined like ivy and it's like an explosion in a Dulux factory.

The rush of sugary alcohol and body heat gets to me, so I go outside. Opening the door there's a distinct contrast between the noise inside and near silence from the town centre. We're just one street away from the market square, but it's as if we're the only people alive.

VP7 meets me as I come back in.

"We were wondering where you'd gone."

"Sorry, needed a breather."

He's on the arm of someone equally gorgeous but slightly shorter, and once again the music takes over.

"We got you a drink!" he shouts, struggling to be heard over George Michael's 'Outside'.

The drink looks like Edgar's outfit though I suspect is far more deadly. "Thanks, what is it?"

"A Rainbow."

"What's it got in it?"

VP's companion butts in. "Vodka, Aftershock, blue and red, Banana liqueur, Blue Curaçao, Crème de Menthe, soda water, lemonade, sour mix and ice."

"You know your stuff."

"He works here," VP says proudly.

It's at times like this I wish I wasn't straight, and didn't have work to go to.

I may regret this in the morning, I think as I down another Rainbow, but I'm too happy to care and too oblivious to notice the familiar taxi driver who's waiting in the foyer tapping his foot… not in time to the music.

Chapter 25 – Garth at The Rover

What did I learn from last night? That whatever the 'date' throws at you, have fun. After a major misunderstanding (I wasn't a gay man), E3 decided to do his own thing, leaving me to fend for myself.

It turns out I didn't have to fend for long as friendly hands clamped on mine and dragged me onto the dance floor where I boogied the night away to songs I'd long since forgotten and couldn't name (sober or otherwise), in between trying cocktails I'd also never heard of.

The venue is a little corner of paradise, tucked away in a town centre side street. From the moment I stepped over the threshold I was welcomed as a long-lost friend and instantly felt like part of the furniture. It goes to show there are small groups of people who forget their troubles, lack of finances or the jobs they hate and give the night everything they have, and, if the people I met are anything to go by, that's a big deal.

Because the 'date' didn't materialise, the rest of this article will be about reader feedback and a couple of technical suggestions surrounding editing and uploading a photo to your profile. After last night's experience, it may have been wise to ask for a photograph beforehand, but if we had, we probably wouldn't have met and after having such a great time, I can't wait to do it all again.

Today's two ticks: Don't think you've seen everything and Do try new things, people and places.

I leave it like that for now, as every keyboard stroke drills into my brain. Even the office lights hurt and they're not particularly bright. At the best of times I'm a bit of a SAD case, especially in winter, when the office seems depressing. I wish I'd brought my sunglasses, but I know that's a big no-no from Karen because it's too 'celeb' and only the über cool get away with wearing them indoors. Apart from a Mike disguise, Donna frowns on sunglasses unless they're super high quality and always tuts whenever we walk past a pound shop with people trying them on, looking in the tiny mirrors or asking their friends if they look okay. Donna would love to tell them, but she's far too polite. I'm too chicken.

After making a huge mug of tea, I see there are three tallgirlnn1 messages, but none that warrant a reply, so I block them and trawl again. I'm on the last-but-one page of my search when I spot a couple of guys who look like fun. After last night, I want to keep that theme going, despite the hangover from hell.

WellyY35 is only a bit older than me, and he's ticked the 'adventurous' and 'fun' boxes, so I type a short reply introducing 'myself'.

Next is StevieBoy who, with a profile name like that, has got to be a laugh. His profile is so packed with information it takes ages to read, which suits me fine as it's black script on a white background and with the screen zoomed in three times, the writing is large enough to find its way through the fog that's called my brain. I scroll down the mouse so I'm almost silent. The office is pretty dead too, and I'm relaxing when Donna comes over.

She takes one look at my face and whispers, "Good morning."

I nod, which is also quite painful. I should have known better than to drink so much on a 'school' night, but, as is often the way, you don't think about that when you're having fun.

"Did you have a good time last night?" she continues, still whispering.

I nod again, this time more slowly. "Have you seen Duncan recently?" I know this is a stupid question because she's even more ecstatic than normal.

"Uh huh," is all I get from her, but she's still beaming. "I want to know about your night first."

We walk (well, Donna springs like Zebedee) into the kitchen to get refills, and I give her a rundown. I know I'm whispering, but my head relays it as shouting to my brain, so a synopsis is all I can manage.

I've recovered somewhat by lunchtime and we cover the last two opticians on Abington Street. This time we try on sunglasses, and I'm tempted to keep them on, but the assistant wants to check the fit of nearly all the glasses on display (which is a challenge in itself as I have a wide nose) and I lose my rag.

Seeing that I've had enough, Donna thanks the assistant, who was convinced she's got a sale, and we scarper.

Fortunately the sales guy in the independent optician's doesn't appear to work on commission. When he hands me his business card, I can see he's the owner, which surprises me as he looks about twelve (now I know I'm getting old). Of all the shops we've visited though, this is the one I'd give my business to; I prefer to support local companies rather than chains. The shop is packed and I realise how many people wear glasses. Some are more Andy Pandy than Andy Warhol, but no doubt Mr 'Almost Young Enough to be My Son' will kit them out.

After a quick trip to Boots for two low-fat meal deals (one for Donna because it's 'research', and the other for me because I consumed enough calories last night to sink a battleship, and have to redeem myself one way or the other) and a detour via their first floor glasses department, we return to the office.

There's no sign of Marion as we walk through reception. She's been temporarily replaced by Mike who, amazingly, isn't eating.

I smile at him, but Donna ignores him. He pays no attention to me, but smiles in Donna's direction, then realises he's wasting his time.

"Did you see that, Donna?"

"What?"

"Mike wasn't eating."

"He's not allowed."

"What?"

"Not while he's on reception. Marion won't tolerate it."

That's Marion all over. Toleration is not her forté.

Speak of the devil. The ladies' door slams shut behind her and she strides along the corridor towards us. I feel like giving her a high five for putting Mike in his place, but that would be like shaking hands with said devil, so I resist.

She looks in our direction, but instead of returning our semi-sincere smiles, she grunts and keeps walking. That's more like it.

I spend the next hour or so finishing the article and put it in William's tray. There's no sign of him, and Janine is typing away.

"Hi, Janine."

She pulls out her earphones and the audiotape stops. "Hey, Izzy. How are things?"

"Bit of a night, last night, but recovering well, thanks."

"The articles are really good."

"Thank you. I didn't realise you read them."

"Most of them – William's unofficial subeditor, you might say."

Janine's clever, so that's high praise indeed. If she wasn't such a good assistant, I wouldn't be surprised if William were to give her the sub job. I smile and go back to my desk. Mmm, sub job.

Five o'clock finally arrives and after a supermarket shop, I'm back in front of my wardrobe.

Being opposite the Saints Rugby Club, I don't imagine The Rover to be pretentious, so it's casual all the way.

Twenty minutes later, I pull into the car park. It's packed and I circle it with no joy, ending up a couple of streets away. I'm five minutes late by the time I get there, and am still swearing at myself as I walk in.

The place is packed with a plethora of football shirts, shorts and scruffy trainers, and I half expect to see Mr Sports Fanatic, but there's no one I think could be Garth. I stand in the doorway for ages and don't have a clue how I'm supposed to recognise him. The noise is deafening and I'm oblivious of blocking the doorway until there's a tap on my shoulder.

I turn round and there are two Saints players looming over me. I recognise them from our back pages – that and a huge team poster over the desk near Donna's: the desk belonging to Andy, our sports journo.

My legs are threatening to give way, my jaw drops open, and I can almost feel drool seeping.

The blond one, no doubt Andy would throttle me for not knowing his name, is the first to speak. "Coming or going?"

"Coming," I say, and giggle like a two-year-old. The guys smile. I mouth "Sorry" and step back, right into the path of a guy carrying a triangle of three full pint glasses.

It's obviously not the first time this has happened to him as he veers out my way like a contestant on *Strictly Come Dancing*. I utter another "Sorry" as I try to look around for a spot I can stand without causing any trouble.

I find a corner and hope Garth can see me. It shouldn't be difficult – I'm the only female on my own. In fact I appear to be the only female in the place.

I'm still here. In my corner. My watch says it's been ten minutes, but it feels like hours. As it's been a few days since we arranged this, I wonder whether I've got the time wrong, so I decide to give him another half an hour and then scarper. No one's paying me any attention anyway.

It's almost nine. I feel like all I need is a dunce's hat. I spot a gap and am deliberating whether to go for it or go home, when one of the rugby players, a dark-haired one this time, takes pity on me.

"Has he stood you up?" He smoulders.

"Looks like it," I whimper.

"Wanna come and join us?"

He looks back at his gang, and they're all equally hot.

I can't believe my luck.

"So?"

"Yes, please." Can I sound any more desperate? I try again. "Thank you. That would be great." I'm not sure that's any better, but he laughs, so I follow him.

I started the evening knowing nothing about rugby and by the time I leave The Rover, I feel like a walking encyclopaedia. Andy won't know what'll hit him tomorrow.

I'm still smiling when I let myself into my house. There was no sign of Garth and I'm glad. For the second dateless night in a row, I've had a ball and wouldn't have changed a thing. Two and a bit hours of raucous hilarity was worth every second of feeling like a lemon.

As I switch off my bedroom light, I can't help rubbing my right cheek – the one a super-cool Saints player kissed as he handed me his phone number.

Chapter 26 – Innes at the Shipman's

What did I learn from last night? Not to take phone numbers from married men.

Yep, that's right. The hot totty was hitched. What did I say before about modern men wearing wedding rings? It should be in their contracts. If I were married to someone like that I'd have his ankle dragging along a ball and chain.

Needless to say, when I got into work I couldn't wait to tell Andy. After putting names to faces, he added marital status (at my very unsubtle request) and the only one I met last night who wasn't married or cohabiting, it turns out, is very gay. And of course, he was the cutest one of all. Typical.

Anyway, it doesn't matter. I'm too busy for a man in my life and, after the past twenty-five days, I've nearly had my fill of male company. The only men I want to spend my evenings with are Ben and Jerry. I've been rather overdosing on Mr Häagen Dazs recently, so Cherry Garcia or Pfish Food for the foreseeable.

Donna's almost waltzing around the office and I'm having to pull her down from the ceiling every now and then. Things are going well with Duncan and I couldn't be happier. Really.

Where was I? Oh yes, married men.

Before you get the impression that last night's date was the married man, he wasn't. At least I assume he wasn't as he didn't turn up. Being surrounded by an army of rugby players and their cronies, I was more than happy to help egg them on with their yards of beer. I was driving so stayed sober, but was feeling the moment by proxy.

So I don't have a 'date' to talk about in today's article, but last night taught me that, despite Northampton changing almost out of all recognition in the last few years (to a cold soulless town, if you go by the comments on our 'text talk' page), *somewhere like The Rover is a place to go to. I may have been an exception to the rule, looking like a lost sheep in a deep dark corner of the pub, but I should play that role more often as it was the beginning of a wonderful evening.*

And it goes to show that, despite the married man letting the side down, rugby is a gentleman's sport.

Today's two ticks: Don't assume that the night is over if the intended date decides to bottle out, and Do have a good time regardless of whether alcohol is involved.

I'm struggling for remaining content, so switch over to my work emails and the readers have done me proud. There are twenty-six feedback emails (direct and via our website's comments box which have been forwarded to me), mostly on the recent articles, but a couple of general ones and three that need redirecting to Aunt Agnes.

These kick off the rest of my article and I deposit it in William's tray with a big smile.

"Something tickled you, Izzy?"

"Had a couple of good evenings."

"Another one last night then."

"Yes, it was very good."

"So another strong article?"

"Thanks to the readers, yes. It's all in there."

"Look forward to it," he says as he takes it from his tray.

I smile and leave him to it. He rarely asks me to change anything, but there's always a first time. There's not a lot to censor with reviews of gadgets, but there have been a few touch-and-go moments during this project, although William seems to have lightened up as the month's gone on. Reader feedback implies happy customers, perhaps the powers that be have patted his back. Then again, he's his own master when it comes down to it. The boat's sailing forward – who are they to rock it?

I detour via Donna's desk and she's peering at her screen, engrossed in something optical.

"Hey, Izzy. Busy. I'm confused with all these sites."

"In what way?"

"There's too much choice."

"Then it's up to Constable Clarke to weed through the mire and give the public a clear choice – the good, bad and the ugly and eek…"

"What?" We both look at the screen.

"That's hideous." At the side of the current website is a mid-surgery photo still and it's not a pretty sight. All of a sudden I don't feel hungry.

"How's Hunky Dunky?"

Her smile says it all.

"Seeing him tonight?"

She nods vivaciously.

"Have a good time."

She suddenly goes bright red and I don't need to say anything else.

Despite it taking forever to answer the reader feedback, the afternoon drags. I'm desperate for an early night, so hope Innes doesn't show. I won't be mad enough to do my dunce act again for another hour, but positive thinking, Izzy. It's going to be fun.

At five o'clock you can't see me for dust. I leave Donna in her pool of drool while she thinks about her date with HD.

Mike's on duty as I walk past the security office and he looks morose. I can't resist knocking on the door and popping in.

"Hi, Mike," I say cheerfully.

"Hello," he drones. Yes, he's definitely not himself. Not that he's the world's brightest spark, but everything about him is grey. Even his foodless blue uniform looks dowdy today.

"What's up?"

"Nothing."

He's not a good liar either.

"Okay." I go to leave when he speaks again.

"Is Donna upstairs?"

Given the amount of CCTV around the place I'm sure he knows she is, but I humour him. "She is."

"Is she…"

I wait for him to continue, but it would appear I'm supposed to know what he's planning on saying next. It's not forthcoming, and I repeat, "Is she…?"

"Is she happy?"

"Deliriously." Oh dear, that came out a little too easily. Still, he was the one who messed things up, playing all caveman-like.

It's then I notice there's no sign of any food. Not even a half-eaten morsel, no packets of tempting delights, nothing. I look at the bin by his feet and while there are scraps of paper (which, by rights, should be in the recycling box) and cellophane from the newly opened blank DVDs sitting on the desk, there are no telltale signs of recent feasts partaken. This isn't like him.

"Is she seeing that guy again?" he blurts.

"That guy?" We both know who he means, but I'm not ready to spill any beans he's not aware of (up to now I'd have thought he'd have eaten those as well).

"Daniel."

"Duncan."

"That's it. And he makes her happy?"

"So far, yes."

"Good," Mike says solemnly, and I feel slightly sorry for him; he's finally realised what he's lost.

"Yes, it's nice to see her happy. There's someone out there for you, you know." After the last three and a half weeks, I feel qualified to say that.

"I've been reading your column," he says.

"You have?"

"Given me a few pointers."

"Ah." I can't think how, but I'm hoping he'll enlighten me.

"Think I might try the lark myself."

"That's good. I'm glad you're being positive."

"May as well do something until Daniel dumps her and she comes running back to me."

Spoke too soon.

He then opens a drawer to reveal an eighteen-pack of mini croissants, a bag of chocolate misshapes and a box of Maltesers. The little bit of sympathy I was mustering for him dissipates and with a half-hearted smile, I leave the office as his right index finger hovers over the buffet.

At home, I get ready for the Shipman's. Although I've never been in, I've walked past often enough, so go for casual.

I take a deep breath as I clutch the door handle. The pub sounds rowdy.

I'm not wrong.

The second thing that hits me is the heat. Thankfully the place only smells of beer.

The third is the number of women. We match the men one to one and, although three sheets to the proverbial wind, everyone looks so at home I can't help but smile.

An arm appears from nowhere and drags me towards the bar.

"Hey!" I shout out instinctively.

"It's all right, love," the bushy-bearded man says. "You look lost. Come join the party."

And that's exactly what it is: a birthday party.

"Who's celebrating?" I shout to Beard, looking around at the colourful '35' banners and embarrassing baby photos.

"Him over there." He points to another beard-swathed patron, who raises his bottle.

"Izzy!"

"Innes?'

"That's me."

"You're the birthday boy?"

"Not really a boy anymore, but I'm what the fuss is all about, yes."

"I hadn't realised, I'd have…"

"Ah no. I'm too old for all that. I get cards, though they take up too many trees. Besides, there's only one way to celebrate."

And I can see they're having a damn good try.

"Charlie, get Izzy here a drink, will you? What'll you be having, my girl?"

It's been a while since I've been called a girl, but I like it. I soon see it's going to be the hat trick of good nights, and wish I hadn't driven.

I'm soon persuaded to get a cab home. Offered a choice of Flying Scotsman (whisky, Italian vermouth, bitters and sugar syrup), a Robbie Burns (whisky, Martini and dashes of Benedictine), or Rusty Nail (Drambuie and whisky), I opt for the latter… for starters.

Innes is sitting at the end of the bar and is more observing than taking part, but looks to be in his element. He lifts his bottle of Red McGregor at whoever catches his eye, and they do likewise with whatever they're drinking.

"You seem to know everyone in here," I say, a little envious. "Do you work here?"

"Yes, I do," he says, raising his bottle again before taking a hearty swig.

A rather drunk and equally Scottish voice from behind me says, "Ach, he owns the place, hen."

Before either of us can say anything, one of the barmaids leans over the bar and whispers something in Innes's ear. He jumps off the stool and goes behind the bar.

This amuses me no end, as I realise he's about five feet tall and can barely see over the bar. He reminds me of the villain from the Shrek movie – the third one? – brilliantly played by John Lithgow, who I've admired since he freaked out about the creature on the plane's wing in the *Twilight Zone* movie.

I finish my Rusty Nail and order another from the barmaid.

"He's just gone to change a barrel," she informs me.

"It's fun watching everyone having a good time," I say as Innes returns.

"Isn't it? It's often like this though. Any excuse for a party. Usually they don't need one, but…"

A chap walks up to Innes and says something I don't understand.

Innes replies and they both laugh.

"What language was that?"

"Russian."

"Russian?"

He smiles. "My mother is Russian."

"Wow."

A Russian-speaking Glaswegian running a pub in Northampton seems to be a waste of his talent, but I've not seen anyone love their job in such a long time, perhaps with the exception of Donna.

"It's a pity you don't speak Polish – there don't seem to be many Russians in Northampton."

"You'd be surprised, hen. Once word gets round… they all come flockin'."

"Flockin' for a lock-in," the familiar drunk voice says to the back of my head.

"Is it true this pub is haunted?" I ask Innes.

"Where did you hear that?"

"I remembered when you mentioned the venue."

"There was something that happened a few years back, before I bought the place."

"Something like… someone dying?"

"There was this guy…" He leans forward as if he's going to tell me a deep dark secret, and I lean forward, as much as my bar stool will allow.

"Harry Franklin, a former manager, committed suicide in gruesome circumstances."

"Really?"

"Oh yes. We've had all sorts of poltergeist activity since then, and I reckon it's all his doing."

The voice beside me pipes up with a childish "Oooh" then bursts out laughing, spraying lager down his front.

"How did he…?"

"Die?"

Innes leans in closer. "Hanging… by the neck."

I wonder if there's any other way. "So he haunts the pub?"

"Aye. His bodiless head searching for the rest of him." He looks deadly serious.

Then he and the drunk guy behind me burst out laughing. I duck to avoid any spray that might be coming in my direction.

The sober me would have felt a bit of a fool, but the me with a stomach full of liquor finds anything funny.

Chapter 27 – Vance at the Deers Leap

What did I learn from last night? That it's not what you know, but who you know.

I'd left home hoping for a pleasant evening, half expecting an average one or pessimistically thinking I'd be stood up again, but, for the third night in a row, I had a ball.

I stumbled into a birthday party and there's one thing about the Celts, they know how to party. The car was abandoned in favour of a taxi home, and a variety of weird and exotically named concoctions passed my lips over those few hours – I admit to having lost count of how many, but feel like I've had no sleep at all, so it must have been quite a few. However, what I lack in slumber was more than compensated by the wonderful company, which, without exception, was high-spirited, but well-behaved.

My 'date' was in fact the birthday boy and the centre of attention. It soon became clear that he was well known by everyone in the bar, except me, but that was swiftly rectified. Although we ended the night being nothing more than friends, I was treated like a princess. Even if I obviously can't say where we were, because that wouldn't be fair on him, if you're in a pub in the town centre and it feels like you're stepping back in time, and you're invited to join the clan, you'll know you've found this 'home away from home'.

Apart from being incredibly tired, I'm surprised I don't have the slightest hint of a hangover. Typing without making mistakes is another issue, but that's what spell-checkers and auto correct are for. Besides, all those red and green squiggly lines make a monochrome screen more interesting, don't they?

I'm on my third cup of tea by ten o'clock and there's still no sign of Donna. Marion doesn't know, or isn't telling where she is. I daren't ask Mike and no one in the office has a clue, so the only person who might is Chloë in HR.

I'm about to knock on her door when I notice the horizontal metal slide bar has been moved from 'Free' to 'In Meeting'.

"Bugger," I say aloud.

"Language."

I swivel round and there's William.

"Sorry."

He opens his mouth to speak as the reception doors fling open and in scurries Donna, jacket half off.

"Did we get dressed in a hurry?" William asks, looking her up and down.

"Err…" she says.

I desperately scrabble around for something to say in her defence.

"It's fine," he says. "You've put a lot of effort in recently." He then looks at me. "You both have. Just don't tell the boss." With that he smiles and strides into the HR office, immediately curtailing the conversation within it.

He shuts the door behind him, leaving Donna and me in the corridor.

"Spill," I say. "Where have you been?"

The smile gives her away.

"Three nights in a row?"

She nods. "We drink lots of wine and talk."

"Uh huh."

"We do!" She feigns hurt.

"Now what was that saying about the lady doth protest?"

"It's true. I want to, but…"

"Cuppa?"

"God, yeah. I'm as dry as a fairy."

An expression that can only come out of Donna's mouth. I didn't know that fairies were particularly dry, but no doubt it makes sense in Donnaland.

We make a drink and return to our desks. Donna's keen to get back to Operation Optic and I'm curious to see if I have any more messages. Although I'm knackered, things will seem a little dull without all the dates. The variety of gadgets are piling up around my desk though, much to Karen's annoyance as her 'presents' are neatly stacked in a cupboard behind her desk, one of which I don't have thanks to the all-in-one fax/copier/scanner/printer that has to be there because it's the nearest point to the kitchen. I know, I don't get it either.

I'm sipping the last of my tea and clicking on 'View new messages' when William saunters past whistling a familiar tune – a mixture between *Grange Hill* and *Rhubarb & Custard* – and, like the last thing you hear when you get out of the car, it sticks in my brain.

I'm still humming it when Donna comes over. She leans forward, looking very serious.

I stop humming. "What are you doing?"

"Do it again."

"What?"

"That tune."

"Which tune?" I ask.

"The one you were humming."

So I hum it again.

"Ah."

"What?"

"Where did you get it from?"

"William."

"Ah ha," Donna says again.

"Ah ha, what?"

"*Sorry* theme tune – he likes his UK Gold."

"Is that where it's from?" I should have recognised it, it was one of my favourites the first time round.

There's a fake cough from behind me and I swivel round to face Karen.

"You're so obvious," she says to me.

"Eh?"

"You and William."

"What do you mean, me and William?"

"You fancy the Bruno Banani off each other."

"The what?"

"Underwear… pants."

"Don't be silly, he's the boss."

"And?"

"He's… well… William."

She bursts out laughing. "Sorry, just teasing. Of course you don't fancy him. He's stuffy."

I feel a little defensive, so turn back to look at his office. I can only see the top of his head and it's shaking in a firm, 'No'.

"Earth calling Izzy."

Donna winks at me and I blush. I've got my back to Karen, but I can tell she's smiling.

Next thing I know, unnecessarily, I feel, Donna scuttles back to her desk. William walks past mine towards the kitchen without saying a word, and I catch the tail end of *Sorry*'s theme tune again.

The office is surprisingly busy for a Saturday, and, apart from the clue of everyone in casual dress, I almost forget it's the weekend. Monday's a bank holiday again, so I assume there's work to be done to make way for the long weekend.

I finally get to log into NorthantsDating to check my messages, and there are three. WellyY35 and StevieBoy have replied and both sound keen, which is great. The third is from Bully4U. Pete Bull's my age, which is a bonus after the mix this month, and loves 'to have a laugh'. I notice he's not online, but the other two are, so Pete gets a quick 'touch base' message with the others warranting proper concentration-with-a-cup-of-tea replies.

Welly, Stevie and I play message tennis and soon dates are set for Monday (Welly has no family commitments) and Tuesday lunchtime (Stevie works nights which is 'cool').

So that leaves one more date for the thirty-first, and by the time I've checked and dealt with my other emails, Pete's come up trumps.

With everything pretty much up to date, I decide to scarper around lunchtime. I know better than to go into town on a bank holiday Saturday. Long weekends are like the end of the world and the place will be heaving.

The town centre's open on a Sunday and parking is cheap (or free, I can't remember; the council keeps changing its mind). The place is usually deserted on a Monday anyway, so this crowding on a Saturday doesn't make sense to me, but Mr and Mrs Public know best. I shouldn't slate them as they pay my wages, but speaking my mind and thinking afterwards is a tried and tested Izzy MacFarlane trait.

What happened to this afternoon? It was just before two when I got home and it's nearly seven.

I'm sitting in my car in the packed car park of the Deers Leap, and am people-watching to kill a few minutes so I'm not too early and end up sitting alone in the pub (or standing as the seats will probably have already been taken) and appearing desperate, which, of course, I'm not.

I spot a guy on his own, so casually get out of my car and walk to the front door. He doesn't see me because I'm a second or two behind him, so he's already at the bar when I go in. He turns as I approach and smiles.

"Izzy?" He looks even younger than speed dating's Rebel Hell.

"Hi, Vance."

"How are you?"

I immediately warm to him. He's not my usual type – light mousey hair receding at either side, a distinctive Roman nose (which I can relate to), v-shaped canine teeth (ditto), and meet-in-the-middle eyebrows which remind me of Mr Hairy Softie.

"Very good, thank you," I reply. "Two days off work."

"Lucky thing, I was supposed to be going away, but I'm going back in tomorrow to do some overtime."

"What do you do?" I ask.

"Call centre customer services. It's boring, but it pays the bills."

"So you do shifts?"

"Just finished nights, and am back on days from tomorrow."

"Doesn't your body clock go all over the place?"

"I've been doing it ever since I left school, so I'm used to it."

"So you've been in the same job for…?" I purposely pause so he can fill in the gap.

"About twelve years."

I don't know whether to feel sorry for him because he's been bored nearly half his life or clip him round the head for being so stupid, but decide the best course of action is to change the subject.

"So you were supposed to be away this weekend?"

"My sister invited me."

"Somewhere nice?"

"Edinburgh."

"I love Edinburgh. Only been once, for a week, but I can see why people move there. It's so clean and the inhabitants are proud of the city's history, with the beautiful castle and–"

"My sister."

His expression implies she's not exactly a tourist attraction. Then it dawns on me. "You didn't cancel to meet me, did you?"

"We don't get on. She's got five wild brats and a ponce of a husband, so you've saved me from torture."

A man after my own heart, except my family's not like that, but I get what he means.

"Do you see them often?" That felt too much like a cheesy chat-up line.

"Once, maybe twice a year. I go up there when I have to, but usually see her when she brings them down to visit our parents."

"I'm lucky. My sister-in-law's lovely, and my niece is smashing."

"How old?"

"Five soon."

"Isobel's are all under five."

"Really? Five under five. She must have had them one straight after the other."

"Triplets and twins."

"Wow." Another of my favourite phrases. "And your sister's called Isobel? That's my name too, Izzy comes from Isobel."

'Suits you though."

"Thanks." I can see we need a change of subject again, but sadly it's one he's intent on progressing.

"I'm a free babysitter."

"Oh dear."

"That's all she wants me for. As soon as I arrive, Donald takes my bags to my room, a tiny attic room, which is freezing, although the view is worth it, and then they bugger off to the pub."

Isobel. Donald. I wonder if they've also got a Jane, Mark, Ellen or Lola. My family mark II. "That seems quite…"

"Shit."

"I was going to say unfair, but you're right, it is… shit."

"So you can see why I don't want to go."

"Can't you say something to them?"

He's about to reply when the barman coughs. We've been there a good few minutes and not yet ordered. The barman has an 'I'm not here for the good of my health' look and I smile apologetically. He relaxes and looks at me to place the order.

I ask for anything non-alcoholic that's apple-related and he nods before turning to Vance, who looks at me.

"Have you eaten?"

"A late lunch. Why, what do you have in mind?"

'They do mean snacks.'

"Sounds good."

"Burger and chips?"

That doesn't sound like a snack to me. It would to Tim the Weeble, but Vance is standard-size proportions – somewhere between Tim and Social Worker Lawrence. Pub burgers however are usually far nicer than burger bar food, so I shrug and say, "Sure."

He turns back to the barman who repeats our food order.

"Can we set up a tab please?" Vance asks. "And I'm not driving, so a pint of Fosters please."

"Right you are. And the table number?"

Vance and I look around the bar – there's no table to be had.

"Can we have them here?" I ask.

"Right you are," the barman repeats and disappears into the kitchen.

I search for another topic of conversation. "So, what do you see yourself doing in five years' time?"

It's a clichéd interview question, but better than the weather, and only leaves music before we hit rock bottom – the hairdresser's question: holidays, and I don't want to go there yet as it may well bring up his sister again.

"What do you mean?"

"You know, job, living somewhere else…?"

"Oh, no, I love my life. I wouldn't want to do anything else."

"But you said your job was boring?"

"The people are nice."

I can relate to that, but it's not a reason to stay somewhere, especially when you're only late twenties, so I change the subject again, getting desperate. "What sort of music do you like?"

"R&B, rap, techno, anything like that."

Like Ollie. "Have you ever been to Groove?"

"Where's that?"

"Top of Gold Street."

"I don't get into town."

"Can't say I blame you. It can be a bit dodgy at night."

"I don't go at all. Don't see the point."

"Where do you do your shopping?"

"Weston Favell Centre."

"It is handy, just down the road."

He nods.

"And where do you work?" I continue.

"Moulton Park."

"That's handy too. Not far to drive."

"I don't drive."

"I thought…"

"I don't have a car."

"Oh."

"What's the point? There's a direct bus."

"That makes sense for such short journeys, but what if you want to–"

"Bus into town then I train up to Edinburgh."

Although I'm pretty sure of the answer, I ask, "Have you ever been abroad?"

"Hate flying."

"I'm not keen," I say, grateful for something in common.

"No, I hate it."

"Where have you been?"

"What you do you mean?'

"Where have you flown to before?"

"I've never been on a plane."

"Then how do you know you hate it?" I can't help myself.

"Afraid of heights."

"Can't say I blame you."

"And don't want to die."

"I don't suppose many people do, but they say you're safer in the air than on the road."

"Which is why I don't drive."

"I think you'd have to drive a lot, and on the motorways, to be at risk."

"You're at risk as soon as you walk out your front door. Something could happen to me while I'm here."

That's what I like: optimism. Change of subject again, I think. "Do you have any pets?"

"No."

"That's a shame."

"Not really."

"Why's that?''

"I'm allergic."

What do you say to that, other than 'Oh' or 'Oh, dear' and if I do I'm going to sound like a broken record.

"You?" he asks me.

I say, "A dog and two cats," so we're as incompatible as possible. He's nice enough, but hard work. At least monosyllabic Nick the librarian was cheerful.

Our burgers arrive and the barman takes another order for drinks. I wonder whether we'll get to a third round. Thankfully having full mouths gives us the excuse not to talk, but I know we'll have to once we've eaten.

Moments later, I'm let off the hook by a girl coming over.

"Hey, Vancie. How are you?"

"Hi, Daisy. Good, and you?"

They then have the longest conversation of the night and I munch on my burger as they gaze at each other. I feel like a spare part although I'm relieved at not needing to contribute. Next thing I know, she's pulling up a bar stool and Vance turns so he has his back to me. I can see how far his receding hair actually recedes. I can't see him getting away without a combover for much longer. It's very cleverly done; you'd never have known from the front.

I've eaten my meal by the time they pause for breath, and I expect him to turn round and apologise, but they yak into another conversation. My second drink's history by the time he finally looks at my plate.

"You were hungry."

His meal is hardly touched and probably cold. Needless to say, I'm not sympathetic.

"I'm going to have to go." I hope he doesn't ask why.

"Sure," he says a little too enthusiastically.

The barman comes over to see if I want a refill.

"Thanks, I'm fine. Could we have the bill though please?"

He nods and returns a couple of minutes later with a slip of paper and a handheld card machine.

"Are we going halves?" Vance asks.

I usually pay for my own, especially when my drinks are cheaper, but I can see he probably needs the money more than I do, and William's still paying, so I repeat his "Sure."

Vance stares at the bit of paper. The barman wiggles the card machine.

"Is there something wrong?" I ask.

"No…" Vance hesitates.

I take the piece of paper and realise he can't work out what 'going halves' would equate to. The bill's £20.14. It shouldn't take a genius. "Twelve pounds each would give a reasonable tip," I suggest.

He nods.

I put down a tenner and a two-pound coin and he does likewise.

"So, why do you have to go so early?" he asks, making me think on my feet.

A conversation with Callum leaps into my brain and I come out with, "I've got an essay to write about the main issues associated with meeting the challenges of international development, in the context of changing global, political and economic circumstances."

"Er, okay," he says, as his sidekick sits there wide-mouthed.

There's nothing left to say, so I smile and head for the exit. I glance back and see my seat's not even cold as he and Daisy pick up where they left off.

I drive home, glad it's nearly the end of the month, although the delicious burger did make up for the strained conversation.

I go to bed with a cup of tea and resume my acquaintance with Elliot, pulling the duvet up to my neck in preparation for what's to come.

Chapter 28 – Ulver at the Swan and Helmet

I so need today's lie-in. After two fairly early starts, I treat myself to an eleven a.m., after which I put on my jeans to go to the corner shop, buy a paper, and go back to bed, only getting out when I've finished reading.

Four o'clock. Dreadful, I know, but hey, I've earned it. I'm not meeting UlverTheIrish 'til eight thirty, so put on my dressing gown, go back downstairs, make a cup of tea and some beans on toast and take it all through to the lounge. I must eat more sensibly, and I know Donna would do her nut, but I can have a salad sandwich or something equally wholesome, later… had I some salad in my salad drawer.

The next thing I know, it's six and I need to think about having a shower. That's the trouble with losing half a day in bed, the rest of it's almost over before you've blinked.

With the long May evenings, I'd normally have walked to the Swan and Helmet, but as we're not meeting 'til late, I play it safe and take the car.

As I drive past the pub, I'm pleased to see a guy standing outside waiting, although by the time I've found a space in a non-double-yellow-lined, non-residential permit parking area and got back, he's gone.

I look at my mobile and I've got two minutes to spare. He did say he might be late, so I duck inside to see if there's anyone on their own, but there's no one who fits the bill (the 'waiting outside' guy is hooked up with his gorgeous girlfriend, so I go back outside.

I've just stepped out on the pavement again when Ulver comes running up to me.

"Sorry." He's slightly out of breath. "Have you been waiting long? You weren't going, were you?"

"No, you're fine." In fact, he's more than fine, he's gorgeous. Six feet of hunky doodle dandy. Piercing green eyes, dark Italian hair and complexion (which is odd as he's Irish) and a great dress sense. Karen would be suitably impressed. "I've just arrived. I went inside in case you were waiting in there."

We get our drinks – him a pint as he lives round the corner (and therefore delighted with my choice) and me the old fail-safe Coke, and we find a quiet table.

I could have done with my seat being a black leather couch for the interrogation that proceeded. Every other statement I make is greeted with "And how did that make you feel?" or "Now why do you say that?" type questions or statements and I begin to wonder when he's going to tell me my time's up.

Every now and then he taps the side of his nose as if something said is top secret.

I buy the second round, he gets the third and we're getting on okay. He's a little hard work, but I'm determined to persevere because I can't take my eyes off his.

Towards the end of the evening, people filter out of the pub and there are half a dozen of us left. As far as I know, neither Ulver nor I have work in the morning, but he downs the rest of the pint and pulls on his jacket.

"I'm off," he announces.

"Oh, okay."

"I won't be the last to leave."

I'm not sure what that means exactly, and he can tell he needs to explain.

"I never stay in a pub until I'm the last person. It smacks of desperation, having everyone clear up around you."

It's not something I'd thought much about. If anything, I'd say it smacks of having a good time, but I guess he's not.

"Thanks, Izzy. It's been interesting."

"You're welcome." I think he is, anyway. He's got my head spinning from how cute he is, but also from the 'twenty questions' (although it seemed like a lot more). I feel like a science experiment or as if I've been caught by a high street market researcher on a lunch break where I have five minutes to get back to work, but must answer their hundred or so vital questions because the fate of humanity depends upon it.

"But we won't be seeing each other again," he states.

"That's a shame," I say, because although it felt like a Spanish inquisition, I'm warming to him.

"I think we both know it wouldn't go anywhere."

I want to say, "I didn't know, but I do now. Thanks for putting me straight, in case I was in any doubt," but cop out with a repetitive, "Oh, okay."

I watch him walk out of the pub and feel deflated. So we probably weren't compatible, but to be told in such a manner was somewhat surprising. This month has been nothing if not that.

I drive home in need of Mr Ben and Mr Jerry, so raid the freezer as soon as I walk through the door. I revel in a late-night horror movie, C-rated at best, and pep up a little by the time I go to bed.

I know this project is work, but somehow I couldn't help but let a part of me get involved and, although I should know better, I feel a little piece of my heart chip away from the rest of it and bob along my bloodstream towards the entity that's my brain.

Chapter 29 – Welland at the Spencer's Arms

Another lie-in today – I could get used to this. With newly bought newspaper, hot buttered toast and cup of tea, I settle down to a catch up of my Sky+ recorded programmes. The planner's only showing twenty-three per cent memory left and the weather is foul (of course it is, it's a bank holiday Monday), so what better excuse than a day vegging?

Starting with the half-hour programmes (comedies then dramas), I progress to the hour longs.

By the time there are just the movies left, it's six thirty. With the exception of another trip to the corner shop, I've been in my dressing gown all day and it's a wonderful feeling.

I'm not meeting WellyY35 'til eight, but it's at the Spencer's Arms, Chapel Brampton, a good ten to fifteen minutes' drive away. With a shower and debate on what to wear (I know I should have thought of this earlier, especially as it's a posh pub), I have to get a move on.

I lean back on the sofa and tip down the remaining contents of the bowl of popcorn. I'm such a slob, but the curtains are closed, so no one can see. Normally I don't like to shut out the sunlight, but there isn't any today. Of course there's supposed to be, but the sky is as black as a number eight pool ball. It looks like I'm going to need a brolly just to get to the car.

I imagine a few thousand people at seaside resorts swearing at the sky, and the Met Office, and the eighty-three million pounds the PWSCG (Public Weather Service Customer Group) spends each year getting it wrong. I know all this thanks to Aunt Agnes's desk neighbour, Bertie. His real name's Cuthbert – he let slip at last year's Christmas party when he and I were in a quiet corner chatting about global warming.

Squeaky clean and dressed in black trousers and a smart aubergine jumper, I make a dash for the car. The rain's eased up a little, but it's still not pleasant.

The drive's a breeze as few people are venturing out, so I make it in ten minutes. I arrive at the car park fifteen minutes early, and decide to hang fire to see if the rain stops, but it only gets worse.

Needless to say, I get the last space in the car park, the furthest away. I make a run for it, but when Mother Nature is throwing buckets of water at you, it feels like a marathon.

My feet are soaking. I'm wearing suede shoes and can almost hear them squealing as they're probably marked for life.

As I burst through the door, everyone inside turns. They soon go back to their conversations with the exception of a fusty-looking chap sitting on a bar stool at the far end of the bar staring at me. I smile uncomfortably.

I can sense eyes boring into me and, without moving my head, turn my eyes and see Mr Fusty's still staring. I fancy something warming, so order a Baileys to have something to occupy myself with while I wait for my date.

As the seconds tick by, and the eyes become more intense, I realise Mr Fusty is WellyY35. I should have guessed as much (and earlier). Although we're just a few feet apart, he waves at me like an aircraft marshal. I'm so pleased that no one else is taking any notice. I move along and sit on the bar stool next to him.

"All right?" he asks.

I put on my synchronised swimmer smile and say, "Yes, thank you, how are you?"

"All right."

Another man with a one-word vocabulary. OK, two words.

"Have you been here long?" I ask.

"A while, yes."

"Sorry. Was I late?"

"No. This is my regular."

"You live in the village?"

"No. Next door."

Unless I'm very much mistaken, next door is technically in the village as the pub is, but I just nod. "That's handy."

He nods back.

Again I'm glad of meeting late and for having work in the morning, as I feel I'm going to need an excuse to get away. I decide to make some small talk to chivvy the evening along. "I thought you lived in Wellingborough from your profile name."

"Why's that?"

"Because of the Welly reference."

"Why?"

"Because the town's called that sometimes."

"I didn't know that." His monotone voice is drilling through my skull like Woody the Woodpecker except not so colourful. He leans across and whispers. "My name's Welland."

"Is that a local surname?" I ask.

"You misunderstand me. My first name is Welland."

"That's unusual." I try to sound enthused.

"My parents used to live near the river, and they were steam rally enthusiasts. They wanted something unusual to go with my surname."

"Which is?" I expect him to say something from one extreme to another, like Smith or Zardfar, but it's neither.

"Yates. As in the pub chain."

I assume no relation. He looks older than his age, maybe even mid-forties, but is wearing a flat cap and everything about him is brown. I like brown; I wear a great deal of taupe, chocolate or khaki, but he's not even gone for the country beige look, but a dull Angela's Ashes era.

Instead of going round the houses and asking about his taste in music, or commenting on the obviously appalling weather, I go for the jugular. "Do you smoke?"

"Oh yes," he says quite proudly, his face showing emotion for the first time. "I have a great collection of pipes."

I can imagine them all lined up above the hearth in his little stone cottage.

"I can pop next door and get some if you like," he chirps.

"No, but thank you."

He looks at what's left of his pint of beer and then at my near-full Baileys. "You not driving then?"

"I am, but…"

He tuts. "Should never drink and drive. Especially not around these country roads. Most accidents happen on country roads. Didn't anyone ever tell you that?"

I think there's more cream in Baileys than whisky, but I would normally agree. "I've eaten a lot today, so that should soak it up. It's such a grotty evening that I wanted something…"

I stop explaining as he's shaking his head. I wonder whether the thirty-five in his profile stands for his year of birth rather than his age, so do some digging.

"Do you have any siblings?" He looks puzzled, so I help him out. "I have a brother."

"Sister, Winema."

Trying not to laugh, I say, "Older or younger?"

"Older."

"By much?"

"Two years."

"Same as me and my brother. He's thirty-two."

I wait for either his or the sister's age, but it's not forthcoming. I decide it doesn't matter, but I like to satisfy my curiosity, so I keep digging. "Are your parents still alive?"

"Just my dad."

"And he is...?"

"In a nursing home."

"That's a shame. He can't be very old."

"No, he's not."

I can see Welland's not the smartest pipe in the rack, and I'm seriously getting nowhere fast, so decide to switch tack. "What kind of music do you like?"

"Anything really."

"Like...?"

"Anything except soul... or rock... or that modern pop rubbish. You can't hear the words and they keep repeating..."

I've lost interest in doing all the work. "Is there anything you want to ask me?" This is beginning to feel like a job interview. And for a job I know I don't want. I'll look at HR Chloë in a new light.

"Um."

"Have you had your profile up for long?"

"A week. You're the first. My sister said I should be careful but..."

"Yes, you should. There are a lot of weirdos out there – not just the men." This last bit comes out unexpectedly.

"She said there are a lot of tarts who'll want to take advantage of me."

The conversation thereafter is not only dead, but cremated. We sit in uncomfortable silence. He stares at me, while I look around the bar at everyone else having a good time. Faced with more silence, I decide to bottle out, and look at my watch.

"Oh dear, is that the time," I say with the conviction of a bad amateur dramatist. "I've got to get home and put my PVC mini skirt and fishnets on for my next date. Time waits for no woman, you know."

His lower jaw drops and in his mouth I see the remnants of his beer and what looks like tobacco. Like the rest of him, it's not a pretty sight. He lifts his head slightly to say something, but it's clear nothing's forthcoming, so he resumes his docile position.

I drive home via an all-night garage where I buy a huge slab of fruit and nut chocolate to munch in the car. One thing we women are also renowned for is comfort eating, and while I don't feel I need comforting, it tastes fecking awesome.

Chapter 30 – Stevie at the Fishmarket Café

What did I learn from Saturday night? That my mobile phone has a calculator on it.

I didn't need it, but I could have lent it to V, my date for the evening. At least this one turned up, but conversation was as easy as creating the Bayeux Tapestry. A fair chunk of the evening was spent with him chatting to a groupie, so I made another semi-rapid departure.

The rest, and most enjoyable parts, were devouring a home-made (pub-made) burger and chips and, I must admit quite cruelly (though without being obvious), watching V trying to work out his (fifty per cent) share of the £20.14 bill.

Figuring my dig is unlikely to get through the William sensor, I save him the bother and delete it (which is a shame because I like it). I may be that cruel, but I don't want my readers to know, so I put a more positive spin on it and come up with the old 'incompatibility' chestnut.

What did I learn from Sunday night? To not take life too seriously. I'd never been in the Swan and Helmet before and it's a typical British pub. Despite it looking like an intimidating corner building, I received a very warm welcome from the staff and my date, U, was apologetically late (which he needn't have been as he had pre-warned me he might be). What he made up for in manners and looks, he sadly lacked in moderation.

Instead of fabric chairs, the pub could have done with a black leather couch and a timer, so I could be told when my session with Doctor U was up. It's a shame because he is very nearly 'my type' and for someone else he would be ideal, but I left feeling as if my brain had gone ten rounds with Albert Einstein.

That said, I'm not knocking intelligence; Mr Einstein would be a welcome dinner guest given the chance, and it's very clear U has oodles of it, but given the choice of Einstein or the Wizard of Oz's scarecrow, I know which I'd rather have.

I've always been rather fond of the scarecrow, but scrub the last bit as I again get into mean mode.

What did I learn from Monday night? That you're never too young to be old. W was the epitome of a pipe and slippers man (and owned both – which, thankfully, I was spared). Again, our conversation was hard work and I felt from the moment I walked through the door that I was under scrutiny – initially from everyone in the pub as I'd got caught in the rain and made rather a grand entrance, but Mr Stuffy didn't let up.

His sister, who I'm pleased to report wasn't there in body, appeared to be equally opinionated when her thoughts were relayed to me by W. I was tarred with the judgemental brush that seemed to run in his weirdly named family, but didn't see the point in attempting to convince him that it didn't apply to me.

Before we'd even got to a second round of drinks, I left the pub implying I was off to do what all we women apparently are good at. I won't tell you what, but suffice to say, it's known as one of the oldest professions.

I then remind the readers that my usual column will reappear later in the week and to let me know of any topics they wish covered. Some of the requests I get whenever I say this are often too weird to review, but it brightens my day.

Something's been bugging me for the last few days, so I aim for the desk of the office's leading gossip queen. "Hi, Donna."

"Hey, Izzy." She's engrossed and doesn't look up.

"I've got a question for you."

"Sure. Fire away," she says, still looking at the paperwork.

"It's Marion. She seems in a better mood recently. Any idea why?"

Donna takes a deep breath and looks up at me with her eyes wide, like she's about to have PKR eye surgery. "I've been meaning to tell you…"

I sit on the corner of her desk and lean in. "Proper gossip?"

She puts her left-hand fingertips over her mouth and through them whispers, "I can't really say."

"Donna."

Without removing her fingers she says, "Okay." It rarely takes much. "She's seeing someone."

"But she's married, isn't she?"

Donna shakes her head. "Divorced, but says 'Mrs' is more professional."

"So who's she seeing?"

"I can't tell you."

"Donna!"

She removes her hand. "All right then." She's such a soft touch. Leaning in to meet me, she whispers.

"No!" I say a little too loudly and she pulls back sharply. "Is she mad? Don't answer that, of course she is. Oh, that's soooo funny!" I clap like a child who's been told it can have the pick of the sweetshop.

I rush over to Karen's desk and whisper the news to her. She bursts out laughing, which gets our car guy Gerry curious, so she turns and leans in towards him. He laughs too and if it was a secret before Donna told me, it isn't now.

I turn round to Donna and mouth "Sorry," but she shrugs. We both know she would have spilled sooner or later.

I do a quick check of tallgirlnn1 and there are four messages. Two are from the remaining dates, StevieBoy and Bully4U, saying they're looking forward to meeting me. I don't need the other two (HotStuff and MickyD), but reply in case Stevie or Bully back out. I'm amazed I only lost two all month and am keeping everything crossed that the last two don't let me down.

I peer at the computer's clock and it's already twelve forty. I'm meeting Stevie at one, so gather my belongings. Donna holds up two crossed fingers as I look over, and I reply with a thumbs up.

To avoid walking down the non-existent pavement alongside the bus station again, I cut through the Grosvenor Centre and out across the top of the market square.

The café in the Fishmarket gallery is fairly tiny and Tuesdays after a bank holiday are notoriously quiet in town, so I reckon Stevie shouldn't be too difficult to miss. And he's not. In fact he's the loudest person in there: clothes and personality. The other people consist of the two female staff, and they're both behind the counter laughing at his every word. At least this isn't going to be boring.

According to his profile, Stevie is thirty-eight. I had my reservations about dating another older man after the previous night, but had high hopes from his profile terminology and messages, but how wrong was I?

"All right, darlin'?"

I can feel the synchronised swimmer's smile coming back. Oh yes, there she is.

I put my hand out to shake his, but he throws his arms around me like I'm a long-lost piece of luggage, and he's got to claim me so I don't escape again. I fight for breath as his twenty-plus stones of muscle squeeze all the air out of my lungs. He then realises my impending destruction and relinquishes his grasp.

I'm glad he speaks next because I don't think I can.

"Sorry, darlin'. Gets a bit carried away. How are ya then?"

"I'm good, thanks. And you?"

He looks back at the counter staff and smiles in a Mary Poppins 'Bert the chimney sweep' kind of way. They giggle and I can tell he's lapping it up. "I got me a posh bird 'ere." I'm looking at Eliza Doolittle's father, except Stevie's dressed like a teenager.

"What would you like, darlin'?"

Through gritted teeth, I ask for a fruit tea and one of the assistants goes to make it and the coffee Stevie's asked for. Turning to the waitress nearest to me, I ask her, in a normal fashion, what kind of sandwiches they do, and I'm impressed by the long list she reels off. I order, via her rather than him, a ham salad baguette and she goes off to make our lunches (after he's said he'll have the same and she's almost drooled in my fruit tea).

"Shall we sit somewhere?" I ask, begging this sideshow to end.

"Sure, darlin', wherever you like."

He pays the other woman, and I smile as she fumbles with the till. "We'll bring them over," she says, almost swooning, and I can imagine them arguing over who will do the delivering.

I walk towards a table at the gallery end, carrying my tea and his coffee while he hovers behind to finish chatting with waitress number two and then they both walk towards me, him

284

carrying my plate, while she carries his. I wonder why he couldn't carry them both over, but the look they give each other confirms he obviously has a 'plan b' if things don't work out with me. Which I know they won't.

By the time we've finished our sandwiches and chatted about music, films and what we both did at the weekend (I, of course, fabricated mine and I'm pretty sure, by the sound of it, his was just as farfetched – unless Sywell Aerodrome really does have sky diving, rock climbing and off-road aquaplaning facilities; ReadyEddie could tell me), it's time for me to go back to work.

"I 'ad a nice time, darlin'. See ya again right?"

I'd love to say 'Nah', but I'm a posh bird, ain't I, so I let him down gently. "Sorry, no. It wouldn't work."

He shrugs. "Can't blame a bloke for tryin'."

Indeed you can't. I thank him for lunch and leave him to it. Before I walk round the corner towards the market square exit, I can't resist looking back. My seat's already taken by waitress number one, and he's got his arm round her.

Feeling like a peeping tom, I can't help smiling as waitress number two realises what's going on and storms over to the table. I don't need to hang around to guess the rest of that scene.

I manage to keep a straight face when walking back through reception. Marion's on the phone, head down, writing a note of some description – perhaps a love letter. I wouldn't put it past her. Work is pretty dull after that. I decide to type up my article in the morning, so with tallgirlnn1 up to date, I reply to the few incoming emails, then wade through two boxes of samples.

Five o'clock eventually rolls around, and I'm out the door faster than you can say darlin'. Donna's still slaving away on her opticians project, but she says it's under control, so I don't feel guilty. She'll soon shout if she needs any more help.

A quick stop at the corner shop for a paper and milk, then I settle in for an evening of reading. After the national newspaper, I read a bit more of *Opaque* and am thrilled to be nearing the end. Not because I want it to be over, but I'm impatient to know what happens.

I'm not quite sad enough to read the ending in advance (never have, never will – some people do before they even buy the book, which I find very strange) and am pleased with myself for reading my first novel in months; I normally prefer short story anthologies, which better suit my impatient brain.

Sadly, I don't get far with Elliot as I fall asleep on the sofa and wake up at gone midnight with a stiff neck. The latter of course had nothing to do with mixing some of the milk with the remnants of a bottle of Baileys.

Chapter 31 – Pete at McNeil, Duffy & Chilson

I arrive at work to an email from Bully4U asking if he can change venues. I reply, asking what he has in mind, then crack on with my article with everything crossed that the last of the month's dates goes smoothly.

What did I learn from last night? That mixing Baileys with milk to make it taste like milkshake doesn't remove the alcohol.

Date thirty was lunch, so no alcohol was consumed anyway (and the Fishmarket Café doesn't have a licence) and by the end of the very quick (under an hour) rendezvous, S (a character and a half) had secured two phone numbers – neither being mine.

Women seem attracted to a man with confidence and I couldn't fault S on his. It was oozing so much that it was rather sickly, but if sickly is what you like, he definitely is the man for you.

I sit back in my chair and struggle for more content. Our conversation was very ordinary (except for the parts where I mentally throttled him for calling me darlin' every few words) and there's nothing else to add, so I continue with general feedback about the NorthantsDating site, that tonight will be my last 'date', and how much I've enjoyed (I find it so easy to lie on paper) the last thirty days. I encourage my newfound readers to keep reading my column once the usual reviews are back in situ and thank everyone for their encouraging emails.

I stretch it out to the required word length and take the printed version to William.

He's coming off the phone as I walk in.

"Hi, Izzy."

"Hello, William."

"How are you?"

"Good thanks. You?"

"Yes, thanks. And the article?"

"It's been an interesting month."

"Are you glad it's coming to an end?"

I'm not sure what I should say, seeing as he gave me the project in the first place, so I go for diplomacy. "In a way, but it's been a great experience. Thank you."

"You're welcome. We've had some excellent feedback on it. The bosses are pleased too."

"Really?"

"You're surprised?"

"I suppose I don't think of them having time to read every article."

"Just the ones that matter."

I'm not sure if 'ones' means bosses or articles, but I say 'Thanks' all the same.

William's phone rings and he looks at the screen. He points a finger to the ceiling, so I assume the bosses' ears are burning; that or telepathy runs fifty miles.

I make my exit and walk back to my desk via Donna's.

"Morning," I say bright and breezily.

"Hello," she says without any hint of a spark.

"What's the matter?"

"I think Duncan's going to dump me."

"What makes you think that?"

"He's cancelled tonight."

"Did he say why?"

"Evening surgery."

"Has he?"

"I don't know."

"You could always ring the reception and try to make an appointment."

"But I don't have a pet."

"You could say it's an emergency."

"That would be lying… and spying."

"You're a poet and you don't even… Has he said when he's going to see you next?"

"Tomorrow lunchtime."

"That's good news. If he didn't want to see you he'd postpone for a few days. Let you sweat."

"He's not like that."

"But you think he's going to break up with you."

"It's a feeling. Something's up."

"You've got…" I look at the clock and it's twelve thirty. "Twenty-four hours. Do you want me to call by on my way home tonight?"

"Thanks, but it's okay. I'm going down to see my mum straight from work, now I'm, you know… I was supposed to go at the weekend, but I saw Duncan instead."

My heart goes out to Donna as she looks as if she's struggling. There's a hint of a smile because they clearly had a lovely weekend, but it's fighting with the worry. "I'll leave my mobile on and will text you later."

When I go back to my desk, I check my messages and Bully4U has replied. Instead of the Abington Park Hotel he's invited me to an office party. Apparently it's his boss's thirtieth birthday and she's throwing a big bash straight after work. He wasn't sure whether it would end early enough to meet me and thought this might be more fun. As if meeting me at APH wasn't going to be fun, but I get what he means.

He also works in town, which is handy, so I reply to say I'll see him just after five. Office parties can be entertaining, especially with a young boss, and I bet there are a few office romances that he can tell me about. When plied with enough fizz.

Donna says she's not in the mood to go out for lunch, but I insist, so we walk down the Wellingborough Road, stopping at the first coffee shop we find. It's very quiet, which suits us. I let her waffle on about Duncan and do my best to reassure her it'll be finc. There's no knowing with men, but Duncan doesn't seem the type to mess anyone around.

We buy the biggest Chelsea bun in the shop (a rare lapse for Donna) and pick at it between us on the walk back to the office.

There's no sign of Mike when we arrive and Marion's on the phone again.

I spend the afternoon wading through and tying up tallgirlnn1 messages, and debate whether to pull my profile. I decide to leave it, in case Bully4U still needs to 'speak' to me or worse, cancels. Half-glass Izzy.

It's soon half four and I get changed into a gorgeous dress Karen's lent me. Sitting next to the über fashion queen has its advantages.

As I walk out of the ladies and go back to my desk to get my matching bag, again thanks to Karen, heads turn. I must admit I feel like a lottery winner in my Julien McDonald turquoise blue shimmering shift and smile at Karen, mouthing, *Thank you*, as I pick up the clutch.

Donna rushes over with her arms outstretched, but seeing the exquisite detailing in the dress, stops.

"It's all right. It's last season's."

Relieved, she gives me a big hug, which I think also makes her feel better, and we're still in a clinch when William walks past. We let go and he smiles.

"If I didn't know better I'd think there was something going on between you two."

I don't know how to react until he laughs, and adds, "Very pretty, Miss MacFarlane." I feel my face go red, which would clash dreadfully with the outfit, but fortunately he's already going back towards his office.

Donna giggles and I growl her name through gritted teeth, but she just smiles and returns to her desk.

As I leave, my dress even gets a smile from Marion. Either that or it's wind.

I feel rather overdressed as I walk past the college towards Abington Street and the main pedestrianised shopping area. McNeil, Duffy and Chilson is above an independent temp agency and an already-shut bakers, and looks to have perfect views for people-watching. I ring the bell on the plain front door and am buzzed in.

Pete's standing at the top of the stairs, and the dress makes an impression on him too.

"Wow!"

"Oh, thanks." I'm tempted to add 'This old thing', but it's a Julien McDonald, so can't imagine it ever being old, even if it were last season (it's not, but it made Donna feel better).

We go through the door on the landing, which is like stepping from a sound booth into the real world, because as soon as the door seals are separated, the noise is deafening.

Pete introduces me to his colleagues. I'm hopeless at remembering names and they're only fixed in my brain for the few seconds it takes to be introduced to the next person.

The name I won't be forgetting is Emily's, the boss, and epitome of female lawyers. She's tall, about the same height as me, although I'm wearing black spangly kitten heels and hers (I look later when it's not being obvious) are a good couple of inches on mine, making her around five feet eight.

Still, I would say, a formidable presence in a courtroom. When I first see her, she has her back to us, but as we walk over, she turns and puts on the same plastic smile I've worn a few times this month. She holds her hand out, waits to be introduced, and Pete duly obliges. I recognise her, but say nothing other than, "Hello." She'll keep.

Most of Pete's colleagues are dancing in the kitchen end of the open-plan office. Because of the computers, the desks haven't been moved, but the copier's been unplugged and relocated, leaving enough space for twenty or so bodies to get up close and personal.

Pete and I have just joined in when the theme tune to one of the Boots adverts comes on to a rapturous applause; everyone seems to know the words to the chorus as they belt out 'here come the girls'. I have it on my iPod, so join in and even manage a bit of some of the verses.

It's clear the alcohol has been flowing for some time, as few are still sober; those few include Emily and me. I wheedle my way towards her, which is easier said than done.

"Emily, hi."

"Hello. Izzy, was it?"

I nod. "Thanks for letting me gate-crash your party. Happy birthday."

"Thanks. It's not until the weekend, but my husband's taking me away somewhere tomorrow for a mini-break."

"How lovely. Do you know where you're going?'

"He won't tell me, but he's a pilot and gets free travel, so it could be anywhere."

A pilot. Of course he is.

We stand in silence for a few seconds, looking at the dance floor. She goes to say something when I blurt out, "We've already met."

Her brow creases. "Oh, I don't think…"

"Twice," I continue.

She shakes her head.

"The Aviator earlier this month."

"No, I think I'd…"

"And the Fish Street café a couple of weeks ago."

"Erm…"

"Tall black guy?"

Her expression changes and I can tell the penny's finally dropped. Then her guard flips back up. "I'm sorry…"

"Izzy."

"I'm sorry, Izzy. I think you must have me confused…"

"Yes, I must. My mistake. Nice ring," I say, looking at her left hand.

She blushes and lifts her glass. "Looks like I need a refill. Help yourself and have a good time."

Oh yes, I'm having a good time all right.

I watch her wander off to chat to a female colleague and of course I'm not in the slightest bit green. Emily's a natural blonde with piercing blue eyes (as have I when I wear contact lenses), a body to kill for (mine's still a work in progress) and perfectly behaved hair.

Mine, on the other hand, only ever behaves while sitting in the hairdresser's chair. Even walking out the door into the lightest of breezes sends it all over the place and it's never the same again.

Next thing I know, Pete's grabbing my arm and leading me to the refreshments. The food must have been done by a caterer, although I wouldn't put it past Epitome Emily to have made it all herself.

"The food looks lovely!" I shout to Pete.

"We've got Emily to thank for that."

Why am I not surprised? "She made it?"

"Oh, no she's a hopeless cook. Her sister's a caterer."

I grin and pick up a plate, helping myself to a selection of goodies. Buffets are my favourite type of food, and I'm so happy to be going out on a high.

A rather short stocky guy comes over and is carrying something weird-looking in his right hand. When he holds it out, I realise it's a pair of devil's horns. He thrusts them at Pete, who's more than happy to wear them and goes back to the 'dance floor' complete with plate of food.

The female colleague Emily was chatting to comes over and helps herself to the buffet.

"Hi, I'm Izzy, friend of Pete's," I say.

"Hello." She doesn't divulge her name. "There are a few of those."

I assume she means the other colleagues until she continues. "He's been out with all the women here."

"Oh."

"Except me."

"Ah."

Pete's a good-looking guy, probably mid-thirties, and is dancing next to Emily.

"Including her," Miss No Name says bitterly.

"Before she was married."

"Oh yes."

"Okay."

"Before… during… probably after."

Miss No Name is glaring at Emily and I can see a catfight ensuing. "She's rich, you know."

"I would imagine she is. She's one of the partners, presumably."

"She's the Duffy, her maiden name of course, married the McNeil."

"As in one of the other partners?"

"Old duffer. Flaunts her affairs under his nose."

"I thought she said he was a pilot."

"I think he has a licence, but just small stuff. She's probably trying to give him a heart attack."

Too much information. "Is he here?"

"No. Left a while ago."

I nod sympathetically. So not quite the charmed life she likes people to believe. Emily and Pete are entwined as they do the Lambada, and I can see other colleagues looking less than impressed.

With all eyes on the dance floor, I wolf down the rest of my food and, picking a particularly sultry part of the song, see this as my cue to leave. As I reach the door, I turn round and see Pete's still oblivious to anyone but his boss, so I close the door behind me, grateful for the tranquillity of the silent landing, and walk back to the office.

The street is nearly deserted and remnants of rush hour traffic edge around the corner of the impressive BBC Radio Northampton building. The town may have changed in the last few years, but the old buildings that remain are defiantly watching over their people.

Marion's long gone and the office is quiet – just William, Janice and Aunt Agnes left.

Keith wolf whistles as he comes out of the kitchen and I smile without saying anything, adding a little wiggle to my walk. He goes back to his desk and I see William look up from his. He smiles too then returns his gaze downwards as Janice switches off her side lamp and picks up her bag.

I gather up my work clothes to go to the ladies.

"That colour suits you," Janice says.

"Thanks. It does feel lovely."

"Ask if you can keep it."

"I couldn't do that."

"I'm sure William wouldn't mind."

"William?"

"You'd have to ask Karen first, but obviously William has the ultimate say."

"Of course, but…"

"You deserve it."

And she's right. I do. I've given up nearly every night for him this month and while some of it's been fun, other nights have been torture. "Will do. Thanks," I say, and follow her down the corridor, disappearing into the ladies while she heads for reception.

I'm Cinderella after the ball. As soon as the dress comes off, the magic is over. Work clothes represent the real me, and, while I love being me, I felt particularly special in a frock I'd probably only buy for a wedding, and I haven't been to one of those since Mark and Ellen's.

I hang up the dress behind Karen's desk, and put the bag in her cupboard. After leaving a thank-you note, I head off home.

Feeling quite low and deciding I'm off men, I reckon I deserve a celebration of my own. It's the end of the project, so I decide to treat myself to a chart DVD or two and some snacks. Asda has a special offer on Ben & Jerry's, what better incentive than to do my weekly shop there.

As I walk through the front doors after grabbing a basket, I remember they're doing their first ever Dating Night. I groan as I see all these single shoppers wearing red heart numbered badges. A smiling chap in green and black offers me a badge of my own as I go through the entry barrier. I raise my hand, so he steps back. I notice the badge I would have been given was number sixty-nine, so I'm doubly glad I refused.

I can't believe that sixty-eight other singletons are wandering around this store in the hope of picking up more than a ripe melon or pack of cheese-topped baps, but as I walk on, I see the place is packed. The only time I want to be surrounded by couples and there isn't one in sight.

After grabbing two bags of mixed salad, I go to the frozen desserts section. As they're 'buy one get one free', I get two Cherry Garcia, a Pfish Food and Vanilla Toffee Crunch.

I'd forgotten to get milk, so walk back an aisle. After adding a litre of semi-skimmed to my basket, I make slow progress along the CD accessories and shop-brand kitchen equipment. I'm tempted by a set of bluetooth speakers, but they've only got them on a higher shelf. I'm five ten but even I struggle to reach. I'm on my tiptoes when an arm appears from nowhere and grabs the box for me.

"Thank you," I say automatically, before turning to my well-over-six-feet knight in white cotton armour.

It's William.

"Why does it not surprise me to see you here?" he says.

"Why does it *surprise* me to see you here?" I reply.

"I'm bored with the other supermarkets, so thought I'd try this."

William's never struck me as the sort of person to get bored with anything.

"I'm on my indirect way home after date number thirty-one," I say proudly.

"How did it go?"

My, he looks good in jeans. Apart from a crisis weekend when he had to interrupt a rare holiday to come in and sort it out, I've only ever seen him in a suit, but he looks doubly good.

He looks at my basket and I cringe. "Eating for two?"

I laugh unconvincingly. "Stocking up the freezer. Taking advantage of an offer."

"Me too," he says, and I see his basket's full of healthy option ready meals.

"Ah, so you're a microwave chef too."

"It's quicker. I need to eat two at a time because there's nothing to them, but–"

"So do I," I say, although I rarely touch the healthy options (unless they're on offer) because they're usually watery.

He looks at my chest, and I look down.

"Sorry," he says, "looking to see if you're taking part in this dating thing."

"God, no. I've had my fill, thanks very much."

"Off men then for a while?"

"For life!" I blurt out but backtrack. "That's not strictly true. I'm waiting for the right one."

"Don't wait too long or your ice cream will melt."

I know the feeling.

We smile at each other, then say "Okay" in unison. He heads towards the checkouts and I stay put.

As I watch him walk away, I can't resist looking at the red tab on his 501s rear pocket.

I put the speakers back on a lower shelf; they're a paltry one watt, which wouldn't cover my understairs toilet, let alone a bedroom or lounge.

With William safely gone, I walk to the alcohol aisle, adding two bottles of buy-one-get-one-free Baileys and a full-price Disaronno to my basket.

I'm unloading my goodies onto the conveyor belt in the basket aisle by the exit doors when I sense someone standing next to me.

"Has it been that bad?"

I look up and, of course, it's William.

"What's that?"

"Your project. Not only is it driving you into the arms of Mr Ben and Mr Jerry, but Messrs Bailey and Disaronno are joining the party."

"I'm just…"

"Stocking up. It's okay." He leans in and whispers, "Your secret's safe with me."

I'm about to speak when he winks and heads for the exit.

"He's cute," the young female cashier says. "Get his number?"

"Oh no, he's…"

"Shame."

With all the 'men' jostling for space in the boot of my car, I drive home with a smile.

As I get home I see Ursula walking up her garden path, arm in arm with Nick. They're oblivious to their surroundings and nattering away. I smile as I unpack the shopping and look forward to catching up with her when I see her next.

I've already promised myself that, come hell or high water, I'm going to finish *Opaque* tonight, so the TV stays off. I text Donna who says she's fine, but will feel better 'when it's all over'. I don't think she literally means that, so I send a 'text me if you need me' reply.

I get comfortable on the sofa under my summer-thin double duvet and look at the nest of tables beside me. The top one is crammed with goodies. A bowl of mixed ice cream takes precedence, but there's also a glass of Disaronno and ice (Baileys would be too much even for me), together with some savoury cheese balls and a small block of fruit and nut Galaxy chocolate.

With Classic FM on low on the radio, I'm all set to reacquaint myself with Elliot, knowing I'm surrounded by a barrage of cushions and comfort food should the going get tough.

Chapter 32 – Mission Accomplished

Yay! I've finished *Opaque*. Oh my God, what an ending. Since starting it, I've bought some of Jack Myler's later ones and am looking forward to getting to know his DCI Ted Dayley.

I don't think I've ever been to Rotherham (maybe passed through, like a lot of people do with Northampton), so it'll also be fun. I don't know if fun is the right word for crime, but getting to know the place should be interesting.

What did I learn from last night? That office parties are all the same. Put supposedly professional people in a room with lots of alcohol, music and flashing lights and they think it's a school disco where it's perfectly acceptable to get off with the married boss.

Today's two items ticked on my 'dater's shopping list' are: Don't get off with the married boss (especially if it puts your job at risk) and Do dress up for the hell of it because you know it makes you feel better.

This past month has been a real rollercoaster of emotions. I've met some wonderful guys and some… let's just say more interesting characters. I hope my column has helped rather than hindered your decision to place a profile should you be single and wish to find the love of your life.

While there's no guarantee to finding him or her that way, as long as you're careful you can have a good time. Don't take it seriously and you may be surprised. Or you may find the partner of your dreams in a supermarket because you're not quite tall enough to get something off a high shelf and he just happens to be there at the right time.

I feel my face flush as I write the last bit, so delete it back to '*good time*'. The fantasy's over anyway. The first of June, reality's back.

Out of curiosity, I check tallgirlnn1 and there are four messages. One I report, as it's gross, and two 'no thanks' (one from Venezuela and the other from Edinburgh – I love Edinburgh, especially having read some of Ian Rankin's *Rebus*, but I'm not into long-distance relationships, although part of me wonders whether it might be Donald Mk 2).

The last is from a gorgeous-sounding guy called 'Milton 6ft4' (he can tick the 'Oh, and did I say tall?' box). He says he's intrigued by my profile and would like to know more about me. He lives in Northampton and has ticked pretty much every box I've ticked.

Although the project's over, he's irresistible and for the first time in over a month, he's a guy I can be honest with, so I pour my heart out to him (in a non-sentimental way, of course) telling him all about me – the real me, not the temporary 'me'.

Despite encouraging my readers to persevere, the last month has convinced me that internet dating isn't for me, so with my reply to Milton 6ft4 sent, I click on the 'hide my profile' button. I'm tempted to delete it, but something tells me to wait a while.

"Izzy?"

Donna. Very pretty but very anxious. She's intent on a spot on my desk and I follow her gaze. Her right thumbnail is scoring a line back and forth in the fake wood. "Have you heard from Duncan?" I ask, looking at her face.

She shakes her head, still staring and fiddling.

"I wouldn't worry. You're still meeting him, right?"

She nods.

"Where?"

Finally looking at me, she mumbles, "Beckett's Park."

"Public yet romantic."

"Yes, so I can't cause a scene."

"Oh, Donna, I'm sure it's not what you're thinking."

"But why else meet me at lunchtime? He wants to get it over and done with, so he knows it won't take any longer than an hour."

"Or he can't wait until tonight."

"So he doesn't waste a whole evening."

"Anyway, it's not long now. You'll know in a couple of hours and knowing is best, isn't it?"

"I suppose so."

I can see that nothing I say is going to help, so I give her a commiserative smile and she plods back to her desk.

As Donna's busy for lunch, I decide to stay in. Before I dig out my sandwich, I refresh my tallgirlnn1 page and 'Milton 6ft4' has replied. He says he's suitably impressed and loves independent women with a strong character who can hold a decent conversation.

I smile as I read on and an excited shiver runs through me when I reply and click on 'send'. I can't believe having dated over forty men that it should be the first one as the real me that gives me goosebumps.

I can't concentrate on my work although looking at the clock every five minutes probably doesn't help the time go any quicker.

I keep checking the corridor and she finally walks through the double doors. It's obvious she's been crying.

We meet halfway and walk into the ladies. I go to put my arms round her as she sobs.

"Donna, what happened?"

"It's..." She sniffs and blows her nose on a very soggy and grubby-looking cloth hankie. It looks horribly familiar. I'm staring at it and remember where I've seen it before: on a desk, surrounded by packets of food, particularly a half-eaten jam doughnut. She's been to see Mike? Oh no, please don't tell me they're back together.

"I met up with Duncan."

I nod and let her continue, breathing a sigh of relief but can't help the feeling of impending doom.

"And everything's great!" She beams but I'm still waiting for clarification. Positive me anticipates a 'Oh, Mike just lent me this because he thought I was upset. Duncan's the love of my life and...' but realistic me is expecting 'Duncan's dumped me and Mike was soooo sweet. I don't know why I ever let him go.' I do.

"Duncan said he was really sorry..." Uh oh.

"...that he's been working so much. There's been some kind of animal flu going around and it's like Noah's ark at his surgery." My insides give a little high-five. Not that I think that's possible but...

She giggles and all's alright with the world again, at least Donna's little part of it. I watch her wash her face before going back outside. She skips down the corridor and back to her desk. I shout "Well done," after her, but her mind is clearly in DonnaAndDuncanLand.

So I go to the kitchen and get us two celebratory cans of fat Coke and two plastic beakers with which to toast the happy couple.

She's on the phone; I pull a chair up from an empty neighbouring desk (the pet advisor/film reviewer – we're a talented lot – only works part time) and pour out the Cokes.

"I know. Yes, really well… happy? Seems to be… me? Of course, I can't wait. Tonight? Sure. Yours or mine? Sounds lovely. I'm missing you too."

I don't need to guess who she's talking to.

"Me too… okay, bye… yes, bye… me too… love you… ahhh… okay, bye." She laughs before finally putting down the phone.

"What's this?" she asks, looking at the drinks.

"A toast."

"I like toasts."

"To Duncan and Donna," I say loudly. "My favourite double Ds."

She swallows a gulp of Coke and bursts out laughing, sending a large dribble of liquid down either side of her mouth. I grab a tissue from her desk and hand it to her.

"Fanks," she says, still full of Coke.

So it's true. I've just seen it for myself.

I make an impromptu visit to reception after a phone call from a supplier informing me of an impending parcel. Marion likes to know these things, which makes it my colleaguely duty to go and warn her (nothing to do with what Donna told me of course). And there he is. Mike, in the twenty-plus-stone flesh, a little too close for innocence.

I can't help grinning as I walk to the perspex screen.

"Good afternoon, Izzy," he says pulling away from Marion.

"Afternoon. How are you both?"

They look at each other quizzically as if I'd meant something by it, which of course I had.

"Good… thank you…" Marion says slowly.

I turn to him. "And how are you?'

"Fine, thanks." He smiles and I can see a hint of leftover lunch in his teeth.

"Great. Marion?"

"Yes, Isobel."

"I'm expecting a parcel. It's samples, no hurry."

"Certainly. I shall ring you when it comes in." This is more than she's said to me in a while, and the most pleasant.

"Thanks." I head for the main office double doors, but turn back to look at them both. "Bye, Marion."

She smiles.

As Mike picks at a tooth – not the fooded one – with his right index fingernail, I say, "See you, Mike," then wink and head back to my desk.

With time running away, I go about finishing the article so it'll reach William's tray by the deadline. I click open the Notes document and look the final version of the shopping list.

Don't do (in no particular order)
- Trainers with smart suit
- Greasy hair or dirty fingernails
- Il/legal offspring or geriatric
- Too short
- No arse/weighs less than me
- Boring conversation (accountant)
- Couch potato
- Nauseatingly smooth
- Geek or trainspotter
- Old-fashioned (pipe/slippers)
- Addiction of any kind
- Wants kids or has brats
- Judge a book by its cover
- Moustache or beard unless goatee
- Too feminine or over emotional
- Hard drugs or smoking
- Too ugly or self-indulgent pretty boys
- Orange suntans/leathery skin
- Slurps his drink or eats like a pig
- Never left Northampton

- BO and other smells
- Sweats like a pig
- Ignorance
- Have wandering eyes
- A short temper
- Judge too quickly/be negative
- Assume poor = no ambition
- Worry what other people think
- Fall asleep on your date
- Wear a wedding ring/be married
- Let your head rule your heart
- Gold digger/money flasher
- Assume hard exterior = hard interior
- Think you've seen everything
- Give up if your date bottles out
- Dismiss the first dress in the shop

Do (in a very particular order)
- Tall
- Funny/good conversation (binman)
- Pay compliments
- Non-smoker
- Ethics
- Intelligent
- Be honest if no spark
- Smart appearance (clean hair etc.)
- Pay attention
- Have some ambition (i.e. not a layabout)
- Be genuine
- Keep up to date with current events
- Judge a book by its cover
- Passionate
- Try new things (including fish and chips, speed dating and gay bars)
- Likes similar music/interests etc.
- Have fun
- Well travelled/interesting
- Sort out things that are bothersome (how old am I?)
- Likes animals

- Tall
- Remember your date's name
- Rugby physique
- Watch out for a suntan circle on finger
- Pays his way
- Have, or at least like, modern technology
- Have a medium patience level
- Have a medium tolerance level
- Think about a person's feelings
- Stand up for yourself and others
- Keep your psychiatrist's head in reserve
- Have a good time, sober or otherwise
- Learn another language
- Dress up because it makes you feel better
- Read good poetry
- Oh, and did I say tall?

When all's said and done, you can write a list as long as the back of your forearm (mine's a shoe size eight – another piece of useless trivia for you), but when you meet the man of your dreams, you can throw that list out of the window… please don't because that would be littering). You can write all the dos and don'ts in the world, but they may well not mean a thing. You can try on all the dresses in all the shops in town, but the chances are you'll go back to the first shop and buy that first dress because it's the most comfortable, most flattering, and the one that has your name written in invisible ink on the inside label. You'll know that moment when you realise the two of you are destined to be together – the moment you realise that your soulmate was right under your nose all the time.

I breathe a sigh of relief as the project is officially over. With more tech goodies promised, I look forward to getting back to normality. Revising it one last time, I make a couple of small changes, press Ctrl and P to print it off, then take it to William's office.

Donna's singing away. Despite her being one of those annoyingly naturally cheerful people, I've never seen her so happy. And that's saying something.

305

It seems to be catching as Janice is chatting away jovially on the phone and smiles at me as I reach for William's door handle.

There's no sign of him so I put the article in his in tray, patting it as I do so, like I'm wishing it bon voyage, and go back to my desk.

As I reach it, William's walking down the corridor. He smiles at me. "Glad it's over?"

I must look puzzled as he continues. "Your dates. Grand job, by the way. Sir Edward's very impressed."

"Thank you." I feel myself blushing.

"Last one in the tray?"

I nod and sit down.

"Thanks," he says, and walks back to his office.

I've barely started looking through my emails when I see there's one from William asking me to go and see him.

He's staring at his computer screen, so I creep in and sit down opposite.

"Ah, glad you're here," he says, as if he'd forgotten his request.

"Oh?"

"There's another project I want to talk to you about."

I imagine another thirty-one somethings in thirty-one days and my clichéd heart sinks. "Is there?" I murmur.

"Yes, something a bit more permanent. I'm just waiting for a call to confirm. You here 'til five?"

I'm curious. "I am, or later if you need…"

"Five will be fine."

As I turn to leave, William stands up from behind his desk, grabs my wrist and pulls me towards him. He looks into my eyes. "First dress in the first shop," he says, before kissing me.

This is the William I've come to know – the passionate man who's not afraid to show his feelings. The kiss is tender and quite overwhelming, and, as we peel apart, he smiles and I must look shocked because his expression changes.

"Oh God! Sorry," he says, and steps back.

"Please don't be. It was lovely. It… you just took me by surprise."

He still looks crestfallen and backs away to behind his desk.

I sit down again then take his hand and lean forward. I want to kiss him again but the phone rings. He studies the phone's display and sighs. I point upwards and he nods.

"I'd better…" he says.

'Sure. Talk later?"

He nods and picks up the phone.

As I stand, I glance at the bookshelf behind him and the file with my name on it. Next to it is something I'd not noticed, or never registered, before: *The Complete Works of John Milton.*

Walking to the door, I'm about to grab the handle when something catches my eye. I look over at the coat stand and alongside his suit jacket is a dress cover. The zip is partially open and as I look closer I catch a flash of pale turquoise.

The End

Rachel Cavanagh

Locations featured in The Serial Dater

Chapter 1: The Picturedrome, Kettering Road
Chapter 2: The World's End, Ecton
Chapter 3: The Charles Bradlaugh, The Mounts, Northampton town centre
Chapter 4: Former Jade restaurant, The Pavilion, Kettering Road
Chapter 5: The Hilton Hotel, near Junction 15 of the M1 motorway
Chapter 6: Frankie & Benny's then Cineworld Cinema, Sixfields
Chapter 7: The Greyhound pub, Milton Malsor
Chapter 8: The Aviator, Sywell Airport
Chapter 9: Groove bar, top of Gold Street (often closes/changes name)
Chapter 10: Chicago's, Market Square, Northampton town centre (currently closed)
Chapter 11: The Moon on the Square, Market Square, Northampton town centre
Chapter 12: Peterborough Greyhound stadium
Chapter 13: The Britannia pub, The Lakes, Bedford Road (on the A428)
Chapter 14: Heather's, Kingsley Park Terrace then later the Cock Hotel, Kingsthorpe
Chapter 15: Speed dating at The Cock, Kingsthorpe
Chapter 16: The Red Lion at Brafield-on-the-Green, near Cogenhoe
Chapter 17: The Red Hot Buffet, Sixfields (subsequently burned down!)
Chapter 18: The Romany pub, Kingsley/Kingsthorpe Hollow
Chapter 19: The Grosvenor Centre then a random café along Fish Street, Northampton town centre
Chapter 20: Abington Park (top half, near the bandstand)
Chapter 21: Delapre Park, London Road
Chapter 22: White Elephant, Kingsley Road/Kettering Road corner
Chapter 23: The Four Pears at Little Houghton
Chapter 24: Boston (formerly Boston Clipper), opposite the town centre bus station
Chapter 25: The Rover (now the Sevens), opposite Saints Rugby Club, Weedon Road
Chapter 26: The Shipman's, Market Square
Chapter 27: The Deers Leap pub, Little Billing
Chapter 28: The Swan and Helmet, Grove Road, off Clare Street
Chapter 29: Spencer Arms, Chapel Brampton
Chapter 30: Fishmarket Café (now the bus station)
Chapter 31: McNeil, Duffy and Chilson, Abington Street (fictional solicitors opposite KFC, Abington Street)
Chapter 32: The office (based on the Chronicle and Echo, now an empty space)

Note from the Author

Thank you for purchasing 'The Serial Dater',
the first novel in the 'Serial' series.

I loved writing it and hope you enjoyed reading it. I will be bringing you more in the series available in the next few months.

I'd like to take this opportunity to also thank all my writing friends – especially Tony, the two Janes, Berni, Pat, Denny and Auriol – for their ongoing support, and to Spinney Lodge Vets for their advice on parrot diseases and for looking after my 'boys', most recently #gustherescuedog.

Thank you also to my ever-patient assistant, Caroline.

I welcome feedback and you can either contact me on Twitter (https://twitter.com/RachelCavAuthor) or via email rachelcavanaghauthor@gmail.com.

I am always grateful for honest reviews.

Rachel's books

Novels

The Serial Dater — 31 dates in 31 days

The Serial Dieter — 31 dishes in 31 days

Oh, Henry — the first in the Henry Houdini series

Short Stories

Various Henry Houdini long short stories

About the Author

Rachel Cavanagh was born a southerner
and will always be at heart.

She transplanted herself, indirectly because of her job at the time, to the East Midlands, UK, in the early 1990s and has dreams of 'retiring' to Sussex, further south than her original roots, where she'd love to write full time with a sea view.

Short stories have always been her first love. A regular at her local library as a child, she devoured novels (sometimes under the covers with a torch) but often returned to short stories. Inspirations include Roald Dahl and Kate Atkinson.

Rachel will always be grateful to her father, with whom she would love to have had more time, especially to hear about his working relationship with Mr Dahl.

Rachel knew how proud her father was of her, and she will always be a daddy's girl.

You can find Rachel at https://twitter.com/RachelCavAuthor.

Published by **August Publishing UK**

Made in the USA
Monee, IL
19 July 2021